P9-CSW-535

APPLAUSE FOR AMANDA SCOTT:

HIGHLAND SECRETS:

"A tempestuous love story that will thrill readers from first to last page. Ms. Scott delivers a highly charged story with passionate characters and lush historical detail."

—*Rendezvous*

DANGEROUS ANGELS:

". . . an exciting Regency romance filled with two great lead characters, a tremendous cast, and a brilliant storyline. If you haven't read the prequel, DANGEROUS GAMES . . . it is strongly recommended that you do so."

—*Affaire de Coeur*

DANGEROUS ILLUSIONS:

"Amanda Scott captures the Regency with a sharp pen and her dry wit, portraying the glamorous appeal and the sorrow of the era to a tee. A true treat."

—*Romantic Times*

HIGHLAND FLING:

"From the pen of a most gifted storyteller, HIGHLAND FLING is a well-crafted romance with a delightful secondary love story, sparkling dialogue, and enough humor to tickle the most discerning funnybone."

—*Romantic Times*

BAWDY BRIDE:

"Ms. Scott captures your interest with the very first sentence and then proceeds to weave a spell around your heart. . . ."

—*Rendezvous*

BORDER BRIDE:

"Hours of reading fun."

—*Catherine Coulter*

ROMANCE FROM FERN MICHAELS

DEAR EMILY   (0-8217-4952-8, $5.99)

WISH LIST   (0-8217-5228-6, $6.99)

AND IN HARDCOVER:

VEGAS RICH   (1-57566-057-1, $25.00)

Available wherever paperbacks are sold, or order direct from the Publisher. Send cover price plus 50¢ per copy for mailing and handling to Kensington Publishing Corp., Consumer Orders, or call (toll free) 888-345-BOOK, to place your order using Mastercard or Visa. Residents of New York and Tennessee must include sales tax. DO NOT SEND CASH.

Highland Treasure

Amanda Scott

Zebra Books
Kensington Publishing Corp.
http://www.zebrabooks.com

ZEBRA BOOKS are published by

Kensington Publishing Corp.
850 Third Avenue
New York, NY 10022

Copyright © 1998 by Lynne Scott-Drennan

All rights reserved. No part of this book may be reproduced
in any form or by any means without the prior written consent
of the Publisher, excepting brief quotes used in reviews.

If you purchased this book without a cover you should be
aware that this book is stolen property. It was reported as "un-
sold and destroyed" to the Publisher and neither the Author
nor the Publisher has received any payment for this "stripped
book."

Zebra and the Z logo Reg. U.S. Pat. & TM Off.

First Printing: June, 1998
10 9 8 7 6 5 4 3 2

Printed in the United States of America

AUTHOR'S NOTE

Clan Maclean has various branches, one of which spells the name Maclaine. The pronunciation of both is exactly the same, and in *Highland Treasure,* as in *Highland Secrets,* the second spelling will be used only when it refers to Mary Maclaine or to members of her immediate family. The official clan spelling is Maclean, and it will be used whenever the clan or its other members or branches are mentioned.

Dedicated to

*Roderick Campbell and his family of Barcaldine
Castle in Argyll; to Doreen Patterson, Eunice Kennedy,
Catherine Stoddart, Carolyn Leach, Mr. & Mrs. Miller,
and particularly to Jim Drennan and the other
members of the Lewis & Clark Study Group, all of
whom contributed to making the author's most
recent adventures in Scotland so memorable.
But most of all, to Terry, who drove.
Thank you all very much.*

Prologue

Eerie echoes reverberated through the mist-shrouded forest as the first shovelful of dirt thudded onto the treasure chest. A second shovelful followed, then a third, as Lord MacCrichton and his elder son, Ewan, worked to bury the chest.

Ewan's brother, Geordie, a huge man with a childlike demeanor, kept a lookout, holding a spout lantern so that its light spilled into the hole containing the ironbound chest. "Hurry," he said anxiously. "We canna see a thing in this mist."

"Set down that lantern and notch the tree," MacCrichton said. He, too, was a big man, though not as large as either of his sons. "You can save us some time."

"Aye, that's a good notion, that is. I'll use my dirk. What mark will I use?"

Impatiently, Ewan said, "Must we think of everything, you daft gowk? Use that rattlepate of yours to think for once. We want to be able to find this tree again."

"Aye, well, then, X marks the spot," Geordie said, drawing a *skean dhu* from his boot top and chuckling as he moved purposefully toward the nearest tree.

For some moments thereafter, the dull thuds of dirt on dirt and the scritch-scratch of metal on bark were the only sounds to be heard, for the denizens of the forest were either fast asleep or keeping their counsel. The air was chilly and damp with mist rising off nearby Loch Creran and drifting over the land in vast, dense clouds. All three men listened intently for anything out of the ordinary, suspecting that more than mere forest creatures might be prowling the nearby woods, and the tension seemed to make Geordie particularly nervous.

Suddenly his hand froze mid-stroke, and he exclaimed, "Hark!" When the other two jumped and Ewan glared at him, he said, "Did you no hear that?"

"What?" Then Ewan heard it himself.

A cracking sound, eerily muffled by the mist, came from the direction of the loch. It sounded like a breaking branch, followed by the rattle of moving pebbles.

"That! Someone's coming. Hurry!" Geordie snatched up the lantern, and just as he shut the spout, its light flashed upon a huge X gashed in the bark.

"By my faith," Ewan snapped, "have you no brains at all? Anyone who sees that X is bound to dig here."

"Och, but that is why men call him Daft Geordie, that is," Lord MacCrichton said with a sigh.

"You said to mark it," Geordie protested.

"Aye, lad," Ewan agreed, "but we never thought you'd mark it so bloody damned well." He fell silent, listening. Then, hearing nothing more that was in any way remarkable, he said, "Look you now, Geordie, help us brush pine needles and leaves over the mound so that it won't look fresh dug, and then we'll notch a few more trees like you did this one. The chest is buried deep, so if this one spot don't shriek out to every passerby to take notice of it, it will lie safe enough, I think."

"Aye, that's a fine notion, that is," Geordie said cheerfully. "Plain to see that you got the brains in the family, Ewan, though I'm no so daft as you think I am."

Ewan did not bother to reply, and they worked as silently as possible, halting frequently to listen.

A quarter hour later, MacCrichton said, "That will do. I'm for bed now."

"You and Ewan go on ahead," Geordie said. "Leave me a

shovel, and I'll cover all our tracks and notch a few more trees before I go in."

"Very well, lad," his lordship said. "Don't be too long, though, and don't trip over any damned Campbells whilst you're about it. They've been watching us for weeks now, thinking we mean to follow the prince."

"And so we do," Geordie said, chuckling again. "Is that no why we're a-burying of this chest, so as to keep the treasure safe till we can return to Shian?"

"We don't want any Campbells getting their filthy hands on it while we're away, that's certain. Come along, Ewan, and mind now, Geordie, don't be long."

"I won't." However, several hours passed before he returned to the well-fortified, round-towered castle of the MacCrichtons perched on its grassy, forest-edged hillside above the loch. The next morning when he met his brother in the breakfast room, he said smugly, "Those damned Campbells will never find our treasure now, Ewan."

"What makes you so certain?"

"Because I've outsmarted them, I have. I thought of things you never thought about, and that's a fact."

Eyes narrow with misgiving, Ewan said, "What did you do?"

"Well, first, I notched every blessed tree for a mile or more, that's what I did. Those Campbells can dig the whole forest up now. They'll never find where we—"

"No, nor anyone else," Ewan snarled as his volatile temper ignited to fury. "How the devil do you think *we* are going to find it again, you daft gowk?"

"But I didna—"

Daft Geordie never finished his sentence, however, for with a single, furious blow, his exasperated brother knocked him senseless to the floor.

One

The Highlands, November 1753

The body of James of the Glen swung gently to and fro in the evening breeze, a stark black shadow against the sun now setting beyond the mountains of Morven and the western shore of Loch Linnhe.

The eerie sound of creaking chains stirred a shudder in the second of a string of ten riders passing through Lettermore Woods in the direction of the Ballachulish ferry. Not that the party meant to cross into Lochaber, for they did not. They were making for the hill pass into Glen Creran, and Mary Maclaine, riding away from her old life into a new one, was already enduring second thoughts.

The effort required not to look at James's body contributed to her depression. The gruesome sight brought back memories not just of James but of Ian, gentle Ian, whom she had loved dearly and whose death had been so sudden and violent, and just as unfair as poor James's had been.

"Don't dawdle, Mary love," the party's leader said. His tone was coaxing, but it held a note of impatience. "We've hours of travel ahead, and there is no use looking wistfully at James of the Glen. Wishing won't stir his body back to life."

"I know," Mary said. "I just wish they would cut him down. It's been more than a year, after all, since they hanged the poor innocent man."

"No one knows better than I do how long it's been," he said with a teasing look, "but I'll warrant the devilish Campbells will leave him there till he's dust."

He was a big, broad-shouldered man with curly fair hair, and she supposed most folks would think him handsome. He was undeniably charming, for although it had cost him a year's effort, he had charmed her into agreeing to marry him despite her firm belief that with Ian Campbell dead she would never marry any man.

Her gaze shifted involuntarily back to the corpse hanging in chains near the high road. All who traveled between Lochaber and Appin had to pass the gibbet. Moreover, its elevated position made it visible to folks along an extensive stretch of Loch Linnhe and Loch Leven, as well.

From where she was, she could see the great square tower of Balcardane Castle on the hillside above Loch Leven, beyond Ballachulish village. The sight stirred more memories of Ian, for the castle had been his home. His father was the surly, too-powerful Earl of Balcardane, and his brother was Black Duncan Campbell, a man of whom many folks went in understandable fear. Mary was not one of them, but she had no wish to think about Black Duncan. Such thoughts as she had of him were wicked, for she could not help blaming him for Ian's death.

"I wish we could just cut James down and bury him properly," she said abruptly, forcing her gaze back to her fair-haired companion.

"It would be as much as our lives are worth to try," he said. "That's why *they* are there." He gestured toward the hut where soldiers guarding the gibbet kept their food and pallets, and could take shelter from the elements. Smoke drifted upward from their cook fire now, and a man stared at them from the hut's doorway.

Mary remembered when the authorities had built the hut, a month after the hanging. Its very presence had been and still was an unmistakable sign that soldiers would remain a good long time to see that no one cut the body down.

Without another word, her companion urged his horse to a

canter. She knew he wanted to be over the hill pass before darkness descended, but she could not help resenting his urgency. Had he presented himself at Maclean House that morning as he had promised, instead of waiting until nearly suppertime, or had they taken one of the faster routes up Glen Duror or south through Salachan Glen, they might have reached their destination well before dark. He had arrived late, however, and still had insisted upon taking this more circuitous route.

Through habit, Mary kept her resentment to herself. When one had long depended on relatives for one's bed and board, one did not express feelings freely. Instead, one tried to prove useful, to present as light a burden as possible.

Mary was deeply grateful to her aunt, Anne Stewart Maclean, for years of care. Lady Maclean was neither a gentle nor a tender woman, but she was capable, kind; and strong, and their kinship was close. Not only had she been one of Mary's mother's six elder sisters, but her husband, Sir Hector, had been chieftain of the Craignure branch of Clan Maclean. Thus, Mary was a double cousin to Diana and Neil, Sir Hector and Lady Maclean's children.

Despite the marital alliance, the Craignure branch and her own family, the Maclaines of Lochfuaran, had enjoyed only brief periods of amity. However, after the deaths of Sir Hector and two of her brothers seven years ago at the Battle of Culloden, followed by the even more untimely deaths of her father and remaining siblings shortly thereafter, no one had remained to protest when Lady Maclean had appeared out of the blue one day to take Mary away to live with her.

Seven years she had lived with her Aunt Anne. Seven years of being brave and cheerful and trying not to be a burden when the very times were burdensome. Men said luck came and went in seven-year intervals, and Mary thought that might well be true. Although she recalled little of her first seven years, living with her large family at Lochfuaran on the Island of Mull, she thought they had been generally carefree. The second seven had been horrid.

In her eighth year, like a bolt of lightning, tragedy had struck, carrying off her mother and the two of the six elder sisters who were nearest Mary in age. The three had died swiftly, one after the other, during an influenza epidemic.

Her father and four other sisters had kept Mary away from the sickroom, of course, but one evening she had seen a shimmering image of her mother, and heard it say matter-of-factly that she was going to heaven now and to be a good girl. Minutes later, Mary's father had come in to tell the shaken, frightened child that her mother had died. Mary told her family about the vision, but everyone agreed that it had simply been a bad dream brought on by all the anxious activity in the house.

The deaths devastated the family, but Mary still had her big, protective father, four generally cheerful brothers, and four nurturing elder sisters to look after her. Then her sister Sarah married and died in childbirth along with her bairn. Their sister Margaret died the following year of a cut that putrefied, and the year after that, Mary awakened one night, sitting bolt upright in her bed, soaked with sweat and shaking. Her sister Eliza, then visiting cousins at Tobermory, had screamed out to her in a dream that she was falling.

In the dream, Mary could not catch her, and thus she wakened with the certain knowledge that Eliza lay dead. She told her brothers and father about the dream the following day, and several hours later word arrived from Tobermory that Eliza had fallen from a parapet while walking in her sleep. She had died instantly.

Years later Mary saw the faces of two of her brothers at what she believed was the moment each had fallen at Culloden, along with a face she later recognized from a portrait as her Uncle Hector. Her other two brothers, her father, and her sole remaining sister had died in the aftermath of that dreadful defeat, at the hands of the man Highlanders called Butcher Cumberland. Mary had witnessed their deaths, too, not by virtue of her gift but from the stable loft at Lochfuaran, where she lay hidden, quaking with terror, beneath a pile of hay. She had never revealed the horrible details of that day to anyone, and now the memory made her shudder again.

She had been fourteen then, and within a sennight her Aunt Anne had swooped in to collect her.

When the Crown seized Craignure and Lochfuaran as punishment for the rebel activities of their owners, Lady Maclean moved her little family from the Island of Mull to an estate in Appin country, owned by the exiled Laird of Ardsheal. Thanks to him, they had enjoyed shelter, food, and relative peace for a number of years at a peppercorn rent.

Then had come the Appin murders, rumors of new rebellion in the making, and the trial and conviction of James of the Glen. Mary still believed James had been guilty of no crime other than of being an influential Stewart in a land ruled by the English and the Campbells.

The murderer's primary victim had been a Campbell Crown factor hated by most of Appin country's residents. His second victim had been Gentle Ian Campbell. It stood to reason that the same villain had murdered both men, and Mary knew that James had had nothing to do with Ian's death. Indeed, she knew only too well who had killed Ian, for she had heard the tale from the murderer's own lips. The authorities knew, too; however, Allan Breck, a Stewart kinsman to her Aunt Anne and thus cousin to Mary herself, remained a fugitive from the law.

Now James and Ian were dead; her aunt and her cousin Neil had left for Perthshire a fortnight before to spend the winter with her cousin Diana, married more than a year now and expecting her first child; and Mary was on her way to Shian Towers to marry its master, Ewan, Lord MacCrichton.

It was after midnight when they arrived. For hours, riders carrying torches had lighted their way through the dark shadows of Glen Creran, aided by a half moon riding high above them, haloed by a misty ring. As they neared the castle, perched on its forested hillside, Mary saw thick mist rising from the loch below. Although she strained her eyes, she could see no sign of anything on the opposite shore that might be Dunraven Castle, which Ian had once told her had long been the seat of the Earls of Balcardane before they assumed ownership of the present Loch Leven castle, a prize of war forfeited by a hapless Stewart after the Rising of 1715.

They rode beneath a portcullis into a torchlit, cobbled courtyard.

"Tired, lass?" Ewan's quiet voice snatched her from her reverie.

"A little," she said. "I still don't understand why we rode so far, sir. We must have added nearly fifteen miles to our journey, for we cannot be but ten or twelve miles from Maclean House now. We've ridden right round half of Appin country."

"Aye, and if we did?"

A note in his voice held warning, but she dismissed it. She had known him a full year now, and he had been consistently charming and considerate to her. Thus she did not hesitate to say frankly, "I should have thought that having chosen such a long route, you would not have wished to leave Maclean House so late, sir, or that having begun so late, you might have chosen a more direct route."

He lifted her from her saddle, setting her down with a thump, but he did not release her. He stood a full head taller than she was, and his hands felt tight around her waist. He said, "Do you find fault with my decision, Mary?"

She could not mistake the warning note this time, and it occurred to her with no small impact that perhaps she did not know him well at all.

"It was not my intent to reproach you, sir," she said quietly.

"Good lass." He clapped her on the shoulder, then slipped an arm around her, urging her toward the entrance stairs.

Like other tower houses built early in the previous century, Shian Towers was a tall, handsome combination of stronghold and dwelling house. Built in the shape of an ell with circular towers at every corner and angle-turrets projecting at the gables, it presented an impressive appearance. Shot holes pierced its walls, and projecting above the main entrance, in the angle of the ell, was a device called a machicolation, which Mary knew was for pouring unpleasantness on unwelcome visitors who managed to breach the curtain walls. The MacCrichton arms surmounted the door, which was huge, iron-bound, and located on the first floor level, twenty feet above the ground, at the top of removable wooden steps.

Ewan hustled her up the stairs and inside, past a stout, woven-iron gate or yett that provided further protection against an enemy attack. As another prevention from assault, door and yett opened onto twisting stone steps that led up to the great hall and down to nether portions of the castle that undoubtedly housed the kitchen and servants' rooms.

Holding her skirt up with her right hand, Mary used her left to hold the rope banister as she preceded Ewan and his men upstairs to the hall. The stairs were narrow and wound in a clockwise direction, as such stairs nearly always did, so that a righthanded swordsman would always have the advantage defending his home against an enemy charging up the stairs.

In the great hall, a thin, fair-haired boy stirred up the fire and one of Ewan's men used a torch to light myriad candles in sconces, revealing a high-ceilinged chamber with dark paneling that Mary saw could use oil and some rubbing. Racks of lances lined one wall, but in accordance with the law they bore no metal tips.

"I suppose your family is abed and asleep at this hour, sir," she said, continuing to gaze about while she took off her gloves, pushed her hood back from her thick, tawny hair, and untied the strings of her long gray cloak. When Ewan did not answer at once, she turned to look at him.

He glanced from one to another of the three men who had accompanied them inside. Then, straightening, he said harshly to her, "There is no family here, lass, only ourselves, my men, and a few menservants."

Stunned, Mary exclaimed, "But how can that be? You said you were bringing me here to be married in the midst of your family, that I need not wait for my aunt and Sir Neil to return or for my cousin to recover after the birth of her child. For a year you've been saying that although your mother and father and younger brother are dead, you still had a large family to share with me. You said—"

"I've said a lot of damned silly stuff over the past year," Ewan interjected. "Not much of it was true, although it is true enough that I've got family to share. There are any number of them buried in our graveyard."

"You said you loved me," Mary said, shaken and trying to gather her wits.

"What if I did? Lots of lads say that when it will do them a good turn."

"What good turn? You know that I have no money or land, that I am completely dependent upon my aunt and my cousin Diana's husband for my keep. I don't even have a dowry. You said that you did not care about any of that."

"I don't."

"Ewan, I don't understand. Do you *want* to marry me?"

"Oh, aye. I don't want any misunderstandings later, and I've got to get myself a proper heir in any event, haven't I?"

"What misunderstanding could there be?" She was uncomfortably aware of the other men in the hall, and of the boy who had tended the fire and now squatted alertly near the wall by the stairs, but she had to find out what was going on.

"You don't need to know any more than that you will be my wife, lass, subject to my bidding."

"I don't think so, Ewan," she said, keeping her temper with difficulty. She was too tired to bandy words with him. "I thought I knew you, but clearly I don't, so I think I had better return to Maclean House at first light."

"Well, that's where you're wrong, Mary Maclaine. I've planned this for more than a year, ever since I learned about you, and I won't let you spoil it now. You will be my wife, like it or not, and that's my last word on the subject."

"Faith, sir, you cannot force me to marry you. No parson will perform the service against my will."

He smirked. "I've read the law, I have. We've no need for any parson."

"You still need my consent, however. A simple declaration

of marriage, while legal if I agree, is useless if I contradict you, and even marriage by promise and consummation cannot be forced. One word of dissent from the bride turns that into rape, Lord MacCrichton." As she said the words, Mary experienced a distinct chill. What good were laws when one was miles from any help?

Ewan's smirk remained unshaken. "You know more than any woman ought to know about the law," he said, "but that will only make you easier to convince. Scottish law provides for all sorts of irregular marriages, my dear."

"I know, for I learned about most of them when my cousin married a man of the law," Mary said. "Hers was a marriage of promise."

"Still, you mentioned only two sorts. There is handfasting, as well. I know a good bit about that one, I can tell you."

"I am not living with you for a year and a day," she snapped, "just so that—"

"Whisst now, lower your voice, Mary, if you don't want to feel my hand across that vixen's mouth of yours."

"How dare you!"

Ewan slapped her, hard.

Her hand flew to her burning cheek. The slap had shocked her, for as a rule Highland men were not violent toward women or children. That trait was unique to Englishmen and Lowlanders—Sassenachs, outlanders. A Highlander might put an erring wife or child across his knee if one needed a stern lesson, but he would never use his fist or lift his hand to any other part of a body weaker than his own.

She stepped back, but Ewan caught her, his hands bruising her arms. Giving her a rough shake, he said, "You will do as I bid you, Mary Maclaine, so listen well. The one law of irregular marriage that you seem to have missed learning is the one you will soon know best, for that law presumes that any man and woman with a habit of cohabitation have become man and wife."

"That cannot be true," she protested. "Men frequently cohabit with women whom no one pretends are their wives!"

"Only if the two come from different classes, lass. You and

I are of the same class, however. Moreover, before long, I warrant you will be only too happy to agree that you are my wife. I mean to see to it."

A shiver raced up her spine at the look he gave her, but rallying quickly, she said, "I shall write to the Duke of Argyll. You may not be aware—"

"Oh, aye, I ken fine that your cousin Diana married a kinsman of Argyll's. That's one reason I bided my time and exerted myself to charm you. I did not want you complaining to him of unwanted attention. I sought you out at the trial of James of the Glen, knowing that you cared for the man, and I've exerted myself for a year to arrive at this moment."

"Then you must know that I have only to write . . ." Her words trailed to silence in the face of his confident grin.

"You will write no letters, lass."

"You cannot mean to hold me prisoner! People know where I am. They will expect to hear from me."

"Aye, well, there's a bit of a rub, for you see, I told your maidservant at Maclean House that we would be traveling into Lochaber for a few weeks to be married from a kinsman's home. That is one reason we traveled the route we did."

"Only one?" She heard the sarcasm in her tone and felt no surprise at seeing a flash of anger in his eyes.

"You will recall that we met one or two folks along the way," he said evenly.

"I do, although we did not meet very many."

"My lads told each one that we were headed for a different destination. Then, forbye, it was dark when we passed through the glen. Most folks paid us no heed. We might have been Campbells or a party of soldiers, for all they saw, and they do not venture out after dark without good cause. Then, too . . ." He hesitated.

"What?"

"I wanted a look at Balcardane to see if Black Duncan was stirring."

"Why?"

"Thought he might take undesirable interest in the lass Gentle Ian wanted."

"Black Duncan takes no interest in me," she said with a grimace. "He and Balcardane did not want Ian to have anything to do with me, which is why we never got properly betrothed. I've told you that many a time before now."

"You had best hope that it's the truth."

"It is. But, Ewan, what do you want? Forcing me to stay makes no sense."

"I've no reason not to tell you, I suppose. I've use for your gift."

"My gift?"

"Aye, sure, and you need not look as if I were speaking in tongues, lass. I ken fine that you're a seventh daughter of a seventh daughter, and that you possess the gift of second sight."

"I still don't understand," Mary said, wholly bewildered now. "What can the Sight have to do with your wish to marry me?"

"Everything," he said flatly. "A seer told me that the only way to find a certain thing that's been lost to the MacCrichtons is through a seventh daughter."

"But the Sight cannot find lost articles," she protested. "Truly, sir, you do not understand. All it has ever shown me is the face of a dear one who died suddenly."

He made a dismissive gesture. "Don't argue. You have the gift of healing, for I've heard many speak of it. Men ask you to wash your hands in the water you use to clean their wounds. People with the Sight can find lost bodies, too, for I've heard of such myself, so why should you not find lost treasure?"

"Treasure?"

He spread his hands. "Just a manner of speaking, lass. Once I've explained the whole, you will understand right enough. First, though, we'll be man and wife."

"I am not going to be your wife, Ewan."

"Aye, then, you are, for another law I've looked into makes it necessary."

"What law is that?"

"So long as you are my wife, what you find belongs to me.

Otherwise, if you find what I seek, the Crown may claim it instead. I cannot have that. We've no need to talk more about it tonight, however," he added. "The hour grows late, and you must be longing for your bed. I'll take you upstairs now."

He signed to the boy squatting by the wall near the stairs. "Bring a torch, lad, and look lively unless you want to feel my whip across your back."

The boy leapt to take a torch from one of the men, holding it aloft with difficulty. Watching him stagger seemed to amuse Ewan, for he chuckled.

With nowhere else to go at that hour, Mary could see nothing to gain by arguing, and despite that chuckle, her stinging cheek reminded her of what the likely outcome of an argument would be. Therefore, she allowed Ewan to urge her in the wake of the child up the twisting stone stairway.

"Bar the gates and set a good watch," he said in passing to a man near the doorway. "I think we've flummoxed the lot of them, but it's as well to take care."

"Aye, master."

The stair went up and up, around and around, past other chambers in which Mary saw carpets and elegant, albeit shabby, furniture. At the top of the stairway they came to a stout oak door. Ewan pushed it open, revealing a room that boasted a once-bright Turkey carpet, but Mary saw that the carpet was threadbare and old. The furniture needed polish.

"This is your bedchamber, lass. Light candles, Chuff. Then be off with you."

The room was spacious enough. A tall, curtained bed stood against the center of the wall opposite the door. One corner opened into a round turret space, apparently arranged as a powder closet. A small fire crackled on the hearth at Mary's right, and thanks to the little boy, light from four tallow candles in plain brass sconces soon augmented the firelight. Her bundles already lay on the floor.

"Thank you," she said quietly, turning to Ewan. "It seems a pleasant room."

"Get out now, Chuff," he said. The boy fled, and the intent

look that leapt to Ewan's eyes as the door shut warned her a split second before he reached for her.

Skipping nimbly away, she said grimly, "If you are thinking of beginning that cohabitation tonight, my lord, you had better think again."

"Why is that, lass?" Grinning, he took another step toward her.

"Because if you lay one more hand on me tonight, I'll cast a spell over the source of your male seed, sir, that will cause it to shrivel up and fall off."

He stared at her in dismay for a long moment, then turned on his heel and strode angrily from the room. The door crashed behind him, but just as Mary was congratulating herself on being rid of him, she heard a key turn in the lock.

Across the loch, at the much larger, far more formidable Castle Dunraven, Black Duncan Campbell looked across the huge desk in his favorite sitting room at the messenger whose late arrival had drawn him wearily from his bed.

"You're certain of this news, Bannatyne?"

"Aye, master. Allan Breck has been seen in Rannoch and also in Lochaber."

"Over the past year men have reported seeing him in any number of places," Duncan said harshly. "He never seems to linger in any of them, however."

"Aye, that's a fact, that is," the shaggy-haired Bannatyne agreed. "No one claims to ha' seen him more than once, but the landlord at the Swan on Rannoch Moor kens him fine, sir, or so he says, and he said Allan Breck drank a dram o' whisky there not a sennight ago. Said he's here to collect more money for the exiled lairds, same as always, only this time rumor speaks of a substantial sum available to him. The name Mac-Crichton were spoken more than once, the landlord said."

"Not the first time, either," Duncan said, absently patting the collie that had followed him in from his bedchamber and now pushed its head into his lap. "The MacCrichtons have long run with the Stewarts of Appin. What's more, they seem to have taken advantage of the Earl of Balcardane's long absence from Creran to increase their power hereabouts."

"Only on the Appin side o' the loch," Bannatyne said loyally. "The Campbells still control this side."

Duncan grunted. "That devil MacCrichton seems resistant to the notion of letting lost causes lie, however. It's time that I had a word with him."

"They say he is nay a man to be trusted," Bannatyne said diffidently.

"Never fear. I don't trust any man." Duncan took a small pouch from the drawer of the desk and tossed it, jingling, to the man. "You've done well, Bannatyne. I'm sorry you had to trudge so far to find me. I came to Dunraven meaning only to move some of my horses from here to Balcardane, but it's as well now, I think, that I *am* here. Shian Towers lies just across the loch, so we'll take boats tomorrow, and I'll pay Ewan, Lord Bloody MacCrichton, a friendly visit."

"You'll nay go alone, sir!"

"I am not a fool," Duncan said. He spoke quietly, but his tone was such that Bannatyne flushed to the roots of his hair. "Though my worthy sire decries the cost of my entourage, I am thought to have sufficient men for my needs. But surely you don't think MacCrichton will be foolish enough to take up arms against me, Bannatyne. That would be against the law, would it not?"

Apparently laboring under the misconception that Duncan required an answer, Bannatyne said, "Aye, sir. It's gey unlawful for any Highlander to bear weapons, and has been since the Disarming Act nigh onto six years ago."

"Do you truly suppose that no Highlander carries a weapon, Bannatyne?"

Looking at the sword belt draped over one corner of Duncan's desk, then down at the *skean dhu* shoved into his own boot top, Bannatyne said with a frown, "Nay, sir. I'd nay put my trust in that."

"Then you are not such a gowk as I thought. Pray, when you

seek your pallet, send one of the lads sleeping in the hall here to me. I've instructions to give him."

When the man had gone, Duncan got up and put another log on the fire. As he straightened, his dark gaze lighted on the portrait dominating the chimneypiece.

A fair-haired youth attired in the blue, green, and yellow Campbell plaid sat proudly astride a sleek bay horse. The artist had painted the lad laughing, with an unhooded falcon perched tamely on his shoulder atop bunched folds of the plaid. At the horse's hooves a brown and white spotted spaniel romped gaily, bearing a bright red ball in its mouth, clearly inviting the rider to play.

Duncan's lips hardened into a straight line, and he felt the surge of anger he always felt when his thoughts turned to his younger brother, Ian.

Solemnly now, speaking directly to the portrait, he said, "I will not rest, lad, until the murderous Allan Breck is dead. And may heaven help Ewan MacCrichton if he knows aught of the scoundrel and attempts to keep that knowledge from me."

Two

Mary wasted no time feeling sorry for herself, knowing she would manage everything better after a good night's sleep. Stripping to her chemise, she snuffed all the candles except for one on the table near the bed, then moved to climb under the covers, intending to say her prayers when she could do so without shivering. With one leg up on the high bed, she glanced back at the door.

Ewan had locked it from the outside, but that would do her no good if he decided to test her nonexistent ability to cast spells. A small wooden side-chair stood against the wall opposite the end of the bed.

Remembering a trick that her cousin Allan Breck had once shown her, she ran barefoot over the cold floor and dragged the chair to the door, tilting it so that its back caught beneath the latch hook and its back legs rested firmly in a crack between two of the dark wooden floorboards. Testing it and finding it steady, she hurried back to bed and slipped beneath the covers, leaving the bed curtains open.

Pale moonlight glowed from the turret room, almost like fairy light, and it made the bedchamber seem friendlier and more secure than it had earlier. Staring up at the tester above her, she said her prayers, taking care to remember her aunt and her cousins, the many deceased members of her family, and Ian. Then, deciding she had done her duty by her loved ones, she added a postscript on her own behalf.

"Dear Lord," she murmured, "I don't know what you can do about my predicament, but I pray you will do something to keep Ewan from succeeding in his plan. You may perhaps decide that, having made the mistake of trusting him, I must suffer the consequences, and if that is your will, I must abide by it. However, I did have reason to think him a kind man, and it is plain now that he is nothing of the sort. He wants only to benefit from the fearsome gift you bestowed on me. Surely, you cannot want that gift employed in such a cause by such a man. I am willing to do my part if you will but show me the way. Thy will be done. Amen."

Hoping He would not think her impertinent for making such a request, especially in view of the fact that a promise to marry—even an informal one like the one she had made to Ewan—was a sacred act. Turning toward the turret chamber, she found comfort in the pale silvery glow, which seemed to have grown stronger.

As that thought crossed her mind, she slept, and although the sun poured in through that small chamber the following morning, she did not waken until she heard a rattling at the door. The rattle was followed by a clanking sound and then what sounded like a curse uttered in a very youthful voice.

"Who is there?" she called.

"Chuff's here, that's who's here, but the master give me a key that willna open this cursed door, so I'll ha' tae gae doon again and tell 'im, and he's as like tae give me a clout on me lug as tae give me another key."

"Wait," Mary called. "Don't go!"

Scrambling from the bed, snatching up one of the coverlets to drape around herself for modesty's sake, she hurried to move the chair away from the door.

"Try it now," she urged.

The key rattled again in the lock, and the latch lifted. She pulled the door open herself and looked down at the little boy, who stared back at her curiously from singularly light-colored eyes fringed with thick dark lashes. He wore a shabby saffron-colored shirt and baggy threadworn breeches held up by a belt of rawhide cords twisted around an oddly shaped piece of metal that served as a buckle. On his feet he wore shapeless leather boots, tied round his ankles with more rawhide strips.

"I brung yer breakfast," he said with a vague gesture toward a tray sitting on the top step behind him. "What did ye do tae the door?"

She hesitated to tell him, but she saw a glint of mischief in his eyes that told her instantly he would not side with Ewan against her. "If you will bring that tray in and put it down on that table by the hearth, I will show you what I did," she said.

With a crooked grin, showing that one of his permanent eye teeth was still growing in, he did as she had asked, then turned expectantly. "Now, show me."

She put the chair back where it had been. "See, the back fits under the latch hook, and the feet stick between the floorboards there, so the door cannot open."

He nodded. "That's clever, that is. I'll keep that in me mind, I will."

"I believe you will, Chuff. Thank you for bringing my breakfast."

"It isna much," he said. "Just porridge and a wee mug o' ale."

"Well, I'm hungry, so it will suit me just fine."

The boy eyed her curiously. "The master said he means tae marry ye."

"I know he did, and I did agree to marry him, but I have changed my mind, Chuff. A lady is allowed to do that, you know."

"Is she then?"

"She is. That is why your master locked the door."

He shot her an oblique look. "I'm tae lock it again, ye ken, when I leave ye."

Sorely tempted though she was to beg him to leave it unlocked or to give her the key, she could not do it. She had heard Ewan threaten to whip him, and she did not doubt that Chuff would suffer if he helped her, so she said instead, "Will you come back again to visit me, Chuff?"

His grin flashed. "I'm tae collect the tray when ye're done, so I can do that." With that, he moved the chair and took himself off, locking the door behind him.

Mary examined the tray and seeing nothing on it that encouraged her to make haste with her meal, she decided to dress first. She had no way to know how long Ewan would grant her privacy, and she knew she would feel much more capable of facing him with her clothes on.

Since the amenities provided for her consisted only of a chamber pot and a pitcher of cold water, attending to her ablutions required but a few moments, after which she put on a fresh gown from her baggage, and brushed her hair. Then, taking the bowl of porridge to the little turret chamber, where she found a dressing stool and a semicircular table, she sat down to break her fast.

Cheerful, warm sunlight streamed in through a casement window, the glass and frame of which were rounded to fit the curve of the turret. When she finished, she stood and unlatched the window, pushing it open to find that despite the sunlight and the consequent warmth of the little chamber, the air outside was brisk and chilly, and the sky not entirely clear. Puffy gray clouds scudded overhead.

For some reason, she had expected the window to overlook the courtyard, but it overlooked the hillside instead. Down to her right lay Loch Creran.

It occurred to her then that the twisting stairway had disoriented her. By the time she reached the top, she had lost all sense of north or south. She had thought, seeing the scene by moonlight, that the loch ended a short distance beyond the castle. Now she could see that it stretched much farther. A moment's thought told her that the castle sat on its hillside at a sharp bend in the loch, for she knew they had approached from the north, along the shore, and now she was looking south with water stretching both to her left and to her right.

She seemed to be in the southeast corner of the tower house. She could see two windows below, but beneath them she saw only ancient arrow loops of the sort designed with a central horizontal space to accommodate crossbows. Farther below, the ground fell sharply away toward the water in a steep escarpment.

To her left a deserted battlement stretched some twenty feet to a corner, and by leaning out she could see a small bit of the courtyard on the other side. It was a pity, she thought, that she could not just fly out of the window and back to Maclean House. Even so, if she could climb down without drawing attention from anyone in the courtyard, the curtain wall would hide her from viewers long enough to follow the escarpment around to the woods behind the castle. Alas, she thought with a self-mocking smile, no outside steps led down from the turret window.

She suddenly thought of a friend whose talents included climbing sheer cliffs and other walls with nothing to aid him but a pair of dirks. He had done so at least once that she knew about, to aid a tower-bound prisoner, but Bardie Gillonie did not even know that she was at Shian, let alone that she was there against her will.

The previous night's mist had gone, and now she could see the far shore of the loch, about a mile and a half away. A lone sailboat tacked swiftly toward the northeast, its sails billowing before a stiff breeze. Beyond it, beyond the far shore, a light sprinkling of early snow dusted forested hills, and she could see two tall black towers rising amidst the trees. She wondered if they belonged to Dunraven.

A click of the latch and a light rap sent her heart thudding into her throat, but they heralded only Chuff's return. With a last look at the water and the two black towers beyond, she returned to the bedchamber to greet him.

He said anxiously, "Ye dinna ought tae lean out o' that window, mistress. 'Tis a fearsome far way doon tae the ground gin ye fall."

"I won't fall, Chuff, although I don't deny that if I could find another way to get down there, I'd do it in an instant. I am here against my will, after all."

"How could ye do it without killing yourself?"

She shrugged. "I don't know, but if I had some rope, I'd try.

I daresay I shall find some other way, however, one that will be safer."

He looked skeptical. "Master doesna mean tae let ye go, mistress. I'm tae tell ye he wants ye below, too, and he isna enjoyin' a pleasant frame o' mind, the day."

Mary sighed. "I begin to think he rarely enjoys a pleasant frame of mind, Chuff. I was much mistaken in your master."

"He is a hard man," Chuff muttered, moving past her into the turret chamber to collect her bowl and mug. From within, he added, "I'll just close this window, mistress. He'd have a fit and all gin he sees it like this."

One of Ewan's men appeared in the open bedchamber doorway, saying curtly, "Mistress, the laird wants you below at once."

Chuff said indignantly, "I just got here m'self, and I tellt her that already."

"You clear up in here and get back to the kitchen," the man said harshly. "And hold your whisst if you don't want to feel my hand."

Chuff passed Mary, muttering darkly as he went to put her bowl and mug back on the tray.

She said hastily to Ewan's man, "I'll come straightaway. I just want to brush my hair and wash my face first."

"He willna care if your hair is tidy or your face is clean, mistress. He said to bring you, and he's that impatient. Come along now. The lad will tidy up here."

He looked grim, and Mary did not doubt for a moment that he would drag her if she resisted, so to preserve her dignity, she swept past him to the stairway.

Holding her skirt up and moving with care, since she had not descended such a stairway since leaving Lochfuaran, she felt overly conscious of the man behind her and of what lay ahead. So concentrated was she on minding her steps that she nearly passed by the entrance to the hall.

Ewan's voice startled her. "Come in here, lass. I hope you've come to your senses by now."

Collecting herself, she stepped into the room, moving to the hearth, where a fire leapt cheerfully. Empty brackets on the chimneypiece suggested that a claymore or musket had once hung there, but the only thing decorating the chimneypiece now was a riding whip that someone had left on the narrow wooden mantel.

"Well, lass?"

Striving to stay calm, she turned to face him and said, "I have not changed my mind about leaving, sir, if that is what you mean."

"That is no longer your decision to make," he said. "You have spent the night in this castle. If you were to leave now, folks would be bound to think the worst."

"I'll take that chance," she said, fearing he was right but determined not to let him know the point had shaken her. "People know me, and they know I do not tell falsehoods. If I say nothing happened, they will believe me."

"Some will, some won't," he said, "but it makes no difference. You will stay until I say you can leave, and by then there will be no question about your having become my lawful wife, I promise you."

His face had reddened, and she knew she would anger him more if she argued, so she said instead, "I still do not know exactly what you expect me to do for you. I would gladly help all I can if your cause is just, sir, without coercion."

"That's better," he said, shifting his position to perch on the edge of the great table that sat in the middle of the hall. "You'll soon learn just how to please me, lassie. I ken fine that you are no fool."

Keeping her temper with the help of long practice, Mary said, "You told me last night that a seer once predicted that a seventh daughter could help you. What makes you think I am such a one?"

"You did not deny it."

"I cannot, for it is true, but who told you about me?"

"Is it such a secret then?"

"No, but I would like to know who told you. I want to know,

too, why you thought it sufficient reason to court and marry me. Just what you think I can find?"

"You've no need to know more than I choose to tell you."

"Faith, sir, how will I recognize what you seek if I don't know what it is?"

"You seek what has been lost to the MacCrichtons," he growled.

She sighed. "Whatever happens, Ewan, I doubt that I shall have a vision of something with *MacCrichton* written across it in bold letters."

He grimaced, but to her relief he did not lash out at her. After a moment, he said, "Very well, then, I'll tell you, but only because you won't be able to tell anyone else. Before we joined the prince in '45, my father, my younger brother, and I buried our family treasure—a chest of gold coins, family jewelry, and such like stuff—so no one could steal it whilst we were away and leave us destitute."

"Surely you must know where you buried it!"

"That's the rub, lass. My brother, Geordie, was a mite daftish. Not crazed or mad, just not sensible like. We notched a tree near the treasure, but then we thought we heard someone coming and I saw that Geordie had made the notch on the tree so eye-catching that anyone would know at once that something lay buried there."

"Who was coming?"

Ewan shrugged. "We never saw anyone, just heard sounds, but Shian stands right on the boundary of Appin county. Yonder, across the loch, lies Campbell land, including the Earl of Caddell's estates and Dunraven, Balcardane's ancient seat. The present earl removed long since to his castle on Loch Leven—the one his grandfather stole from the Stewarts and renamed to match the earldom the English gave him. Still, all the land south of here crawls with Campbells to this day."

"So what did you do when you heard the noise?"

"I got a notion to notch more of the trees around us, and I set Geordie to helping me. Then my father said we had done enough and ought to go inside. Geordie was to do a few more trees and bring the shovels in, but the daft lad stayed out most of the night. I waited up a bit for him, but when he did not come, I thought he had gone off to visit his woman. We were leaving the next day, after all. Instead, I discovered that the fool had notched well nigh every tree in the forest."

Mary felt a bubble of laughter forming, but she suppressed it, saying, "Did your brother not remember where the chest lay buried, either?"

"Geordie died at Culloden," Ewan said shortly, "like my father."

"You never told me that, only that they died fighting for the prince. Even so, did you not make an effort, the pair of you, to find it again before you left Appin?"

"I lost my temper and hit him," Ewan said. "Anyone would have done the same, but he refused to discuss the treasure after that, saying only that he would show me when we got home again that he was not so daft as I thought him."

"But he never came home," she said quietly.

"No."

"Why are you in such a rush now? It's been six years since Culloden, and you waited a full year for me."

"After Culloden I hid out in the hills with the prince," he said harshly. "I was certain someone would betray us, too, because the damned English offered a bounty of thirty thousand pounds for him. A fortune, that was."

"An astounding amount," she agreed. "I warrant the English still cannot understand why no one betrayed him for such a vast amount."

"Aye, well, I was tempted myself more than once. Might have done it had I not thought they'd chop my head off along with his. Still, we got safe to France, and by biding my time and playing it shrewd, I was able to arrange a full pardon. They even let me keep Shian and my title, though unlike Campbell titles, it don't count for spit outside Scotland. I returned just in time to hear James Stewart sentenced."

"Where you met me," Mary said. "I don't understand,

though, what led you to believe that my powers include the ability to find things. I cannot do that, sir."

"You will," he said. "Part of the agreement I made to obtain my pardon included a substantial payment to the Crown. I'd expected to make it easily once I'd recovered the treasure, but I've dug up nearly every inch of that forest, and I can't find it, so you must. What's more, we'll be man and wife before we dig it up."

"Ewan, I will certainly tell you if at any time I have a vision revealing the whereabouts of your treasure, but I simply cannot marry you now."

"You'll do as you're bid," he snapped, hefting himself off the table and striding to catch her by the shoulders. He shook her. "Do you hear me, lass?"

"Aye, I hear you," she said grimly, "but I won't marry you."

"That's where you're wrong, Mary Maclaine. You need to learn a harsh lesson, my lass, but learn it you will, and right speedily. The sooner you know that you've got to do what I say, the better." With that, holding her tightly by an arm, he dragged her to the hearth, and snatched the riding whip from the mantel.

Having risen before dawn to finish the few remaining tasks he had set for himself at Dunraven, Black Duncan ordered most of his men to ride north with his dogs and all the horses until they could ford the loch at the narrows. When they had a good start, he would take the three remaining men with him and sail across the loch. The breeze remained brisk, so his crossing would be swift. With only three companions, his party would not look threatening to MacCrichton.

He doubted that the ex-rebel kept many men with him. Though he was doing his best to behave like a law-abiding citizen now that he had made his peace with the authorities, he did not fool Duncan. MacCrichton was a leopard who would never change his spots, and his friend Allan Breck was just such another.

Duncan knew, for Breck had admitted as much to others, that

he had murdered Ian. Of course, Breck, who had been in Appin illegally on one of his frequent forays to collect money, second rents, for the exiled rebel lairds, had insisted the death was accidental. Evidently, Ian had surprised him, and afraid the lad would betray him to searching authorities, Breck had struck him down.

The authorities had certainly been searching high and low for Breck at the time, because they suspected him of conspiring to murder Crown factor Colin Glenure. Indeed, many believed he had fired the shot that killed the man. Duncan had had no great love for Glenure, but from the day he learned of Breck's part in Ian's death, he had sworn to have his revenge.

The night Ian died, he had been going to visit the bewitching Mary Maclaine. Entranced by rumors of second sight and her knowledge of healing remedies, the lad imagined himself in love with her, and no one could convince him of his folly. That Duncan had ordered him to stay away from Maclean House, and had warned him never to walk or ride through Stewart country without an escort to protect him, only made him angry now whenever he thought about how right he had been.

Anyone could see that Ian simply had been infatuated with the sly but winsome lass. She was different from others he had known, with her fey ways and her silver eyes that looked like serene moonlit pools of water.

Ian had been particularly vulnerable to her spell. Doubtless the poor lad had felt isolated at Balcardane, which lay in the midst of Stewart country, far from his fellow Campbells. Eager to make friends, Ian had believed that because he cared nothing for politics or causes, the local folk would forgive him his antecedents.

They had certainly pretended to do so, tramping the hills or sailing with him, inviting him into their homes, and calling him Gentle Ian. But he had been foolish to think that Stewarts, Macleans, and others of their ilk, still bemoaning the failure of a rebellion doomed from the start, still grieving for their idiot Young Pretender, could forget that Ian was a Campbell. As a result, Allan Breck had murdered him in cold blood one dark night simply because they had met unexpectedly.

The fury Duncan felt toward Breck had threatened more than once to overwhelm him. Because he blamed himself as much as anyone for Ian's having failed to accept his excellent advice, he had flung himself into a depression afterward that had come near to ending his sanity. He had drunk too much and gamed too much, fought too many demons, and generally had infuriated his father.

He had even fought with his cousin Rory Campbell, Lord Calder, because Rory had insisted on marrying Diana Maclean. Bad enough that he was marrying into the wretched Maclean clan, but Rory had announced he would do so without waiting the full year that Duncan thought appropriate for mourning Ian's death.

When Rory had said callously that if Campbells were to put off marriage for a full year after every Campbell death, they would never marry at all, Duncan had leapt at him and tried to knock him down. To his humiliation, Rory had just stepped aside and told him he was drunk and to go soak his head.

Thinking about that now, Duncan's lips twitched with sudden grim humor. They had nearly come to blows more than once, the pair of them, but somehow (doubtless because Rory had better control over his temper than Duncan had over his) they had never fought. Had they done so, he knew the end would have been a near thing, because Rory was nearly of a size with him, but he thought he would have prevailed. He had had more practice, after all, with violence.

Having taken the field during the late uprising, he had proved himself in battle, while Rory had followed in Argyll's train, spending more time in London than in Scotland. Not that Duncan held that against him. He had come to respect his cousin deeply. He even liked him, but he was glad that Rory was in Perthshire now and not in Argyll. Rory would not approve of what he meant to do about Allan Breck, and he would strongly disapprove of any visit to MacCrichton.

"The lads are ready now, master," Bannatyne said from the doorway. "The breeze blows from the west."

"Too bad it's not from the south," Duncan said, getting to his feet. He picked up his dirk from the desktop and shoved it into his boot, adjusting the boot top so the weapon did not show too easily. Then, taking a dark-blue wool cloak from the back of a chair where he had tossed it earlier, he flung it over his shoulders, picked up his gloves and hat, and strode past Bannatyne across the hall and outside.

The air felt crisp and cold, and dark clouds were gathering in the north, but the wind, as Bannatyne had said, blew straight from the west. Perhaps the forthcoming storm would miss them, but he knew that he might find himself returning to Dunraven instead of going on to Balcardane after he paid his visit to Mac-Crichton. Someone would have to bring the boat back, in any event.

The other two men were waiting, ready to set sail the minute he and Bannatyne were aboard. The boat was good sized, a seaworthy craft, requiring a crew of at least two or three. Loch Creran was not wide, but it was six miles long and emptied into the Lynn of Lorne near its confluence with Loch Linnhe. Good boats were assets, and several that he had seen sailing the loch qualified more as small ships than as mere sailboats.

They had the loch to themselves, however, when they set out. With the wind coming from west they could not sail straight across, and tacking to the east took time. Watching the far coast, Duncan soon saw with satisfaction that the rest of his men had reached their position. They would move no farther unless he signaled to them, or did not reappear within an hour after entering the castle.

No one challenged them when they approached the wooden dock below the water gate at Shian, but Duncan could see a watchman standing at the corner of the battlements, overlooking the main track to the castle as well as the loch approach.

Duncan exchanged a look with Bannatyne, saying, "Perhaps MacCrichton posts guards as a matter of habit."

"Aye, sir, we do the same at Balcardane."

Disembarking, they left two men with the boat and climbed the steep escarpment to the water gate, which remained closed. The watchman, however, had moved nearer. He stood just above them now.

"Ho there," Duncan shouted. "I want speech with the laird."

"Who are you?"

"Duncan Campbell, Master of Dunraven. Tell him I request hospitality."

The man nodded and turned away. Several moments later, the water gate opened, and another man bade them welcome and led them toward the entrance.

Duncan looked around curiously. He counted seven men, none of whom seemed obviously to carry arms. He did not think for a moment that they could not defend themselves, however.

Bannatyne muttered, "Shall I stay here in the courtyard, master?"

"No, we'll stay together. I don't want to come out again to find you spitted over a slow fire. The lads can cast off if they must, but you'd be all on your own."

They followed their guide up the wooden stairway to the entrance, where he pushed open the heavy door without ceremony and went directly up a spiral flight of stone steps, clearly expecting them to follow.

So intent was Duncan upon obtaining a clear picture of the castle layout that he did not instantly pay heed to a masculine voice raised in anger above. However, as they neared the first doorway in the stone wall, he distinctly heard, ". . . a harsh lesson, my lass, but learn it you will, and right speedily. The sooner you know that you've got to do what I say, the better!"

Duncan's guide had reached the opening, and he stopped there, clearly stunned. Looking back at Duncan, clearly having second thoughts about having brought him there, he looked again into the room.

Just then, Duncan heard cloth tearing and a shriek of terror or fury.

The man above him on the stairs, apparently having made up

his mind, turned back toward him, saying urgently, "We'd best
go back d—"

He did not finish, for Duncan pushed roughly past him into
the great hall, where he saw MacCrichton with one arm around
the waist of a fiercely struggling female. Her bare backside
faced Duncan, and slim bare legs flashed furiously as she tried
to kick her captor, but MacCrichton held her firmly bent over
his knee. Thick tawny hair covered her face. Her dress lay in
tatters at his feet, and her chemise had bunched up above the
muscular arm that held her. In his free hand, raised to strike,
MacCrichton held a riding whip. One fiery red line already
striped her bottom.

His attention diverted to the doorway, MacCrichton snarled,
"Get out!"

Behind Duncan, his guide said anxiously, "He claimed hospitality, laird. Said he wanted speech wi' ye. 'Tis Black Duncan
Campbell, laird."

"The devil it is. Well, if you've come for the lass, Duncan,
you're too late. She's a wild piece, but she agreed to marry me
and she's spent a full night here, so I have every right now to
tame her as and when I please. Here, lass, stand up and bid a
civil good-morning to Black Duncan."

The girl had gone utterly still, and she did not move until
MacCrichton dumped her unceremoniously to the floor. Then,
hastily pulling her chemise down to cover her, and pushing her
thick hair back from her face, she looked at Duncan.

She was the last person he had expected to see at Shian Towers. Concealing his shock, albeit with difficulty, he said evenly,
"Accept my compliments on your marriage, mistress. You have
come by your just dessert, I believe."

Three

Mary's shock at seeing Black Duncan in the great hall at Shian Towers suppressed the agony of the single whip stroke, but embarrassment and humiliation washed over her when he spoke. She would have begged help from almost anyone just then, but when his scathing words and sarcastic tone made it clear that he would ignore her plea, she decided she would rather die at Ewan's hand than give Duncan that satisfaction.

Ewan chuckled. "As you see, her manners need mending, but perhaps that does not surprise you, since she was friendly with your brother, Ian."

"They were acquainted," Duncan said curtly. "You say you are betrothed to her, MacCrichton?"

"I am," Ewan said, shooting Mary a look that dared her to deny it.

"I wish you happiness then and thank you for your hospitality."

Cursing herself for cowardice, Mary held her tongue and reached for the frock Ewan had torn from her body. Gathering it close, she watched him warily, but his attention had darted back to Black Duncan.

"You don't require hospitality," Ewan snapped. "My people ought never to have let you in, and I'll have something to say to them, I can tell you." He glared at the man who had accompanied Duncan.

Near them, standing quietly, Mary saw the man who had

brought her downstairs. Another, in the stairwell, she suspected was Duncan's man. Knowing he frequently traveled with a tail that would do a clan chief proud, and wondering how many had accompanied him to Shian, she drew her frock closer and inched away from Ewan toward the table in the center of the room. Ewan paid her no heed, but Black Duncan was watching her. Perhaps, if he meant trouble, as he generally did, she would find a way to escape during the confusion.

Duncan said in his usual curt way, "I come in peace, Mac-Crichton. I want information from you, which is why I claimed hospitality from your people. They are Highlanders, so they had little choice but to grant my request. Surely you do not deny hospitality to anyone who requests it."

"That depends on how many men he brings with him," Ewan said.

"Just three, laird," his man interjected hastily. "Two remained in the boat."

Ewan grunted and went on without taking his eyes off Duncan, "Even so, you Campbells have a reputation for abusing hospitality that goes back nigh onto a hundred years. Or perhaps they do not teach Campbell children about Glencoe."

"That was a hundred years ago. My home is not far from there, you know."

"Aye, and Balcardane is yet another example of Campbell thievery," Ewan said harshly. "That castle belonged to Stewarts for three hundred years, sir, before your lot snatched it away."

"That, like the massacre, occurred before I was born," Duncan said. "I came in peace to hold private speech with you about a matter of importance to me."

"Did you now?"

Mary straightened, gathering the remnants of her frock around her. Still moving steadily away from Ewan, she edged toward the doorway.

Abruptly, Duncan said, "Send the lass and your men away, and I will send my man downstairs. We can talk better without an audience."

"I'll keep one of my men," Ewan said. "I don't trust any

Campbell, and I'd as lief have a witness to what you say to me. You stay, MacSteele." He gestured to the one who had escorted Mary from her room.

"In that case, I'll keep my man, too." Duncan stood his ground, his very posture a challenge to Ewan to argue the point.

"As you will then," Ewan said. "I can attend to the lass later. I've given her something to think about, at all events. She's run her own course for far too long, but I am not a man to let a lass twist him round her thumb."

"I'll wager you are not," Black Duncan said, sounding almost amiable.

Mary waited no longer, hurrying to the doorway and bolting past the men, then upstairs to the tower bedchamber, where she found Chuff on the point of departure. The boy had swept the hearth and made up the bed. The tray with her dishes waited for him at the top of the stairs.

"Oh, Chuff, I'm glad you are still here," she exclaimed when he stared at her in astonishment. "Can you fetch me a rope, a long rope? Strong, too," she added.

"I might," he said with a shrewd look. "What happened tae your dress, and why are ye wanting the rope, forbye?"

"I must get away from here, Chuff. I cannot stay."

"The laird tore your gown off." It was a statement, not a question.

"He did more than that, and he means to do more yet. I must get away!"

"I'll no lock the door, then. He'll be wroth wi' me, I'm thinking, but—"

"Thank you, but it would do me no good. His men guard this stairway, and even if I could sneak down a service stair, I could never get beyond the courtyard without the men there seeing me. And what he would do then . . ."

Chuff shuddered. "Ye needna tell me, but what good can a rope be?"

"If it is long enough, I can tie it to the bedpost and climb down it to the ground outside the wall."

"Nay, then, ye'll fall!"

"No, I won't. Oh, don't argue with me, Chuff. Will you do as I ask?"

"Aye, then, I will, but only if ye tak' me with ye. I ken fine the woods behind the castle, and the ridge beyond them, too."

"Oh, Chuff, I mustn't do that. It's too dangerous, and cold besides, and——"

"Then ye shouldna go either, and I doot I'll find ye a rope."

Mary hesitated. If she agreed to take him, and if Ewan caught them, she did not even want to think about what he would do to either of them.

Evidently taking her hesitation for reluctance, Chuff said, "I canna stay here if I help ye. The laird . . . It isna that I am a coward, so ye needna be thinking I am. There are things ye dinna ken. I can tell ye all about it, if ye like, but it will tak' a deal o' talking, and so——"

"You can go with me. Just hurry, Chuff, and mind now, get a long rope!"

The boy hurried off, leaving the tray where it lay, and Mary shut the door. For a moment, she considered her chances of slipping down into the courtyard and out by the postern or water gate, but she dismissed the thought as foolish. The only chance she had lay in getting away while Ewan talked with Black Duncan, and the courtyard would never be empty of men while an enemy remained inside. As it was, she would fail if Ewan had taken it into his head to post guards to watch for any more of Duncan's men who might be approaching from the hills.

That thought stirred her to action. Swiftly, she cast aside her tattered frock, and found a fresh one in her case, of plain brown camlet with a simple ankle-length skirt and matching jacket. The outfit was one she generally wore to walk in the hills or by the shore. Slipping the dress on, she struggled to fasten all the buttons, which marched down the back and with which she generally required help. But she finished the task unaided in record time.

Quickly donning the jacket, she replaced the thin shoes she had worn with half boots, and as a second thought, found a pair of leather gloves and her cloak. It was cold out, and she did not know if she could reach Maclean House in a day. If she went toward Loch Linnhe, and the weather held, she could make it, but that was the most likely route for her, a fact that would not escape Ewan's notice.

She decided to go up Glen Creran. Ewan would not look for her that way until he had tried the other, and she could seek refuge with Bardie Gillonie, whose cottage lay in a small side glen near the top of Glen Duror.

She finished dressing before Chuff returned, all the while listening carefully for heavier footsteps on the stairs. Her tension increased by the minute. Pacing, she thought of a dozen things that could go wrong.

The most likely was that she would fall. She had never climbed down a rope before, and she suspected that it would prove harder than she imagined rather than easier. Knowing what Ewan meant to do to her after Duncan left lent her courage, however, and when she finally heard Chuff returning, she rushed to meet him. With relief she saw that he carried a thick coil of rope slung over one thin shoulder.

"I thought you were never coming," she said.

"I had tae nip round the laird's men," he said. "D'ye want me tae help? 'Cause if I'm tae meet up wi' ye, I'd best be skipping out afore anyone finds I mean tae go."

"Yes, go at once," Mary said. "If someone catches me at this, I don't want them suspecting that you helped me. Take that tray with you when you go, and hope they think I found this rope under the bed, or that someone else gave it to me."

"But can ye manage it all on yer own?"

"Go, Chuff!"

He obeyed, albeit with clear reluctance, and the moment he had gone, Mary set the side chair under the latch hook, anchoring it firmly between floorboards. Then, hurrying, her mind focused solely on her task now, she tied one end of the rope to a stout bedpost, uncoiled the rest, and flung it out of the open window, noting with satisfaction that it reached nearly to the top of the steep escarpment.

* * *

Despite his words to her, Duncan had found it hard to ignore MacCrichton's treatment of Mary Maclaine. He had often thought he would like to skelp the lass himself for exerting her feminine wiles to draw Ian to her side on the fatal night. But thinking such thoughts and seeing a burly man like Mac-Crichton take a whip to her had proved to be two entirely different things.

He had more important matters to deal with at the moment, however, so he forced himself to concentrate on learning the whereabouts of Allan Breck. That, after all, was why he had come to Shian Towers. It was no business of his what Mac-Crichton did with the woman he meant to marry.

Duncan waited only until the door had shut behind the wench. Then, drawing up a chair near MacCrichton's, he said, "I want to ask you about the outlaw Allan Breck. I'm told that you might know where I can find him."

"What name was that again?"

Barely controlling a surge of impatience, Duncan said, "Allan Breck. He is a Stewart, related to Ardsheal and suspected of conspiring with James Stewart in the Appin murders."

"Half of Appin claims kinship to Ardsheal," MacCrichton said. "As to the Appin murders, your father and the others who investigated still think those same folks conspired to murder Glenure. Ardsheal's exile has accomplished little."

"He betrayed his country," Duncan said evenly. "He is fortunate to have escaped to France. In any event, it is not about the Laird of Ardsheal that I seek information. Tell me what you know of Allan Breck."

"Breck . . . Breck . . ."

"Don't muck about, MacCrichton. I know that you are acquainted with the man, so equivocation will only lead me to count you as his friend. You don't want that, for you will soon find that you cannot move a step away from Shian Towers without men following and watching where you go. They'll also watch all who come and go here. I don't think you or your real friends want that."

MacCrichton grimaced. "I do not. What a thing to do to a

man! Still, it won't be as easy as you claim, what with winter coming on and all."

"By the time the heavy snow flies, Breck will be back in France, but you will still be here," Duncan pointed out. "I want him, and I think he is in the Highlands now. Believe me when I tell you that you don't want to be the man who keeps me from getting my hands on him."

"Here now," MacCrichton began, glaring at him, but when Duncan gazed grimly back at him, he did not continue. Instead, after swallowing visibly, he cleared his throat and said in quite a different tone, "Fetch ale, MacSteele."

Duncan did not press him, but MacCrichton's hesitation had not surprised him. Though the two were of comparative size and weight, he had watched even larger men blench when he grew angry. He waited until MacCrichton's man poured their ale. Then, sitting on a bench by the table and stretching his legs toward the warmth of the fire, he said, "What do you know about Breck?"

MacCrichton drank deeply. Then he said, "I do not know why you think I'm your man. I'll not deny I know Breck. Nor I won't deny that I know many hereabouts think he killed Glenure and that you think he killed your brother."

"I know he killed Ian. He confessed as much to his own cousin."

"What, to Mary? She never said he confessed to—"

"I don't know if he told her," Duncan said impatiently. "He told his cousin Diana Maclean. Your Mary has lived with Diana's family these seven years and more, however, and since they are cousins, then Breck . . ."

"She don't like him much, that's certain," MacCrichton said. "She's hinted as much to me more than once this past year." His gaze shifted.

Duncan waited, knowing the man had more to say and would be more likely to say it if he did not press him.

MacCrichton grimaced. "Aye, then, she did say she holds Breck responsible. Said he killed Ian in a fight, but Breck said—" He flashed an angry look at Duncan. "You needn't look at me like that. She don't blame him for Ian's death near as much as she blames—" He glanced at Duncan, cleared his throat again noisily, then muttered, "It don't matter what she thinks. She's just a foolish woman."

Duncan got up and set his mug on the big table with a bang. "You are trying my patience," he snapped. "Tell me what you know about Breck, and I'll go."

"I know he's in the district," MacCrichton said, capitulating, "but I'm speaking God's truth when I say I don't know where he is. You might find him on Rannoch Moor, for he has friends there, and his mother. I cannot think why you came to me."

"Then I will tell you," Duncan said grimly. "I've come because I heard that he expects to receive a large sum of money this trip, more than usual and enough to begin yet a new movement in France. Perhaps here, as well. Whenever men mention that unusual sum, MacCrichton, your name comes up. Now, what about it?"

MacCrichton turned pale. Then, even as Duncan began to doubt his sources, he leapt to his feet, and just as quickly as his color had fled, it returned, reddening his face with anger.

"My name," he cried. "What the devil would my name have to do with anything?"

"Look, I'm just telling you that—"

As if Duncan had not spoken, MacCrichton went on furiously, "If I had money to give someone like Breck, would I not have paid what I owe to the Crown for my pardon? I've only till Candlemas to produce two thousand pounds, and that sum is nowhere as great as the sort of money you're talking about. Do I look like a bloody philanthropist? For that matter, do I look like the sort of man to entrust my money to a chap like Allan Breck?"

"You fought for the same cause," Duncan reminded him.

"Aye, and I know what manner of man he is. Don't forget that until a year ago I was in France myself. Had I known the whereabouts of such a sum, and wanted to donate it, would I not have asked him to fetch it then, when the movement was stirring and in sore need of funding? Use your head, damn you!"

At first, MacCrichton's diatribe shook Duncan's belief in his connection to Allan Breck, but the more he protested, the less uncertain Duncan became. He could not doubt that something in what he had said had shocked the man. Nor could he doubt MacCrichton's sudden fury, but he did not seem to be directing that fury at Duncan. Waiting until he was certain the other man meant to say no more, Duncan said quietly, "Might Mistress Maclaine have knowledge of Breck's whereabouts?"

"Ask her," MacCrichton growled.

His quick agreement made Duncan wonder if he was eager to shift the focus of the questions away from himself to Mary. Still, Breck had visited Maclean House on more than one occasion. Perhaps the lass did know where he was.

"Send your man to fetch her back here then," Duncan said.

MacCrichton gestured to his henchman, and Duncan noted with satisfaction that Bannatyne followed the man into the stairwell to make certain he went up and not down. Bannatyne was a good man.

"Have some more ale," MacCrichton said with a sigh. "I've no quarrel with you. In point of fact, I feared when I saw you that you had come for the lass."

"Why would I do that?"

MacCrichton shrugged. "She was close to your brother. I thought you might feel some responsibility toward her, and I did not think she had told you about our intention to marry."

"Did she tell anyone?" Duncan's tone was sarcastic.

"Oh, her people know we intend to marry. They will be surprised to learn we are doing so at once, I suspect, but the lass wanted the security of a home of her own. We were to wait until spring, but when her kinsmen decided to journey into Perthshire for the winter, she grew lonely and tumbled into my lap, so to speak."

"True love, then." Duncan heard the edge in his voice and said no more. He did not want to reveal his feelings about Mary Maclaine to this man.

MacCrichton had heard the edge, for he said hastily, "Don't be thinking she did not really care for Ian, for nothing could be farther from the truth. She insisted upon a full year's mourning, and more, for she mourned James Stewart as well. But we agreed that she would be wiser to get herself settled before winter set in, rather than spend the whole season alone. Since she had decided not to travel into Perthshire with her aunt and cousin, it seemed an excellent notion."

Duncan frowned. "Somehow, MacCrichton, I did not perceive that the pair of you were wildly in love."

MacCrichton chuckled. "You mean because I put her across my knee? Lord, man, she's been leading me a dance, and she thought she could call the tune here the way she's called it the past year and more. I just decided to show her where her duty lies. She defied me, and I showed her the error of her ways."

"Well, don't do it again until I've gone. I won't trust information that has to be beaten out of the lass."

"I doubt she'll say much at all if we don't press her."

"You leave me to ask the questions then, for I can promise you, she knows me well enough that she won't dare lie to me. I'll find out what she knows."

MacCrichton shrugged, getting up to refill his own mug, then looking impatiently toward the door. "Can't think what's keeping them. She's had time and more to put her clothes on, and MacSteele knows better than to keep me waiting."

Just then a clatter of boots sounded on the stone steps.

Bannatyne stuck his head in, saying to Duncan, "He's coming now, sir."

MacSteele hurried in, his face red. He was alone.

"Where the devil's the girl?" MacCrichton demanded.

"She willna open the door, laird."

"You have a key, man. Use it!"

"I tried, laird, but though I turn it, the door willna open. She wouldna answer when I called, either. Mayhap she's had a fit and all."

"Nonsense," MacCrichton said, striding toward the door.

Duncan followed, wondering if MacCrichton had done more to her than he had seen him do. There had been only the one stripe, and she had not been screaming hysterically. One stripe and one scream seemed insufficient cause for a fainting fit, or worse. More likely, the lass was being obstreperous. Lord knew, the Maclean women were not known for being soft or submissive.

They soon reached the top of the stairs, and Duncan suddenly found himself suppressing laughter at the sight of MacCrichton and his henchman both trying to open the door at once. The area was small, lacking adequate room for both men to move about in the small space. MacSteele quickly gave way to his master, however, and MacCrichton rattled the door, then banged on it angrily.

"Open this door, lass! I'll make you sorry if I have to break it down."

Silence greeted him.

He pounded again. "Open this door at once! Do you hear me?"

More silence.

Duncan said, "Are you sure your man unlocked the door? What if it was unlocked before, and when he turned the key he locked it?"

MacCrichton stared at him, then looked at MacSteele. The henchman said quickly, "Mistress Maclaine ran up here, laird, and she didna have a key. The lad, Chuff, had one, and he must have been here when she came or the door would not be locked now. It takes a key to lock it, ye ken, and it canna be locked from inside."

"That's just what Black Duncan said, you fool. If the lad left it unlocked because she had not yet returned, she would just have closed it, not locked it. Are you sure you did not lock the door instead of unlocking it?"

"Aye, I'm sure, but ye can try for yourself, laird. Here's the key."

Snatching it from him, MacCrichton put it in the keyhole and turned it, trying to lift the latch at the same time. The latch would not budge.

"See, laird, it's like I said. The door willna open either way."

Turning the key again, MacCrichton nodded. "You're right,

so what the devil is wrong here? She's done something to it."
Raising his voice, he snapped, "Mary, come open this door, or
by God I'll flog the skin right off your backside!"

No reply came from within.

Duncan said, "How solid is that door?"

"Not solid enough to stop me from getting in," MacCrichton
said grimly. Gathering himself, he flung his body against it, but
there was little room to gain momentum, and he fell back with
a grimace of pain. The door had not budged.

"Stand back," Duncan said. "I think it must be blocked inside. Let me see how it feels."

"If it's blocked," MacCrichton said, standing back to make
room for him, "it's something bloody effective. That door won't
budge."

Duncan saw at once what he meant. Turning the key, he could
feel the lock mechanism move, but no matter which way he
turned it, the latch remained stuck. "There is no great mystery
about which way the key must turn," he said.

"It's like any other," MacCrichton said. "The devil fly away
with the wench. I'll take her apart for this trick. See if I don't."

Duncan ignored him, surveying the door thoughtfully. "Since
it's the latch that won't move, we can assume she has not put
the bed or some other heavy piece of furniture in front of it."

"She couldn't move that bed alone," MacCrichton said con-
fidently. "The only other furniture in there is a table or two, a
stool, and a pair of side chairs. She's jammed the latch, that's
what she's done."

Duncan nodded. He had come to the same conclusion himself. Bracing himself with his hands against the stone walls on
either side of the doorway, he brought up one leg and kicked
the door hard at latch level. He felt it give slightly, but it remained shut. "Brace me from behind, both of you," he ordered.

With the two men holding him, he was able to put more
power behind his next kick. With a loud crack and the sound
of wood fragments scattering across the floor, the door flew
open. What remained of a small side chair, broken into numer-
ous pieces, lay just beyond the open door.

"What the—" MacCrichton stared at the remains.

"She jammed it under the latch hook," Duncan said. "Where is she?"

MacCrichton hurried across the room, kicking chair pieces out of his way, and peered into and under the curtained bed. The curtains hung open, and Duncan could easily see that the bed provided no dark space large enough to conceal a grown woman. Nonetheless, MacCrichton jerked off the featherbed and shook it, as if he expected to find her stuffed inside or underneath it.

A swift look around told Duncan that she was not in the bedchamber. He strode into the small adjoining turret chamber.

"Here, MacCrichton," he called seconds later as he leaned out of the open window to pull in the rope that dangled a dizzying thirty feet or more to the ground. "I'm afraid that your love bird has flown away."

Four

Terrified that someone would look up from the courtyard or come around the wall from the dock or the main gate and see her climbing out of the window, Mary had wasted no time once she decided what she had to do. The action soon proved more difficult than the thought, however.

She had realized at once that she could not climb down a rope in her cloak, so she had dropped it to the escarpment. After some trial and error, she discovered that by using the rope, she could sit on the window ledge and balance there, but it was quite another thing to ease over the edge holding nothing but the rope. At first she did not think she could do it, but fear that someone in the courtyard might look up and see her, added to the greater fear that Ewan would soon come in search of her gave her the motivation to do it. Nonetheless, the plan nearly came to an untimely end when her skirt got wedged in the angle of the window opening.

Hanging there ungracefully, legs flailing, her skirt caught just above her, she could think of only one thing to do. Drawing a breath and saying a quick prayer, she let go with one hand to reach up with the other to yank the material free. For a dizzying moment, her weight seemed to be too much to hold, and the hand gripping the rope slipped. Then her other hand grabbed hold, and the moment passed.

Glancing toward the one corner of the courtyard that she could see, and taking courage from the fact that it remained unoccupied, she began to let herself down hand over hand. She had hitherto thought her hands and arms quite strong from doing housework and riding, but she quickly realized that she was not strong enough to dawdle. The turret being near the battlement helped once she was below the latter's top edge, for by swinging slightly she could push against the curtain wall with her feet. That relieved her hands of the weight and made her descent easier.

Not until she reached the end of the rope did she realize that it was not as long as she had thought it was. Some six feet of open space remained below her, and the top of the steep escarpment was barely narrow enough for a foot path. If she stumbled, or tripped on the cloak that was lying there, she would tumble some fifteen or so feet farther into the icy waters of the loch. She did not think the fall would kill her, but it would certainly do her no good.

Turning so that her left side was against the rough wall, and resisting a strong impulse to shut her eyes, she drew another breath and let go. She landed, bending her knees to soften the shock and grabbing the wall to steady herself.

She had done it. Glancing quickly around, she saw no one. The water gate lay around the corner in front of her, however, and she wanted to reach the hillside behind the castle as quickly as possible without being seen.

The path on which she had landed was no more than a foot wide, but it seemed to go right round the castle, so picking up her cloak and putting it on, she turned and followed it, regretting that she had no way to retrieve the rope now that it had served its purpose. There was none, however, so she dismissed all thought of it from her mind and hurried to the next corner, pausing there long enough to peek round it and be certain that no guard awaited her. None did. The hillside was clear.

Hugging the wall, knowing it would be less likely for someone to see her in the shadows there, she hurried along till she came to where the distance to the trees seemed shortest. Just as she was about to make a dash for it, someone hissed at her, and she nearly jumped out of her skin.

She had been watching the woods and listening for sounds from above that might warn her of guards looking over the battlements. Now, seeing Chuff emerge from a narrow opening just ahead, clutching a small duffel, she remembered that she had told him he could go with her. To her shock and dismay, however, she saw that he held a little girl tightly by one hand.

"Chuff, who is this?"

"She's me sister," Chuff said. "I'll explain it all when we get safe. There is nay time the noo for blethering."

Mary agreed wholeheartedly with the last statement, so she said no more, asking instead how they had got outside the castle walls.

"Postern gate," Chuff said.

"Did no one see you?"

"They paid us nay heed," Chuff said. "Black Duncan's wi' the laird, ye ken, and one o' his men be just inside the door. The other two stand by his boat, and the laird's men who dinna be watching the doorway be watching them."

"Is there no one on the battlements, then?"

"I didna see anyone. The laird keeps only six or eight men here the noo."

"Well, if Black Duncan has only the ones he brought with him, it will be the smallest tail he's commanded in a long while," Mary said thoughtfully. "We must take great care, Chuff."

"Aye, I ken that fine, mistress. We must whisk across quick, though, or they will be after us. That dangling rope will tell them all they need tae know."

"I blocked the door," Mary said. "Perhaps that will delay them for a bit."

"Aye," Chuff said doubtfully. "We'll see. I dinna like that sky."

Mary did not like the darkening sky either. As they sped across the open space to the safety of the forest, she saw that the gathering clouds loomed darkest in the north, the very direction they would head. For a moment she hesitated, wondering if it would be wiser to take the shore road along Loch Linnhe. It was cold enough for snow, and they would be less likely to meet with any if they avoided the passes, but no sooner did the notion cross her mind than she rejected it.

"Do you know this forest, Chuff?"

"Aye, a good bit of it," the boy said. "Flaming Janet lives yonder." He pointed to the left.

"Who is Flaming Janet?"

"She's by way o' being our mam."

"Do you mean she is your foster mother?"

Chuff shrugged. The little girl imitated the shrug and said not a word. Her blue eyes seemed overlarge in her thin, freckled face.

"Do you want to go to her?"

Both children shook their heads fiercely.

"Where exactly does she live?"

"I'll no tell ye," Chuff said. "Ye'll tak' us there whether we will or nay."

"What is your sister's name?"

"She's Pinkie," Chuff said. "She doesna talk much."

"I can see that," Mary said, smiling at the little girl, whose fair hair and thin body were draped in a thin plaid shawl that she held clutched shut beneath her pointed little chin. "Will she be warm enough, Chuff?"

"Aye, she's a tough lass, is Pinkie. Where will ye go, mistress?"

"I want to go up Glen Creran," Mary said. "That's the one where the loch below us begins. It's some distance to the river glen from here, though, and we dare not show ourselves in the open or along the shore, so we must keep to the woods as much as we can. I don't know these woods, though, and we will all find ourselves in deep trouble if we should become confused, or get lost."

"I willna get lost," Chuff said. "I ken fine a good bit o' the way up the glen."

"Once we get into the glen, I shall know the way," Mary assured him. She had been looking around the dimly lit forest, and only now did it strike her that nearly every tree she could see had a slash mark on it, as if someone had scarred the bark with a knife. Recalling what Ewan had told her, and hiding a smile at the memory, she looked at Chuff to see that he was watching her with solemn curiosity.

"Do you know why the trees are all marked like that, Chuff."

The boy shrugged. "They been like that long as I can remember."

"Me, too," Pinkie said, speaking for the first time.

"How old are you, my dear?"

"She's seven," Chuff said.

"Seven," said Pinkie.

Mary chuckled. "And how old are you, Chuff?"

"Nine," the boy said. "Least the laird said I was nine and so I'm old enough now tae work harder, but Pinkie's too small yet tae work in the scullery. I didna like them in the kitchen touching her. We go this way," he added, drawing Pinkie forward with a gentle tug.

Watching them walk ahead of her, Mary wondered what on earth Ewan had been thinking to set the fragile little girl to work in the scullery. She had seen no sign of ordinary maidservants anywhere at Shian, and to think of the child working for the rough men she had seen there made her shudder.

"How came the pair of you to be working at the castle?"

Glancing back at her over his shoulder, Chuff said, "Flaming Janet said it was time we earned our keep."

"If she is your mam, why do you call her Flaming Janet?"

"It's her name," Chuff said simply. Then, apparently deciding he could trust her with some small part of their history, he added, "She isna our real mam though, only like you said, a foster one. Our real mam was her sister. She was called Red Mag MacLachlan, and she died when Pinkie was nobbut just borned."

"Then Flaming Janet is your aunt. But why did she send you to Shian?"

"She said it was the laird's duty tae look after us," Chuff said. He came to a sudden halt, drew Pinkie close behind him, and cupped a hand to one ear. Then, lowering his voice to a murmur, he said, "There's men and horses below, mistress."

Mary heard the murmur of voices, and then a dog barked,

but she could see no sign of them, for the forest was thick. Leathery green and yellowing bracken covered the ground, and despite the seasonal lack of leaves on the deciduous trees, thick conifers mixed amongst them allowed little daylight to filter through. The children appeared to be following a deer trail.

She said quietly to Chuff, "We have been walking toward the loch shore, have we not?" When he nodded, she said, "Those may well be more of Black Duncan's men. You will recall that I thought it odd for him to have only three men with him, since he usually travels with many more. I wonder if any of them saw us when we crossed the open hillside to reach the woods."

"It willna matter," Chuff said. "They canna ken which way we turned."

She gazed around thoughtfully. This part of the forest was too thick for any party of men on horseback to follow them. "The laird must be looking for us by now," she said. "Odd that he hasn't called up Black Duncan's men to help him."

"Why would Black Duncan care where ye went?"

A bubble of laughter formed as she said, "You are quite right, Chuff. I am of no importance to him. I had been thinking that he dislikes me and thus would not pass up an opportunity to do me harm, but you put the matter in perspective."

"I did?"

Pinkie's eyes widened. "He did?"

"He did indeed," Mary said, reaching out to feel the little girl's cold cheeks. "We must keep moving, so we can stay warm, and so we'll not worry about Black Duncan. He is more likely to demand that the laird attend to his wants before he will allow him to chase after me, so we shall make haste while we can."

They made their way along the hillside, keeping to the trees until they were well past the party of horsemen. Then, in the interest of covering as much ground as fast as they could, and hoping their pursuers, whoever they might be, would search first along the road to Loch Linnhe, Mary urged the children to the hilltop above the forest. Though the trees grew sparse, bracken and heather still covered the ground. Although the thick fernlike bracken hampered their progress at times, they still were able to make better time than in the forest, and at last, Mary saw that the shoreline of Loch Creran lay well behind them. They were above the narrowing river glen.

She kept her charges near the crest of the hillside. Although someone with a keen eye riding along the trail by the river might see them, greater danger existed in the fact that their pursuers might overtake them if she and the children followed the river trail themselves. The higher they climbed, the more rugged the terrain grew, but she knew the territory now. She had often walked these hills with her cousins and Bardie Gillonie.

"I dinna ken this place," Chuff said an hour later, as they made their way across a barren granite outcropping.

"We are nearing the hill pass into Glen Duror," Mary told him. "I am very proud of you both. I have not heard a word of complaint from either of you, and we have come very far for such short legs."

"My legs are not short," Chuff said indignantly. "They are just right."

"Mine, too," Pinkie said, looking down at them.

"So they are," Mary agreed, chuckling. "Forgive me, both of you."

They eyed her curiously, as if they did not know what to expect next.

"You know," she said, "we have been in such a hurry, and we've been concentrating all this while on walking, so we have not talked much. This place is protected from the wind, and it's sunny at the moment, so I think we can perhaps sit down for a few minutes now to rest a bit. No one can see us here from below."

The children plopped down at once, and despite the sunlight, she saw Pinkie pull the little shawl closer around her. Chuff took a bun from the little duffel he carried and broke it into pieces, giving the first to his sister and the next to Mary.

She accepted it with thanks. "You are truly amazing, Chuff. I did not even think about food, I'm afraid."

"Well, I've no got anything else o' that sort," he said, "but

I did just take the bun from the kitchen, because I knew Pinkie would get hungersome."

"You take good care of her, I think."

"I canna always take care o' her. That's why I decided tae leave."

"We need to talk about that," Mary said. "I think perhaps there are folks who would say that I have done wrong to let you come with me, but I did not feel that it was wrong at the time, and I generally follow my instincts. Perhaps you would not mind telling me just a little more about yourselves, though, so that I can decide what will be best for me to do with you."

"Canna we just stay with ye, mistress?"

"Aye," Pinkie said solemnly, "that would be good."

"I do not have the right to make that decision," Mary said. "I live with some of my kinsmen, you see, so my house is not my own. I am sure my Aunt Anne would want to help you, but she is not presently at home, so we cannot ask her. You can stay with me through the winter, I expect, since she and my cousin Sir Neil Maclean intend to remain in Perthshire, but I cannot promise more than that until I have laid the matter before them."

"You can tell them we work hard," Chuff said.

"I will, but there is also the likelihood that the laird will object, and there may be others who hold authority over you. Tell me more about Flaming Janet. Does she perhaps have red hair?"

"Aye, but there is nay more tae tell," Chuff said, dismissing his foster mother with a gesture. "She is just Flaming Janet. She does not count for much with us."

"But she cared for you most of your lives after your mother died."

"Because our daddy gave her money tae look after us and a wee good-luck charm he said he would take back when he came home. But after a time Flaming Janet grew a fierce temper on her, because she said there is no way tae mak' siller out o' air, charm or no charm. And so, when the laird did come home again—"

"Just a moment," Mary said as an unpleasant thought struck her. "Do you mean to tell me that the laird is your father?"

"Nay, then, he's not," Chuff said, grimacing expressively. "I'd no want him for my daddy, either."

"Nor me," his small echo said. "He isna kind, the laird."

"I see. Well, go on. What happened last year when the laird came home?"

Grimacing again, Chuff said, "She went tae him the day she heard he was at the castle, and she tellt him he should look after us. At first he wouldna do it—said we was nobbut handfast brats—but she kept at 'im till he said he would tak' me."

"Not Pinkie?"

"Nay, not till a fortnight since when Flaming Janet just left the wee lass at the gate wi' nobbut that dress and her wee shawl tae keep her warm. The laird couldna find her after that—"

"Flaming Janet, you mean?"

"Aye, she just up and left, and there was no females at Shian, only our Pinkie, and the men tease her and dinna treat her well. The cook give her a clout on the lug once that near laid the lass oot. But then the laird said he was for marrying, so we waited till he brought ye home, only then . . ." He spread his hands, adding, "When ye said ye was for running, I decided we should both of us come away, too."

Mary's throat ached, and she felt a prickling of tears in her eyes. Though she knew the notion was nonsensical, she felt as if by fleeing she had unwittingly betrayed the children. At all events, she did not want to hear more.

Chuff said, "Pinkie's getting cold."

"So am I," Mary agreed. "Shall we go on?"

"How far is it tae your house?"

"We are not going there at once," she said. "Darkness would catch us before we could get there, and in any event, I think we will do better to seek some advice first. I have a good friend who will be glad to help us."

Chuff pulled Pinkie to her feet. "Is your friend nearby?"

"Not far," she said, getting up and moving ahead so they could follow her. "His name is Bardie Gillonie, and he lives in a wee glen just beyond that pass yonder. We have only to make our way there without getting lost."

She had little real worry about losing her way, because the hillside they followed would lead to the path through the pass, but she realized there were some obstacles in their way; and the sunlight had disappeared.

For some time the dark clouds she had seen earlier had been growing more ominous. Now a light rain began to fall, hardly enough to dampen more than their spirits, but it was enough to make the granite over which they traveled rather slippery. Mary feared it would grow worse before it grew better, and she began to wish they had taken the river path after all. However, as they came to a scattering of boulders, a shrill whistle sounded from below, putting that wish to instant flight.

"Quick," she said, "take cover. I don't know if they can see us from down there, but most likely it's Black Duncan and his men, so we mustn't let them."

The children scampered ahead of her, diving behind the big rocks, and she hurried after them only to hear Pinkie shriek, "I'm falling! Catch me, Chuff!"

The boy cried out in terror, and horrified, Mary rushed to his side, only to skid to a halt when she realized they had come to a precipice overlooking a steep tumble of boulders and deep, rugged crevices. "Where's Pinkie?"

"She slipped and fell on her backside, then she just up and disappeared," the boy said frantically. "I'll gae doon and look for her."

"No, wait," Mary said, grabbing him. "Pinkie, can you hear me?"

Distantly, and with an odd echoing sound, the little girl's voice came back on a sob. "I'm in here. Oh, get me out, Chuff, get me out! It's dark and horrid, and it hurts something awful, Chuff. Get me out!"

Struggling to free himself from Mary's firm grip, the boy tried to lunge toward his sister's cries, but Mary managed to hold him. "Wait," she said, "we must find the safest way to get to her. It will do her no good if one of us gets killed trying to help her."

"She's afraid. She needs me!"

"Yes," Mary said calmly, "she needs you to be sensible."

Getting down on her hands and knees, she leaned over and saw that there was a narrow cavity or crevice in the cliff side some six to ten feet below them where a thin jagged-edged slab of granite had split away from the primary mass, opening like a pocket in a coat. Below it lay twenty feet of open space, then a steep rocky slope. Nausea swept through her at the thought of how close the child had come to death, but she forced herself to sound confident when she said, "Pinkie, we are here. Think, darling, and look around you. Can you not climb out of there?"

"Nay, I'm stuck, and I canna move me foot. It hurts. Oh, get me out!"

"We'll get you out as quickly as we can, darling, but you must be patient. I think we must get some help."

"Dinna leave me alone," Pinkie shrieked.

"No, of course we won't leave you alone." Mary looked thoughtfully at Chuff. "I cannot climb down there, Chuff, because if I fall, both of you will be alone here, and I'm no hand at climbing in any event. Moreover, I cannot tell from here how deep that crevice is or even if I could fit into it."

"I can fit, and I can climb doon there and see," he said urgently.

For a moment she was tempted to let him try, but it was raining harder now, and she knew they could not take the chance. Speaking firmly, she said, "Chuff, even if you could get down to her, she is hurt. Would you be able to pull her out of there by yourself?" When he hesitated, she said, "You know you cannot be sure of that, and I will not be able to help you from here. Perhaps if we had a rope—"

"Aye, sure, but we've no got one. It's hanging from yon turret at Shian."

His tone was bitter, but Pinkie called out again just then, and Mary said to him gently, "You must be strong for Pinkie, Chuff. If I leave you here with her and go for help, I must know that you won't do anything foolish. Can you promise me?"

He eyed her with grave displeasure. "How long will ye be away?"

"No longer than I must. If Bardie is at home, I will return

in less than an hour. It will seem like a very long time, though, so I must know that you will obey me. It won't help anyone if I fret myself to flinders, worrying about whether you will be sensible. Nor will it help Pinkie in the least if you try to climb down there to her and you fall. Think how it would terrify her."

"I think it would terrify me, too," Chuff said with a sudden glint of humor.

She ruffled his damp hair. "I'll be as quick as I can. I can get down from here to that granite slope over there to the right, so you'll be able to watch me for a time. I should easily reach the path through the pass from there, and it's no more than a ten-minute walk from the top of the pass to Bardie's cottage. Keep talking to Pinkie, Chuff. Reassure her that we'll soon have her out of there."

He nodded, and Mary hurried away, taking greater care than before because the ground beneath her was growing treacherously slippery. The rain had eased, but she felt colder and feared there would be snow before she returned.

When she reached the granite slope, she looked back and waved to Chuff, hoping he would keep his word to her and do nothing foolish while she was away. Realizing, even as the thought crossed her mind, that he had never actually promised to stay put, she knew the likelihood was great that she would return to find him perched at the edge of the crevice, or even down inside it with Pinkie. There was nothing she could do about that now, however, other than send up a prayer and hope that God would keep watch over both children.

Once she was on grass again, she increased her pace, recognizing more landmarks as she went until, rounding a clump of aspen and birch, she came upon the hill path. Relieved to have reached it at last, and glad that the rain had stopped for a time, she stepped onto the path, her attention fixed on the way she meant to go. Thus it was that she nearly lost her footing when a stern voice behind her said, "You seem to be in an almighty hurry, Mistress Maclaine."

Whirling, she found herself face to face with Black Duncan Campbell.

Five

Trying to conceal her dismay, Mary said, "Wh-what are you doing here?"

He was leading his horse, giving her to suspect that he had seen her earlier and dismounted to wait for her, but he said only, "I should be the one asking that question, not you. I'm here because I told MacCrichton I'd keep my eyes open on my way home for a foolish wench who'd most likely got lost in the woods. Now, come, I'll take you back to him."

Stepping hastily back, she said, "No! You have no authority over me, Duncan Campbell, and I have no wish to go anywhere with you or to return to Shian Towers. Ewan was keeping me there against my will."

Duncan's eyebrows rose sardonically. "If you are claiming that he abducted you, how is it that you failed to mention that fact earlier?"

Blushing furiously at this reminder of the scene he had witnessed in the great hall, she nevertheless managed to say with a semblance of her normal calm, "He did not abduct me."

"I thought not. A dangerous thing to do, abducting a wench."

"I agreed to go with him, but he deceived me."

"He said he means to marry you. I heard him say it myself. I must say," he added in a harsher voice, "it didn't take you long to recover from Ian's death."

A surge of fury nearly overwhelmed her, but her long years of practice at controlling her temper served her well. Forcing the words, she said, "You do not know what you are talking about. Now, let me pass. I'm in a frightful hurry."

"I could see that. You scrambled onto this path without so much as looking to see who might be coming. That argues either a clear conscience or sheer folly, and even on our short acquaintance I can guess which is more likely. If you agreed to marry MacCrichton, then he has every right to order your coming and going, so I think you would do well to return to him at once. From what I know of the man, he is nearly as dangerous an enemy as I am. Can you afford two of us, mistress?"

"I am going," she said, turning abruptly on her heel.

He easily blocked her way. "Tell me first exactly why you left. I find it hard to imagine a deception so grave as to make you cry off after agreeing to marry him."

"It may begin to snow soon," she said, growing desperate, "and my personal life is of no concern to you. For that matter, nothing about me should concern you."

"You will nonetheless have to indulge me before I will let you run off."

"Were you really searching for us? I did not think you any friend to Ewan."

He frowned. "Is that what you call him? I was merely keeping an eye out, as told him I would. I thought I saw movement near the crest of the hill, so I rode up here to see what it was. My men are just behind me, however."

"All of them?"

Amusement glinted in his eyes. "You make them sound like an army. I had but three with me at Shian Towers, although I don't suppose you noticed. As I recall it, you did not even bother to offer me a civil welcome." There could be no doubting his amusement now.

Stiffly she said, "You need not taunt me with what you saw, Duncan Campbell. I know you are no gentleman, so I won't point out that a gentleman would say nothing about interrupting such a horrid scene. But you had more than three men with you, for I saw them myself. Heard them, anyway," she added conscientiously. "I'll wager there were at least ten more waiting where the woods run down to the loch."

"You're observant, lass."

"I'm also in a hurry," she said, trying again to step past him.

"Not so fast," he said, grasping her arm. "You still have not told me what I want to know. Moreover, there are other questions I would ask of you."

"You will just have to endure your curiosity, sir, because I cannot stand here talking to you." When he still did not let go, she stamped her foot. "Let me pass!"

"Guard your temper, lass," he said. "In truth, I did not know you had one."

"You do not know me at all," she snapped, as angry that he had stirred her temper as for any other reason. "I tell you, I do not want to answer your foolish questions and I do not want to marry Ewan MacCrichton. Indeed, sir, I will *not* marry him, and he and you can both go to the devil!" Wrenching herself free, she began to stride up the hill, but he caught her again and pulled her back to him.

Struggling, increasingly frantic, she kicked him. "Let me go! Please, you must. A child's life may depend upon it!"

Duncan's hand tightened on her arm, but the expression on his face altered ludicrously. "A child? What child? Here now, tell me at once. What nonsense are you spouting now?"

"You wouldn't believe me. Just let me go. I don't want your help."

"Now you're being petulant," he said, and to her amazement he no longer sounded angry or as if he were mocking her. He went on steadily, "I have no cause not to believe what you tell me, Mary Maclaine. I've accused you of many things in the past, but I have never accused you of being untruthful. I doubt that anyone in Appin country has ever accused you of that."

She looked at him and saw that for once he was sincere. "Would you help?"

"Of course, if I can. What happened? What child are you talking about?"

It occurred to her that he might disapprove as much as Ewan

would of her having let the children accompany her, but Pinkie's plight was too desperate to worry about that. She said, "Two children came with me from Shian, sir, and one of them has slipped into a crevice in the rocks above here. We cannot get her out without help."

"Children, eh. Might one of them have possessed a rope earlier today?"

"He has not got it now," she said tartly. "Will you help us, or will you not? Because if you refuse, I must go at once to find someone else."

"Don't be daft," Duncan said in a tone nearly as sharp as hers. "I am not nearly the villain you believe me to be. Of course, I will help." Turning, he gave a piercing whistle similar to the one she had heard before. Shortly afterward, three men on horseback, followed by a black and white collie, rode up the hill toward them. When they had drawn rein, Duncan said, "Denoon, you stay with these horses. Bannatyne, you and Coulter come with me." Handing his reins to the one he called Denoon, he turned back to Mary. "Which way, lass?"

"Have you got any rope, sir?"

"Bannatyne?"

"No, sir, any we had was on the boat."

"Bannatyne seldom disappoints me," Duncan said, "but I think we can manage well enough without rope. Now, where is the child?"

"This way." Hurrying, she led the men back up the hill and across the granite slab. It was drying now that the rain had stopped, but she could tell by the sky that the respite would not last for long. They clambered over the rocks to the top, and when she did not instantly see Chuff, she hurried to the edge. Just as she had feared, the boy was below, balanced precariously on the narrow, jagged ledge that served as the outer lip of the crevice. "Chuff, what are you doing down there?"

"Pinkie were scared," he said. "I didna try tae climb doon in, though. I knew ye'd be angersome gin I did. I meant tae get back up afore ye came back," he added, "but I couldna find my footing, and I feared that I might fall in, too."

"Then you were wise to stay put, lad," Duncan said. "Here, reach up your hand to me."

"Did ye come tae help us, then?"

"I did. Give me your hand."

"I told him to stay up here," Mary said, watching with her heart in her throat while Chuff maneuvered to reach a hand up to Duncan.

"Don't scold him now," Duncan said. "First, we'll get him and the lass safe."

"I don't mean to scold him at all," she said.

"That shows one difference between us then," he muttered. He was on his belly, leaning over as far as he could. When it became evident that he would not be able to reach the boy so easily, he edged forward, finally ordering Bannatyne and Coulter to hold his feet. "I can't just jump down there," he explained. "He's balanced on the outer edge of the crevice, so there's open space below him on both sides, a good twenty feet of it to the slope. And that's naught but scree and gravel."

While the men held Duncan's feet, Mary looked over to watch. Seeing again that sinister dark cleft in the granite wall, she thought again how miraculous it was that the child had somehow slipped into it instead of falling to her death. "How far down is Pinkie?" she asked Chuff when Duncan hauled him up at last. "I can see only blackness in that crevice after the first few feet."

Chuff looked at her, then at Duncan and the other two. "About as far as if Himself there was tae stand on top o' that 'un," he said, pointing at Coulter, who was short and stocky, barely reaching Bannatyne's shoulder, let alone Duncan's.

Duncan frowned. "So she's in that crevice, is she?"

Mary nodded. "Can you get to her, sir. She must be terrified."

"Pinkie was crying afore ye came," Chuff informed them solemnly.

"We'll soon have her out of there," Duncan said, patting the boy's head.

Imagining Pinkie's terror sent shivers up and down Mary's spine. Only too easily could she imagine the eerie depths of the dark, damp crevice. Her breathing quickened, and she could almost hear the thudding of her heart. "Oh, hurry, sir!"

"Steady, lass, we'll get her. Bannatyne, give me a hand. I mean to climb down where the lad was and take a closer look."

Moments later, he called up to them. "I cannot reach her, and she says the sides are too steep for her to crawl out. I can barely see her, for that matter, so I'd guess she's farther down than the lad estimated, perhaps fifteen feet."

"She said she hurt her foot," Mary told him.

"Aye, she told me that, as well. Are you lads wearing belts?"

They were, but the three belts fastened together did not reach. Chuff unwound the twisted rawhide-strips that served him as a belt and handed them down, but it was no use.

"We could tie all our shirts together," Bannatyne suggested.

"Don't take your clothes off yet," Duncan said. "I don't think she can simply hold on to a makeshift rope even if it reaches her, especially if she tries to climb that steep slope with an injured foot. We'll have to contrive a loop of some sort for her to slip one hand through."

"Can't you get down to her?" Mary asked him.

"I'm too big. I can get my head and shoulders in, barely, but I'd never be able to maneuver, and if I got stuck, we'd really have trouble."

Coulter said diffidently, "I'm smaller, master. Perhaps I can fit."

"Come down then and try," Duncan said. "Help him, Bannatyne. I can guide his feet from here, but you'll need to steady him from up there so he doesn't fall."

Soon Coulter stood precariously beside him on the narrow lip of the crevice, but a moment later Mary saw the smaller man shake his head.

"He's no so small as all that," Chuff said, clutching his baggy breeches to keep them from falling down. "Ye should put me doon there."

Feeling desperate now, Mary looked at Duncan. He appeared to consider the boy's suggestion for a long moment, then said, "Do you think you could hold her, Chuff? Don't just say aye now. Think about it, because she could get hurt much more than she is now if you misjudge your strength. We can tie the belts around you, but you'd have to reach down to her, even so, and pull her up by one hand so that you can maneuver with the other."

Chuff said stoutly, "I would niver let go o' Pinkie."

"I know you would not. What I must know is if you are strong enough to climb while you are holding onto her. Only one of us will be able to help, because there's not room enough for more, and Pinkie will be frightened, you know."

Chuff raised his chin. "I must try. We canna leave her there."

"What about Mistress Maclaine?" Coulter asked, looking at Mary. "She might fit, and she'd be stronger than the lad."

Mary froze. The icy chill she had felt before had been nothing to what she felt now, but before she could think about its cause she said, "Of course I'll try to reach her. Here, help me down there."

"Wait," Duncan said. "There is not room enough for three of us to stand here on this ledge. As it is, I just kicked a chunk of it down into the crevice. Let Coulter climb back up there before you come down."

Uncertain whether the strong aversion she felt stemmed from the knowledge that Duncan would be below her while she climbed down, or from what she faced once she got there, Mary had all she could do to master her feelings and let his men lower her to him. He eased her down until he could catch her firmly around the waist, then lowered her to stand beside him—much too close beside him.

Bracing herself with a hand against the cliff wall, and holding his arm with the other, all the while avoiding so much as a glance into the chasm, she trembled.

"Cold, lass? We'll get her up as quickly as we can."

Mary was cold, but she knew her chill had nothing to do with the weather.

"I'll just fasten one end of these belts around your wrist," he said. "That will help you hold onto it once you've got the child. Both walls slope inward, so work your way down feet first by bracing yourself against them. Watch your skirt now."

Gritting her teeth, trying desperately to ignore the wave of icy fear that washed over her at the thought of going down into the crevice, Mary moved as he guided her. At the top, the opening was long and gaped two and a half to three feet from the granite face, but it narrowed quickly inside.

With Duncan's help she managed to slide in until she could sit on the edge. But when she looked down into the dark, narrow open space below, sweat began streaming from every pore. Her hands grew so clammy that she found it hard to gain purchase on the granite. The leather belt felt slippery in her hand, too, and when her skirt caught on an outcropping of rock as she slipped farther into the black chasm, she cried out, unable to stifle her panic.

"Come out of there," Duncan said harshly, reaching down and grabbing her wrist. Without protest, she let him haul her out in much the same rough and ready way that he had hauled Chuff to the cliff top. "What the devil is wrong with you?"

She swallowed hard. "I-I—"

"Hoots, below! D' ye require assistance?"

Overwhelmed with relief at the sound of the familiar voice, Mary looked up and cried, "Bardie, is that you?"

"Aye, lass, it is myself," Bardie Gillonie said, leaning over to peer down at her. From her perspective, the dwarf's large head with its thin-lipped mouth, big bony nose, luminous dark eyes, and bushy eyebrows looked particularly ridiculous, but she felt no urge to laugh. She was too glad to see him. "What's amiss," he demanded, straightening his water-beaded tie-wig, "and what the deevil are ye doing down there with Black Duncan Campbell of all nefarious felons?"

She glanced uncertainly at Duncan, and seeing his quick frown, she shouted back, "You must not call him names, Bardie. He is trying to help us."

"These chaps here say there's a wee bairn got stuck in the rock."

To Duncan, she said urgently, "Bardie can get her, sir. He is very strong, and he can fit into places where no normal-sized man can go."

"I'll wager he can, and while he makes the attempt, perhaps you can explain to me how it is that a lass intrepid enough to climb down a thirty-foot rope from a tower window— Oh, yes, I know exactly by what means you chose to leave Shian, so how is it that such a fearless lass grows cold with terror at the thought of slipping into a crevice to rescue a helpless child? You must not care as much as I thought."

"I do care about Pinkie, very much," Mary said, but she felt ashamed of herself, and Duncan's words did nothing to soothe her feelings.

He helped Coulter and Bannatyne hoist her to the top, and then Bardie, with but a little help from the others, scrambled down beside him.

Duncan climbed up himself then. "Coulter, go help Gillonie," he said. "I want to talk to Mistress Maclaine."

"Canna ye help our Pinkie then?" Chuff demanded. "Ye said ye could help, and ye're sending that wee little man tae do it instead forbye!"

"Hold yer whisst," Duncan said, taking the boy's chin in his hand and making Chuff look up at him. "You must learn patience, lad. Go watch them now, and you'll see how they get your sister out. And," he added in a much sterner tone, "the next time someone tells you to stay put, you stay put. Do you hear me?"

Meeting his gaze, Chuff said, "I didna promise, and Pinkie was scared."

Mary saw Duncan's fingers tighten, and Chuff's eyes grew wide. Duncan said in the same stern tone. "How do you think Pinkie would have felt if, in trying to reach her, you had fallen and smashed yourself to bits on those rocks instead?"

Chuff swallowed visibly. "I didna think about how she would feel."

"That's why you should do as you are bid. Now, go watch how they get her out. I'll wager she will be as glad to see you as you will be to see her."

With a look of relief, Chuff ran to stand beside Bannatyne. Duncan turned to Mary. "Now then, lass—"

"I am grateful for your help," Mary said with dignity, cutting in before he could continue. "Nevertheless, you have no call to speak so to me. I know you have formed the habit of issuing orders to others, who generally obey you, and doubtless you see me just as someone new to control, but I won't submit to your commands."

To her surprise, he said, "What more do you think you know of my habits?"

"Why, nothing! I did not mean to imply—"

"I doubt that. Did Ian talk about me to you?"

She wished that she could say no, for she did not in the least want to tell him what his younger brother had said of him, but she could see by his expression that he already knew the answer. She said, 'You know that he did."

"I warrant his comments were not complimentary."

"If they were not, can you blame him? His most common complaint was that you continually issued orders that he did not wish to hear."

"If he had obeyed them, he might still be alive," Duncan said harshly.

"If you had not constantly tried to control him, he might not have felt such a strong urge to defy you," she said before she thought.

Duncan's face whitened, and Mary felt a tremor of fear. Then he said with a calm more frightening than if he had lost his temper, "What do you know of such matters, that you dare to speak so to me?"

"I should not have said that," she admitted. "Ian rarely blamed you for anything you said to him. He knew that you cared for his safety above all else. He just felt constantly constrained, sir, and he frequently wished that you had more faith in his ability to look after himself."

"We saw how capable he was of that the night he was murdered."

Bannatyne shouted, "The dwarf's got her, sir. He's bringing her up now."

"Oh, good," Mary said, turning to join the others.

"One moment," Duncan said, catching her arm. "Who are those children and what do you intend to do with them now? If you took them from MacCrichton—"

"They came with me from Shian Towers, but if you are thinking I abducted them, it was no such thing. They insisted upon accompanying me."

"I can well believe you were in no good position to argue with them, but what will you do with them?"

"I did mean to stay tonight at Bardie's cottage, and take them to Maclean House in the morning. I don't think Pinkie can get far on an injured foot though."

"You can take one of our horses for the children," Duncan said, "but you must not return to Maclean House."

"Faith, sir, do you still mean to issue orders to me? I was just beginning to think that you had changed since we last met."

"I mean to make you see reason, Mary Maclaine. For you to go home now would be foolish."

"Thank you very kindly, but I do not know where else you think I can go. In any event, I will decide for myself what I must do, and what I decide does not concern you. You have not adopted us, sir. You have merely given us aid."

"Now, see here—"

"They are calling us. I must see if Pinkie is truly safe."

"No, you don't. I have not finished speaking to you."

"Then finish. I don't want to stand here till dark."

"Ungrateful little fool," he growled. "I am not speaking just to hear myself talk, you know. You cannot go to Maclean House for the simple reason that it is the first place MacCrichton will look for you."

"Then just where would you have me go, sir?"

"Go to your aunt."

"And how am I to do that? You must know she has gone to Perthshire with Neil to your cousin Calder's house. Diana is expecting her baby soon after Christmas, and they knew if they were to get there to be with her, they would have to go before the heavy snows begin."

"You should go to Perthshire," he said stubbornly.

"Would you have me walk there from here? No," she added curtly when he opened his mouth. "You must see that's impossible. I shall stay at Maclean House, just as I'd planned to do from the start."

"Now, look," Duncan snapped, "if you have taken those children from Shian without MacCrichton's permission, you have given him another reason to be angry with you. I saw how he reacts to your defiance, or do you deny that defiance was the cause of that little scene I interrupted when I first saw you at Shian?"

"That will do, Duncan Campbell. You have no right—"

"Don't babble at me about rights! You gave me the right to speak when you asked for my help, and I say you haven't spared a thought for any consequences. You acted impulsively, your actions endangered two innocent children, and . . ."

Mary stopped listening. It was clear to her that he meant to have his say, and that there was nothing she could do to stop him, but she knew she had done nothing to endanger the children. They had chosen to accompany her, and Pinkie's fall had been no more than a horrible accident. Even Black Duncan, were he thinking clearly and not just losing his temper again, would admit that no one could have expected her to hold their hands all the way to Maclean House.

He ran out of things to say at last, and she said, "If that is all you want to say to me, sir, perhaps you will excuse me now. Pinkie is calling me."

With that, she turned and left him, hurrying to hug the little girl.

Chuff said in surprise, "He saved her, and he isna much taller than me."

"No, he isn't. This is Bardie Gillonie, Chuff. I hope you thanked him for his help. Did you have any difficulty, Bardie?"

"None tae speak about, lass. Me shoulders made for a tight fit, but I just wriggled a bit, and the wee lass were so glad tae see me, that I didna mind a whit. Ye should ha' come tae fetch me straightaway."

"I was on my way to you when I met Duncan," Mary said.

Amanda Scott

"We did not realize how much we would need you, Bardie, but I am very glad you came."

"I were passin' above," the dwarf said, "and I heard a ruckus, so I came tae see what it was. The lass canna go far, though, I'm thinking."

Mary had bent to examine Pinkie's foot, and she saw that the ankle had swollen. After prodding a bit and receiving no more than mild protests from her patient, she said, "I do not think it is broken, but it's badly twisted. Fortunately, Black Duncan has said we can take one of his horses. Would you children like to ride a horse?"

"Aye, we would that," Chuff said, his eyes sparkling.

"We would," said Pinkie.

"That's fine then." Turning back to Duncan, she said, "We will accept your generous offer, sir."

"Good. I take it you mean to stay with Gillonie for the night at least. Perhaps he can talk some sense into you and persuade you to stay longer."

"Oh, I don't think we need beg Bardie's hospitality for more than a bite of supper," Mary said airily. "Now that we have a horse, I think I'd rather get back to Maclean House as soon as we can."

"Now see here," Duncan began, but she interrupted him again.

"You have had your say, sir, and I thank you kindly for your concern, but I have made up my mind. No one would dare try to take me from my home, and you are mistaken if you think Ewan will care enough to come for the children. Indeed, I daresay he has realized by now that he is well rid of all of us."

"But—"

"I do not want to quarrel with you," she said, smiling and extending her hand to him. "You have been more kind to us than I ever thought you could be, and I would be wickedly ungrateful to say otherwise. So if you will just tell us which horse we should take, we can part friends, and the children and I will be on our way. Bardie, you do mean to accompany us, I hope."

"Aye, sure, lass," Bardie said, but he was watching Duncan.

Mary looked back at Duncan and suppressed a sudden urge to smile, for fierce Black Duncan was staring at her as if he could not believe his ears. For a moment she feared he might explode, but then with a surly look at his men, and another at Bardie, he grunted and told Coulter he could give her his horse.

"I'll carry the child down to where we left them," he said. "You can walk from there till we rejoin the others. Then you can ride one of the Dunraven horses."

Avoiding Duncan's eye, Mary followed the men silently to the path and waited while Coulter and Bannatyne put the children on the horse. Then thanking the three men equally, she turned to follow Bardie, leading the borrowed horse.

The dwarf lumbered ahead of her, his awkward gait carrying him faster than one might expect. He said nothing until they had topped the rise. Then he stopped and said, "Ay-de-mi, but I never thought he'd let us walk off like that. I never before saw such a look as the one he gave you when you walked away from him to join us, lass. His jaw fair dropped tae the ground. What did you say tae him?"

"Nothing at all, Bardie. I was perfectly polite, I assure you. Well, at the end, at all events," she amended, thinking of some of the things she had said earlier. "He tried to give me orders, which I think is simply a habit with him, you know, but he has no call to think I will obey them. I let him have his say, thanked him for his concern, and told him that I mean to return to Maclean House with the children. I hope you won't tell me, like he did, that I must not."

"Nay, then, why should I? It is your home, is it not?"

"It is."

"Then I hope you told him tae hold his whisst."

Mary smiled. She might not have said it in so many words, but she had certainly silenced him. Before her smile faded, however, a niggling thought stirred, that she might live to regret having angered Black Duncan Campbell.

Six

Ewan MacCrichton, having reached Loch Linnhe without finding Mary, was not in a good mood. Seeing a lone rider approaching as he and his small party of men rode north along the shore road, he muttered a curse.

MacSteele, riding beside him, said, "Who is it, laird?"

"The devil, I'm thinking. That's Allan Breck, and he's a dangerous man, so don't let him engage you in conversation. He knows too damn much already."

"Aye, I remember him, but I canna say he looks like much of a threat," MacSteele said critically. "Ye could break him in two wi' your bare hands, laird."

Ewan did not reply, for he thought Breck might be near enough to overhear. Instead he drew rein, signing to his men to do likewise, and waited.

"A fine good day to you, Ewan MacCrichton," Breck said cheerfully. He was a slender man of medium height in his late twenties with curly black hair, deep-set grey eyes, and a long narrow face marred by smallpox scars. Crooking one thick black eyebrow, he said, "I was just on my way to Shian to offer my felicitations."

Ewan looked him straight in the eye. "Were you now?"

"Aye, I heard that you took my advice and convinced the wench to tie the knot at once instead of waiting till spring."

"Aye, I did that," Ewan said, "but I did not know the news had spread."

Shrugging, Breck said, "You told me you have to pay your fine by Candlemas, and lenient as the Barons' Court has been in such matters, I could not help thinking you would not expect another extension."

"You said as much when you advised me to press her as soon as her aunt and cousin had left Maclean House. What made you think we had gone to Shian?"

"Considering that half the authorities in the Highlands are looking for me, and the other half would shoot me on sight if they got the chance, it behooves me to keep an ear to the ground. Moreover, she is my kinsman, although she makes much of telling folks we are not close. I must say, though, you cannot have made it clear to folks where you mean to hold the ceremony. I've heard that you went into Lochaber, even that you went to Perthshire so that she could be married from Rory Campbell's house. I knew that last one was a fabrication, and since I had just come from Lochaber myself without hearing a word about your presence there . . ." Spreading his hands, he fell silent.

"I took her to Shian," Ewan said. He added grimly, "I've heard things myself, man, and I cannot say I liked what I've heard."

"If that lass has been telling tales out of school again—"

"It was not the lass. It was Black Duncan Campbell who told me."

"Black Duncan!" Breck frowned. "That cannot be. You are hardly on speaking terms with that villain."

"Nevertheless, it was he who told me that you have been blethering all over Rannoch Moor and Lochaber about how you mean to take a great deal of money back to France with you this time. Mentioning my name at the same time, he said."

Breck's eyes shifted, but he said defensively, "What if I have spoken of money? That has naught to do with you. It is ever my custom to take the second rents with me when I return to the lairds in France."

"Aye, but those rents have been growing scarcer by the day," Ewan said. "You told me yourself that folks resent being made to pay both the government and their exiled lairds. They were willing enough to support them for a time, but they cannot afford to do so any longer. I can understand that. I have enough trouble collecting enough from my tenants to pay my men. Had to sell half my sheep just to feed and house them."

"Well, tenants must pay." Breck's eyes narrowed as he added, "As for you, I *will* say this much. I shall expect a generous portion of whatever the lass helps you find. You'd not have known about her gift had I not told you, and our cause needs more funding."

Ewan kept his temper with difficulty, and only because he knew Breck's reputation. An affable and popular man when sober, Breck turned ugly in his cups or when someone thwarted his will. Of his nerve there could be no question, for as a wanted felon, he risked the rope each time he set foot in Scotland. A chance encounter with an army patrol or a convivial evening in the wrong dram-house could be the end of him, yet here he was, riding the open road as casually as any man out for an airing.

Deciding it would be as well to change the subject, Ewan said casually, "I take it you have come from Maclean House."

"Aye, I spent the night there last night." Breck grinned, his good humor apparently restored. "I doubt I'd have been welcome if my aunt were there, but I passed a pleasant night forbye."

"Was anyone there?"

"Not a soul in the house. A few herds about the stables, but they paid me no mind. Even the housekeeper, Morag Mac-Arthur, was away for the night." His eyes bowed again with sudden suspicion. "Look here, why do you want to know that? Where's Mary?"

"She ran away," Ewan told him.

"You bloody fool! You must have frightened her."

"Like as not, she had a vision, telling her she'd been wrong about me being desperately in love with her," Ewan said sarcastically.

"Nay, it wouldn't be that. The lass never has visions about herself."

"She says she don't have visions about finding things either," Ewan snapped.

"She will if that seer of yours said she will," Breck retorted. "She's the only seventh daughter hereabouts. You'd best find her and tame her a bit, my lad."

"Oh, I aim to do that, right enough," Ewan growled.

Duncan was furious. He had been feeling generous, even noble, knowing that Mary Maclaine had not expected him to help her, or anyone with her. She knew that he disliked her, and she knew why.

Still, whatever she might think of him, she ought to know he would not have left any child in that crevice. Such a tiny thing, too. It made him angry just to think how far she had had to walk from Shian. Not that she had looked any the worse for that walk, but still, there it was.

His men rode silently behind him. Not even Bannatyne ventured to ride alongside, let alone speak to him, and Duncan could not blame any of them. No doubt they imagined steam rising off his clothing from the heat of his anger.

He told himself he was a fool to let any wench get under his skin the way she had. But the way she had stood there, listening politely to him, *humoring* him, while he explained the dangers of her situation and challenged the stupid decision she had made to return to Maclean House— Even now, just thinking about her unruffled calm in the face of his displeasure made him angry all over again. Women!

For her to thank him for his concern as if he had been an elderly advisor of some sort to whom she had felt obliged to listen patiently, and then to announce that she was going to do the very thing he had advised her most strongly against, showed plainly that the woman was an idiot with a reckless disregard for the danger she courted to herself and to the others. The sheer folly of it dumbfounded him.

Perhaps she did not know she had made a treacherous enemy by infuriating MacCrichton. She had probably never even seen him angry. But that thought stirred the memory of an upraised whip and her scream, and he quickly revised it. She had cer-

tainly seen MacCrichton angry. Even so, she had not seen the
look Duncan had seen when MacCrichton discovered she had
chosen to risk her life by climbing down a slender rope from
the high turret, rather than stay with him.

Duncan had managed to keep the man from instantly setting
out in search of her, but thinking back, he wondered why he
had exerted himself. At the time he had thought it urgent to
find out if MacCrichton had lied about his relationship with
Allan Breck. Now, having obtained no more information at all
about Breck, he knew he had asked more questions only to
delay MacCrichton.

He had even tried to convince the laird that he would do
better to tell his men that Mary had strayed by accident, to keep
them from learning that she had run away. MacCrichton had
said flatly that he did not care what his men thought. He wanted
the lass back. At that point, the hour he had allowed himself
nearly spent, Duncan had offered to search the Glen Creran trail
on his way back to Balcardane.

When MacCrichton agreed, he had dismissed any plan to
return to Dunraven. Keeping Bannatyne with him, he had sent
the other two men back with the boat, and with only minutes
to spare, he and Bannatyne had rejoined the others waiting for
them. Following the river track, he ordered all his men to keep
their eyes open for anyone walking through the woods or above
them on the ridge.

He knew that MacCrichton had agreed to the offer only because he believed Mary would take the shortest way possible
back to Maclean House, but Duncan did not think the laird
knew about Bardie Gillonie. Knowing from past experience that
the dwarf enjoyed a close friendship with the residents of
Maclean House, he also knew that Bardie's cottage lay near the
hill pass from Glen Creran into Glen Duror. Bardie had a well-
deserved reputation for shrewdness, and in the absence of her
family, what had been more likely than that Mistress Maclaine
would seek help and advice from a wily friend?

Thick woods hugged the river Creran, but they thinned
quickly up along the sides of the glen, until naught remained

but bare granite near the ridge. He had been tempted more than once to send a couple of men to walk the hill route in search of her but decided that would call too much attention to what was, after all, another man's problem. That he spotted her himself had been entirely fortuitous.

Even then he had not known what he meant to do. He had not known about the children, but he had certainly led Mac-Crichton to believe he would return Mary to him if he found her. Still, he had taken care not to promise anything. His conscience would remain clear on that point, although he suspected MacCrichton might not see the matter in the same light if he learned that Duncan had found her.

In any case, he washed his hands of her. He had done his Christian duty by helping to rescue the child and by explaining the dangers of Mary's present position to her. That she endangered the damned dwarf now, as well as herself and two children, was certainly no reason to concern himself further. He and Bardie Gillonie had never been friendly, because the latter had an unfortunate knack for annoying his betters. And although the dwarf was wise enough to see the danger if the wench told him the whole tale, Duncan doubted that even Bardie would be able to persuade her to take precautions now that she had taken the bit between her teeth.

It occurred to him that Mary might have been more reasonable had someone other than himself pointed out the error of her ways, but he rejected the notion. Logic was logic, and facts did not alter simply because a listener wanted the person reciting them to be wrong. In the end, she would find that he was right, of course, and she would learn a hard lesson. With increasing annoyance, he felt the first drops of icy moisture begin to fall. In moments, sleet was pelting down at them.

The sleet began while Mary and Bardie were preparing a simple meal for the children and themselves in his cottage. Pinkie's injured leg was responding well to an herb poultice, and Mary soon realized that it would be foolhardy for her and the children to leave before the storm stopped. Darkness fell long before then, however, and so they passed the night with Bardie, leaving his cottage shortly before dawn.

Mary led the compact, well-muscled bay gelding that Black Duncan had lent them, with Chuff and Pinkie clinging happily to its back. As she walked along the familiar track, leading the gelding, she turned her thoughts to her aunt and cousins, and wondered what they would think of her decision to keep the children with her. They would not expect her to turn them out, but she knew they would not be overpleased, either, to learn that she wanted to add two more mouths to the household. Doubtless they would expect her to find positions for them in a suitable household, but try as she would, she could think of no such place.

Things had come to such a pass in Appin—and, indeed, throughout the Highlands—that most folks had all they could do to feed their own. Even an assurance that Chuff would work hard for his keep would not tempt most to take him on, and Pinkie was so young and so small that it was hard to imagine how she could truly earn her keep.

Again Mary found herself mourning the loss of James of the Glen, for over the years, he had taken many children into his household and fostered them to adulthood, including the outlaw Allan Breck. In that case, however, his efforts had gone unrewarded. Indeed, they had led to his death, for the authorities, convinced that James had conspired with Allan to murder the Crown factor, had tried and convicted him of the crime, and had hanged him.

Despite offers of huge rewards and frequent rumors of Allan's presence in Scotland, no one had turned him in, but then many still thought him a hero. No one had betrayed Bonny Prince Charlie in the months after Culloden, either, although the English had offered thirty thousand pounds for his capture. Mary approved of the prince's successful escape to France. She felt otherwise about Allan Breck.

"What are ye thinking on, mistress?"

Chuff's voice startled her from her reverie, and she glanced over her shoulder at him to say, "I was woolgathering, I'm afraid."

"I dinna see any sheep."

Mary chuckled. "That is what one calls a figure of speech, my dear. It means that I was lost in a daydream."

"Thinking," the boy said flatly.

"Yes, I was thinking."

"Aye, sure, and isna that what I asked ye? What are ye thinking on then?"

Mary stifled her amusement. Chuff had spoken earnestly, and she did not want him to think she was laughing at him. Pinkie, too, peering solemnly around her brother, seemed to be waiting for Mary to explain.

"I was thinking how much I will enjoy having you stay with me," she said.

Chuff frowned. "Did ye live all alone afore the laird took ye tae Shian?"

"I wouldna like that," Pinkie said.

"I have never lived alone," Mary said. "I have lived with my aunt and cousins for some years now, but they are presently visiting in Perthshire."

"D' ye no have a daddy and mam, then?" Chuff asked. "Like us?"

"No, my mother died when I was about your age, Chuff, and my father died six years ago. Even so," she added quickly, not wanting to expand that subject, "I do not live alone. Our housekeeper, Morag MacArthur, lives with me."

"Will she like us?" Pinkie asked.

"I am certain that she will," Mary assured her, "but she will not be at Maclean House when we get there. I gave her leave to visit her brother when I left for Shian Towers. There are men who work the land, of course, and tend the animals, but they do not live in the house. We shall be on our own for a few days, I think, so that we can think about what to do next."

Chuff frowned. "Ye willna send us back, will ye, mistress?"

"Not unless I must, Chuff," she promised. "What authority has the laird over you? Do you know?"

The boy shrugged. "Like I said afore, Flaming Janet said she didna want tae keep us any longer, because the laird wouldna pay for our keep and we were too sma' tae work for it, so she sent us tae live wi' him."

"But you are certain that he is not your father."

"Nay, our daddy and mam are both dead."

"You said your mam died when Pinkie was born," Mary said. "When did your father die?"

"He went wi' the old laird tae follow the bonnie prince," Chuff said. "Flaming Janet said it was a good thing, but not so good that he niver came back. When the siller give out, she had nobbut the charm he left, and that only a bit o' plain brass, she said. She give it tae me," he added, fingering his odd belt buckle.

Looking at it, Mary could see why Flaming Janet had not been impressed. It was no more than an oddly shaped chunk of black metal, interesting only to a child. "Your father must have been one of the laird's tenants," she said, thinking aloud. It was clear to her that the children knew little about their antecedents, but she could be absolutely certain that the sister of a woman with the interesting name of Flaming Janet had not been a member of the gentry.

They continued for some time in silence before Chuff said, "Will Himself come tae see us, mistress?"

"I certainly hope not," she said, "but if Lord MacCrichton shows his face at Maclean House, you need not fear him, my dears."

"I wasna speakin' o' the laird," Chuff said. "I thought Himself would ken what Pinkie and me should do wi' ourselves."

"Faith, do you mean Black Duncan?" She repressed a chuckle at the notion that he could think of Duncan in terms generally reserved for the chief of a clan, but Chuff nodded vigorously. Pinkie nodded, too, and faced with their earnest solemnity, Mary could not bring herself to reveal her dislike, so she said matter-of-factly, "I do not think he will bother his head about us. He is a very busy man."

"Aye, and so I thought," Chuff said.

"It's darkening up again," Pinkie said, looking at the sky. "Will it snow?"

"Perhaps," Mary said, "but I think we will be home before it does."

The weather held, and they reached Maclean House shortly before noon. Mary turned the bay gelding over to one of the men who worked for the family, asking him to have someone return it, with her thanks, to Balcardane Castle. Then, holding hands with the children, she led them toward the house, noting with satisfaction that Pinkie walked now with only a slight limp.

"This is nice," the little girl said, looking around the yard.

"Yes," Mary agreed. "Maclean House is a pleasant place to live."

Inside it was not as pleasant as usual, however, because the parlor was chilly without a fire, and sounds she was accustomed to hearing from the kitchen were absent. She was not one to dwell upon such deficiencies, however, and quickly set about lighting a fire on the hearth, and another in the kitchen. To her surprise, the wood baskets in both rooms were nearly empty.

"Chuff, there is a woodpile just outside the scullery door," she said, pointing the way. "Go and fetch some wood for the baskets, will you, please?"

"Aye, I'll go."

"I'll help," Pinkie said instantly.

"Let me look at that leg again first," Mary said. Though it was still angry looking, it was healing well, so she saw no reason to keep the child in. When they had gone, she poked up the kitchen fire and took the kettle from the hob to fill at the scullery pump. A bowl, a platter, and a mug sat in the sink, used but unwashed.

She frowned as she filled the kettle. It was not like Morag to leave the house without washing her dishes.

The children returned, their arms laden with wood, which they took into the parlor. Mary heard thumps and chuckles as she put the kettle back over the fire, and then the children returned, passing her without a word on their way outside again.

Moving to set places for them all at the kitchen table, she

saw crumbs on its surface—as if someone had sliced bread there—and a ring the size of a mug.

Listening intently, she heard only the children's voices outside and the crackling of the nearby fire. She glanced at the ceiling, forcing herself to remain calm. No sound came from above, but she hurried to the stairway off the parlor and went quietly upstairs. Finding her aunt's bedchamber empty, and the one she had shared with her cousin Diana in a like state, she entered Neil's room and stopped, staring in puzzlement at the rumpled bed. Clearly, someone had slept in it.

Her first thought had been fear that Ewan had broken in to wait for her, but she knew he would not have gone away again so quickly. Having failed to overtake her, he would know she had taken another route. He would know, too, that she could not reach Maclean House as quickly on foot as he could on a horse.

Hearing the children in the kitchen, she put her worries aside and went downstairs again. "Shall we make something to eat?"

They agreed with enthusiasm, and she took them out to the byre to show them where the hens laid their eggs. "If you will gather eggs for me, I will go back to the kitchen and see what else we can fix for our supper."

At Balcardane, despite a near sleepless night Duncan had begun the morning by attending quite early to several matters of business before seeking out his father's steward in the estate office just inside the main gate of the castle.

"Good day, Master Duncan. How did you find Dunraven, sir?"

"Well enough, MacDermid. We should increase the flocks there, however. The land can sustain a few more per acre, and the wool they produce is particularly fine. You might note, as well, that I authorized two new pumps and told them they can put new roofs on the dovecote and the stable in the spring."

"What's that, Duncan? New roofs, you say! Would you beggar me, lad?"

Having assumed—clearly incorrectly—that the steward was alone, Duncan started at the sound of the earl's voice. With a sour look at MacDermid, to which the man returned a blank gaze, Duncan turned and said, "Good day, Father. I have no intention of beggaring you, sir, but both of those roofs are caving in. They have patched them enough to get them through the winter, but—"

"Then let them be, damn you! I did not agree to your running Dunraven just so you could empty my pockets with foolish extravagance." The earl, a full-bodied man of medium height, straightened his periwig and glowered at his son, adding, "You and your mother both seem to think I'm made of money. She's inviting the whole countryside to dine on Christmas Eve. Money is power, lad. Don't waste it."

A familiar sense of frustration threatened to make Duncan forget the duty he owed his prickly parent, but he gritted his teeth, saying only, "You cannot think it foolish, sir, to keep the birds from leaving and the horses from dying of exposure. Purchasing new stock would prove vastly more expensive."

"If you've already authorized it, I won't embarrass you by sending contrary orders to Dunraven," the earl said sternly, "but next time have a care, Duncan. I trust your trip was otherwise uneventful."

"Not exactly," Duncan said, "but it was interesting."

"You shall tell us all about it when we sit down to breakfast," Balcardane said. "Serena will want to hear the tale as much as I do, and your mother, too, of course." He winked at Duncan. "The lass truly admires you, you know—Serena, not your mother. I can see it in those beautiful blue eyes whenever she looks at you."

Instead of the Lady Serena Caddell's eyes, Duncan's memory presented him with a pair of silver-grey ones, their irises outlined in black, their dark lashes long and thick. He blinked the memory away, saying bluntly, "I hope you are not still thinking of making a match between us, sir. I have no objection to Lady Serena's making her home with us here for as long as you wish her to stay—"

"Devil take it, Duncan, it wasn't my idea for her to stay. Just another mouth to feed, come to that, but when Caddell said she wanted to get away from Inver House until her sister-in-law's bairn is born, I couldn't refuse to welcome her."

"No, sir, I just don't want you thinking I have an interest in that direction. You've suggested more than once that the connection would be advantageous."

Balcardane frowned. "I think it would, Duncan. Anyone can see that the lass is hot for you, and Caddell favors the union. She'll have a devilish good dowry."

"I warrant she will. Did you have more you wanted to say to MacDermid?"

"Aye, I do. Mind, now, no more roofs without you talk to me first."

Duncan held his temper, but the thought of trying to enjoy a meal while his father complained about his spending and his mother and Serena pitched questions at him about his trip soon convinced him to find something else to do. He would not ride to Maclean House, however. The fool wench had chosen her path, and she would just have to take the consequences. She was no business of his, and he had no interest in what became of her, and that was that. No matter what. Absolutely.

The children helped Mary clear up after their meal. The sky still looked threatening, but not a single snowflake or drop of rain had fallen. The waters of the loch lay calm and dull gray, and the hills beyond it looked dreary. It was, Mary thought, as if all the color had faded from the day.

She was certain that someone had been in the house. Morag would have left fires ready to light and the wood baskets full, and she would never have left dirty dishes behind. Fear flashed through Mary's mind that something had happened to the housekeeper, but then she remembered Neil's bed. Someone had slept there. Surely, she thought, no one would hang about who had harmed the housekeeper.

Whoever it was, she hoped he would not return, for as certain as she was that it had not been MacCrichton, the most likely housebreaker was Allan Breck. He had not paid Maclean House a visit in over a year, and no one had given him cause to expect a welcome, but he was arrogant enough to think that Lady Maclean would forgive a faithful member of her clan for any transgression. Allan believed clan loyalty was sacred, although his definition of loyalty itself was certainly flawed.

In any event, he would not expect Mary to be glad to see him, so if he knew that she had returned, surely he would stay away.

Sending the children out to play by the loch, she lighted lamps and stirred up the fires again. Then, taking her aunt's tea chest from its place atop a cabinet in the kitchen, she brewed herself a hot cup of the precious tea, and sat down to write a letter to Perthshire. Although Sir Neil Maclean was titular chieftain of the Craignure Macleans, she addressed the letter to her aunt, for it was certainly her ladyship who would decide what they should do about Chuff and Pinkie.

She had finished her letter and was heating wax for her seal when she heard horsemen ride into the stable yard. Forcing herself to remain calm, though her heart began thudding hard enough to jump out of her chest, she dripped her wax onto the letter and pressed her thumb down to make the seal. Then, setting the letter carefully aside, she went to the parlor window and looked out into the yard.

Ewan MacCrichton was striding toward the front door.

Seven

Mary's palms were sweating, and she wiped them on her skirt, but she refused to let Ewan see her fear. Raising her chin, she opened the door.

He stood on the step, a hand raised to knock. Letting it drop, he glowered at her and said, "So you did come back. I thought you would."

"You are not welcome here anymore," she said. "Go away, or I will call our men in from the stable and the yard to put you off the property."

"Do you think they could do it, lass?" he said, jeering. "I've five men with me, all armed and ready for whatever comes. I don't think your lads will be much of a match for them. I'm going to take you home, and that's all there is about it."

"Your home is not my home, my lord." Hearing movement and whispering behind her, she realized that the children had come back in. She had kept the door partially closed, and now, behind it, she motioned to them to get back out of sight. She kept her eyes fixed on Ewan, however, and saw his expression change to anger.

"You've given your promise, lass, and I don't mean to let you break it," he said. "Come now, don't be foolish."

She started to shut the door, but he shoved it open and walked inside.

Glancing swiftly behind her to be sure the children had left the room, she exclaimed, "You can't come in here!"

"I am in, so you'd better behave," he snarled. "I've come to take you back, Mary Maclaine, and there's no one here to stop me. Where is your cousin?"

"My cousin? You know perfectly well that Sir Neil and my aunt have gone to stay in Perthshire until Diana's child comes, and perhaps for the entire winter if heavy snows come early."

"I am speaking of Allan Breck," he snapped.

"I don't claim that villain as a cousin," she retorted.

"He is kin to your mother's folk, is he not?"

"He is a Stewart, and so certainly there is kinship, but you know why I am not quick to acknowledge it. Even my aunt does not recognize him now."

"Well, I thought he might be here. In any event, you are not to speak to him if he approaches you. He wants my treasure to finance a resurgence of the cause."

"How does he even know about the treasure?"

"He does not know everything, but I told him once that I could pay my fine if I could recover something that had been lost, and about the seer's telling me I needed a seventh daughter. Breck's the one who told me about your gift."

"Well, he won't ask me to help him learn more about it," she said, watching Ewan warily. Despite his apparent willingness to converse with her, she knew he still hoped to force her return to Shian. "Allan knows that I believe the Jacobites lost their cause at Culloden, if not long before. That cause cost me my father, an uncle, two brothers, and a sister; and Allan himself cost me more when he killed Ian."

"Just see that you don't talk to him, that's all. He'll winkle what he can out of you one way or another if he can get to you."

"He can scarcely winkle out information I don't have," she said tartly.

"You just put your mind to it, lass, and you'll know soon enough where the treasure lies. Now then, I doubt you need to collect anything since you left all you took with you at Shian, but fetch a cloak if you've got one. It's devilish chilly out."

"I'm not going, Ewan," she said, folding her arms across her chest. "I know I said that I'd marry you, but a woman can change her mind. I have changed mine."

"No one else knows that, however," he said, "and I mean to see that you don't tell anyone. As soon as we have consummated—"

"We are not going to consummate anything, sir. As for not telling anyone, I have already told Black Duncan Campbell that I don't want to marry you. If you try to force me, I shall claim rape, and *that's* all there is about it!"

He slapped her hard enough to make her stumble, and began to undo his belt.

"Dinna touch our Mary!" Chuff shrieked, rushing into the room. "Ye'll no beat her, laird, or I swear tae ye, I'll kill ye wi' me own hands!"

Mary cried, "Chuff, no!"

Ewan backhanded the child, sending him sprawling to the floor.

Mary leapt forward. "Leave him alone!"

Holding her off easily with one hand, Ewan looked grimly at Chuff, who sat up slowly, gazing resentfully up at him. "So," Ewan said, turning back to Mary, "now I see how you were able to escape. Chuff, my lad, you'll soon regret betraying me. When we get back to Shian, I promise you the skelping of your young life."

"I'll go with you, Ewan," Mary said instantly, "but only if you will promise not to hurt the children."

"Children, eh? So the brats are both here. Well, you'll all come with me, and I'll make no bargains. I don't stand for defiance in my household, as you'll all learn before you're much older. Leave us now, lad," he added. "Fetch your sister, and prepare to leave. We'll go just as soon as I've attended to my lass here."

Mary backed away, but Ewan grabbed her, paying no more heed to the boy. She cried, "Run away, Chuff! Go, run, and take Pinkie with you!"

Ewan laughed unpleasantly. "They won't get far. My men

are all around the house." Jerking her forward, he added, "We'll tend to our business now."

"Please, don't beat me again. I've said I'll go with you."

"Beat you? I'm not going to beat you. Not yet, at all events. I asked a few folks if they'd heard of any wench who could curse a single part of a man's body. They said only a witch can do that. Are you a witch, Mary Maclaine?"

Recognizing his true purpose now, she swallowed hard and shook her head.

"That's what I thought. I'd have preferred a bed, lass, but the carpet will do." He drew her close, seeming to enjoy it when she resisted. He was too strong for her, and ignoring her struggles, he began to kiss her.

When she kicked him, he did not seem to notice, and when she writhed in his arms, he chuckled. "You've no choice, lass, and once the deed is done, you'll give me no more trouble. Then, when you've got accustomed to marriage, you can just tell Black Duncan how you changed your mind again, and how happy we are."

She tried to scream, but his mouth swiftly covered hers, and his arms clamped so tightly around her that she could scarcely breathe.

As he bent her toward the floor and reached to pull up her skirt, the door burst open and a man dashed in, crying, "Laird, Black Duncan's coming!"

"Let him come," Ewan snarled, tumbling Mary to the floor.

From the moment Duncan had watched Mary Maclaine walk away from him with the two children, after she had so foolishly rejected his excellent advice, he had wanted to wash his hands of her. She had given him every reason to do so, and he told himself that she deserved whatever consequences befell her.

He had told himself so several times on his way home to Balcardane, and many more times since, but he could not seem to put her out of his mind.

Since leaving his steward, he had found his thoughts fixed

often on Mary. Was she safe? Had MacCrichton found her? Was there anyone who would protect her? He had heard rumors that Allan Breck was back in Appin. Could the villain have sought refuge at Maclean House? Would he do anything to protect her from MacCrichton if he had?

Having put these thoughts and others of their ilk aside to deal with matters that had been neglected in his absence, he nonetheless found his thoughts constantly returning to Mary. So it was that despite his determination to have nothing more to do with her, instead of joining his family for dinner, he found himself sending orders to his men to saddle horses and prepare to ride out with him at once.

Assuaging his hunger with ale and mutton from the kitchen, and taking a loaf of bread to stave off hunger pangs along the way, he snatched his sword from its hook near the hall door and hurried outside, stirred by an odd, inexplicable prick of urgency. A flurry of activity in the yard told him that the men were nearly ready.

He took fifteen with him. Not a chief's tail, by any means, but then he was not and never would be the chief of his clan. Still, he was a Campbell and knew what was due to his position as Master of Dunraven.

The sense of urgency increased, and he set a fast pace, for he could not resist its pull. If he found nothing bothersome at the end of the trail, he would tell his men he had been testing them, if he chose to tell them anything at all.

With a deepening chill in the air, he had expected snow to follow the heavy sleet of the day before, but although the sky remained overcast and the air icy cold, there had been no more precipitation. Mist had risen from Loch Leven all morning, but it had not drifted far from the loch, nor did it appear likely now that they would meet with any from Loch Linnhe. The water there was clearly visible now and calm for once, slate grey beneath the dismal grey sky.

Still, the pace was exhilarating. His cheeks stung, and he could see his breath in a cloud when he exhaled. Clouds of steam wafted from his mount's nostrils, too.

When they passed the Kentallen Inn, and the northern end of Cuil Bay came into sight, he spurred his mount to an even faster pace. The dirt track was hard-packed, and the other horses pounded behind. Since he had not yet pressed the big black horse he rode, the others kept up with him easily and without incident.

Fifteen minutes later, near the south end of the bay, he turned uphill onto the track leading to Maclean House. The house sat at the back of a large meadow overlooking the loch. A dry stone dike surrounded house and grounds, and before he and his men reached the timbered gate, Duncan knew he had been right to come. A number of men and horses occupied the stable yard.

He slowed his pace, allowing his own men to bunch up behind him.

Bannatyne drew in alongside to ask, "How many, sir?"

"Five, maybe six," Duncan said. "I don't see their master."

"D' ye ken who he is, then?"

"Aye, it's MacCrichton. Look at those saddle blankets. Though they are stripes, not plaids, the colors are his. Tell the others to await my signal here. They are to cause no trouble until they hear me whistle for them."

"Aye, sir."

Hearing doubt in the man's tone, Duncan looked at him. "Do you doubt my ability to look after myself, Bannatyne?"

"Nay, sir, I ken fine that ye can look after yourself, but that MacCrichton is no man to trust."

"Just do as I bid you. If you see them rush the house, or if more join them, you may consider that as good as my signal—and if they attack you, of course."

Grinning, Bannatyne said, "Aye, sir, we'll take them then, right enough."

Duncan rode into the yard. He could see now that there were five men and seven horses. Either MacCrichton had taken a bodyguard in with him, or someone had seen them and carried warning to the house. In the latter case, it did not seem as if MacCrichton had responded.

The others stood silently, watching Duncan. He was certain

they would not have remained passive had he ridden up with his entire company, however.

Riding right to the front step, he dismounted and dropped his reins, knowing the horse would stand where he left it until commanded to move. Without pausing, he strode to the door and thrust it open.

"Good day to you, MacCrichton," he said from the threshold with a false cheerfulness that did nothing to soothe his fury at the sight that met his gaze.

MacCrichton scrambled hastily to his feet, leaving Mary Maclaine in a tumbled heap on the floor.

Movement from the left caught Duncan's eye, and flicking a glance that way, he saw the man who had been missing from the courtyard. Meeting his gaze briefly, Duncan shifted his sword belt, then swiftly returned his gaze to MacCrichton.

"What brings you to Maclean House?" he asked him. "Something tells me that Mistress Maclaine did not invite you."

"Nay, then, she certainly did not," declared a childish voice that Duncan recognized as Chuff's.

He did not look to see where it came from, but without taking his eyes from MacCrichton, he noted obliquely that Mary was getting slowly to her feet.

"You shut your mouth, brat," MacCrichton snapped at the boy. "You've just earned yourself a few more strokes of my whip across your backside, is what you've done." Still bristling, he took a step toward Duncan. "Your memory must be failing, Duncan Campbell. I told you yesterday, the lass has promised to marry me."

"That would explain why she risked her life to get away from you, I suppose," Duncan said sardonically.

"Aye, then, explain that part o' the tale, laird," Chuff said, chuckling.

"She left because of a misunderstanding, that's all," Mac-Crichton said grimly, shooting a ominous sidelong look in the direction of Chuff's voice. "I've come to take her home again, and the brats as well."

Knowing even without Bannatyne's warning that Mac-

Crichton was capable of mischief, Duncan studied him carefully. If the man was armed, however, he was not advertising the fact. Duncan glanced swiftly around the rest of the room.

"Good day, mistress," he said when his gaze came to rest upon Mary.

She did not reply. She had backed into the shadows near the most distant corner of the room, and at first he thought she was alone. Then he saw the children close beside her. Both returned his look solemnly, but neither said a word. When Mary stayed where she was, he wondered if he had missed something.

He remembered from certain earlier visits that Lady Maclean employed at least one servant, but there was no sign of the woman now. From what he remembered of her, he was sure that if she were on the premises, she would be here with Mary and the children.

Mary still did not speak, but MacCrichton moved then, drawing Duncan's attention sharply back to him.

"You've seen all you need to see," MacCrichton said gruffly, "so leave us be. This is no affair of yours."

"Perhaps it is not," Duncan said, "if the lass does want to marry you. The fact is, however, that she told me only yesterday that she has no such wish."

MacCrichton chuckled, shaking his head. "If you had as much experience with wenches as I've got, you'd know you cannot trust their word on such matters."

"Can I not?"

"Nay then, for they'll always tell you the thing you least want to hear. The plain fact is she was wroth with me yesterday, because I'd made her obey me. She had expected, after a year of keeping me on her string, that she could rule the roast in my house, as well. When she found that was not so, she tried to teach me a wee lesson by running off. It was a quarrel between lovers, that's all it was."

"A quarrel?"

"Aye, the sort any man and lass have from time to time. I warrant you've had a share of them yourself. But she's come about now, so I'm taking her home."

"She has not," Chuff said stoutly, "and we don't want to go home with you."

"No, we don't," Pinkie echoed in a small voice.

"They don't want to go," Duncan said.

"They have nothing to say about it," MacCrichton snapped. "They are only tenant's brats bound to work at Shian. They'll go back with me, in any event, and they will swiftly learn what a mistake they made in running away."

"I don't think so," Duncan said evenly.

"What? You've got nothing to say to any of this, damn you."

"We'll see about that. First I want to hear from Mistress Maclaine that she has truly agreed to marry you."

"Then ask her. I doubt that she will lie about having given her promise."

"Mistress, what say you?" When she was silent and did not step forward, he had a sudden fear that MacCrichton had done worse this time than give her a stripe across the backside. "Come out here where I can see you," he commanded harshly.

To his relief she stepped forward at once, and her clothing, although mussed, appeared to be generally intact. As his gaze moved upward to her lovely serene eyes, it stopped at a livid red mark on her cheek, already darkening to a bruise.

A surge of rage threatened to overcome his common sense before she said calmly, "I did promise to marry him, I'm afraid, sir."

"There," MacCrichton said triumphantly, "you see?"

"Good God, mistress, were you mad?"

"I think I must have been," she said with a sigh.

"No such a thing," Chuff declared loyally. "Laird took ye for a gowk, is all."

"Aye, gowked," Pinkie said.

The small interruptions helped Duncan regain uncertain control of his temper. He said as gently as he knew how, *"Did* he mislead you, mistress?"

"Aye, for he pretended to feel tenderness toward me, and I believed him."

"What blithering nonsense," MacCrichton snapped. "It is always the same. If you upset them, they say you don't love them. If you say you love them and then correct their behavior, they say you misled them. I tell you to your head, Campbell, if you would just take yourself off, I could settle this in the blink of an eye."

Duncan was watching Mary, and he saw her eyes widen with fear. Until then, a voice deep inside him had been suggesting that he had overstepped his mark, that MacCrichton's argument made sense and the man had every right to try to sort things out with her. But that look of fear decided Duncan's course.

Grimly, he said, "What say you, mistress? Would you return with him?"

Mary swallowed hard. After the way they had parted the day before, Duncan's appearance on the scene had shocked her, and she could scarcely believe, even now, that he was here in her house. Still, she would accept help from the devil himself if it would enable her to escape Ewan and protect the children from him.

She glanced at Ewan, seeing frustrated anger in his eyes and furious tension in his posture. She turned back to meet Duncan's stern gaze.

"I told you the truth, sir. I have no wish to marry him. The misunderstanding to which he refers took place when I believed he cared for me and wanted to provide a home for me. Over and over, he professed to love me, and for a year he pressed me to respond, although I told him repeatedly that I could not return his regard, that any passionate sentiments I might have possessed died with your brother Ian." Seeing Duncan's flinch of pain, she fell silent.

Ewan said sharply, "Damn it, I do care for you, lass. You've only to come home with me and keep to your part of our bargain to see how much I care."

"Indeed, mistress," Duncan said with obvious reluctance, "if you are betrothed to him, there is—"

"There was no formal betrothal," Mary hastened to tell him.

"I think the truth is that I missed my cousin Diana dreadfully when she married your cousin and went to live in Perthshire. After my aunt and Sir Neil went to join her for the birth of her child, I was terribly lonely, although I had urged them to go without me, thinking I would be glad to have the time to myself. Thus I was particularly vulnerable, I think, to the promises he—"

She broke off, seeing by his expression that he was no longer really listening. This was no time to try to explain the myriad of emotions through which she had struggled, or that the pain of the struggle itself had finally led her to accept Ewan's offer. Black Duncan would not want to hear that pride could make one vulnerable. Indeed, even she was not ready yet to admit that to anyone but herself.

He was looking at Ewan now. "It sounds to me, MacCrichton, as if you took advantage of Mistress Maclaine the moment her protectors left her alone. If you never arranged for a formal betrothal—"

"Man, there was no need," Ewan protested. "She has no dowry, no one to act for her, and she's well past the age of consent. I promised I'd take care of her and I will, so damn it, Campbell, get out of it. She gave her word, and I mean to hold her to it if I have to take her to court. Breach of promise works two ways, you know."

"Did you promise, lass?"

Mary hesitated, but the truth was the truth. She nodded.

"There, you see," Ewan exclaimed. He turned to his henchman. "You heard her, MacSteele. You're a witness, man. There are others who heard her make that first promise, too," he told Duncan earnestly. "Don't be thinking there are not."

"Then take your case to court," Duncan said abruptly, astonishing Mary, who was certain her case was lost. "Perhaps you'll convince a magistrate that she has no right to change her mind, but until you do, she remains under my protection."

"What about us, then?" Chuff demanded.

"Aye," Pinkie said, her blue eyes wide in her thin little face as she watched Black Duncan anxiously. "What of us, then?"

Mary kept silent, hardly daring to breathe, not even certain that something good had just happened.

Duncan looked at the children. "The children, too," he said.

"You have no right," Ewan cried. "By God, I won't let you, either. You come strutting in like the lord of the manor, but you are no such thing. You've got no right here, no power over her or me. So get out, or I'll have you thrown out."

"If you think you can, go ahead," Duncan said calmly.

"You talk big, but it's only talk. Oh, I see your great sword, too, but it won't do you much good in its sheath now, will it?" Snatching a pistol from his pocket, Ewan aimed it at Duncan with a shaking hand.

Mary gasped, grabbing Pinkie and Chuff and shoving them behind her.

"I ain't afraid of 'im," Chuff muttered, clutching her hand.

"Hush," Mary warned, watching Duncan while her heart pounded.

He had not moved. As calmly as if he were standing in a meadow watching clouds roll by instead of looking down the muzzle of an illegal, undoubtedly loaded pistol, he said, "Before you pull that trigger, MacCrichton, perhaps you should tell your man here to look out in the meadow in front of the house."

Ewan gave a curt nod, and his man rushed to a window. "I dinna see— Ay-de-mi, laird, there be nigh onto a score of armed men out there!"

"You have five men in the yard, MacCrichton, plus this lout here. From the look of them, however, I doubt they are foolish enough to be carrying much in the way of illegal arms."

"I'm carrying a weapon. Why would not they?"

"Castle Stalker lies not far from here, at the south end of the loch," Duncan said, referring to a famous Campbell military stronghold. "Coming here, you were too likely to run into the odd patrol of soldiers for your men to take the chance."

"Do you think I'm more foolhardy than my men, then?"

"Doubtless, you think yourself safe, since no member of the gentry has yet been arrested for carrying weapons, but don't be too cocksure. If you go in peace, I'll overlook the fact that you waved a pistol in my face, but if you don't, I promise you the authorities will listen when I report that you threatened me with one."

"What about the lass? She's mine, I tell you!"

"I'm a man of my word," Duncan said. "You can take your case to court if it amuses you to do so. I won't try to stop you."

"I think I'd rather kill you where you stand," Ewan said. "I'd be doing the whole of Appin country a bloody great favor if I did."

"That is another alternative, certainly," Duncan said with the same amazing calm. "You would not then be able to take your case to court, however."

"No, and why not?"

"Because, you great stupid lout, you will be dead within a minute of firing that shot. Your pistol holds only one bullet, and even if you've got another in your pocket, you won't have time to load it before my men rush this house, and if you think they'll reward you for murdering me, you are a fool as well as a lout. They revel in making sport of traitorous knaves like you."

Ewan paled but said stubbornly, "You would still be dead."

"True, and that's why I won't object to your peaceful departure. I don't want to annoy you so much that you put your life second to the joy of stealing mine."

Behind Mary, Chuff stirred.

Fearing that he would say something to irritate Ewan, she reached back and touched his arm warningly. The silence lengthened then until her knees felt weak.

Ewan said, "I don't trust you."

Duncan said, "Have you heard anyone accuse me of breaking my word?"

Ewan hesitated, then shook his head.

"You won't find anyone, either. My word is good, even when I offer it to the likes of you."

"I'm keeping my pistol out, nonetheless," Ewan declared with bravado. "At the first sign of any man drawing arms, I'll shoot you or the lass."

"So very much do you love her," Duncan murmured gently.

"I meant the wee lass," Ewan spat. "No one would even miss her, but I warrant you don't want harm to come to her, all the same."

Mary's hand tightened on Chuff's arm, but he reached out with his free hand to draw Pinkie closer.

Ewan was watching Duncan.

"I've made my offer," Duncan said.

"Aye, and I'll take it for now, but that lass is mine. I mean to see to it."

Silently, Duncan stepped aside to let Ewan and his henchman pass, making no move to follow them.

Mary said hastily, "Your men won't—"

"They'll do nothing unless they are threatened, mistress. My word is good."

"I did not mean to imply that it isn't, sir. I feared that without word from you, your men might act impulsively."

"They know better. Come here."

She moved obediently to stand before him, then started when he caught her chin and tilted her face to look more closely at her cheek.

"Why did he strike you?"

"He threatened to make me his wife by habit of cohabitation. I expect you know what that is." When he nodded, frowning, she said, "His intention was to force my submission here and now, believing I would then make no objection to returning with him. I said I had already told you I did not want to marry him."

"And that's when he slapped you?"

"I-I said I would claim rape if he laid a hand on me."

"That was foolish," Duncan said, releasing her. "You should not have taunted him, mistress."

"I suppose you think I should simply have lain back and welcomed his attentions," she retorted bitterly.

"Don't fling your sarcasm at me," he said, turning to look out into the yard. "I am not your enemy."

"I'm not so sure," she muttered.

"Have you things to pack?"

"Goodness, what for?"

"You cannot stay here."

"Why not?"

"Don't be daft. Because he will come back for you, of course. I told you as much yesterday, and you did not believe me. Surely, you see now that I was right."

"Won't he fear that you will go after him if he tries it again?"

"Fear won't stop him. You saw that he nearly decided to shoot me just to see me dead before my men came for him. Had I not believed he might, I'd never have made such a bargain with him, but for all I knew, his man had another pistol. In any event, once I was dead or badly wounded, they could easily have killed you and one or both of the children before my men could have stopped them. I couldn't take that chance, nor will I chance trusting him now. You will not stay here, mistress."

"I prefer to make my own decisions, sir. You have no authority over me."

"We have seen where your decisions lead," he said flatly. "If you have nothing to pack, we can leave at once."

She made a last attempt. "I don't want to go, and you cannot possibly want to be saddled with the children. In any case, where would you take us?"

"To Balcardane, of course. Get your things."

"Faith, sir, you cannot take us to Balcardane. Your father won't want us there, nor will your mother. For that matter—"

"Mistress Maclaine, I have already exerted more patience today than anyone has a right to expect. If you don't want me to pick you up and carry you out of here without a stitch of clothing other than what you stand in, pack your damned clothes. We leave in five minutes' time."

"Ye canna talk to our Mary like—"

Duncan snapped a grim look at Chuff, and the boy instantly fell silent. His small echo did not utter a sound.

"That's better," Duncan said softly. "Do not think for one minute, young man, that I will treat impertinence as gently as MacCrichton did, for I will not. Have you anything more to say to me?"

Chuff shook his head, looking at his feet.

"I would like a proper answer, if you please."

"No, sir."

"Good." He glared at Mary. "Does your singular lack of movement mean that you've got nothing to fetch?"

She fled upstairs, where she flung into a battered satchel an old dressing gown, a clean chemise, her gloves and hat, and a pair of old dresses that she had not thought worth taking to Shian. Looking swiftly around, knowing that Duncan might come in search of her at any moment, she snatched up a pair of her aunt's shoes. They wore the same size, and she knew she would be grateful for something to wear later in place of her half boots. Shoving them into the satchel atop everything else, she tied it shut and hurried down to the kitchen to fetch her box of remedies. She had not taken any to Shian, but with the children, she decided she would need them.

When she returned to the parlor Duncan was waiting, holding her gray cloak. The harsh look in his eyes eased, and he said, "I thought you would take longer."

She met his gaze. "You must think me very brave then, sir."

To her surprise, he smiled, and although it did not quite reach his eyes, it softened his expression. She did not think she had ever seen him smile before.

"You'd better hope," he said dryly, "that the day never comes when I tell you exactly what I think of you or your behavior, Mary Maclaine. I can promise you would not enjoy the experience."

Eight

The children enjoyed the ride to Balcardane Castle more than Mary did. Not only did they each get to ride pillion behind one of Duncan's men and make new friends, but Mary felt nearly as resistant to Duncan as she had to Ewan, as if she really had accepted salvation from the devil. Rather than feeling as if Duncan had rescued her, she felt as if she had been a bone over which the two men had fought, a bone that Duncan had successfully carried away with him.

She was riding in the same direction that she had ridden only two days before, but the journeys were vastly different. After all, she had at least gone with Ewan voluntarily, and as she thought now about the disastrous result of that, she imagined that the end to this journey could only be worse.

Once again, they passed the desiccated body of James of the Glen, hanging in its horrid chains. But in the dim gray light of an overcast afternoon, the sight was not nearly so stark as when it had cast a grim black shadow against the orange and gold blaze of a setting sun. No breeze made the chains creak today, either, she noted thankfully, but although the corpse hung still and silent, it stirred sad memories nonetheless. One of the soldiers guarding it saluted Duncan. He nodded, and Mary turned away, gazing resolutely ahead.

"You should have brought a warmer cloak," Duncan said, interrupting her reverie. "If those clouds open up, it's cold enough to snow."

"Do you think it will?" she asked. The low-pitched, even sound of his voice was more pleasant than her drifting thoughts, but she did not want to discuss her choice of clothing with him.

He glanced at the sky. "It might hail or sleet instead, I suppose."

She did not want to discuss the weather either. She really did not want to discuss anything with him. The farther they rode from Maclean House, the more she wondered what he would do with her at Balcardane.

Without thinking about the wisdom of bringing up such a topic, she said, "Your father will not welcome me to his house, I'll wager."

A glint of amusement lit his dark eyes. "What do you imagine he will do?"

She had not expected the question, but it diverted her thoughts from the gruesome sight they had passed. "I don't know what to expect. He is your father. I know he does not approve of me or my family, for he forbade Ian to visit our house."

"I, too, forbade him to visit Maclean House," Duncan reminded her.

"We have discussed that before, sir." Remembering some of what she had said then, she decided she owed him a partial apology and said at once, "When you said you supposed that Ian had never spoken kindly of you, I replied that you had only yourself to blame. I believe that is true, sir, but I may have misled you a trifle."

"Only a trifle?" The look he gave her was derisive.

Determined not to let him bait her, she said carefully, "I should also have told you that Ian knew you cared, sir. He knew that you were only trying to protect him. I would not want you to believe that he was unaware of your regard for him."

"I could wish that awareness had kept him home that night, but clearly what little influence I wielded was no match for your wiles, mistress."

"You dislike me, sir. You make no secret of the fact, so why are you helping us? You cannot want to see my face ten times a day at Balcardane."

"Perhaps I am doing it for Ian's sake. Did you think of that?"

"Perhaps you would do that," she said doubtfully.

He looked sharply at her. "Do you think it so impossible?"

"Not impossible, only unlikely," she replied honestly. "I confess, I find you much different now from what you were just a year ago. Nevertheless, I think it more likely that you still just order people to do what you think is best for them without considering what they might prefer."

"Do you?" A note of danger sounded in his voice.

She smiled. "I have offended you again, but you asked the question, you know. You should not ask questions if you do not want to hear honest answers."

"I'll give you more good advice, mistress. You should think before you speak. Experience with MacCrichton must have taught you how dangerous it can be to say whatever comes into your head, and although you may not know it yet, he is far less dangerous than I am."

Mary wrinkled her brow thoughtfully. "Perhaps that is so, sir, but I fear him. I do not fear you."

"That would be your second sight at work again, I expect."

She could not mistake his sarcasm, but she said, "I don't think the Sight has anything to do with this conversation. I merely state facts, sir. Perhaps you would also beat me if I angered you sufficiently, but I do not think you would knock poor Chuff halfway across the room with the back of your hand, or threaten to shoot Pinkie merely to convince someone of your fierce nature."

She saw the muscles in his jaw tighten before he said, "Are you telling me that MacCrichton hit the lad, too?"

"Aye, and I believed he would shoot Pinkie."

"I, too, but although I do not brutalize children, mistress, I will tell you what I told Chuff. Don't think you can disobey me without consequence, because I will enforce my orders as and when I find it necessary to do so. Do you understand me?"

"Aye, sir," Mary said with a sigh.

They fell silent after that. Ahead, on the hillside overlooking Loch Leven, she saw the great square tower of Balcardane above the trees, and a few minutes later the formidable grey stone castle loomed into view.

Concealed on the hillside above Maclean House, Ewan had watched Black Duncan's party ride out of the stable yard. He remained still, glowering at them, wishing he had the means to murder Duncan and all his men and carry the vixen away with him. He would soon teach her to mind him.

He did not speak to anyone on the way back to Shian, and no one tried to engage him in conversation. As they rounded the curve in the road overlooking Castle Stalker's island, he recalled Duncan's warning about patrols. He had seen none, but he knew Duncan had been right. The soldiers might not arrest him for carrying a pistol, but given the slightest chance, they would harass and threaten him. They were Campbells, after all, paid by the English government to enforce the laws it had imposed on the Highlands after the tragedy at Culloden.

Darkness had fallen by the time he and his men rode into the courtyard at Shian, and Ewan tossed his reins to MacSteele with an order to see to the horse. Thinking now only about getting his dinner, he strode inside and up the spiral stairs, coming to an astonished halt on the threshold of the great hall.

"Welcome home, MacCrichton," Allan Breck said, raising a glass half full of wine toward him. "I wondered when you would return. Did you find her?"

"What the devil are you doing in my house?"

Breck shrugged. "Seemed the safest place for me just now, unless of course you've murdered someone and you've got a patrol at your heels."

"Don't be absurd. I don't want you here."

"Well now, I think we ought to discuss that. Did you find my pretty cousin?"

"Aye, I found her."

"Then where is she?"

"Black Duncan Campbell's got her; that's where she is."

Breck took a sip of his wine. His expression gave away none of his thoughts.

Accepting that Breck was not going to leave, Ewan went to fill a glass for himself from the sideboard. "At least you didn't drink all my claret."

"It's palatable, but I prefer brandy. What is Duncan doing with her?"

"He *says* he's taken her under his protection," Ewan said sourly.

Breck snorted, but then his expression turned thoughtful. "If rumor does not lie, Balcardane has plans for Black Duncan. I'm told that he envisions an alliance between his house and the house of Caddell."

"More suitable, that. Caddell's another damned Campbell."

"Aye, and his land lies between Dunraven and the Duke of Argyll's seat at Inveraray. Balcardane thinks first about his pocket in all things, they say, and the Lady Serena stands to be a considerable heiress."

"She's got a brother, hasn't she?"

"Aye, and he's married, too, but he's sired five daughters with nary a son. They say his lady will be in the straw again soon, but no one is holding much hope. In any event, Caddell has only the one daughter, so he is bound to dower her well."

"Perhaps I should cast an eye in her direction."

"Much good it would do you. The winsome Serena is already a guest at Balcardane, and you've small hope of breaching any wall of that stronghold."

"How do you know so much about it?"

Breck smiled over his glass. "I've eyes and ears the length and breadth of Argyll and Lochaber, my lad, but don't look so glum. I've decided to help you."

About to tell him he could take his help and himself straight off to hell, Ewan held his tongue. He harbored no illusions about Breck's reason for the offer, but the man's abilities were legendary. It might be wiser, he thought, to exploit those abilities until he had no further use for them, or for Breck. One thing was certain. Allan Breck would not get his greedy hands on the MacCrichton treasure.

When the riders entered the courtyard at Balcardane, Duncan jumped down and lifted Mary off her horse before she could dismount. His hands felt firm and warm around her waist, and until then, she did not realize how cold she was. He urged her toward the impressive entrance, but her legs felt stiff and reluctant to obey. Pausing to look up at the Earl of Balcardane's crest, carved and colored above the doorway, she knew her reluctance had nothing to do with stiff knees.

"Bannatyne," Duncan said as they reached the front step, "take these children around to the kitchen and see that someone feeds them and looks after them."

"Aye, master. Come along, you bairns."

"Just a moment," Mary said, halting the three in their tracks. Turning to Duncan, she said, "Do you have other children in the castle, sir?"

"I have no children at all that I know of, mistress."

"I meant servants' children, of course," she said, not bothering to conceal her exasperation.

He shrugged. "I don't pay heed to scullery brats. Bannatyne?"

Shooting Mary an apologetic look, the man said, "I don't know, sir."

Mary said, "If your cook is unaccustomed to children, she may dislike having these two cast into her kitchen without so much as a word to her about them."

"She will do as she is told," Duncan said.

"Very likely she will," Mary said, grimacing, "but Pinkie has already endured abuse in Ewan's kitchen. I don't want that experience repeated, and before you say it would not be, sir, let me suggest that you won't know anything about it."

He looked ready to explode, but he controlled himself, muttering through clenched teeth that perhaps she might also like to suggest what he should do instead.

"I don't know," she admitted frankly, "but until you can offer more options than merely to fling the child into someone else's care, I would like to keep her with me. Chuff is accustomed to hard work, and I daresay you can find a place for him in the kitchen."

"Someone can find one for him, certainly," Duncan agreed harshly.

Chuff said, "I'd like fine tae be a stable lad, I would. I dinna like kitchens."

Hastily, Mary said, "You must do as you are bid, my dear. Now, go along with Bannatyne, and take Pinkie with you to get something to eat. When you have finished, perhaps someone will show her where I am to sleep, and she can wait for me there." She looked challengingly at Duncan. "Have you an objection, sir?"

"None. See to it, Bannatyne. And now, mistress," he added, giving her a little push toward the entrance, "perhaps you will allow me to take you inside."

Her misgivings returned in full force. That she was on Campbell soil, in the heart of the sole Campbell stronghold in country that once had held only Stewarts and others loyal to the Stewart cause, seemed more than incongruous. No one would want her here. If the earl did not order his strong-minded son to fling her outside the gates at once, he might order her locked up or even thrown into the pit he doubtless kept for serious miscreants.

Since Culloden, most Scottish noblemen no longer held the powers of the pit and gallows, but she did not think anyone would try to prevent a man as powerful as the Campbell Earl of Balcardane from exercising his ancient rights and privileges. Just thinking of the pit chilled her very soul.

The reality of meeting his lordship was quite different from what she had expected, however. Crossing the threshold, she and Duncan entered a great hall two stories high with a wide, elegant angle staircase soaring up from the left rear. Tall double doors opened off the hall to left and right, with a third, smaller one at the back, just visible in the shadowy alcove beneath the stairway's half landing.

Shadows and shapes on the dark paneled walls showed that many weapons had once hung on them, as they had in most Highland households that could afford to display their strength. The sight reminded her of the hall at Shian, with its racks of pointless lances.

Here, however, a musket hung over the fireplace in what seemed a direct defiance of the ban. Not that anyone would complain about actions taken by a kinsman of the mighty Duke of Argyll, of course. The oddity was that they had taken down the other weapons. Mary wondered if they lay hidden somewhere or had been turned in to the authorities, as the law said they should have been.

"We'll look for my father first," Duncan said, gesturing toward the pair of tall doors on the left side of the hall.

Mary felt her heart begin to pound. She had met Balcardane only once, when he had visited Maclean House the night of Ian's murder. The earl had been dazed with grief then, but later, when she had several times seen him from a distance during James's trial and hanging, he had shown no weakness and no compassion. He was a hard man with an ingrained hatred of Jacobites, and Mary's kinsmen had been, to a man, strong fighters for the cause. The earl represented their enemy.

The room they entered proved to be a large library, for which someone had collected an astonishing number of books. Shelves of them lined two walls from floor to ceiling. A third wall boasted two tall windows overlooking the courtyard, with an arched, gilded pier glass between them. Candles in girandoles on either side of the glass, along with the cheerful fire and a lamp burning on the huge desk near the hearth, cast a friendly glow throughout the room.

The burly, gray-haired figure rising awkwardly from behind the desk to greet them dispelled the warmth of that glow, however, leaving her feeling stiff and chilly. After one hasty glance, she kept her eyes modestly downcast in the manner she knew such a powerful man would expect.

Duncan stepped forward. "With your permission, sir, I have extended the protection and hospitality of Balcardane to Mistress Maclaine and two servant children who find themselves dependent upon her."

"What led you to do such a thing?" The earl's voice was as gruff and gravelly as she remembered it. He went on in a carping way, "More visitors, Duncan? It's winter, lad. I hope you realize that we cannot simply ride to Fort William if we run out of supplies."

"I don't think her presence will tax the castle stores much, sir. She isn't very big, as you can see for yourself, and both children are accustomed to working for their keep."

"Aye, well, but still, she's one of that Maclean lot that fought so hard against us in the late rebellion, and again when we were trying to put an end to James of the Glen and his lot of damned conspirators."

"James was not guilty, sir," Mary said quietly, looking up and then quickly down again, careful not to let Duncan catch her eye.

Balcardane snapped, "Nonsense, of course he was guilty, but we won't fratch over him, lass. He's dead and gone now, and that makes one plotter the less to worry us. You must agree that Appin's been devilish quiet since he met his Maker."

"She can do nothing to alter that," Duncan said, relieving her of the necessity of contradicting her host. He added evenly, "You will not deny her simple Highland hospitality, sir. No proper Highlander would do that. Moreover, had I left her where I found her, Ewan MacCrichton would have forced her to marry him."

"That villain! I've no more use for that man than I had for James. Ever since the king pardoned MacCrichton—a grave error, in my opinion—he has been trying to control south Appin and has even dared to stick his oar into Campbell country."

"I've just returned from Dunraven," Duncan reminded his father. "Our men have things well in hand there. I doubt that MacCrichton wants to do more than crow on his own dung heap, but I could not allow him to abduct the lass."

When Balcardane did not reply, Mary regained enough of her confidence to look at him at last, only to find him regarding her in a measuring way. Meeting that scrutiny by raising her chin, she was nonetheless shocked by his altered appearance. He was not the man she remembered. His grey-green eyes were flat, as if the once fierce light in them had gone out. Dark hollows lay beneath them, his sunken cheeks looked grey, and his mouth seemed to have turned down permanently.

"I'm sorry to be a nuisance, my lord," she said quietly, "but Black Duncan insisted that I come here. I hope you are not vexed."

"Nay, lass, not vexed. Your presence brings back sad memories, that's all."

She swallowed hard, understanding at once why he seemed but half the man he had been. Grief had taken a sad toll of the earl. With sincerity, she said, "If the memories are too sad, sir, I can simply go away again."

"Where is Sir Neil? Why ain't he looking after you like he should?"

Giving her no time to reply, Duncan said, "He and Lady Maclean have gone to Perthshire, sir. You know that Rory and Diana are expecting her confinement soon. It is not so amazing that her mother desired to be with her."

"Everyone is having bairns except you, Duncan," the earl complained. "I should have thought Diana's cousin would want to be with her, too."

"I can go to Perthshire if my presence here distresses you, my lord. I would prefer that myself now, I believe, if it comes to that."

"I suppose you think you can just get on your horse tomorrow and ride off to Perthshire," Duncan said harshly. "Or do you perhaps imagine that I will supply you with an escort of my men?"

"Here now," Balcardane protested, "we're not sending a lot of your chaps into Perthshire. They're expensive enough to keep here. Think what it will cost for board and keep when they're cut off by the snow and have to stay there all winter!"

Meeting Duncan's sardonic gaze, Mary said, "I would not want to put you to so much trouble as that, sir, but if you will take me back to Maclean House, I promise I will set forth at once. I can take some of our men with me, I expect."

"Which ones?" Duncan demanded.

Pressing her lips firmly together to keep from snapping at him in a like tone, she took a deep breath before she said, "I do not yet know which ones. That will depend upon who amongst them knows the direction and can protect me."

"That means none of them," he retorted. "Your men are naught but shepherds and hinds, lass, and the minute Mac-Crichton gets wind of your departure, he will be hard on your heels. You'll stay here, and there's an end to it."

Mary had never thought herself a violent woman, but a sudden overwhelming urge seized her to throw something at him, preferably something hard and heavy that would knock some civility into him. With nothing of the sort at hand, she managed to keep her temper, saying firmly, "We shall see about that, sir."

"We'll see nothing. It's decided. Now the next thing is to figure out what you can wear while you are here. You cannot possibly have stuffed enough clothing into that little satchel you brought to serve you properly here; however, my mother may be able to help, or perhaps Serena will have a few things you can borrow."

"Serena?" She looked blankly from one man to the other.

Balcardane cheered up at once. "Mistress Maclaine will make excellent company for Serena. She is Caddell's daughter," he explained to Mary, "and I think she must be very near you in age, for she is but one- or two-and-twenty."

"I shall be twenty the end of January, sir."

"Just as I thought," he said, nodding. "Duncan, you take her along to your mother and Serena, lad. They'll look after her, and I'll see you both at dinner."

Back in the hall, Mary said, "He did not ask anything about the children."

"No reason that he should. He does not concern himself with servants. That is his steward's duty, and I will tell MacDermid about them when I see him."

Crossing the hall, he opened the double doors opposite the library and let Mary precede him into a pleasant yellow saloon. At the far end, four tall, narrow windows overlooked Loch Leven. At first she wondered if such windows might invite enemies to attempt an invasion, but soon she saw how steeply the grassy hillside fell away below. Although the saloon was apparently at ground level, its windows were fifteen feet or more above the ground.

A plump lady wearing a frilly white cap and a gown of flourished golden-brown paduasoy sat on a claw-footed sofa near one of the end windows. She held a tambour frame, plying her needle with a lassitude that suggested the task did not enthrall her. Even so, she did not look up at once when they entered.

"Good afternoon, ma'am," Duncan said.

"Bless me," she said, starting and looking over spectacles that had slipped down her nose, "is that you, Duncan? And who is that with you? I do not think your father will approve of your bringing another young woman here, particularly with Caddell thinking you and Serena will make a match of it and your father hoping the same. I shall not mind if you don't, but I have nothing to say about it, of course. Serena is pretty enough, but she talks only about how dull it must be now at Inver House whilst everyone waits to see if her sister-in-law has a boy after producing a string of girls, and I did hope you would find a wife who liked lively conversation. I scarcely ever have anyone to talk with, you know, and you and your father rarely listen even when you are in the same room. When your brother was alive—"

"This is Mistress Maclaine, ma'am," Duncan said, cutting in without apology. "You know her family, I believe. Her aunt is Anne Stewart Maclean."

"Oh, you were Ian's friend," Lady Balcardane said, removing her spectacles and smiling at Mary in such a way as to tell her that she had just been elevated to a class above that of a mere *someone else*. She went on warmly, "How kind of you to visit us. Do come and sit beside me. We miss him dreadfully, you know."

"Yes, ma'am," Mary said, glancing uncertainly at Duncan.

He shrugged, so she went to sit beside Lady Balcardane, saying, "I miss him, too, ma'am, very much. He was such a kind and gentle person."

"Oh, yes," Lady Balcardane said with a deep sigh. "Dearest Ian."

"Mother, Mary is going to stay with us for a time. There has been some unpleasantness at Maclean House, and Lady Maclean and Sir Neil are away in Perthshire, at Rory's, for the winter, so Mistress Maclaine has been alone there. I brought her here where she will be well protected."

"How frightening for you," Lady Balcardane said sympathetically.

"Yes, it was," Mary agreed, shooting a speaking look at Duncan.

He said evenly, "She was able to bring only a meager wardrobe with her, ma'am, a problem that I am hoping you can help her rectify?"

"Do you expect me to buy clothing for her, Duncan? Because unless you pay for it yourself—which I cannot think wise, because people are bound to talk, you know—your father won't stand for spending so much money, particularly since I applied to him only this morning to fund our annual dinner for the villagers and our neighbors on Christmas Eve. His own father began the tradition, hoping to foster peace with his Stewart neighbors, so one would think your father would not cavil so at spending the money, but he does, every year, and I'm certain he will not want me to spend more. Not that clothing need cost so much as all that," she added, "but he will think that it must, and he will fly into the boughs just as he always does."

"I don't mean for you to purchase new clothing, ma'am. She brought things with her but only a few. I don't want to relate all her troubles. It is for her to decide how much she wants to tell, but she had to leave most of her belongings elsewhere and had little left at home from which to choose. I doubt that the things she brought will be sufficient, or that they are stylish enough to suit your taste or Serena's."

"As if I should let that bother me! When, I ask you, was the last time I had any stylish new clothes myself? If it were not for friends sending me drawings of the things they see women wearing in Edinburgh, and Serena bringing pattern cards to show me, I should not have a notion of how one ought to dress. Only think how embarrassed I was when his grace of Argyll last paid us a visit!" She looked Mary up and down. "I do think I might have one or two things for you, my dear. They won't be the height of fashion, but I daresay few people hereabouts know what that is, so we shan't let it trouble us. If I am to dress her for dinner, Duncan, you will have to tell them to put it back an hour. I was just waiting here now for Serena and your father to join me." To Mary, she added, "We generally dine at four, you see, my dear, and we breakfast each morning at ten. Where shall we put her, Duncan?"

"Serena has taken the tower bedchamber," he said.

"You won't put her in that little room below it! There is no fireplace there."

"No, I think she will have to go into the south wing," Duncan said. "She can have the room next to Ian's, if that will not distress you."

"Of course it will not, and I daresay she will like to be close to his room. It is just as he left it," she said, patting Mary's knee, her eyes filling suddenly with tears that spilled over and trickled down her plump cheeks. "Oh, my poor sweet laddie!" She burst into sobs.

Mary looked helplessly at Duncan, but his expression had hardened again, and he turned on his heel and left the room without a word. Knowing no other course, and fully in sympathy with the plump little woman, Mary put her arms round her and held her until the worst of the emotional storm had passed.

"There, there," she said when the sobs had abated at last. "Have you got a handkerchief, ma'am? I don't have one to offer you, I'm afraid."

Drawing a ragged breath, Lady Balcardane gestured distractedly toward her sewing box. Correctly interpreting the gesture to mean that she would find a handkerchief inside, Mary soon pressed a lace-trimmed one into her hand.

Lady Balcardane clutched it to her bosom for some moments before she dabbed her eyes, and then suddenly blew her nose hard with it. Folding it tidily, she blotted her eyes again, and said, "How kind you are, my dear. I am so dreadfully sorry to have wept all over you, but when I think of my poor darling Ian just lying there dead at the side of the road. Not that I saw him there, for they would not let me look at him, but still, one's imagination paints pictures, you know."

"I do know, ma'am. I did not see him either, and I admit that I'm grateful—"

"What's this? Why are you crying, ma'am? Has something gone amiss?"

The voice, high-pitched and childlike, announced the arrival of a lovely young woman in a blue gown that looked like silk to Mary, and expensive silk at that. The dress hugged a slender waist and billowed over a hoop that would have been more suitable in an Edinburgh drawing room. Elegant matching slippers peeped out from beneath the young woman's wide skirt. Over her shoulders, caught up at her elbows, she wore a bright Paisley shawl. Mary, in the camlet jacket and dress she had worn far too long, felt like a mouse in the presence of a butterfly.

The newcomer's hair was the color of pale new corn in bright sunlight, and she wore it in a dazzling, complex arrangement of twists and curls piled atop her head. Her face was perfectly oval, its features delicate and well formed. The eyes gazing curiously at Mary were a shade of blue so brilliant as to startle her.

She swallowed, gathering her wits, more aware than she had ever been of her dowdy old camlet walking dress and her thick tawny hair that, as usual, she had twisted into a knot and pinned in place. She could feel strands tickling her face and neck. Worst of all, she felt as if she ought to jump up and curtsy to the other girl.

Lady Balcardane patted Mary's knee, saying kindly, "This is Serena, my dear. I am persuaded that the pair of you will become excellent friends."

Nine

Mary stared at Lady Serena, who gazed back expectantly. It did not take second sight to realize that the other young woman, an earl's daughter, expected her to rise and, if not to curtsy, at least to greet her with the extraordinary civility to which her rank had no doubt accustomed her. Moreover, if they were to live together in the same house, even for a short time, amicably, Mary knew her duty.

Putting aside all thought of her own appearance, she rose, saying politely, "Forgive me if I seem to have lost my wits, Lady Serena. I was a little stunned, I suppose, for I cannot recall when I have met anyone as beautiful as you are."

Lady Serena smiled, and if the smile did not quite reach her eyes, it was nonetheless a lovely smile. Mary sighed inwardly as she held out her hand in greeting, aware that her own teeth were not nearly so straight. One front tooth slightly overlapped the other, and although she had never thought it a defect before, since her teeth were remarkably white and unblemished, she did think it one now.

Serena said bluntly, "Who are you?"

"Oh, gracious me," Lady Balcardane exclaimed with a watery laugh, "if I have not failed in my duty to present you, my dear. This is Mistress Maclaine, Serena, and Duncan has brought her here to stay with us for . . ." She looked blankly at Mary. "How long shall we enjoy your company, my dear?"

"I do not know, ma'am," Mary said. She nearly added that

she was not there by her own choice, but it occurred to her that she might upset her hostess with such a statement, so she said only, "I hope to join my kinsmen in Perthshire soon."

"Maclean kinsmen?" Lady Serena turned abruptly to her hostess. "Did you say Duncan brought her here, ma'am? How very odd."

Lady Balcardane blinked, then dabbed her watery eyes again. Mary saw that the redness in them was fading, and she saw, too, where Duncan had come by his dark eyes. His mother's were the color of coffee beans.

Lady Balcardane said, "Why is Duncan's bringing her here so odd, Serena? I'm sure he has brought guests to stay at Balcardane many times before."

Lady Serena laughed lightly. Catching up her skirt and turning with a rustle of swirling silk to sit on a nearby sofa, she said, "I should think he'd take care not to show up with unknown young women—especially unknown Maclean women—when he is trying to win my hand, that's all. It is bad enough that he has been at Dunraven nearly since I arrived. To be collecting females of any sort when he has only just returned . . ." She spread her hands. "I ask you, ma'am, is that civil?"

Mary decided that she and Lady Serena were not destined to become fast friends. She had no more desire now than before to join her relatives in Perthshire, but Serena's attitude did make the journey begin to look more appealing.

Lady Balcardane picked up the tambour frame she had set down earlier, and said as she put it into her workbasket, "I cannot imagine why you should think it uncivil to offer hospitality to a visitor, my dear. I am sure everyone does that, and Duncan only brought her here because he thought she would be safe—"

"Safe!" Serena turned back to Mary. "Were you in real danger? I find that hard to believe."

"I am not certain if you mean that I don't look as if I would ever meet with danger or simply that I don't look like the sort of woman Black Duncan would rescue," Mary said evenly. "But doubtless you did not mean to imply that her ladyship is mistaken."

"Really, Serena, that was unkind," Lady Balcardane exclaimed. "I do not know the whole, for Duncan would not tell me. He said it was for Mistress Maclaine to tell us about her troubles, and only if she wishes to do so, so we must not press her for information. Oh, and that reminds me," she added, slipping her spectacles into her reticule, "Duncan asked if we would help her find something suitable to wear. He does not think she has brought enough appropriate clothing."

"I am very sure I have not," Mary said, struggling to keep from looking again at Serena's gown. "We do not keep such state at Maclean House, ma'am."

Lady Balcardane got to her feet. "Then we must go and see what we can do about you right now, my dear, for it is nearly four o'clock, and although Duncan will have told them to put things back an hour, here you are, still looking just as you did when you arrived. I daresay he did not so much as show you where you are to sleep. Will you come with us, Serena?"

"No, thank you, ma'am. I think perhaps I should stay here in the event that Duncan wishes to see me before we dine. You will do much better without me, in any event, but perhaps you could send someone to pour me a glass of wine."

"Yes, of course," Lady Balcardane said, nodding. "You must do as you please, my dear. Come along, Mistress Maclaine."

"I do hope you will call me Mary, ma'am," she said, turning to follow. "I am not accustomed to such formality."

"Well, I will then, and gladly." Lady Balcardane paused and looked pointedly at Serena. When that young woman gazed limpidly back at her, she said, "I am persuaded that Serena would like you to be more informal with her, too."

"I don't mind, I suppose," Serena said.

"There, you see," Lady Balcardane said cheerfully.

Mary was not at all certain Serena had meant her words to be taken quite the way Lady Balcardane had taken them, but she was not going to argue. The formality Serena clearly preferred would make any relationship between them even more difficult than Mary already expected it to be. Therefore, she smiled sweetly and said, "Thank you, Serena. You must certainly call me Mary."

"Oh, I will. I do hope you can manage to find something that will become you." Her tone left Mary in no doubt that she thought the task an impossible one.

Lady Balcardane took time to ask a hall boy to fetch wine for Lady Serena. Then she led the way up two flights of stairs and along a short corridor to the bedchamber Duncan had allotted to Mary.

"I must first see if you have something you can wear," she explained as she pushed open the door. "Men generally know so little about these things, you know, although I will say that Duncan displays quite good taste in his own clothing, and frequently compliments mine."

"I can certainly see why he would, ma'am, because if that dress you are wearing is any indication, your taste is exquisite. Moreover, I can assure you that nothing I brought with me will please you. I do own gowns that, while they do not compare with the one Serena is wearing, are certainly suitable for dining in company, but I was able to bring none of them with me."

"Dear me," Lady Balcardane said. She opened her mouth, doubtless to ask for an explanation of Mary's lack, but turned her head suddenly and said instead, "Who can have left that window open? No doubt someone intended to air out this room, but it's like an ice house in here." She moved quickly to shut it, giving Mary a moment's respite to look around her new bedchamber.

"How very pleasant this room is," she said when her hostess turned back again, the window fully locked behind her.

"Do you think so? I think it rather dismal myself. That paper has been there since the castle came into my husband's family, and I daresay this Turkey carpet is even older. But then I don't like red in a bedchamber."

"I think it makes the room seem warmer," Mary said, glancing at the little fire crackling in the hooded fireplace.

"The fire would have warmed it properly if the girl had not

left the window open," Lady Balcardane said over her shoulder as she opened the large wardrobe. "But where are the rest of your things? There are only two old frocks in here."

"They are all I brought."

Lady Balcardane gaped at her, speechless for once.

Mary could not recall having felt so embarrassed by her circumstances before. The Macleans were a strong clan, and had once been a wealthy one. After Culloden, when the Crown had demanded forfeiture of their lands, she, her aunt, and her two cousins had found themselves reduced to living in a house much smaller than those they had known on the Island of Mull. But nearly everyone they knew or cared about then had been in a similar circumstance.

She had not visited a home grander than her own in seven years, and before that she had known few grander than Lochfuaran Castle. It was easily the equal of Craignure, where she had lived briefly before they had all left Mull for Stewart land in Appin. In the long ago days at Lochfuaran, although stately dinners and elegant apparel had doubtless been customary, she had been too young to indulge in them.

"This simply will not do," Lady Balcardane said abruptly.

"I beg your pardon, ma'am?"

"This!" She gestured toward the barren wardrobe. "No one owns only two dresses, Mary. I know that many persons hereabouts have fallen on hard times, but you are well bred, my dear, and I cannot believe that anyone related to Anne Stewart Maclean has no more than these few paltry things to wear."

Suddenly an image of her formidable aunt swept into the room, and Mary felt herself stiffening in defense of her, and of herself.

"I know they are not suitable, ma'am," she began, speaking with careful control over her surging emotions. "However—"

"Oh, pray, do not take a pet, my dear," Lady Balcardane exclaimed, looking stricken. "I did not mean to offend you, indeed I did not, but I cannot believe this is all you own. I simply must know what horrid thing befell you to bring you to

such a pass. I do hope it was not Duncan's doing! Oh, pray, tell
me it was not!"

"No, ma'am, of course it was not," Mary said swiftly. Despite
the words, however, she was thinking unkind thoughts about
Duncan, for although he was not responsible for her dresses
having been left at Shian Towers, he was certainly responsible
for her present plight. She would not be facing it if he had left
her comfortably at Maclean House. Gazing unsteadily at Lady
Balcardane, she said, "It a long story, ma'am, but I will tell you
if you want to hear it."

"I certainly do," Lady Balcardane said. She picked up her
skirt and walked to the door, talking all the while. "But you
come along with me to my bedchamber whilst you tell it, because I mean to ring for my woman at once. Between the two
of us, we will find you something to wear. Now, come, come!"

Mary followed her downstairs to a much larger bedchamber
than the one they had just left. It was a bit chilly, like every
room in the castle, but the fire looked cheerful and the embroidered peach-colored bed curtains looked like velvet.

Lady Balcardane tugged the bell cord vigorously, then moved
to a larger version of the wardrobe in Mary's room and pulled
open the doors. A cloud of varicolored materials billowed forth.

The next half hour passed in a daze while the constantly
chattering countess supervised Mary's dressing. Her woman, a
tall, angular woman in a black dress, named Sarah, soon responded to the bell and set to work.

Lady Balcardane's figure was much plumper than Mary's, but
among all the gowns in the wardrobe they found several from
her younger days that would suit a more slender body. Sarah laid
them out on the bed and over chairs and stools. She held them
up, twitched them about, then flung each in its turn over Mary's
head to be buttoned, laced, tucked, pinned, and rearranged until
finally all three women agreed upon the one gown.

In stays and petticoats, Mary sat at the dressing table so that
Sarah could do her hair. She could scarcely breathe, for the
countess and her woman had insisted that she lace her stays
tightly. Since she rarely did so, she was half afraid the laces

would pop, but she had only to sit while Sarah deftly wielded the curling iron that she had previously heated in the fire.

"That will do for now," Lady Balcardane said when Sarah stepped aside to let her see. "I daresay we ought to cut and curl it into a more modern style, but she has beautiful hair, and you have done well with it, Sarah. Now, for the gown."

Mary stood up to let them put it on her, trying to see herself, but able to see only bits and pieces at a time in her ladyship's looking glass.

"Stand still, my dear," Lady Balcardane said when everything was in place. "Let me look at you."

Mary stood nervously, waiting for the verdict.

Made of pink brocaded damask, the gown was of the sort called a sack with a closed skirt over plain dimity petticoats. Mary was two or three inches taller than the countess, but the skirt was full enough to accommodate the round hoops worn twenty years before, so over the more modern fan-shaped hoop, with but a few tucks and stitches, it draped at just the right length. With full sleeves, a low, snug bodice, and creamy lace trim, Mary felt elegant, but Lady Balcardane was frowning.

"Fetch my jewelry box, Sarah."

"Oh, no, ma'am," Mary protested. "I couldn't!"

"Don't be foolish. Here now, let me see," she added when Sarah presented her with an open box chockful of glittering baubles. "Ah, yes, put this on, my dear." She held out a pink velvet ribbon with a small gold locket attached. "It is no more than a trumpery kickshaw, but it will look well with that gown."

Mary looked into the glass to tie the ribbon, but to her dismay her hands shook. Sarah took the ribbon from her and tied it around her neck.

Tears pricked her eyes when she turned back to say, "Thank you, ma'am. You are very kind."

"Fiddlesticks, we have enjoyed ourselves immensely, have we not, Sarah? I have never had a girl to dress, you know, having borne only sons, and them not wanting me to have a thing to do with their dressing once they were out of short coats. But come, my dear, we must go downstairs now. How Duncan and

Balcardane will stare! We have done very well, I think, very well indeed."

Mary was not so certain. Her hair looked and felt odd to her, for she had become accustomed simply to twisting it up and pinning it in place whether she was dressing up or not. It curled naturally, but the riot of curls that Sarah had created looked very different from her soft natural ones, and made her imagine she was seeing someone else altogether in the mirror.

When they returned to the yellow saloon, she saw that Balcardane had joined Serena, but Duncan was not there.

"How vexing," Lady Balcardane murmured beside her.

The other two did not seem to have noticed their arrival. They remained deep in conversation, and it was evident from the earl's chuckles that he enjoyed flirting with Serena. He looked at them only when he could no longer avoid doing so, and his eyebrows rose in mild surprise as he got to his feet to greet them.

"Can this be the same young woman I saw not long ago in my library? I swear, I would not have recognized you, mistress."

Lady Balcardane folded her fan with a snap and said, "If that is all you can say, my lord, I am prodigiously disappointed in you. Why, I can remember when you were a dab hand at paying a pretty compliment, sir."

"He still pays pretty compliments," Serena said, smoothing her skirt.

The earl's cheeks flushed, and Lady Balcardane said, "Where is Duncan? They will announce dinner soon."

"Aye, so they will," Balcardane said, "and we shan't wait long for him."

They did not have to wait at all, however, for Mary and Lady Balcardane had no sooner taken seats than Duncan entered. His gaze rested first upon Mary, but before he could speak (if, indeed, he had intended to do so), Serena jumped to her feet and hastened forward to meet him.

"Lud, sir, how very late you are! I had expected to see you long before now, and I can certainly tell you that when I am Countess of Balcardane, I shall not stand for such shabby treatment."

"Have you plotted to murder my mother and marry my father, Serena? Because if you have not," he added in the face of her speechless astonishment, "I cannot imagine how you intend to become Countess of Balcardane."

Recovering quickly, she said with a nervous laugh and a glance that darted to Balcardane and back to Duncan, "Why, I protest, sir, I never meant I should do so at once. I was referring, I hope, to the far distant future. You need not fear that I have come to prefer your papa over you," she added, giving his arm a familiar squeeze.

Duncan said, "Mistress Maclaine, that gown becomes you well, but you ought to wear pearls with it instead of that trumpery locket."

Feeling sudden, inexplicable sympathy for Serena, Mary said quietly, "Thank you, sir, but I am quite happy with the locket your mother very kindly lent to me."

Lady Balcardane said, "You are right, Duncan, of course, but I knew she would never accept pearls. Why, the poor dear scarcely knows me, and it is prodigiously awkward to borrow jewelry from anyone but one's mother or sister. Not but what I should have been perfectly happy to lend Mary anything she liked, and you must admit she looks quite elegant, even without pearls."

A lackey entered just then, and Balcardane said, "It looks like they've got dinner ready to serve at last. Will you take my arm, my dear?"

To Mary's surprise, he extended his arm to her, but she understood more clearly when he added, "Duncan will escort Serena."

"Then I shall be pleased to go in with you and her ladyship," Mary said, putting a hand on his outstretched arm.

"What? Oh, yes, of course. Come along, madam. Not but what you don't know your own way, I'll wager," he said, adding to Mary with a laugh, "The dining parlor lies just above this room at the top of the stairs."

At the table, Mary sat alone opposite Duncan and Serena, with his lordship at the head and Lady Balcardane at the foot.

A lone servant served the first course, then placed side dishes on the table and left the room. Lady Balcardane talked incessantly, and although Mary did her best to respond to such gambits as seemed to require a response, she quickly realized that the others had developed a habit of ignoring her ladyship's constant chatter.

Conversation between Serena and the two gentlemen continued in spite of Lady Balcardane, and Mary soon found that she could easily listen to everyone, since no one seemed really to require a response from her. All in all, the meal proved relaxing. No one expected her to do anything but eat her food.

When the servant brought in a decanter of claret and set it on the table, Lady Balcardane arose at once, shaking out her skirt in preparation to withdraw.

Serena said hastily, "I hope you gentlemen mean to join us soon, for I think we would all enjoy a rubber of whist this evening, don't you agree?"

"An excellent notion," Duncan said. "Why don't you join the ladies down in the saloon now, sir, and I'll attend to those letters you asked me to write."

Serena said in dismay, "We want you to play, Duncan!"

"You have not counted, Serena. There are five of us."

Before Mary could say that she would be perfectly happy to go to bed, Serena said with a heavy sigh, "In that case, I daresay no one will want to play."

"Suit yourself," Duncan said. "I've still got letters to write."

"I'll come with you," Balcardane said. "I'm in no mood for cards either. Bring the claret to the library, Donald."

"Aye, m' lord."

So it was that the three ladies went alone to the saloon, where Mary soon pleaded exhaustion and asked to be excused.

"Of course, my dear," Lady Balcardane replied instantly. "Can you remember the way to your bedchamber?"

"Yes, ma'am, thank you. Good night."

"You will need help undressing. Just pull the bell and someone will come."

"Yes, ma'am, I will. Good night, Serena."

After a brief pause, Serena said, "Good night, Mary."

Leaving them, Mary hurried across the shadowy hall, but the library door opened before she reached the stairway, and Duncan said, "Mistress, is that you? One moment please. I want a word with you."

Wondering what she had done now to annoy him, she turned reluctantly.

"You should have a shawl," he said, as he approached. "You must have been chilly throughout dinner. That dining parlor is never warm."

"I sat near the fire, sir. I have not been cold till just now."

"I won't keep you. I wanted only to assure you that the children are faring well. Chuff has already made a friend of the cook, and she is determined to fatten them both up."

"I'm glad of that, sir. Thank you for telling me."

"You will find Pinkie awaiting you in your bedchamber," he said. "Don't coddle her, though. You will do the child no favor by spoiling her."

"Both of them could do with some spoiling, I think," Mary said. "They have not enjoyed a pleasant life. I do understand you, however, and I will try not to let her acquire notions above her station. Is that all you wanted to say to me, sir?"

"Aye, for now. Good night then, Mary Maclaine."

He turned on his heel, but a moment later when the library door shut behind him, Mary still had not moved. She stood staring after him, thinking that perhaps Balcardane Castle cast some sort of odd spell over its inhabitants.

The earl was nothing like she had expected him to be, bearing little resemblance to the ogre she had long thought him.

As for Lady Balcardane, she was like no one Mary had ever met. The plump little woman seemed never to cease talking, but beneath the chatty exterior beat a warm and generous heart, and Mary already loved her dearly.

Black Duncan certainly had changed. The man who had just bade her good-night could not be the same man who had ordered Ian to stay away from her, or the one who had once angrily accused her of bewitching innocents. She tried to imagine any of those men married to Serena, found herself suddenly chuckling, and took herself off to her bedchamber, where she found Pinkie curled up on the high bed in a tight little ball, sound asleep.

Shutting the door quietly, Mary put a log on the fire. She poked at it until the flames began leaping merrily, then drew the coverlet gently over Pinkie, and sat down at the dressing table to let down her hair.

Fortunately and despite her tight stays, she could undress herself, and she did so at once, hanging the lovely dress in the wardrobe. Performing her ablutions hastily, she snuffed the few candles that lit the room and climbed into bed in her chemise, taking care not to waken the sleeping child.

Darkness surrounded her like heavy, suffocating black water. When she tried to move her hands and arms, they felt heavy, clumsy, almost as if someone else directed their movement. She could not see them. Moving her hand before her face seemed to take forever, and it did no good. She could not see it at all.

She touched a finger to her nose. She could feel it, but still she could see nothing. It was growing harder to breathe. Her chest felt tight, her lungs constricted.

She was leaning against solid rock, rough rock, damp and slimy rock. When she realized she had been leaning against it, that the slime had touched her hair and the back of her gown, she felt sick.

She was in some sort of cave or cavern, then, but what was she wearing? She could not tell, and she tried to remember what she had put on earlier, but she had no memory of an earlier time. It, like the hand before her face, was a total blank.

The fear increased slowly but steadily, till it threatened to swallow her. She could feel the blackness, the total lack of light. Added to that dread was the sense of being caged, closed in, and unable to break free. She did not need to stand up or step forward to know that the rock wall surrounded her, that it offered no way out.

She knew more. Someone was with her, someone she did not want to touch or to speak to. If she stayed quite still, he would not know she was there. He could not hurt her.

The wall moved, pressing against her. Involuntarily, she tried to cry out, but no sound emerged.

Fear blossomed to terror. She wanted to shriek for help, just to hear herself scream, but although she moved her lips, her throat tightened till she could not seem to breathe, and she could speak not a word, not a sound.

An inhuman screech sounded right in front of her, making her fling her head back against the wall, and suddenly light glowed as a threadlike gold line opposite her formed a rectangle in the thick blackness. Briefly, she saw Duncan's image in what looked like the bed of a wheelbarrow. Then Allan's long, narrow face flashed close to hers, pressing her back against the rocks again, blotting out the other image.

Rocks began falling all around her, and above her shrieks of terror, she heard whimpering and the cries of a child. It sounded like Pinkie's voice, coming from above, but Pinkie was not there. A translucent shape appeared against the blackness, oval, green, shimmering, and Pinkie's cries grew louder, nearly as loud as her own.

Ten

"Mary, Mary!" Pinkie's voice seemed closer than before, but at the same time, the pitiful whimpering grew clearer.

Small hands tugged at her sleeve. Little fingers pinched and pulled at her arm and shoulder. "Mary, Mary, stop! Oh, please stop!"

Feeling much as she imagined one might feel at being dragged from the depths of the sea, but mercifully aware that the horrid sounds in the cavern had begun to fade behind her, Mary relaxed and allowed the voice to draw her upward.

In that moment of release, as the horror rapidly receded, only the whimpering remained.

"Oh, wake up! Wake up, Mary!"

The whimpers ceased.

Blinking, starting a little at seeing Pinkie's anxious face so close to hers, she felt confused and disoriented, unable to remember where she was or why Pinkie was there. Had the whimpers come from the child or from herself?

Muttering disconnectedly, she tried to sit up, but every muscle felt weak and useless. The dream that had seemed so real that it had drained all her strength faded and disappeared.

"Mary, are ye awake, then?" Pinkie's small hands gave her another shake.

Drawing a deep breath to steady her agitated nerves, Mary said, "I'm awake, Pinkie. You can stop shaking me."

Pinkie burst into tears, flinging herself atop Mary, holding her tightly, her thin arms convulsing as she sobbed.

The child's distress put every other thought out of Mary's head. Summoning strength and resolution that she had thought beyond her reach just then, she sat up, holding the little girl and murmuring reassuringly.

Reaching behind to shift her pillows so that she could lean against them, she said, "Pinkie, hush, you are quite safe. Hush now."

The little body jerked again, and more sobs poured forth.

Mary smoothed the child's hair, saying softly, "Very well then, lovey, have your cry right out."

The sobs diminished soon after that to an occasional gasp or sniff, which did not surprise Mary, since in her experience, the moment someone told her it was perfectly all right to cry her eyes out, the impulse to do so disappeared.

She said quietly, "What is it, lovey? Why were you crying?"

"Ye were screaming in your sleep!"

Memory of her dream flashed, then faded. "I was screaming?"

"Aye, and cryin'," Pinkie said, shuddering. "I never heard a grown woman scream like that afore. Why did ye, Mary?"

"Is that why you were frightened?"

Pinkie nodded vigorously against Mary's bosom. "Ye were shriekin' and cryin' like ye was beset by devils. D' ye no remember, Mary?"

Mary tried to catch the last, lingering vague threads of her dream, but they were wisps now, eluding her. She remembered only that the cavern had seemed terribly real at the time, not at all like something in a normal dream.

"I must have had a nightmare," she said. "It was certainly frightening, Pinkie, but I cannot even recall what it was about now. That is the way of such dreams, you know. It was dark," she added, frowning as a last wisp of memory flitted through her mind like a mischievous ghost, taunting her to catch it.

"Aye, it was dark," Pinkie said, snuggling against her, "but it's growing lighter the noo. Chuff will be up and working, I think. Must I go doon tae the kitchen, Mary? I mean, Mistress Mary," she added quickly, guiltily, as if she had just remembered her place in the order of things.

Mary smiled. Then, realizing that she had not thought much about what the children would do at Balcardane, and remembering what Chuff had said about kitchen duties, she added, "Do you like the kitchen, Pinkie?"

"Aye, I like it fine. It smells good."

"Does it?" Wrinkling her nose, Mary became aware that the little girl did not smell good. "Pinkie, have you ever had a bath?"

"A bath?"

"Have you ever sat in a tub of water to clean yourself or let someone else clean you," Mary explained. "With soap."

There was enough light now to see the child's frown. "Nay, then, no in a tub, I never, and never wi' soap neither. Me and Chuff, we played in the burn near Flaming Janet's cottage in the summer, but we'd catch our deaths did we do any such daftie thing now!"

"Aye, you would," Mary agreed. "I think we will both get up now and go down to the kitchen."

"Ooh, mistress, will ye work there, too, then?"

"No," Mary said, "but I want to see this place that smells so good, and I want to meet the cook."

"Ah, she's a fine woman, is Cook," Pinkie said, scrambling out of bed. She had not taken off her clothes, so she had only to pull on her ragged shoes to announce herself ready for the day.

Mary took longer, but having only the three outfits she had brought with her and the pink gown she had worn to dinner, she had no great decision to make about what to wear. Dressed in a plain stuff gown with a gathered skirt and a modest bodice, and shivering in the frosty air, she sat down to brush her hair, twisting it deftly into its usual knot and pinning it firmly in place.

Pinkie watched her curiously, and Mary felt tempted to tackle the little girl's hair, but she resisted the temptation. She had grander plans for Pinkie.

"Come along, lassie," she said, taking the child by the hand. "Show me this fine kitchen of yours."

Pinkie giggled. "It's no my kitchen, miss. Belongs tae Himself, Chuff says."

Realizing that both children thought the castle belonged to Black Duncan, Mary wondered if she should try to explain but decided not to make the attempt. They would understand their surroundings in time, and the strong possibility existed that they would not remain at Balcardane long enough for it to matter whether they comprehended the difference between the earl's powers and those of his son.

Pinkie remembered the location of a service stair, and they found the kitchen easily. The child was right, Mary thought as they entered. It did smell good.

The kitchen was much larger than its equivalent at Maclean House, with a well-swept stone floor and a big central table. A huge fire roared at the oven end of the great fireplace, warming the whole room, and heating the huge black kettle on the iron swey above it.

Over coals at the other end, a joint turned on a clockwork bottle jack, and the aroma of sizzling juices filled the air, accounting for some, at least, of the pleasant odors that had so impressed the little girl.

A tall, lanky woman strode briskly across the room to meet them. She had a gypsy look about her, with a hawk nose, beetling black brows, and a firm thin-lipped mouth. Her black hair, streaked with grey, had been combed back into a tight bun beneath a plain, neat cap. Wearing a simple blue dress with a voluminous white apron over it, she bore an air of confidence, even of command.

"What's this? Has Master Duncan decided I'm to have another drudge?"

Mary said with quiet dignity, "Are you his lordship's cook?"

The woman's expression altered swiftly. She nodded, saying respectfully, "Aye, miss, and I can see now that ye must be the young lass Sarah told me aboot. I should ha' known when I saw ye wi' the wee lassie."

"I wanted to meet you," Mary said, glancing around for any sign of Chuff and seeing none. "Pinkie has spoken kindly of you. Have you a moment? I know it is Sunday morning and you want to be off to the kirk when the morning chores here are finished, but I would like to request a favor."

Nodding, the woman looked over her shoulder and called out, "Jessie, slice up the rest o' that ham now, and get a move on. They'll be down to eat it in a wink." Turning back to Mary, she said, "I like the bairns, miss. That Chuff's a treat, and though this 'un's wee yet, she's willing."

"I am glad to hear that," Mary said, giving Pinkie's thin shoulder an approving squeeze. "Do you think perhaps some-one could bathe them?"

The woman's eyebrows rose. "The lassie's hair needs a good combing, I'll grant ye, miss, but a bath? This time o' the year?"

"Yes, please, and some clean clothing if there is any at hand," Mary added. "Both of them are very ragged, Cook."

"I'm Martha to the family, miss."

"Thank you, Martha, though I am not family, you know."

"The mistress likes ye fine, and that's good enough for me. I'll see they get bathed then, and I'll scare up something for them to wear." She glanced toward Jessie and the ham. "Will that be all, miss?"

"Just keep them warm, Martha," Mary said, smiling at her.

"Aye, I'll do that. Not that I ken where that Chuff has got to. I set the lad to watch the joint, I did, but he up and vanished soon after. One o' the stable lads came in about then, though, so I dinna doubt but what the wee rascal's run off with him. You come along with me," she added to Pinkie, "and I'll give you a bowl of porridge and a jammy piece before you help Jessie with her work."

Bidding Martha good-day, certain now that the children were in good hands, Mary returned to her bedchamber, where she found a lively fire burning in the fireplace, and the bed already made. The ewer on the washstand contained warm water, and a fresh towel hung on the hook. As she moved to wash her face, the door opened again behind her and Sarah entered with some dresses draped over one arm.

"Och, there ye are, miss. The lass that lighted your fire was that surprised to find ye gone from the room."

"Good morning, Sarah. I woke early and went down to the kitchen with Pinkie, who is one of the two children who came to Balcardane with me. I wanted to thank the cook for looking after them, and see about getting them some clothing."

"They dinna be gentlemen's bairns, miss," Sarah said, frowning.

"No, but I feel responsible for them, you see, and their clothes are sadly shabby. I spoke to Martha about it. Since you clearly know about the children, I collect that you and she are friends."

"Aye, miss, we've kent one another since we was lassies. If Martha Loudon is looking after them bairns, ye've naught to fret about, I promise ye."

"Thank you, Sarah, and thank you, too, if you came here expecting to help me dress. As you see, I am accustomed to waiting on myself, so there is no need."

"Och now, Miss Mary, if I may call ye so, the mistress did send me with these frocks for ye to try. She said she kent ye wouldna want to go to the kirk this morning with the Lady Serena, looking like a dowdy, and if that dress is all ye've got to wear, she is in the right of it, I'm thinking. So let's have that auld thing off ye, and see which of these dresses will suit. The mistress says ye're to tak' all ye want, since none o' them will fit her anymore and she ha' tired o' the fabrics."

Having not the least inclination to argue, Mary let the woman help her take off the old stuff gown.

"Hoots, then, but I ha' near forgot," Sarah exclaimed, pulling a folded piece of paper from her sleeve. "Someone's sent ye this wee message, miss."

Mary took the paper and unfolded it to read, *"I need to talk to you. Come up the hill toward the pass alone when you return from kirk services. I'll show myself when I can see that no one is with you. If you don't come, you'll be sorry.*" He had signed it with the single initial: *A*.

"Where did you get this, Sarah?"

"One of the lads from the stable brought it into the kitchen, miss. He told Martha a messenger brought it. Martha gave it to me."

"I see," Mary said, wondering what on earth Allan Breck thought he could have to say to her.

Duncan had risen early, too, and as was his custom, he had gone out to visit the stables before breaking his fast.

One of his best mares had presented him with a promising young chestnut colt late in the summer, and fearing the colt was too young to survive the winter without special care, he kept a close eye on its welfare.

Light flakes of snow drifted down, swirling round the courtyard. They were not falling thickly yet, but they were sticking to the cobblestones, making them slippery, and Duncan wondered if the storm that had been threatening for two days now would prove to be a strong one. Through the open coach house door, he saw two lads polishing his father's coach in preparation to harnessing the horses, and he smiled slightly at the futility of the task. On his arrival in the stable, he found Chuff brushing the colt while it munched contentedly from a bucket of oats.

"What are you doing here?" Duncan demanded. "You're supposed to be in the kitchen."

"Aye," Chuff agreed, nodding without looking at him, "but the colt was hungry, and tae my eye, he needed a bit brushing. He's a fine, braw laddie, he is."

"He is. Look at me when I talk to you."

Chuff turned and faced him, holding the oval curry brush with both hands. His hair was tousled, but his cheeks were pink and his eyes bright with interest.

When Duncan did not speak again at once, the boy said with a touch of indignation, "They set me tae watching the meat turn aboot. Now, I ask ye, since it can turn by itself on that hook, what need had they for me tae watch it?"

Duncan experienced unexpected difficulty in maintaining a stern look. He said evenly, "You must do as you are bid, lad, that's all. Perhaps whoever set you to that task wanted to find out if you are dependable."

Chuff frowned. "Seems daft tae me. They could ha' found that out by setting me tae do something reasonable."

"Do you like horses?"

"Aye, I like them fine."

"Then, perhaps you can help in the stable from time to time, but only if your other chores are done. Have you had anything to eat yet this morning?"

"Aye, Cook gave me some porridge and a bit jammy bread. Bramble jam," he added with a nod of approval.

Duncan said, "I'm glad you liked it, but you may find yourself in trouble when you return, you know."

Chuff eyed him thoughtfully. "Not if you was tae tell them I ha' been helping here in the stable with the wee horse."

"Well, I'm not going to do that. If you left without permission, you will just have to face the consequences when you return. But if you behave yourself in the future, I promise I'll let you help out here from time to time."

Chuff grimaced, then glanced at the colt, which was still munching its oats. "Can I finish brushing him first?"

"If you make a quick job of it," Duncan said.

Chuff grinned. "I'll do that, right enough."

"Where's Wull?"

The boy gestured with his head. "Back yonder with the harness. Said he had a pile and all tae polish and that I was a good lad tae look after the colt." Shooting Duncan a sudden worried look, he added, "Ye willna skelp Wull for letting me!"

"No, but you behave yourself."

"Aye, then, I will."

Hiding a smile, Duncan turned and walked back to the tack room, where he found the stable lad Wull standing at a table piled high with oddments for polishing. "I see you found your-self an extra helper," Duncan said.

Wull was a tall, thin lad, who, like his father and brothers before him, had worked in the Balcardane stables since he was old enough to carry a water bucket. He looked up from his task with a smile and said, "Aye, the wee lad fair dotes on that colt. He seems to be a fine, good worker."

"I told him he can help from time to time, but he's to stay in the kitchen for now," Duncan said. "He'll need warmer cloth-ing before he can work out here."

"Aye, sir, I saw that for myself. My mam might still have an old coat o' mine about that would fit the lad. I can ask her if ye like."

"Tell her she'll have my thanks if she can find one," Duncan said, picking up a bridle and an oiled cloth and beginning to help with the polishing. "Are you the only one here just now? Where are the others?"

"Out and about," Wull said. "What with the snow starting, they're helping the herds bring in stock afore kirk. Jock said they could pen some of the younger sheep inside the castle walls, but they must put the cattle into yon pasture by the loch," he went on, referring to Jock Burnett, the earl's captain of guards. Wull shot Duncan a look, then added casually, "I took a message in earlier, Master Duncan."

"A message? I got no message. Was it for his lordship?"

"Nay, then. 'Twas for the lass."

Duncan's first thought was that someone had sent Serena a message, but he realized even as the thought crossed his mind that Wull would never refer to Serena so casually. He did not know Mary Maclaine, however, only that Duncan had brought to the castle two ragged children and a wench whose clothing wasn't much better than theirs. "Do you refer to Mistress Maclaine?"

Eyeing him now with misgiving, Wull nodded. "Aye, sir, if she's the one ye brought in yesterday."

"What sort of message?"

"A paper folded up. One o' the lads bringing the young sheep in said a chappie sprung up out o' the bushes and said he should give it tae the lass—tae Mistress Maclaine, that is. I took it in tae the kitchen and gave it tae Martha."

"Did you read it?"

"Nay, then, why would I do such a thing? Are ye vexed wi' me?"

"No, Wull, but I don't like the sound of this." Turning away, he thought of something else and turned back to say, "Don't leave Chuff to blanket the colt alone, and make sure someone looks in on it frequently. I don't want it ridding itself of the blanket and freezing to death."

"I know."

"And send the lad back to the kitchen when he's finished. Don't let him cozen you into letting him do more chores for you out here."

"Aye, sir. He's a scamp, that one."

Leaving him, Duncan went back into the house, wondering grimly just which acquaintance of Mistress Maclaine's had dared think he could slip a message to her right under her protector's nose.

In the dining room, Mary was silently cursing the snow. Although the light blanket of white that already covered the land as far as she could see was beautiful, she knew that snow would make it difficult for her to leave Balcardane.

She had not noticed it earlier from her bedchamber, but upon entering the dining parlor, where windows overlooked the hillside and the loch, she saw at once that the world outside lay under a blanket of white. Not only would it make meeting Allan difficult, if not impossible, but her hope of leaving Balcardane for Perthshire would prove fruitless unless the snow melted soon and warmer weather followed.

"Good morning, my dear," the countess said cheerfully. "I see that Sarah was successful. That dress becomes you better than it ever did me."

"Lud, Mary," Serena said, "do you have no clothing of your own?"

"I do, but it is unavailable to me at present, I'm afraid," Mary said, smiling at her. "It is particularly kind of her ladyship to be so generous with her dresses."

"Cast offs," Serena said disparagingly. "I am quite certain that I have never worn a cast-off dress in all my life, certainly never to attend kirk services."

"How fortunate you are, to be sure," Mary said.

"Oh, indeed, she is," Lady Balcardane said. "Why, I daresay Serena has never wanted for anything, for you must know that her father, the Earl of Caddell, is a very wealthy man. He is part of Argyll's entourage, you see. He spent time with the duke in England last year, or was it the year before, Serena? I think it must have been then." She went on talking, giving Serena no chance to interject more than brief comments, and Mary was grateful, for once, for the countess's habit of chatter.

Taking a plate from the warming shelf by the fire, she selected a breakfast of sliced ham, porridge, and toast, then took her place at the table.

She was smearing bramble jam on a slice of toast when Duncan came in. Looking up, she saw at once that he was displeased about something, but he said only, "Good morning," before crossing the room to take a plate from the warmer.

His mother said, "Bless me, Duncan, are you just now coming downstairs? You must hurry. I came down later than usual myself, and I have not yet seen your father. I hope he remembered to order the coach for us."

"The coach will be ready, ma'am. I went out early to have a look at the colt."

"You fret more about that colt than about me," Serena said flirtatiously.

He glanced at her. "Why should I worry about you? You are inside, warm and well cared for. The colt spends its days in a cold stable with only a blanket and warm mash to keep it from freezing to death."

"I protest, sir, you are too cruel! I hope you mean to mend your ways."

"Why should I? Fetch me some ale," he added, speaking to Jessie who came in to clear away used dishes.

Lady Balcardane said, "I'll have some chocolate, Jessie, and perhaps Lady Serena and Miss Mary would like some as well."

Mary disclaimed a desire for chocolate. She was still watching Duncan, although she had lowered her eyelids slightly in the hope he would think she was attending only to her toast.

He took his seat and began to attack, with visible appetite, a plateful of eggs scrambled with onions and herbs, ham, roast mutton, and potatoes. He did not seem disposed to talk, but when Serena said brightly that she wondered just how many of the countess's dresses Mary would require, he looked up.

"Is that another one of my mother's gowns?"

"Aye, sir," Mary said, putting down her fork and knife. "She has been most generous, and was kind enough to send her woman with a selection this morning."

"Excellent," he said, "I like that shade of blue on you, but don't let her dress you in scarlet or black, and don't let her cut your hair, or curl it all up and about like she does. I like it better the way you usually wear it."

Serena said with surprise, "All twisted in a knot with bits hanging all over her face and neck? You can't mean it. Surely you prefer this more fashionable look. You purchase fashionable clothing for yourself, after all."

"I don't fuss about with wigs, though," Duncan pointed out. "Never could stand them, so unless I am required to wear one, I never do."

Lady Balcardane tilted her head to study Mary, and said, "You are quite right, Duncan. Those curls sticking out at the sides of her head don't become her. She looks better with her hair brushed back smoothly, away from her face, but I do not know that I approve of the way it was all falling down yesterday."

Mary set her napkin on the table and said, "You are all very kind to interest yourselves in my appearance, but I must write a letter to my aunt. I wrote one yesterday, but I left it at Maclean House, and in any event, I must inform her of my whereabouts now, and I should like to do so before we leave." To Duncan, she said, "Is there someone who can take it to Fort William to catch the post, sir?"

"I'll send a lad, but don't go yet. I want to talk to you."

Serena said with the same playful tone she had used before, "I cannot think what you could have to say to her, sir."

"No," Duncan said evenly, "I don't suppose you can."

Mary said, "I would like to write my letter as soon as possible, sir."

"You can write it later, and I will see that it gets to Fort William tomorrow, but you will wait for me now, if you please."

Without being rude, she could think of no way to defy him, so she sat quietly until he had finished, trying in the meantime to ignore Serena's barbed remarks.

At last, Duncan pushed his chair back. "You may come with me now."

"Dear me," Serena said, "you cannot mean to be private with Mary, sir. That is not at all the thing, you know, particularly on a Sunday."

"Don't be foolish," Duncan said, holding open the door for Mary.

He said nothing until they reached the library, but once he closed the door, he said bluntly, "Who sent you the message?"

She nearly gasped, for it had not occurred to her that he might learn of it. She had not decided if she would try to meet Allan, but she certainly had not intended to mention the note to Duncan. After all, Allan was a fugitive wanted for more reasons than one. She had no liking for him, and no reason to protect him, particularly since he was responsible for Ian's death. Still, the Campbells were not noted for fairness. They had tried poor James before a jury composed solely of their own, thus assuring his conviction. Even if Allan were guilty, he did not deserve that.

"Well?"

She licked suddenly dry lips. "M-message?"

"Don't try to lie to me. I asked Martha, and she said the lass who cleaned your room took the message to Sarah. Sarah said she gave it to you. I want to know who sent it. Was it Mac-Crichton?"

She shook her head. "No, sir, it was from Allan."

"Allan Breck?" The astonishment in his tone did not surprise her, but another note in it did, for it sounded like satisfaction, or even thankfulness.

"Aye," she said. "He wants me to meet him."

"Where?"

She sighed, aware that the message lay in a drawer of her dressing table. He would find it in an instant if he searched, and she had no doubt that if she prevaricated, he would know and would institute a search at once. Therefore, she said, "He said to walk up the hillside toward the pass and he would find me." When he frowned, she added hastily, "I had not decided if I would go or not, sir. I do not trust him any more than you do, and I cannot imagine what he could want with me."

"He's in a league with MacCrichton. That's what he wants with you. But I have some business with him that must take precedence. Did he name a time?"

"No, he just said he would find me."

"We've got him then. You are not to go outside the castle walls, lass—not to meet him, not for anything at all. Do you understand me?"

"Aye, but—"

"No buts. You will obey me in this, or I will make you sorry you did not. Both Breck and MacCrichton are dangerous men, and whatever they want with you, neither one means you any good. You'll obey me, Mary Maclaine." The last words sounded more like a growl than a simple statement.

She sighed. "Very well then, I won't try to meet him."

"Don't worry about that," he said. "I'll meet him for you." But although he rode out at once with a party of men, risking the wrath of the parson by missing the service, they returned long before dark without finding a trace of Allan Breck.

Mary knew that Duncan set men to watch for Allan, but despite those precautions, she received a second message the following Friday:

"Mary, I've offered to give Ewan MacCrichton the names of several people who will swear they know you promised to marry him. He means to sue you for breach of promise and with their testimony, he will succeed. Meet me by nightfall or you will be sorry. A"

Eleven

Standing in her bedchamber that Friday afternoon, Mary stared at Allan's second message with irritation, thinking that he was the most arrogant, cocksure man she knew. Nonetheless, in honesty, she felt angrier with Ewan MacCrichton.

She had never seriously believed Ewan's threat to sue her before a magistrate. At the time, he had obviously been blustering, trying to intimidate Duncan into abandoning her. The thought that Ewan apparently believed a court of law would compel her to marry him astonished her. That one actually might do so was inconceivable.

She crumpled Allan's note in her hand and looked thoughtfully at the maid who had brought it.

"I hope it wasna bad news, miss," the girl said.

"Who gave it to you, Ailis?"

"One o' the herds brought it in to the kitchen, miss. Said a man he didna ken gave it to him yesterday."

"Near here?"

"Nay, miss, 'twas up the brae, he said. Now that the week's snow has begun to melt, the herd and his collies was searching for stray sheep, to bring them inside the walls. A chappie came along and helped him catch one, he said. Asked him was he from the castle, and said the herd could save him a trip. Did he do wrong, miss?"

"No, Ailis, I just wondered how you came by the note."

She knew that Duncan would not remain long in ignorance

of the message. Indeed, it was because she wondered why he had not intercepted it already that she had questioned Ailis. Nevertheless, and despite Allan's threat to make her sorry if she betrayed him, she went down to the library to look for Duncan.

Balcardane was alone, however, sitting behind the desk. He looked up when she entered and smiled at her. "Good day to you, lass. Were you looking for me?"

She smiled. "No, my lord. I was searching for your son."

"He's out and about somewhere, but he'll be in for dinner."

"Is he away from the castle, sir?"

"I expect he is in the estate office, or more likely, in the stable. Can I not be of service to you? You're such a quiet lass, I scarcely ever see you except in the dining parlor table. I hope you are comfortable here."

"Yes, sir, thank you, I am quite comfortable. You are very kind to let me stay at Balcardane."

"Bless my soul, there's no kindness in it. Duncan said you needed a safe place, and there's none safer than this in all of Appin. Stands to reason, don't it? In Stewart country a Campbell house has to be well fortified if anyone is to have any peace. I harbor no ill feeling toward anyone, so long as he's peaceable, lassie, and you are certainly that. You're welcome to stay for as long as you like."

"Thank you, sir," Mary said. "I did not mean to interrupt you, so if you will excuse me now, I think I will fetch my cloak and go out for a walk. I have taken little exercise this week because of the snow, but most of it seems to have melted now, so if I can pick my way amongst the drifts and puddles, perhaps I can put some roses in my cheeks."

He warned her not to catch a chill, but he made no effort to delay her. Convinced that she would deal better with Duncan if she could tell him about the message before someone else did, she hurried upstairs to fetch her cloak and clogs, then went outside and made her way across the slushy courtyard to the stable.

Since her arrival she had learned that most of the important outbuildings at Balcardane stood inside the castle walls for protection, and the most prominent was the stable. A small barn to store hay and oats flanked it on one side; and, lined up on the other, against the castle's north and west walls, stood a byre for the cows, pigs, and sheep kept for household purposes; a smithy; and a brewery. Next to these, nearest the house, stood the bakehouse and the dairy.

Inside the stable, familiar horsy smells assailed her nose, and Mary soon found her quarry at the end of the inner row of stalls, watching while Chuff carefully examined the hooves of a handsome bay colt.

Duncan raised his eyebrows at the sight of her. "I trust you were not thinking of going outside the castle walls, mistress."

"No, sir, I came in search of you. What is Chuff doing out here?"

"He thinks he's of more use in the stable than in the kitchen, and I am beginning to believe him. He's been taking very good care of my colt."

"I have that," Chuff said, grinning over his shoulder. "I'm a dab hand, I am."

"Are you, my dear? You certainly seem to have made friends with that colt."

"Aye, I have, and all. He likes me fine, he does. I take care o' the other horses, too, and I muck out stalls and fetch hay and oats, and Jock said I—"

"Silence, brat," Duncan said. "What do you want with me, mistress?"

Glancing back at Chuff, whose attention had already returned to the colt, she said quietly, "Perhaps we could walk outside, sir. I have taken little exercise this week and I utterly yearn for a walk in the fresh air."

He nodded, gesturing for her to precede him. She heard him say something to the boy, and then heard his footsteps in the straw before he caught up with her.

Outside the stable, she hesitated, uncertain which way to go. The courtyard was a mire of brown slush and icy cobblestones.

"We can walk down to the loch if you like," he said. "The

path is open, and I've got men out clearing the road and the coach track leading down to it."

She knew he meant that no harm would come to her while she was with him, but she agreed without comment, too grateful for an opportunity to get outside the castle's formidable walls to chance saying anything that might make him change his mind. For that reason, she walked silently and without mentioning the message she had received until they were halfway to the loch. Then she drew the note from her sleeve, and silently handed it to him.

Unfolding it, he read swiftly as they walked, and she heard a quick intake of his breath when he realized what message the note contained.

"Who dared bring this to you?"

"I was curious myself about how it got inside the castle," Mary said calmly, "but it seems to have arrived in all innocence. One of your shepherds' was out with his dogs yesterday, gathering sheep that had strayed during the storm. He told Ailis today when he brought it that a man who helped him catch one gave him the note so the man could save himself a trip to the castle."

He frowned. "I told Martha and most of my own men to let me know about any messages that arrived from strangers, but I certainly did not make a great noise about it. If the herd gave it to Ailis, and she said nothing to Martha . . ."

"Ailis cleans my room, sir," Mary said. "She brought it up as a kindness. I don't think either she or the shepherd should bear any blame for this."

He flashed her an enigmatic look. "Afraid I'll eat them, are you?"

"Your temper is legendary," she reminded him.

"You don't seem frightened by it."

"No, but I don't suppose you have ever directed the full blast of it at me."

"Take care that you don't give me cause," he warned, but he smiled when he said it, and the warmth of that smile surprised her. He said thoughtfully, "Where does Breck expect you to meet him? He leaves that particular detail out of the message, as if he expects you to know the right place."

"If he expects that, he is mistaken, for I have no idea. In truth, I was more distressed by the news that Ewan intends to pursue his suit than I was about meeting Allan. I wish you would believe that I have no desire to meet with him."

"I do believe you," Duncan said, adding bluntly, "I also believe he will send another message. Would you agree to meet him if it would help us capture him?"

"Aye, sir, I would, and without misgiving. He is a confessed murderer, and although he seems to think I will protect him because we are kinsmen of sorts, I feel no obligation to do so. Not only do I want him to pay for Ian's death, but I never liked him and I do not believe in blind loyalty."

"You surprise me. I did not think you would betray him so easily. As I recall, you were reluctant to tell me about the first message."

"I had scarcely had time to think about that message before you confronted me with the fact that you knew about it," Mary pointed out. "If I did not tell you at once, it was because I feared you might murder him."

"I might."

"Then I can only tell you, sir, that I do not condone murder no matter who commits it. Moreover, don't count Allan Breck caught before he is in your net. Men have tried to trick him before, many times."

He did not reply, and they walked silently until they came to the confluence of the loch and one of the burns flowing out of the hills. Snowdrifts still hugged the leafless shrubbery, but the day had warmed noticeably, and Mary noted a sun-filled hollow where nettles, some celandine, and a pair of hardy dandelions had easily survived the storm. She drew a long, appreciative breath of the tangy fresh air as she gazed out at the waters of the loch, sparkling blue beneath the sunlit sky.

"Still thinking about MacCrichton?" Duncan asked.

She looked at him. "I did not think he would pursue me like this. Of course, Allan may have said that about Ewan only to frighten me. I cannot imagine who he thinks can testify. Allan certainly can't. He never heard me promise anything."

"He cannot testify, because the minute he appears near any courtroom they will hang him from the nearest tree," Duncan said.

"Can a court force me to marry Ewan, sir?"

He did not reply, and his hesitation told her more than she wanted to know.

At last, slowly, he said, "A court might well find that you *should* marry him. Unless you enlist someone to fight for you, I doubt if you can prevail against him."

"But surely, the rules of polite society have not changed," she protested. "A lady can still change her mind, can she not?"

"One would think so," he agreed, "but your position, as I understand it, may be slightly more tenuous. Although I still don't understand why he is so set on marrying you, even I heard you agree at least once that you and he are betrothed."

Stiffening with indignation, she said, "If you are referring to your entrance upon that horrid scene at Shian Towers, may I remind you, sir, that he was beating me! *He* told you we were betrothed. I did not!"

"The point is, lass, that you did not deny it. Moreover, I'll remind *you* that I was not the sole witness to that scene."

"That's a mere quibble, sir, and you know it. I was in no position then to say anything, particularly since the first thing you said to me was that I was getting what I deserved. I certainly never thought you would support me against him."

"Still, you do agree even now that you promised to marry him," Duncan said, his voice still maddeningly calm, "and since he can produce witnesses, even without the ones Breck promises to produce, he can make a case for breach of promise. A magistrate still might determine that you have the right to change your mind, of course, particularly since MacCrichton cannot produce any formal betrothal."

"Thank heaven he never asked me to sign one," she said fervently. "I don't doubt that I would have done so."

"Well, don't volunteer that information to any magistrate. As

I see it, you have a slight chance of winning, but only if Mac-Crichton does not get his hands on you before his case gets to a court. If he succeeds in consummating the union, he will have the most powerful weapon of all, because no magistrate would refuse then to find in his favor, and would believe he was doing you a great favor."

"A favor," she said scornfully. "Turning me over to a man who will treat me shamefully would be no favor, sir."

"In the eyes of the court, however, a woman is always better off married than not married," he said. "Marriage provides her with protection, after all, and since few men want to marry damaged goods, if the man who rapes her agrees to marry her, that is universally thought to be the best resolution. And in this case, when he had a promise of marriage, as well . . . Not that any of that will matter if he lays hands on you, of course. Once he gets through with you, even you won't want—"

"Enough," she said, grimacing. "I understand what you are telling me, sir, but such a viewpoint seems most unfair to women."

"Then I suggest that you apply to Rory Campbell for help. Not only is he married to your cousin, but he is still a member of the Barons' Court, is he not?"

"You know he is, but that court concerns itself generally with land matters, not with the finer points of marriage law."

"Still, Rory can hire an experienced man of law to represent you, and oversee his actions. Rory's influence alone—"

"I don't want to ask him," Mary said hastily. "I have no real claim on his protection, you know, although I confess that I have been thinking more favorably lately about going to join my aunt and the rest of them in Perthshire."

"Don't be foolish," he said harshly. "The most that would do is delay the matter. In any event, the weather could turn again at any moment, and you could easily be caught in a much worse storm than the last one."

At the moment Mary had mentioned Perthshire, she realized that no thought of going away had occurred to her for several days. Knowing she did not really want to go, she said stubbornly nonetheless, "If a bad storm comes, any messenger I sent would be caught in it, too."

"It is a messenger's business to be caught, however."

"Now, you are being obstinate simply because I will not take your advice."

"I am never obstinate. Moreover, I give good advice."

"Perhaps you do, but I have no money of my own, and I don't like begging for more help when Rory has already been so generous to all of us. If Ewan forces me to go to court, I suppose I shall forget my scruples and send a plea for help at once, but I still find it hard to believe that Ewan will do any such thing."

"You are being a fool, Mary Maclaine, but I understand your reluctance."

Surprised at the last words, and the sigh that preceded them, she shot a glance at him, expecting to see mockery. But he was staring out at the loch, and his slight frown told her nothing. A minute later, he said evenly, "We had better go in. You will want to change your clothes for dinner, and so must I. We will say nothing further about this today, but when you hear from Breck again, be sure to let me know. Do not try to deal with him alone."

"No, sir," she said meekly. "I won't."

A short distance away, Ewan MacCrichton and Allan Breck, concealed behind trees in hillside woods east of Balcardane, looked down on the scene in disgust. Allan coughed, smothering the noise hastily into his handkerchief.

"A fine notion this was," Ewan snapped.

"You don't have to tell me. I've probably caught my death, but how was I to know Black Duncan would turn out the entire castle today to clear away the snow?"

"You gave your message to a herd, you said, so you knew at least that there would be men driving stock inside."

"Aye, and what of it? None of them would have paid heed to the lass while she strolled up the hill on a sunny afternoon. We could have snatched her and been away before anyone did, I tell you."

"Well, we can scarcely do it whilst she walks with Black Duncan," Ewan retorted. "They *strolled* all the way to the loch, and we could not have touched them even if my men had been nearer at hand."

"You haven't got enough men to take Balcardane," Breck said with a sneer, "so it's just as well that they are not too near. Someone would be bound to see them. Look there's the Ballachulish ferry coming," he added, gesturing toward the east. "They're going to lose that wagon in the loch if they don't take care."

Ewan grunted. "From what I hear, they lose something at least once a year there. It's no concern of ours, though. You'd do better to keep your eyes on Black Duncan. I'll wager the lass handed your message right over to him."

Allan sneezed and blew his nose before he muttered, "I doubt that she told him anything, but even if she did, he will guess nothing from it."

"Not about us, perhaps, but don't forget how badly he wants you, my lad."

"Oh, I've no intention of hanging about here long enough for him to catch me," Breck said, tucking his handkerchief into his sleeve. "Not today, at all events."

"We won't get the lass this way," Ewan grumbled. "She's too well guarded here, and with Black Duncan at hand—"

"What you lack is a creative imagination. We cannot storm the castle walls, that's true enough, but there is more than one way to influence those inside. We have the lovely Lady Serena Caddell on our side, for one."

"We don't have her at all," Ewan retorted. "Just look at the pair of them now, will you? My Mary's smiling at that villain as if she likes him."

"Well, she don't. You can take my word for that. As for the lovely Serena, you can take my word that she won't like her smiling at Black Duncan any more than you do. I hear tell Serena don't even like Mary being at Balcardane."

"And just how the devil would you know that?"

Allan grinned. "I told you, my lad, I maintain my freedom

by keeping eyes and ears all over Appin country. Is it so surprising that I've got one or two inside Balcardane?"

"You do?"

"I do," Allan assured him as he stood and drew his companion silently back from their vantage point. "We'd best be on our way, just in case Black Duncan calls out his men. Mary won't come out again today, but as I see it, you've got less than two months to find what you've lost, turn it into good coin of the realm, and pay your fine. With the weather against you, as it soon will be, that don't give you much time to tame our precious seventh daughter, so you need to stir things up a bit."

"Since you know so much, perhaps you can tell me what I should do."

"That's simple. If the lass remains obstinate, find yourself a tame magistrate and force her into court. That don't mean we stop trying to get our hands on her, of course. Your best argument to any magistrate is already to have bedded her, and the fact that she promised to marry you will absolve you from a charge of rape."

Inside the castle, Duncan parted from Mary in the great hall, and went into the library, glad to find it unoccupied for the moment. He wanted to think. If he could manage to set a trap for Allan Breck, he would certainly do so, but he thought the lass was right. Breck would be on the lookout for just such a trick. It would be better to lure him to Balcardane, if only he could think how to do it.

It was a pity, he thought, that she did not give him the note before they left the castle. He might have set his trap that very day, but he could not doubt now that Breck had been somewhere up there, watching the castle. Nor could he doubt that, having seen all the activity, the man was long gone.

Duncan tried to keep his thoughts on planning a trap, but they kept shifting to Mary instead. His reaction to the message had surprised him. His first thought, for once, had not been of capturing Breck. Like Mary, he had reacted first to Mac-Crichton's intention to pursue his suit.

What, he wondered, could the man be thinking? He must know that such a marriage could not prosper. She would hate him for forcing her to marry against her will. MacCrichton must want something more from her, but what on earth did he think the lass could bring him? She had nothing of value, except herself.

MacCrichton must be mad for her, he decided, and the lass had simply underestimated his feelings. Nothing else would explain his persistence. The thought of her married to Mac-Crichton disturbed Duncan more than he had thought possible. He had heard long since that the man was courting her and had sneered at the news, thinking how quickly she had abandoned her pretense of loving Ian. Now that he knew her better, however, he believed she had cared deeply for his brother. Indeed, he was finding it hard to continue blaming her for her part in Ian's death. In any case, no woman deserved such a marriage as the one MacCrichton promised.

He thought of the first time he had seen her with the laird, and his hands clenched in anger at the vision that leapt to his mind. He remembered the look of humiliation on her face when MacCrichton dumped her on the floor and she had turned and seen him standing there, watching them.

She had covered herself quickly, or as much of herself as she had been able to cover. Remembering how much of her body he had seen before that, he suddenly found himself wanting to smile. The wench was well formed, and no mistake.

He did not remember noticing that particular, interesting fact before that moment at Shian. Always before, when he had thought of her at all, he had thought only of her eyes and the entrancing serenity of her expression. That serenity had pricked at him whenever he thought of how she had bewitched his little brother. It was as if she had dismissed the danger into which she had beckoned Ian. Frequently he had wanted to shake her, to make her see that she was bewitching the lad, making him forget his duty to his clan, his loyalty to his family.

Now Duncan found himself far more aware of her clear,

smooth skin, the slight dusting of freckles across her tip-tilted nose, the fullness of her lips, and the soft curves of her breasts and hips. He remembered lifting her from the saddle, his surprise at how small her waist was, how firm and supple her body.

Shaking himself from a reverie he wanted to believe was pointless, he glanced at the clock on the desk and realized that he would have to make haste if he meant to change his clothes in time for dinner.

At the table, Mary noticed at once that Serena was in a brittle mood. They had no sooner taken their places than she had said archly to Duncan, "What can you and Mary have had to talk about down by the lake for so long, I wonder."

He looked at her in surprise. "Perhaps you ought to have joined us, Serena. Doubtless Mary would have invited you to accompany her had she known that you, too, longed to take some air."

Lady Balcardane said, "Oh, but Serena did not want to walk, Duncan! When I suggested that she join you—she saw the pair of you from the drawing room window whilst we were discussing food for Christmas Eve, you know—she said it was too cold and the ground far too muddy for anyone of sense to enjoy a walk."

"Well, and so it was," Serena said, growing pink. "That was why I wondered what you could be doing down there for so long. Why, it must be all one can do to keep one's footing in all that muck and slush."

"I see what it is, Duncan," Balcardane said with a chuckle. "The poor lass is jealous. She don't like seeing you walking about with another pretty female, and that's understandable, damme if it ain't!"

"Bless me," Lady Balcardane said, looking with dawning comprehension at Serena, who was now staring down at the plate in front of her. "Why your cheeks are as red as fire, my dear. I do believe Balcardane has hit upon the truth of it after all. You know, Duncan," she added cheerfully, turning her twinkling eyes on her son, "you could settle all this in a trice, merely by arranging for a formal betrothal between the pair of you and setting a date for the wedding."

"What wedding? I have not offered for anyone, ma'am."

"Oh, but it is just a matter of the details," Lady Balcardane said, chuckling. "Why your father and Caddell had it set between them ages ago, and I am persuaded that dear Serena has expected these three or four years past that one day you would make her an offer. Bless me, sir, why else do you think your father agreed that she should come to us when she wrote me to say how dreadfully dull she felt at Inver House, with everyone in alt over her sister-in-law's impending confinement?"

"Since I was not a party to that decision, ma'am, I gave it no thought at all," Duncan said brutally.

Serena pouted. "Lud, sir, but you are being prodigiously cruel to me tonight. You must know that my papa and yours settled the issue of our marriage long ago."

"In all fairness," Balcardane said, "I must say that it was never, as you say, *settled* between us, my dear. Your papa and I talked about it, I grant you, but we signed no papers, you know. Still and all," he added, looking sternly at his son, "if the lass has got it into her head that you've intended all along to marry her, I am not certain that plain courtesy don't demand that you do just that, lad."

Duncan shot him a look of acute dislike. "Are you trying to tell me, sir, that because you and Caddell indulged yourselves in a few air dreams, and because somehow Serena became aware of them, you now think I am somehow bound to marry her? You are being as absurd now as she is, I think."

"Now there you're wrong, lad, damme if you ain't. Most folks would think just what I'm thinking now, and I won't have a son of mine gaining a reputation for playing at ducks and drakes with a lady's sensibilities, leading her to think you want to marry her and then leaving her in the lurch. Damme, Duncan, it just ain't done!"

"I am not the one guilty of leading her astray," Duncan pointed out with what Mary thought was more patience than anyone could have expected from him.

"Point is, though, that the lass herself has come to believe you will marry her," Balcardane said. "Ain't that right, Serena?"

"Why, yes, certainly, sir, and although I have never made any secret of my belief, not before I came to Balcardane or since, I am sure that he has never said anything to make me think I might be mistaken. Surely, if he did not intend to marry me, he ought to have said so long before now."

"She has you there, lad."

Lady Balcardane said thoughtfully, "You know, Duncan, that is quite true, and you must allow that it is, for I have myself heard Serena say in your hearing that she was going to be your countess. If you will recall, my dear, she said so just a few days ago, and you teased her, wanting to know if she meant to murder your father to gain you the title. A most improper thing to say, that was."

Indignantly, Balcardane snapped, "It most certainly was. As if we have not had enough of that sort of thing in Appin during these past few years. You're an unnatural son, Duncan, that's what you are."

Shoving back his chair and getting angrily to his feet, Duncan said, "If this is your notion of how to get an offer out of me, Serena, you have gone the wrong way to work. If I failed to scotch your notions outright, it is because I never took them seriously. They were no more important to me than the prattling of a foolish child."

"How dare you, sir!"

"Oh, I dare. Since you seem to want the matter put plainly, I tell you here and now that I have no intention of marrying you, nor have I ever had any such intention. And if that does not make clear to you how very much I dislike the notion, let me put it this way: I would much rather marry Mary Maclaine!"

With that, he strode angrily from the room, leaving his astonished audience to stare blankly after him.

Twelve

Mary did not know which way to look after Duncan left the room, and she was certain that if she opened her mouth she would say something truly regrettable. Lady Balcardane recovered her powers of speech before anyone else.

"What a prodigiously odd thing for Duncan to say," she said, looking from one to the other of her companions, as if she expected someone to agree with her. When no one else spoke, she went on in a thoughtful tone, "I cannot think why he would want to marry you, Mary. Not that you are not perfectly charming, but I am certain that he has indicated on more than one occasion that he does not even . . . That is . . ." She cleared her throat. "I believe he has never before thought of you as a possible wife, my dear. I cannot think what has got into him."

Serena raised her chin and said firmly, "He is merely being cruel, ma'am. Surely you have noticed how Duncan positively delights in teasing me."

"Aye," Balcardane said with a heartiness that rang false, "that will be it, sure enough. The lad never did take well to a heavy hand on his bridle."

"Bless me, sir," Lady Balcardane exclaimed, "you make him sound like a horse, although I believe it is quite true that no one ever made Duncan do anything he did not want to do. Why, even when he was a little boy, he took his own road. Dearest Ian was far more tractable. Do you really think Duncan is only teasing, Serena? Because I must tell you that I have never known him to tease anyone before. No one has ever accused him of levity. He is far more likely to say what one least wants to hear than to be playful, but I think that is because he generally says precisely what he thinks. Oh, I am getting my thoughts jumbled, you will say, and I cannot deny it, but I do think one is wiser to believe what he says than not to do so."

"He'll do as he's told, by God," Balcardane said curtly.

"Do you think so, my lord? Were we not just agreeing that Duncan rarely does what he's told, and nearly always does what he says he will do? It is not such a bad thing, either, because with men who say one thing and do another, one never knows what may happen next. At least, with Duncan, one has only to ask him."

Balcardane snapped, "He will not dare to disobey Argyll, I believe."

Silence greeted this awful pronouncement.

Mary thought Serena looked smug. Lady Balcardane, on the other hand, still looked doubtful, and evidently her lord and master thought so as well.

"Do you doubt me, madam?" he demanded.

Coloring, clearly flustered by his tone if not by the question itself, she said, "I would never doubt you, sir. I trust that I know my duty better than that, but do you mean to say that you believe Argyll will order Duncan to marry Serena?"

With exaggerated patience, he said, "I am saying, madam, that the potential alliance between our house and Caddell's is one of which his grace knows and approves. He believes it will strengthen our resources in Lorne, particularly if Duncan removes with Serena to Dunraven after their marriage."

"But Duncan can live at Dunraven no matter whom he marries," Lady Balcardane pointed out. "He does not even have to wait until then if he does not want to do so. He is already Master of Dunraven, and has been since his birth."

Serena signed to a lackey to carve her some more mutton, saying casually, "I shall enjoy being a countess, I think, but I can tell you that I will not allow him to keep me buried at

Dunraven, ma'am. I mean to see Edinburgh and even London whilst I am still young enough to enjoy them."

So strong was the picture that flashed in Mary's head of the scene that would follow Serena's making that declaration to Duncan that for an instant she thought Ewan had been right, that her gift might let her see more than the last moments of those she loved. It was just as well, she thought, that no one was paying heed to her.

Just then Lady Balcardane said, "His grace has quite a strong respect for your Aunt Anne, does he not, my dear?"

Mary jumped, realizing that while she had been indulging in fantasies—for the image had been nothing like one of her visions, which were extremely physical in nature—Lady Balcardane had been chattering on. The countess was regarding her now with the inquisitive air of one who expected an answer.

"I beg your pardon, ma'am," she said, flushing. "I am afraid I let my attention wander for a moment and did not hear exactly what you were saying."

"I am quite accustomed to that, my dear, I promise you, but I was just observing that if Duncan should offer for you, perhaps his grace would not object as strenuously as he might to someone else in your particular circumstances."

"Argyll thinks Anne Stewart Maclean is a damned interfering woman," Balcardane growled. "If you think that is any indication that he will sit still for a union between her family and ours—"

"But he has already sat still for such a union, my dear. Her daughter married his cousin, after all, and Rory is our cousin, as well, come to that."

"Rory Campbell will never be the Earl of Balcardane, however."

"No, sir, but he is a powerful man in his own right. You cannot deny that."

"I don't attempt to deny it," Balcardane said testily, "but it's got nothing to do with the matter at hand, madam. Duncan must learn that while he may be Master of Dunraven, he is not entirely his own master. He must answer to those in authority over him, and that includes Argyll, by God; and the duke will not want my son to marry another penniless wench from the Maclean clan."

Lady Balcardane chuckled. "You make it sound as if he's already married one, my lord, though I do not believe that is what you meant for us to believe. As to penniless, as I understand the matter, Mary's father owned quite a large estate on the Island of Mull before his part in the late rebellion forced him to forfeit it after his death. Though how someone can forfeit anything after death, I do not know, but there it is, and the same was true of Diana before she married Rory. Nonetheless, as I understand it, his grace is making an arrangement to award Castle Craignure—"

"You know nothing about such matters," the earl snapped, "and the point has nothing to do with this matter. Duncan will not marry Mary Maclaine, and that's my last word on the subject." He glanced ruefully at Mary, adding in a gentler tone, "Not that I mean to cast aspersions on you personally, mistress. I am sure you are all that is amiable, and I trust you will not take offense at my candor."

"None at all, sir," she replied. "You may rest assured that your son does not want to marry me, nor I him. I daresay that he would be shocked to learn that words spoken in haste, and only to show how little he cared for the union suggested to him, have stirred such a rousing debate."

Balcardane frowned at her for a long moment, then said, "He may not care for it, lass, but he'll soon learn to take good advice when it is offered to him."

Mary smiled. "You know him better than I do, sir, and duty makes him more likely to listen to you or to the Duke of Argyll than to others. In my experience with him, however, I have found him much more likely to give unwanted advice to others than to accept any himself."

"That's just what I said," Lady Balcardane exclaimed. "It is Duncan's besetting sin. Indeed, I have heard you say as much yourself, sir, many times."

"Still and all, he'd be a fool to turn down the sort of dowry Caddell's offering," Balcardane said. "Duncan is many things, madam, but he is no fool." He smiled at Serena. "Don't you fret, lassie. We'll soon sort this out."

She rewarded him with a flirtatious look and tossed her head. "I won't fret, my lord," she said. "In point of fact, I must tell you that if I were to choose for myself I would not marry Duncan, for he is not at all romantic in his ways. My mama said I should take advantage of my time here at Balcardane to teach him to be more attentive to me, but I confess, I have made no progress in that endeavor. Still, I daresay I shall do much better once we are married."

Mary kept her gaze firmly fixed on her plate and did not look up again until Lady Balcardane managed at last to change the subject.

Over the weekend, the weather improved, and on Monday afternoon, when Mary saw Chuff lead the bay colt out through the postern gate, she experienced a strong sense of envy. She had not laid eyes on Duncan since the incident at the dining table, but as much as she would have liked to enjoy a walk outside the walls with the boy and the colt, she did not think it would be wise to go. Whether it was fear of finding Ewan or Allan waiting for her that stopped her, or simply a certainty that Duncan would find out and be angry, she did not know.

He had ridden out with some of his men Saturday morning, without informing anyone of his destination, and he had not yet returned. Although there had been no further discussion of Serena's apparent belief that he intended to marry her, Mary could tell that relations had become strained between the earl and his son. She feared there had been more words between them, for Balcardane remained withdrawn and coldly angry after Duncan left the castle.

Serena, too, seemed out of sorts, but she said nothing to explain her frequent moody silences, other than to complain that her maid had caught a cold in the head, and to express the feeble hope that it would not prove contagious.

When passing days brought no more notes or word of pending court action, Mary began to believe that Allan had merely been testing her to see if she would obey, or trying to scare her.

While she remained at Balcardane, the notion that Ewan could force her to marry him seemed increasingly absurd; therefore, when she went to bed on Wednesday night, she slept quite soundly at first.

This time, despite the oppressive blackness that swirled around her like a menacing presence, Mary knew that if she groped behind her, she would touch a slimy stone wall. She was aware, too, however, that she was not alone. Thoughts of another presence ought to have reassured her, but they did not, for she felt unable to move, like a rabbit frightened to stillness by a lurking enemy.

When the golden thread of light appeared before her, it seemed to release her from her immobility. As the thread formed a rectangle before her eyes, she forced herself to reach out and about, and finally down toward the floor.

At first it seemed like just a pile of clothing. Then she touched a cold and clammy hand, and panic seized her, for such a hand could belong only to a corpse.

Mary awoke sitting straight up in her bed, her throat still closed tight over the scream she had fought to utter in her sleep. This time details of the nightmare lingered, and she knew it was much like the one from which Pinkie had wakened her. Fortunately, Pinkie no longer shared her room, for the children had missed each other and now shared a pallet by the kitchen fire, willing to tolerate being rousted at an unseemly hour each morning in exchange for the companionship they enjoyed.

Although Mary tried to go back to sleep, she succeeded only in dozing fitfully until Ailis arrived at her usual time with a pitcher of hot water and a pot of hot chocolate, when she got up with relief. After joining the others for breakfast, she spent the rest of the morning sorting threads for the countess and answering a letter that Lady Maclean had written and sent by ordinary post, and that Duncan's man had brought from Fort

William when he posted Mary's letter. Since her aunt's was a response to one Mary had sent to inform her of her decision to marry Ewan at once, rather than waiting for spring, she approached the task with little enthusiasm.

"That is the third time you have crossed out what you have written," Serena said crossly, "and that pen makes a dreadful scratching noise. It is doing nothing to help my headache, I can tell you."

Looking up from the list she was making to peer over her spectacles, Lady Balcardane said, "If you are not feeling well, Serena, perhaps you ought to go to bed and put a hot brick at your feet. Indeed, you might ask Mary for a remedy to make you feel better. She is a dab hand at such things, I'm told."

"I don't want a brick or a remedy. I want Duncan to come home. He is being very rude, considering that he has scarcely been here at all since I arrived to visit."

Such conversation as there was proceeded in a similar fashion until Mary begged to be excused shortly after one and retired to her bedchamber. Lack of sleep had robbed her of usual tolerance for Serena's behavior.

Unable to remain idle for long, however, she took out one of the gowns Lady Balcardane had given her, and engaged herself in replacing the cherry-colored ribbons that had adorned it originally with some peach-colored ones the countess had given her while she sorted threads that morning. "For I know," Lady Balcardane had said with a smile, "that Duncan will say you ought not to wear cherry, my dear, and he would be quite right about that. Softer colors become you best."

"Lud, ma'am," Serena had chimed in, "I should think that with her pale eyes and yellow hair, poor Mary would do better with brighter colors, but I daresay you know more about these things than I do."

Lady Balcardane had replied complacently, "Why, yes, I am thought to have prodigiously keen eye for colors, Serena, but how kind of you to say so."

Though the countess had come off with the honors, Mary had known that Serena would not abandon her incivility. She was never overtly rude, always coating her barbs with an air of innocence—like fish hooks wrapped in worms, Mary thought—but Mary was finding her daily more difficult to tolerate. Never had anyone tried her patience more. Thus did she sit quietly in her bedchamber, stitching and enjoying her solitude, but wishing she had more freedom.

She had finished attaching new lacing, and narrow ribbons above the lace trim on the sleeves, when a tapping at the door drew her attention.

"Enter," she said, looking up from her work.

The door opened, and Pinkie looked in, her eyes red-rimmed, her cheeks streaked with tears.

Mary jumped to her feet. "What is it, lovey? What's happened?"

"A lady said she will make Himself send us away, miss. Can she do that?"

"What lady?" Mary asked, shutting the door and drawing the little girl to the window, to sit beside her on the bench. "Tell me."

"She's very pretty," Pinkie said sadly. "She said she saw Chuff in the stables, and one of the lads tellt her there was two of us, so she come tae find me. When she said we have no business here, I told her it was Himself that brought us when he brought you, but she said if that was true, she would soon put a stop tae such goings on, because his lordship willna stand for any more mouths tae feed."

"Oh, dear," Mary said, "what a thing to say to you!"

"Who is his lordship, miss? Will he send us away? Where will we go? Will he send us back tae the laird? Dinna let him send us back!"

"Hush, Pinkie," Mary said, smoothing the little girl's hair, soft now and neatly arranged in plaits after daily brushing. "Lady Serena—for I believe that is who frightened you—does not rule Balcardane. His lordship is Master Duncan's father. He is the Earl of Balcardane, and this is his castle."

"I thought it belonged tae Himself!"

"I know you did, but it makes no difference in this instance.

Lady Serena lacks the authority to send you away, and Master Duncan will not let her do so." Putting her arm around the child, she was relieved to feel her relax. "Come now, look out the window with me, and watch for Chuff to return. He has been taking the little colt outside the walls each day for exercise. Do you know the one I mean?"

"Aye, Chuff showed me. He calls him Wee Geordie. Chuff let me pat his nose, and he'll eat sugar out o' me hand, will Geordie."

"What does Himself— That is, what does Master Duncan call the colt?"

"I dinna ken, miss. I never went out whilst he was there. I wouldna!"

Mary had been idly watching activity below, and now she saw the postern gate open. "Look, Pinkie, I think Chuff is coming back now."

It was Chuff, but he was not alone; and, seeing the lurching walk of his companion, Mary gave a cry of pleasure. "Oh, look, Pinkie, it's Bardie!"

At that moment, she saw one of Duncan's men stride purposefully toward the dwarf. Holding no illusions about the man's intent, she jumped to her feet, ordered Pinkie to return to the kitchen, and hurried downstairs as fast as her legs would carry her. Reaching the great hall, she picked up her skirts and ran across it to the front door, flinging it wide and hurrying out to the courtyard, unmindful of the fact that she had forgotten her cloak until the chilly air reminded her.

Ignoring the cold, she hurried to intervene, for she could see that, as she had expected, Duncan's man intended to put the dwarf outside the walls again.

"Wait!"

The man turned, tugged his cap, and said, "This 'un's no welcome here, miss. It'd be as much as my position is worth tae let him stay."

"He has come to see me," Mary said firmly. "No doubt he brings me news of my home. Do you think your master would deny me that?"

"Nay, miss, but—"

"Fine, then he can come inside with me. You go and help Chuff see to the colt." Intercepting an indignant look from the boy, she held his gaze until she saw understanding dawn.

Chuff said, "Aye, ye'd best come along. Ye're always tellin' me I don't put the blanket on 'im proper. Just come and see if I've got it right yet, will ye?"

With a last, lingering, doubtful glance, the man went with the boy.

Bardie chuckled. "I like that lad. He's got an old head on young shoulders, and a quick tongue tae boot."

"Come inside, Bardie. I'm freezing out here."

"Aye, and so ye should be, standing about in no more than that thin frock."

Hurrying back inside, she led him into the library and shut the door.

He looked around appreciatively. "A bit too spacious for my taste, but well appointed nonetheless. The auld earl does himself proud, he does."

"It's wonderful to see you," Mary said, drawing a stool near the hearth for him, and a side chair for herself. The fire had burned down nearly to coals, but she did not think the earl would appreciate it if she wasted wood on herself and the dwarf. "Have you been to Maclean House? Have you seen Morag?"

"Aye, and she said that scoundrel Allan Breck's been staying there without so much as a by-your-leave. He cleared out when she got back from her brother's place, because he feared she would reveal his presence tae the authorities."

"I don't know that she would," Mary said. "Morag feels strong loyalty to the Stewarts. I doubt she would betray him."

"Aye sure, but Allan Breck don't ken that. She had another visitor, too, lass," he added bluntly. "That's why I've come."

"Who?" But Mary's heart sank, for she was certain she knew. "MacCrichton."

"What did he want?"

"Morag said he's taken his case tae the magistrate in Fort

William. Ye'll soon get a summons, commanding ye tae appear before him right after Christmas."

"Straightaway then," she said with a sigh, for the holy day lay less than a week away. "I hoped he had given up, Bardie, but clearly he will not."

"Aye, I ken that fine. What's more, that cousin of yours told Morag that ye *should* marry the laird. Said ye're a fool if ye willna do it."

Since she already knew that Bardie did not agree with those sentiments, she did not bother to dignify them with comment. Instead she pressed him for news of friends, and he was easily able to oblige her, for he supported himself (or, as he said, kept himself in snuff) by selling the produce of his gardens. Although his store of fruits and vegetables was sadly depleted at this time of year, he always kept herbs and remedies at hand for those who needed them.

Once while they were chatting she thought she heard a rustling sound at the door. She stopped talking, thinking the earl about to come in, but no one entered, and she decided she must have imagined the noise. Bardie left soon afterward, and she was surprised to note that the afternoon was nearly gone. Already light was fading from the courtyard.

Duncan and his men returned as darkness was falling. The pale moon already riding high above the loch wore a halo, and clouds floated across it, harbingers of the snow that his shepherds had told him to expect that night. The warning had brought him home at last, despite his reluctance to face his family and Mary.

It was bad enough that he had embarrassed her in his anger at Serena and his father. It was worse that he had not taken the time before leaving to apologize to her, but he had not wanted to face her. Instead, he had convinced himself that, having left Dunraven without seeing that all was in train for winter, he was doing no more than duty demanded to return for a day or two. However, his failure to make things right with Mary, and the fact that he had quarreled with his father before going, had soon made him feel as if he were running away to pout, like a child.

A night at Dunraven had cleared his thoughts, making him realize that to leave her and the children alone at Balcardane when he had promised them his protection was behavior he would condemn in any other man. He would have returned the next day, had his tenants not learned of his presence at Dunraven. He had wakened to the news that despite its being Sunday, a number of them wished to speak with him. By the time he had seen to their needs, three more days had passed, and it was not until Thursday morning that he was able to leave Dunraven.

Having noted with satisfaction that Shian Towers showed definite signs of its master's presence, he had passed much of his return journey in a mental rehearsal of an apology he could make to Mary that would not grievously offend his pride. Then it had occurred to him that, quite likely, Allan Breck had attempted to communicate with her again in his absence. After that, he found himself in a fret to reach Balcardane, hoping she had kept her promise not to meet the villain alone.

That he would also have to deal with his father, to explain certain promises that he had made his people at Dunraven, and to persuade the earl to part with the funds to cover them, suddenly seemed of less consequence than his fear that Mary might have felt obliged to do something foolish. He increased his pace, but the niggling fear that had touched him then refused to go away.

He rode into the stable, half expecting to find Chuff there, but although the colt gazed solemnly at Duncan, the boy was nowhere to be seen. Pausing only long enough to turn his mount over to one of his men and to see that the colt's blanket had been well secured, he crossed the courtyard and went inside.

In the great hall, he went toward the stairs before he noticed light under the library doors. Deciding to speak to his father first, he had turned that way when he heard his name spoken from the half landing. Turning back, he saw to his surprise that Serena had appeared there like some sort of genie. She hurried down to him.

"How glad I am that you are home, sir! We have missed you." She sneezed.

"Good evening, Serena," he said warily. "I must not stay, for you will not welcome me at the dinner table in my riding dress."

Pulling a handkerchief from her sleeve to blow her nose, she said, "I know you must change your clothing, sir, but I need your advice. I've learned something I think his lordship should know, but I do not want to make trouble for anyone."

"What is it, Serena?" He failed to conceal his impatience, drawing a quick frown from her, but he did not apologize.

"Oh, dear, now you are vexed, but truly, I do think someone ought to speak to her, for I am sure she does not comprehend the perils of such behavior."

"What the devil are you talking about? Is this about Mary, Serena? What has she done to put you in such a pelter?"

"She was closeted for nigh onto an hour this afternoon with a man, sir, right in your father's library! I did not recognize his voice, and I could scarcely stand about eavesdropping, for no lady can do such a thing, but I know she was not talking to his lordship, for he did not come inside till some time after that."

Fury leapt in him at the thought that Breck or MacCrichton had somehow dared to penetrate Balcardane, and although he remembered noting the latter's presence at Shian, he said nonetheless curtly, "Is she still here?"

"Why, of course, she is. Where else would she be?"

"You are certain she did not go out."

"Of course, I am. She is upstairs, dressing for dinner. I saw her."

"Go and tell my mother that I am home then, and tell her with my apologies that I am going to order dinner put back half an hour or so."

"Lud, sir, can you dress so quickly?"

"More quickly than that. I want to speak to my father first."

She hesitated, as if she would say more, but then she turned away and he went into the library to find Balcardane pouring himself claret from a decanter. The earl paused and glanced at Duncan. "So you're back, are you?"

"Yes, sir. I've been at Dunraven. I behaved badly, sir. I want to apologize."

"Been spending more money, Duncan?"

He grimaced. "Dunraven will pay for itself next year, sir. I know I have not taken the care of it that I should. I take full blame for that, although by the time you agreed to let me run things, it was already taking more money than it paid us."

"Aye, land is expensive to run, just as I keep telling you, and now I learn that those two brats you foisted onto me are still here. Are they yours, Duncan?"

"No, sir, they are not," he replied, striving to keep his temper. "Moreover, both of them are earning their keep. The boy is a particularly hard worker, and although the girl is only seven, Martha Loudon tells me she cheerfully does any task she is asked to do. Has someone complained about them, sir?"

Balcardane handed him a glass of claret and gestured for him to sit down. "In truth, I think Serena fears they are yours. She came in here to tell me she was surprised to find such small children working in the castle, but I'll wager it was not that at all, for there must be servants' children and the like at Inver House."

"Serena is a great deal too busy," Duncan said harshly.

"You'll soon set that to rights when you are married."

Determined not to quarrel again, Duncan managed to hold back the hot retort that sprang to his lips, but he did not linger longer than it took to finish his wine. Hurrying upstairs, he changed his clothing in record time, and reached the landing again just as Mary shut the door of her bedchamber, in the opposite corridor.

Looking toward the sound, he stopped and waited for her. For an instant he thought she looked pleased to see him, but by then he had remembered Serena's tale. Taking an angry step toward her, he saw her pleasure change to alarm.

"Who was with you with in the library earlier today?" he demanded.

"Bardie," she replied at once, though her expression remained wary. "I am sorry if you do not like his being here, but

I wanted to hear news of Morag and our friends. One of your men tried to put him out, and it was cold, so I brought him in."

Feeling foolish, and knowing he deserved to, he pushed a hand through his hair and said, "Lord, what a fool I am! Look here, did Serena know it was Bardie?"

"I don't know."

"She told me she overheard you talking to an unknown man in the library."

Her brow cleared. "You feared it might be Allan. I do not think he would be that brazen, sir, or that foolish."

"Well, I don't think Serena made any attempt to learn who it was. There must be half a dozen people who could have named Bardie or described him to her."

"Yes, at least that many, for he came into the castle with Chuff, and there were several others in the yard when I went out to rescue him from your man."

"Mary, I . . ." Talking was harder than he had thought it would be. "I have spent the entire journey from Dunraven thinking how to say this, and now . . ."

When he fell silent, she said in her serene way, "Is that where you went?"

He nodded. "You will be glad to know, at least, that Mac-Crichton looks as if he is fixed there for the present."

To his surprise, she frowned, saying, "That may be so, sir, but he has not changed his mind about his suit. Bardie said Ewan has put the matter before the magistrate at Fort William. I am to expect a summons straightway, commanding me to appear right after Christmas."

"The devil take him!"

"My very thought, sir, but that cannot be what you wanted to say to me."

"No, it isn't. Mary, I should never have spoken as I did the other night. No matter how much I disliked being pressed by my father and Serena, I had no right to say that being married to her would be even worse than being married to you."

Her silvery eyes began to dance. "Is that what you said, sir?"

"You know it was."

"Then you believe it would be better to be married to her?"

"No! By God, I would far rather be married to you." Hearing what he had said, he nearly stopped breathing.

She seemed to have done the same. Then, in a much smaller voice, and with no light in her eyes, she said, "I will not marry you, however."

"I know you don't want to. I don't blame you in the least. I don't want marriage either." Lord, what was he saying? Before he could catch his thoughts, his tongue went on, seemingly of its own accord, "Still and all, maybe it's the right answer, lass. Maybe it would resolve big problems for both of us."

"You are daft, Duncan Campbell."

"No, listen to me," he said, unable to believe he was pressing her like this but feeling the same perverse need he always felt to prove an opponent wrong. "My father and Caddell between them are determined to make me marry Serena, and I cannot imagine a worse fate. Can you?"

"No, but you have only to say no," she pointed out.

"Aye, and I don't doubt that I could make it stick, even if Argyll lends them his support. But they'll plague the life out of me, Mary. What with them insisting that somehow I led Serena to believe I want her, I am not at all sure that they won't be able to present the same sort of case, in their way, that MacCrichton means to present for the magistrate at Fort William. Don't you see? I'd be doing it for my sake as well as yours. I can protect you from MacCrichton, and you can protect me from Serena. Believe me, marriage to her would be worse than death."

Her lips twitched, but she did not speak.

"Don't say no yet. I know I've treated you badly, that I blamed you unfairly for Ian's death. You cannot possibly think of any reason that I might want to marry you, but I don't think I would dislike it as much as all that, or that you would, and I've got to marry someone one day, if only to secure the succession to the earldom. My father expects that, and he has every right to do so, because it is my duty. You must marry, too. I know you don't want to hang on Rory's sleeve all your life, and if you don't marry someone else soon, MacCrichton will force you to marry him."

She looked at him. "Very well then, sir, I will marry you."

Thirteen

Duncan stared at Mary in astonishment. Until that moment, ne did not know how convinced he had been that she would refuse. He could think of nothing to say.

She looked uncertain, too. "Did you hear what I said, sir?"

"Aye. Aye, I heard you. I just don't know if I can believe my ears."

"Then it is just as I thought. This whole notion is absurd. You don't really want to marry me, nor I you."

"No." Realizing that she had misunderstood him, he added hastily, "What I mean is that I don't agree with you, lass. I cannot deny that your acceptance rendered me speechless, but you are wrong to think I don't want to marry you. I meant what I said about that. I just did not think my arguments would persuade you. That's why your acceptance surprised me so."

"Me, too," she muttered. "For one thing, who will protect me from you?"

"Look here, Mary, I cannot swear I'll make you a good husband. I could not swear that to anyone, for I'm certain that I'd make a devilish husband for any woman. I don't blame you in the least for feeling reluctant, especially after things I have said about you in the past. I was wrong to say them. I know that now."

"You have disliked me forever, sir. How can I believe you want marriage?"

"I admit the notion would not have occurred to me had my

father not made it plain that he and others will press me to offer for Serena. Still, the more I think about it, the more I believe that marriage between us is a good notion. If you agree to it, I promise I'll do all I can to see that you don't regret it. I won't touch you till you say I may, and we'll work to create a partnership that will benefit us both."

She was looking into his eyes, and he felt the same startled sense of awe that he always felt when his gaze met hers. Her eyes were so clear, so guileless, so calm. He felt as if he were looking into her soul. Though he hesitated to search his own soul for fear of what he might find, he did his best to meet her steady gaze.

"Perhaps you are right, sir," she said at last. "Such a marriage is certainly not the answer I would have sought, but I do believe that you can protect me from Ewan and any others who might wish me harm."

"I can do that. As soon as we are wed, I'll send proof of the ceremony to that magistrate. That will put an end to MacCrichton's nonsense, at least."

"I shall be most grateful for that, sir. I cannot promise I will ever become a loving wife, but I will do my best to be an amiable one."

"And an obedient one, Mary?"

She blushed. "I must try, sir, since I shall have to promise as much before God, but in a partnership, does one partner constantly expect to prevail?"

With a wry smile, he said, "I'll try not to demand too much of you."

"There you are!" Serena exclaimed. Hurrying up the stairs toward them, holding her wide skirt up with both hands so that she would not trip, she went right on talking. "We have been waiting to go to the dining parlor! Your mother went to fetch a shawl and was to join us there, Duncan. She will be waiting for us now."

"I had something of importance to say to Mary," he said repressively.

"In faith, sir, you should not be alone with her, even here. It is quite shadowy here, you know. I believe you must enjoy making me feel jealous."

"You have no cause for jealousy, Serena."

"No, of course I do not, but still, sir, think how it would look to others. Here they are, my lord," she said over her shoulder, adding playfully, "Come here at once, if you please, and take my side in this matter. Duncan says I have no cause to be jealous, but I ask you, sir, if anyone were to find your handsome son and Mary standing alone in the shadows like this, talking secrets—"

Balcardane brushed past her to confront Duncan. "What the devil is the meaning of this, sir?"

"You see, Duncan," Serena said sweetly. "People *will* think the worst in such instances, sir. I know you do not mean to hurt me, or cause me distress—"

"Believe me, Serena," Duncan said, cutting in before she could say more, "I don't wish to distress you. I understand that your father, and mine, may have led you to think I might offer for you; but, now that you have spent several weeks in this house, I don't know how you can continue to believe it."

Her eyes widened, and she clasped her hands soulfully to her bosom. "What can you mean, sir? Surely, after what your father said . . ." Her words trailed to uncomfortable silence when Duncan shook his head.

As gently as his exasperation with the situation would allow, he said, "Truly, Serena, you cannot expect me to answer for what my father or yours have led you to believe. I will swear that I never said anything to make you think that I hold more than a cousin's affection for you, if that." He could not resist the rider; but, catching sight of Mary's disapproving frown, he added swiftly, "I do apologize if anything I said or did caused you to misunderstand my sentiments."

"That's all very well, sir," she said with a forced laugh, "but even if it has not yet come to a declaration between us, you should not be alone with Mary."

"Faith, that's true enough," Balcardane said, "though damme, Duncan, I still think you are bound to marry Serena. I cannot think why you don't want her when Caddell's offering a most excellent dowry to the man who takes her off his hands."

"I don't require a large dowry from my wife," Duncan said evenly.

"Nonsense, a large dowry is essential for any marriage to prosper."

"You may think so, sir," Duncan said, watching Mary, "but I shall manage without one. Perhaps I ought to explain that the reason Mary and I were alone just now is that I have asked her to marry me and she has agreed."

"What?" Balcardane and Serena spoke as one.

"We'll be married on Christmas Eve, I think, if I can persuade the parson to overlook calling the banns and perform the service that soon. Since Mary's safety might depend upon it, I daresay he will agree."

"Good God," Balcardane exclaimed.

Serena looked pale with shock.

Mary said quietly, "Christmas Eve, sir?"

He began to declare that he had made up his mind to it; but, remembering certain complaints she had made in the past about his domineering ways, and determined that she would not instantly regret her decision, he said, "I believe we can be married then if you will agree to it, mistress."

"That is four days hence, sir."

"So it is. I can arrange it sooner if you prefer." He knew that she had not meant the delay was too long, but he could feel impatience stirring. Ruthlessly, he suppressed it, ignoring his father and Serena to focus on Mary.

She regarded him steadily. "I was thinking that rather too soon, sir, but if you wish to arrange it so, I will not object."

"Then so be it."

"Good God, Duncan," Balcardane sputtered, "what are you thinking? Not that she ain't a good lass, for she is. I've grown amazingly fond of her."

Mary smiled at him. "Have you, my lord? That is kind of you."

"Aye, but I don't want my son marrying you, lass, and that's the plain truth of the matter. Why, you haven't got a penny to bless yourself."

"That is true, sir. I haven't."

Balcardane glared at her, then shifted the glare to Duncan. "You ain't going to hand me a load of nonsense and tell me you love her, are you?"

"No, sir, I won't insult your intelligence. The plain fact is that you were quite right to suggest that it's time I settle down with a wife and beget a few heirs."

"But I meant Serena!"

"Aye, and once it became apparent to me that you had got it into your head that I was to marry her, and had put the same notion into her head—not to mention Argyll's—I knew I'd have to act quickly if I was to have a choice in the matter."

"But damme, Duncan, you can't want to marry a penniless Maclean wench!"

"More important to me, sir, is that *I* choose the woman I marry. I do not want to offend Argyll by refusing to marry Serena when he tells me the union has his approval. I can think of no one else whom I would prefer over Mary, and I've no desire to begin a search on the small chance that I might find someone quickly enough. As for Mary herself, she has her own reasons for accepting my proposal."

Balcardane looked sharply at Mary. "Look here, she ain't . . . that is, you haven't gone and got her—" Breaking off in confusion, he glanced awkwardly at Serena. "Perhaps you ought to go on to the dining parlor, Serena, lass. You can be the first to tell her ladyship what her son proposes to do."

"No," Duncan said flatly.

Serena had not moved, but Balcardane bristled. "Now, look here, Duncan, damme, that is no way to speak to your father. I want to know—"

"I know what you want to know, sir, and I will answer your questions gladly, but it is my privilege to tell my mother about this, not Serena's. If you want to send her away, that is between you and Serena. She's welcome to stay if she wants."

"Too kind," Serena muttered.

Gritting his teeth, Duncan bit off the words that leapt to his tongue and said instead, "Mary is not with child, sir."

Mary said evenly, "Duncan's proposal must have surprised you, Serena. It surprised me, too, but I hope you will not dislike it too much if I say that I am grateful to him. You know that I have reason to fear Lord MacCrichton, that he has already attempted to abduct me. Duncan can protect me from him, and—"

"Lud," Serena said, "now I see how it was. I'd have thought that a mouse like you would be too terrified of him to marry him, but perhaps I should have looked at it the other way round. Were you too frightened to say no, Mary?"

"Duncan does not frighten me," Mary said with dignity.

"Lord bless us, I should hope he don't," Balcardane said. "Although, come to think of it, it wouldn't be the first time he had frightened the liver and lights out—"

"Forgive me for interrupting you, sir," Duncan said sharply, "but this conversation grows pointless. If you want to discuss my plans with me, I shall be happy to wait upon you later. Just now, however, I have been reminded that my mother deserves to hear this news from me at once. So perhaps we should adjourn to the dining parlor so that I may tell her. Come, Mary."

As he held his arm out and turned abruptly away, it occurred to him that she might not obey, but then he felt the gentle touch of her fingers on his forearm, and the moment passed. To his astonishment, he felt profound relief, even gratitude, that she would obey so curt an order without protest.

Then she murmured for his ears alone, "A partnership, sir?"

"Sorry, lass," he said, drawing her nearer. "Sometimes—"

"Don't explain," she said, and to his surprise she was choking back laughter. "I do not expect you to change, you know. You are much too arrogant and domineering ever to do so, I fear. I must just learn to cope, I suppose."

Nettled, he retorted, "Do you think you *can* cope, mistress?"

"Oh, yes, I expect so," she said.

He would have liked to debate the point, but his father and Serena had caught up with them by then, and moments later they entered the dining parlor to find Lady Balcardane impatiently awaiting them.

"I thought you were coming straightaway," she said, looking accusingly at Serena. "Indeed, I thought you would all be here before me, but I have been sitting here this age, and with the poor servants quite eager to serve dinner."

"Well, you won't want your dinner when you hear this," Balcardane announced grimly. "Your son thinks he is going to marry Mistress Maclaine."

"Mary?" She looked blankly from Duncan to Mary and back again. "Surely you have made a mistake, Duncan, although I cannot think how you came to ask the wrong girl to marry you."

"I didn't." He held Mary's chair for her while his father attended to Serena.

"But I thought it was settled that you are to offer for Serena, dearest," Lady Balcardane said, signing to the servants to begin serving. "Indeed, though you have not quite liked the notion, your father has said a thousand times that she will make an excellent wife for you, and just the other day he said you must do as you are bid because Argyll approves the match. Moreover, he is particularly pleased with her dowry, and I must say that if anyone has mentioned Mary's having money, I never heard them. You must have made a mistake," she added, looking bewildered.

"I made no mistake, ma'am," he said, affecting a patience he did not feel. "I have decided to marry her, and since I believe I am my own master, I need not explain my reasons for doing so. We shall be married on Christmas Eve."

"Christmas Eve? But, Duncan, how can we arrange a wedding so quickly? You cannot have thought about it! We will have guests on Christmas Eve, of course, just as we always do, and even minstrels and a great deal of food, but a wedding requires much more. We must send out invitations and announcements, and Mary's people will want to come, of course. But they are in Perthshire, you said, and cannot depend upon getting here at all if it snows again, which it looks like doing even now. And the banns! Why, no proper wedding could take place in so short a time, sir, but do not despair. Perhaps we can manage to arrange a ceremony in March, if you still want one then, although I do think that April would provide more reliable weather, or even June."

"Christmas Eve," he said firmly. "I'll make the necessary arrangements. With travel as difficult as it is this time of year, you are right to point out that we cannot expect guests to come from any distance, so we'll just make do with those already invited to share the evening with us. In fact, not to put too fine a point on it, I don't want a great noise made about this, ma'am. Mary's safety may depend upon it."

"But her family—"

"We will inform them, of course, but legally, although she is still a minor and I believe they changed the law in England some months ago, forbidding minors to marry without their fathers' consent, in Scotland a girl past the age of twelve still requires no one's permission. At least—" He looked at Mary. "I hadn't thought about it, lass, but is there anyone whose permission you believe you do require?"

"No," she said. "Neil might think he has some authority as my cousin and chieftain of his branch of the Macleans. If he were here, I would certainly ask him to give me in marriage, but there is no one left who wields real authority over me."

"Excellent."

"It is not excellent, Duncan," Lady Balcardane said fretfully. "Your father certainly does not think it is excellent. Pray, recall that you are his sole remaining son, my dear. I should think that you would have a care for his feelings, and—"

"Aye, he should have," Balcardane snapped. "Here's poor Serena, not knowing what to think, and how I shall tell Caddell about this, I do not know. You might have thought about that before you asked Mary Maclaine to be your wife."

Serena sat in chilly silence, attending to her dinner and taking no part in the conversation, but Lord and Lady Balcardane went on at length throughout the meal, and afterward, in the yellow saloon. As usual, they often talked at the same time and without paying heed to each other, but Duncan managed to keep his temper.

Although it was clear to him now that his father's discussions with Caddell had been more serious than Balcardane had suggested, it took no more than a glance at Mary to soothe any stirring annoyance. No sooner did his gaze meet hers than the serenity in her eyes calmed him. He therefore made no attempt to stem the tide of his parents' discourse, and felt no inclination to coax Serena out of her sullens.

He had been concerned at first that they might upset Mary, but his betrothed replied in her tranquil way whenever one of them appealed directly to her for a comment. In less time than he had feared it would take, he was able to bid his parents and Serena good-night and usher Mary out of the room.

Accompanying her upstairs, he apologized for his family, but when she smiled, saying it was nothing, he left her at her bedchamber and turned with relief to his own. Kicking the door shut behind him, he greeted the sleepy dog thumping its tail on the hearth rug, then rang for his man. But if Hardwick expected conversation he was disappointed, for Duncan went silently through his ablutions while his mind skipped from one subject to another. One moment he found it difficult to imagine what could have possessed him to propose marriage to anyone, let alone to Mary. The next he found himself wondering what his wedding night would be like.

It had been quite a night, Mary thought, watching Ailis lay out her night shift. So much, she thought, for her firm principles. Black Duncan Campbell had made a declaration, and as if she had not had a brain in her head, she had said yes.

She could accomplish nothing good by reminding herself again that he could protect her from Ewan. That had not been the reason she had accepted his proposal. She could not even pretend that she had agreed in order to help him evade marriage to a woman he could not abide. Not for a moment did she believe Duncan needed her to do that. Why then, had he proposed?

Moving to stand before the listless fire, and reluctant to add more wood, knowing that the earl would disapprove, she told herself yet again that she could not imagine why Duncan had proposed or why she had accepted him.

She bit her lip. The last was not quite true, for she knew she had accepted on an impulse. She had been on the verge of saying no, and the word had come out yes, as if she had had no control over her lips or her voice. Clearly, she was mad.

"Shall I brush out your hair now, miss?"

"Aye," Mary said absently, moving to sit on the dressing stool.

If she was crazy, what was his excuse? She had listened patiently to his explanation about Serena and Aunt Anne; but although it was true that Argyll showed more respect for Anne Stewart Maclean than for most women—or most men, for that matter—Mary did not believe for a moment that Duncan feared the duke, or that Argyll would take an excessive interest in Duncan's marriage.

Frowning, she wondered if that last was true. Marriages must always be of importance to powerful men, and no one in Scotland was more powerful than Argyll. He would care if he disapproved of Duncan's choice for a wife, and if he had approved of Serena, would he not disapprove of Mary Maclaine? Duncan could get himself into trouble—in more ways than one, now she came to think about it.

"I should have told him," she muttered.

"What's that, miss?"

"Nothing, Ailis. Pay me no heed." She had not intended to speak aloud, but the errant thought had startled the words from her. Duncan still did not know about the MacCrichton treasure. He knew only that Ewan wanted her, and doubtless he believed Ewan had fallen in love with her. It must have seemed so to many people, she realized, because of the persistence with which Ewan had courted her.

"Ye look a bit unweel, Miss Mary," Ailis said, "like Lady Serena. I hope ye ha' no taken her woman's cold, too. Ay-de-mi, but ye'd think it would ha' taught the silly lass no tae go walking oot with her young man in such fractious weather."

Diverted from her thoughts, Mary met the maid's gaze in the mirror and said, "Serena's woman has a lover here?"

Ailis shrugged. "As tae his being her lover, I dinna ken, miss, but she slips oot the noo and again tae meet someone. She was oot again the day."

"It's probably all a sham, poor girl, and he does not mean a single honeyed word he whispers to her," Mary said grimly, thinking again of Ewan.

Ailis looked bewildered, as well she might, Mary thought, knowing her words must have sounded a bit daft. Surely most men were not like Ewan, but how many who had witnessed his courtship of her had doubted his sincerity?

Certainly, Duncan questioned it now because of what Ewan had been willing to do to her, but even so, she decided, he probably thought Ewan's love merely a bit twisted. Unless she told him about the treasure, he would never know the whole truth, but if she told him, would he not insist that she use her gift to find it anyway, for the Campbells? Might he not prove as greedy in his cause as Ewan and Allan were in theirs? If he did, he could make her life miserable.

"But if I don't tell him . . ."

"Tell who, Miss Mary?" Ailis said, putting the brush on the dressing table. "I dinna like the look o' ye, miss. Shall I brew ye a posset? It will help ye sleep, miss."

"I do not require a posset, Ailis, but thank you. I have just been thinking about some things. Just fetch my cap, and then you may go. I can manage the rest."

"Aye, miss." But the maid looked doubtful.

Mary got ready for bed quickly enough, but it was long before she slept.

Next morning, Lady Balcardane came to her room, bearing in her arms a lovely pale blue silk gown trimmed with white lace. "It was my wedding dress, my dear, and there is no one else to wear it, but I hoped to have a daughter one day, and now I shall. I'd be so pleased if you would wear it. 'Marry in blue, love ever true,' you know. I've given Duncan one of my rings for you, as well, my dear."

With unexpected tears in her eyes, Mary hugged her and said,
"I would be honored to wear your dress, and your ring, ma'am.
You are so very kind to me!"

"Well, you know, I thought about some of the things I said
last night, and I am not very pleased with myself, Mary, but
the news came as such a shock, you know. I am certain that
Duncan never gave anyone the smallest reason to believe that
he was contemplating matrimony of any kind. But he must have
been thinking about it, you know, for a man simply does not
blurt out a declaration like that without having thought about
it a great deal."

"He surprised me, too, ma'am."

"Do you love him, Mary?"

The question caught her by surprise, and when she did not
answer, Lady Balcardane said with a self-conscious laugh, "I
know that persons of our sort do not fall in love. Balcardane
says that even the thought of it is vulgar, but this happened so
quickly, and I thought that perhaps . . . since you have no
dowry . . ."

"I see how it was that you came to wonder, ma'am, but I am
afraid I accepted simply because it seemed the wisest thing for
me to do. Duncan wants a wife who will not . . . That is, he
said that he thought I should be conformable, you see."

"I do see," Lady Balcardane said with a chuckle. "Serena
drives him to distraction with her nonsense. Balcardane ought
to have known within a week of their meeting each other that
his scheme would not succeed, but I don't suppose he expected
it to lead to this. I have given the matter much thought, myself,
and I shall not be at all surprised, my dear, if the pair of you
don't suit each other down to the ground. You will not mind
Duncan's temper tantrums, for I have seen how little they affect
you, and he will be grateful for your calm and composure. I
daresay the two of you will lead a pleasant, placid life together."

Since the thought of such an existence made Mary feel rather
sick, it was as well that she did not believe life with Duncan
would be anything of the sort. If she had believed it, events in
the week that followed would quickly have disillusioned her.

More than once Balcardane urged his son to change his mind, pressing him to do so until Duncan did lose his temper, making it clear that everyone around him had better tread cautiously.

Even Mary, determined to help the countess as much as she could in the many preparations for the Christmas Eve festivities, took extra care not to irritate him. In addition, she managed to put up with Serena's continued barbs, constant complaints, and her megrims.

When Mary made the mistake of telling Duncan she thought Serena truly disappointed by his choice, she instantly found herself the target of his exasperation.

"Don't even speak to me of that selfish chit," he snapped. "I have had all I can tolerate of her jibes and whining. She can thank the Fates that I did not wed her, for I am very sure I'd have beaten her soundly before the wedding night was over, and afterward at least weekly until she learned to keep her fool mouth shut."

"Dear me, how violent you are, sir," she said placidly. "Until I met Ewan, I did not think Highland men generally were given to beating women or children. I do hope you will not ever beat me."

His eyes gleamed with appreciation. "Don't tempt me, lass."

"Certainly not, sir."

Although his mood improved for the moment, with his father frequently pinching at him, and Serena constantly suggesting reasons that he would regret a marriage to Mary, it was not long before he was out of temper again.

Christmas Eve arrived at last, however, and Mary found herself in Lady Balcardane's blue silk gown, standing at Duncan's side in the yellow saloon, facing the parson and reciting the lines of the marriage service. Behind her, the buzzing crowd included Lord and Lady Balcardane, a number of surprised and delighted folks from Ballachulish village and the local Appin gentry, all of whom had submitted to a rather unusual welcome for such a festive occasion.

Over Lady Balcardane's indignant objections, Duncan had insisted that each guest be identified upon arrival and that no one be admitted who was not known by at least two others. Only when he explained that he did not want to chance admitting any-one who would cause trouble, did Lady Balcardane agree.

The audience also included Serena, still suffering from her cold, as well as any men at arms who were not on guard duty, the servants, Chuff, and Pinkie.

Despite such company, Serena's displeasure was almost tac-tile. Mary felt it even when she was not looking at her. When Duncan put the ring on her finger, and they turned so the parson could present them as man and wife, Lady Balcardane dabbed her eyes with a handkerchief. Beside her, Serena's eyes sparked fire. She said all that was proper, but her tone was brittle, and she did not deceive Mary.

Finding herself alone with Duncan for a few moments while everyone moved toward the hall, where tables had been set up for dinner, Mary said quietly, "I am sorry she is so distressed, sir. I simply don't know what to say to her."

"She wants a good skelping," Duncan said curtly. "Ignore her."

After dinner, Lady Balcardane bustled up to them and said briskly, "I know Duncan said you do not want to move into his room, Mary dear, but I do think it would be more convenient for you to have one a little closer to him. I did not like to suggest one of those when you arrived, of course, because it would not have been seemly to put you so near him. But if he should come to visit you where you are, it might be just a little disconcerting to be . . . that is . . ." She looked helpless for a moment, then added in a rush, "To be right next door to Ian's room, you know!"

A little dismayed, Mary said, "Oh, but, ma'am, truly, we do not intend—" Duncan's hand on her arm silenced her.

He said smoothly, "Mary and I will deal with all that soon enough, ma'am."

Mary's gaze flew to meet his, and she saw gentle mockery in his eyes. Collecting herself, she said, "Aye, sir. I didn't think." Wondering if he had changed his mind about giving her time to adjust to their marriage, she waited only until they could speak privately again to ask if he meant to visit her bed that very night.

"Worried, lass? I keep my word. I just did not think we ought to advertise to the castle at large that my wife is not yet ready to sleep with her husband."

Mary bit her lip, but later, when the guests had all gone home and she had dismissed Ailis for the night, she began to wonder how long it would be before everyone knew exactly how matters stood. There were few secrets in a castle full of servants. Then, too, she wondered what Duncan expected of her. Did he think she would tell him when she was ready to consummate their marriage, that one night she would just invite him to join her in her bedchamber?

As she snuffed her candle and pulled the covers up, she assured herself that she could not imagine doing either one, but her dreams soon proved her wrong. Duncan appeared in every one, and not one portrayed him as patient or casual. His hands and lips touched her everywhere, making her squirm with delight. Just the sound of his voice strained her senses—and her imagination—and never did she try to avoid him. She was enthusiastic, ardent, even wanton, and in her dreams, none of this very unMarylike behavior seemed the least bit unusual.

Duncan lay alone and sleepless in his bed. The fire had died to ashes as he lay staring up at the dark tester. The dog had crept onto the bed, and for once he did not object, grateful for the extra warmth. He found it hard to believe that he was married. He found it harder yet to stop thinking about his bride.

Had he been a fool to agree to leave her alone? His imagination kept suggesting things he might be doing with her, right now, and he began to wonder if she would prove passionate. He had heard men talk of quiet girls proving to be even more ardent than those who seemed to be the opposite. Still waters ran deep, they said. He wondered if Mary's passions ran deep. He suspected that they did.

She had a temper, for he had seen the signs more than once, and tempers demanded passion. But Mary generally kept her fires well banked. Thinking of her that way stirred his imagination, which in turn stirred sensations to life in his loins. He shifted uncomfortably. He was indeed a fool.

How long did she think this state of affairs could continue before the servants made a gift of the news to everyone else in the house? Serena would certainly hear of it, and his father. The disturbing sensations ebbed when he imagined how the pair would react upon learning that he had not touched Mary on their wedding night. He would have to make her see the wisdom of consummating the union quickly.

Grimacing, he remembered that his trying to make her see wisdom had annoyed her in the past, and he remembered certain things she had said. She was right. He was accustomed to telling others what to do, while he did as he pleased.

He recognized no master. The thought pleased him but irritated him, as well. He could change, as he had promised he would, but he would never yield to anyone when he knew he was right. Surely it would be enough to discuss his reasons with her before he issued any ultimatum that concerned her welfare.

Her hands were so white, her complexion so smooth, and if what he had seen at Shian was a sample, her skin was like that all over. He had the right now to see and touch it, and his curiosity nearly overwhelmed him. Her lips always looked soft, and the way her body moved when she walked made him think of a graceful woodland creature. When she drew in a quick breath or turned quickly, responding to someone's voice . . . Duncan groaned at the images his mind produced.

He slept at last, but his sleep was so restless that the dog soon sought the hearth rug again, curling tight against the cold.

Even without its warmth, Duncan was not cold. His body burned, and in his dreams, his bewitching bride obeyed his every command. Her skin was smooth and flawless, her breasts soft and springy to his touch, her moans responsive and filled with passion, her tongue warm and wet wherever it touched him. When he took her, she writhed beneath him, urging him on, her body leaping to welcome his.

When he awoke in a tangle of bedclothes, his body was awash with sweat that soon threatened to turn icy in the freezing room.

Fourteen

"It's snowing something strong," Ailis told Mary as she drew back the bed curtains, "but I brought ye a Christmas bicker o' new sowens tae warm ye, madam."

The new form of address being a powerful reminder of her marriage, Mary wondered why she felt no different from the way she had the day before. Not only was it Christmas Day, but she was now and forevermore a married lady.

Accepting the wooden porridge dish that Ailis handed to her, she sniffed at its contents, a distinctive mixture of oatmeal husks and siftings boiled to the consistency of molasses that most Highlanders received early Christmas morning while still in their beds. When Mary had finished hers, she got up, shivering in the chilly air to perform her morning ablutions.

As she washed her face, she saw Ailis steal several sidelong looks at her.

"I expect you stayed with Master Duncan for a long time last night," the maid said at last, very casually, as she bent to stir up the fire.

It was a good thing, Mary thought, that Ailis was not looking at her just then, for she could feel her cheeks burning. She nearly denied having done any such thing before she realized that she would be wiser to keep silent. The last thing she wanted was for the servants to begin talking about her relationship with her husband. Duncan's man, Hardwick, would not say a word about his master's business, however, and she did not think Ailis would dare press her now to say more.

She said with quiet dignity, "I will wear the dark blue wool, Ailis, please."

Her cheeks reddening, the maid said hastily, "Aye, madam, and will ye be wanting a cap tae wear, as well?"

About to refuse, Mary changed her mind. "I believe I will, if you can find me a suitable one. I am a married lady now, am I not?"

"Aye, madam, and the mistress has any number of lovely ones. Nay doot she'll be that glad tae lend ye one, so ye can wear it tae the kirk."

Half an hour later, her hair tidily arranged beneath a fetching lace cap, Mary descended to the dining parlor, where she found Balcardane, his wife, and his son, augmenting the Christmas sowens with a substantial breakfast. Serena evidently had either chosen to sleep late or was dressing even more carefully than usual for kirk.

Lady Balcardane said enthusiastically, "Good morning, my dear. How very becoming that gown is on you. I declare, it never became me so well."

"Thank you, ma'am."

"What the devil have you got on your head?" Duncan demanded.

"I am wearing a lace cap, sir, as you must be able to see for yourself." Turning to Balcardane, she added, "Good morning, my lord. Happy Christmas."

Balcardane returned her greeting, but he was watching his son. Although both men had risen to their feet at her entrance, only Balcardane resumed his seat.

Duncan remained standing, regarding her critically. "I don't like that thing," he said. "I'd rather look at your hair."

Lady Balcardane protested, "But it is the fashion, Duncan. Married ladies do not go about with their heads uncovered."

"Why not?"

"Well, I do not know precisely. It is not the thing, that's all."

"Mary?"

She met his stern gaze calmly. "Yes, sir?"

"Would you prefer to please your husband or certain critics of fashion?"

She pretended to think about it, then tilted her head to one side and said, "My husband, sir, looks as if he did not sleep well. Perhaps I had better do as he bids."

"Just what I was thinking," he said. Amusement crept into his eyes, although he ignored his father's chuckles. "I thought you did not fear me, Mary."

"Oh, I don't, sir, but vexation is certain to increase your weariness, and it is my duty to give you comfort and solace—when it is possible, at all events."

He stepped around the table, his gaze still locked with hers, and for a moment she thought he was going to take her out of the room, perhaps to scold her for her impertinence. Instead, coming to a stop directly in front of her, he reached for the cap.

"Take care that you remove only the pins holding it, sir, or you will have my hair tumbling down around my shoulders and I shall have to do it all up again before we leave for kirk. That is," she added with a questioning look, "I assume that we will attend services today."

He was too near. Her heart was pounding, and she found it hard to keep her voice calm. She was unusually aware of his size, and the spicy scent of his clothing seemed to fill her senses. His hands touching her hair stirred sensations that shot right to her toes and back up again, settling somewhere near her midsection.

"To be sure we'll attend services, lass," Balcardane said. "Parson would read out our names did we not attend, and we must set a good example, even," he added with a chuckle, "if we did not get much sleep. My men have begun to clear the road, but we'll not trust the coach. They'll hitch up the sleigh when it is time to go."

Duncan handed her the cap, kissed her on the forehead, and said evenly, "That is much better. Don't wear that thing again. It does not suit you."

Clutching the cap in one hand, she waited until he had returned to his chair before she tucked it into her sash and moved to help herself to sliced ham, toast, and an apple from the sideboard. Trying to ignore the burning sensation where he had kissed her forehead, she watched in a daze as Jessie served her hot chocolate, and set a pot of bramble jam nearby on the table for her toast.

While they ate, Lady Balcardane maintained her usual light chatter, and for once Mary was grateful for it. She felt self-conscious, and the feeling was new to her. She had not missed Balcardane's chuckle, and could only hope that he stood in too much awe of his son's volatile temper to question him about his wedding night. At least, she thought, the earl would not do so in front of anyone else.

She avoided Duncan's glances, hoping he would think she was as calm as always, and that she took interest only in her breakfast. Most of all, she hoped that he would ascribe any extra color in her cheeks to the chilly morning air. Even with a fire crackling on the hearth, the dining parlor was not warm. More than once she cradled her chocolate cup with both hands to warm them, and she shifted her feet frequently, rubbing them together in search of warmth.

The men talked quietly, their conversation providing an undercurrent to Lady Balcardane's continual stream of light comments. Mary murmured a response to one, more out of politeness than because she was paying close attention. When a sudden silence ensued just as she took a bite of toast, she looked up in surprise.

The others were staring at her as if she had said something odd. She looked from one to another, letting her gaze come to rest on Duncan.

"My mother just said that she hoped you do not regret your hasty marriage," he said wryly. "You said, 'Indeed I do, ma'am, thank you.' "

Nearly choking on the food in her mouth, she swallowed and looked ruefully at Lady Balcardane. "Oh, ma'am, I beg your pardon! Of course, I do not regret my marriage. My mind was wool-gathering, I'm afraid, and I must have misunderstood your comment. Pray, say that you will forgive me."

"Of course, I will, my dear. Why, I remember that I scarcely got a wink of sleep on my wedding night, so I daresay you are not at all yourself this morning. You said that Duncan looked tired, and I must say, that you do not look too well rested yourself. I should have seen that you were listening with but half an ear."

Doing her best to conceal her embarrassment, Mary said firmly, "It was unconscionable of me not to listen with both ears, ma'am. I should be well scolded, but you are always so very kind to me that I daresay you won't do it. Nonetheless, I am a wretch to repay your kindness with such discourtesy."

"Well, it is no great matter, my dear, after all."

"Have you finished your breakfast?" Duncan asked.

Mary's gaze snapped to meet his, but she could tell nothing from his expression. "Why, yes, I suppose I have, sir."

"Good, then you may take a walk with me, and I'll see if I can do something about that scolding you deserve."

His mother protested. "Duncan, don't be absurd! I have taken no offense, I promise you, and if I have not, I cannot think why you should do so. I am sure *you* never listen to half of what I say!"

"Then you should take me to task for *my* bad manners, ma'am," he said, grinning at her as he got to his feet and went to hold Mary's chair for her.

Lady Balcardane stared at him in astonishment. "Why, I don't believe you mean to scold her at all! I cannot recall the last time you made a jest, Duncan."

"Was I jesting, ma'am? I'll wager Mary is not so certain of that as you are."

Mary said not a word. She allowed him to draw her hand through the crook of his arm, thinking it odd that she had never before been so sensitive to the roughness of wool as she was now with her hand resting on Duncan's sleeve.

Just outside the dining parlor, they met Serena, and Mary saw at once what had kept her. The other young woman looked particularly lovely in a magnificent straw-colored silk gown with a narrow edging of lace at neckline and sleeves. Over it she wore a gaily embroidered white silk apron.

"I thought you would still be breaking your fast, Duncan," she said, pouting. "The snow lies so thick on the ground that I was persuaded you would play slug-a-bed. Now I shall have to breakfast alone, I suppose." She did not look at Mary.

Duncan said, "My parents are in the dining parlor, Serena, so you will not be alone. As for sleeping late, chores do not wait upon the weather, nor will the Christmas kirk services. We will all be out and about today as usual, I believe."

"Won't you come back into the parlor until I have eaten my breakfast?"

"I want to speak to Mary before I go to the stable. Perhaps afterward she will return to bear you company for a short while, until we depart for Ballachulish."

Serena sighed. "You are being cruel again, Duncan."

Seeing his jaw tighten, Mary said quickly, "Perhaps you will be kind enough when we return from kirk to show me how to do that stitch you used to embroider those roses, Serena. That is some of the most exquisite work I have seen."

"They are lovely, aren't they?" She glanced speculatively at Duncan, then said with apparent graciousness, "I will be happy to show you if you like."

"Come along, Mary," Duncan said. "You two can talk stitches later, but if Serena wants more to eat than her Christmas sowens, she had better hurry."

As he ushered her downstairs toward the library, Mary said, "I hope you do not mean to scold me, sir, although I know I deserve it. Your mother has been exceedingly generous, and I should not have treated her so shabbily. I don't know how I came to let my mind wander so."

"Don't refine upon it," he said. "I promise you, she does not. She spoke the truth when she said that none of us listens to her as we should. Once, Argyll nearly surprised us with a visit despite her attempts to warn us that he was coming. My father thought she was talking about a cousin of hers whom he particularly dislikes, and he kept cutting her off. We all nearly landed in the suds that time."

She chuckled. "Did the duke have any notion of his part in that tangle, sir?"

"No, thank heaven. My father kept telling her she was not to order more food and supplies, because her idiot guests would eat everything she ordered and more, and she never quite understood his error, because he always complains about how much things cost. To hear him go on, one would think him a pauper."

"I suppose he is not as purse pinched as he makes himself sound."

"He is not. His steward keeps me well apprised of the state of his finances, but my father has everyone so bamboozled that I found young Chuff trying to pick oats up off the floor of one of the stallions' stalls to feed my colt. He'd heard my father ranting at another lad for wasting feed, and Chuff worried that he would be the next to be scolded. I tried to reassure him, but I am not certain I succeeded."

"I should think perhaps you did," Mary said, smiling. "Do you know that Chuff and Pinkie both still refer to you as Himself, as if you were a clan chief? They were surprised to learn that you have a father, let alone one who bears a title."

Duncan laughed, and she realized that she liked the sound. She had not heard it often. Indeed, until recently, she had not heard it at all. It was, she thought, a particularly warm and pleasant laugh.

"Why aren't you wearing a shawl?" he asked her abruptly as he opened the library doors and gestured for her to precede him inside.

"I chose not to," she said, moving to warm her hands by the fire. The library was warmer than the dining parlor had been, and she wondered why that was so. It was a larger room, and on the ground floor, which ought, she thought, to make it colder. It had no proper windows, however, only ancient glassed-in arrow slits, and its walls were particularly thick. In any event, she welcomed the fire's warmth.

"You will catch Serena's cold if you are not careful," he said, hesitating with the doors still open. "I can send a servant to fetch a wrap for you."

"No, thank you. I am warm enough for now, and in any case, I shall need to fetch my cloak and gloves, and tidy my hair, before we leave. If you did not bring me here to scold me, sir, why did you bring me?"

To her surprise, he equivocated. "Is it beyond reason that I should want to have a private word with my wife?"

"No, but you made the decision so abruptly that you cannot be amazed if I wonder what brought it about."

"Perhaps not. Look here, Mary, is Serena going to drive you to distraction with her reproaches and laments?"

"Is that it?" She searched his expression but could not tell if that had been his real reason. "I shouldn't think so," she said. "She is disappointed, but in truth, sir, I believe that is because she will not someday become a countess, not because she will not be your wife. If that offends you, I apologize—"

"Don't be foolish. I know Serena does not care a snap for me. She has never made a secret of that. She behaves more as if she had been denied a treat than as if she were broken-hearted. I merely want to know if she will annoy you."

"I cannot answer that," she replied honestly. "Perhaps she will desire to return home, now that her hopes have been dashed. I know that with the weather in such a state, it will be no easy journey—"

"I would arrange it, nevertheless, if I thought she would go. She won't though, and my father would kick up the devil of a fuss, because we'd have to send any number of men to protect her, and they would have to stay with folks along the way. Moreover, at this time of year, we could not allow such a party to descend on folks without providing food and supplies for them."

"You would have to accompany her, too, would you not?"

He began to shake his head, then grimaced and said with a sigh, "I suppose I would at that. Caddell will choose to be grievously offended, I'm afraid, especially since I know that I can't count on Serena to smooth things over with him."

"Indeed, I think she would delight in making trouble for you just now."

He was silent for a long moment. Then he said with the curtness she had come to expect of him, "That isn't why I wanted to talk to you."

"No?"

"No. Look, Mary, I know I said that I would be patient, but I have thought more about it now, and I just don't think patience is the wisest course for us."

She did not have to ask what he was talking about, for she understood him all too perfectly, but suddenly she found it hard to meet his gaze. Rubbing her hands together over the warmth from the fire, she struggled for her usual calm as she said, "Why do you think it unwise, sir?"

His hand on her shoulder caught her by surprise, and she jumped, but she turned obediently to face him. Without taking the hand away, he said gently, "A significant reason for our marriage, lass, was to confound Ewan MacCrichton. I am not altogether sure that he cannot overturn the marriage even now if he can manage somehow to have his way with you before we consummate our union."

"Surely not," she said, staring at his waistcoat. "I thought you said the magistrate would accept written proof of our marriage, and stop Ewan's nonsense."

Whatever Duncan might have said to that remained unspoken, for the doors opened and Balcardane strode in. He came to a halt, clearly surprised to see them. "What are you two doing here? They are hitching a team to the sleigh, and we'll be leaving for the kirk in just a few minutes. I thought you were fetching your coats. I do hope you don't mean to keep those horses standing long in this weather."

Exchanging an apologetic look with Duncan, Mary excused herself and hurried upstairs to fetch cloak and gloves, and to tidy her hair. She also replaced the lace cap. It was all very well to please one's husband, she thought, but people would ask why she did not wear one, and she did not want to supply them or

the magistrate with more food for gossip than her hasty marriage had already provided.

Duncan also excused himself to the earl, for not only did he
want to don his outdoor clothes, but he wanted to be certain
that the sleigh contained enough rugs and furs to keep the ladies
warm. Not that he would mind overmuch if Serena caught a
chill, he thought with a mild renewal of his earlier exasperation.

He was well out of that entanglement, he knew, for entanglement it would soon have become with the vixen so hot to marry
him. It made him shudder just to think of the riot and rumpus
Caddell and Argyll might have stirred up in order to press him
into obliging her. Better to be safely wedded to the unflappable
Mary. She would not enact him a tragedy every time he failed
to dance to her piping.

His confidence suffered a slight setback, however, when she
rejoined them in the hall, for the first thing he saw was the lace
cap on her head beneath the cloak's fur-trimmed hood. She met
his gaze with her usual serenity though, merely raising her eyebrows as if she wondered why he looked stern.

Making no comment on the cap, he handed her into the sleigh
with the other ladies and tucked the furs around her with his
own hands. He had not liked the way she had kept trying to
warm hers, both in the dining parlor and in the library.

He and Balcardane had chosen to ride. The rest of the castle's
inhabitants, including servants and stable hands, the herds and
their families, would follow on foot. A few guardsmen would
stay behind to mind the castle, however, for even on Christmas,
one could not depend upon enemies to love their neighbors.

A light snow was falling, and the only sounds were the hushing of the sleigh runners and the crunching of the horses' hooves
in the snow, punctuated now and again by a masculine voice,
or comments from his mother. It was not far to the village of
Ballachulish or to the wee steepled kirk around which it had
grown.

When the party from Balcardane entered, an instant stirring

greeted them. Good manners suggested that folks already in their places ought not to turn to peer at newcomers, but even before Balcardane had unlocked the family pew, heads turned and whispers could be heard.

Duncan saw Mary push back the hood of her cloak. She stood proudly, her chin up, her shoulders straight, the little lace cap like a crown on her golden hair.

When she would have followed Lady Balcardane into the pew, Duncan reached forward and stopped her with a touch, gesturing for his father to precede them. Balcardane glanced at him, then nodded and moved on. Duncan put his hand lightly in the small of her back to urge her forward, a possessive gesture that he knew the onlookers would not miss.

Many, but not by any means all, of those present had attended the Christmas Eve festivities at Balcardane. Still, by the time the parson got round to announcing the recent marriage of Duncan, Master of Dunraven, to Mistress Mary Maclaine of Lochfuaran, Duncan was willing to wager that although the news could not yet have reached every corner of Argyll, it came as a surprise to no one sitting in the kirk.

His mind proved unwilling to focus on the parson's sermon despite its being Christmas. Grand religious festivals no longer held the preeminence they once had held in the Highlands, for the dour Protestant church disapproved of such goings-on, and Duncan found himself wondering if Mary, who doubtless had not been raised a Protestant, had been accustomed to more cheerful Christmas celebrations in the past.

From that point his thoughts drifted to Mary herself. She was so close to him that he could smell the tantalizing lilac scent she wore and feel her slightest movement. He wondered if she smelled like lilacs all over.

Perhaps he had not made himself plain earlier. Had she understood his intent to consummate their marriage, and the very excellent reasons for doing so?

He did not trust Ewan MacCrichton. The wonder was that the man had not already caused more trouble, and once he learned of their marriage, no one knew what his fury might lead him to do. If he managed to rape her, declaring a belief that her promise entitled him to her virginity, he might still prevail before his magistrate, especially if Duncan had to admit that the marriage had not yet been consummated. Clearly, the sooner they completed their union, the better it would be for her safety.

The necessity of sitting through the long service made him restless, as did the ritual of receiving felicitations from those members of the congregation who had not been present for the ceremony. Duncan forced himself to speak pleasantly for Mary's sake, even greeting Bardie Gillonie without the impatience he generally felt toward the impertinent dwarf.

Bardie was not impressed with Duncan's forbearance. He glowered at him. "What did ye do tae the lass? I swear she never wanted tae marry wi' ye afore."

"Hush, Bardie," Mary said, smiling at Duncan. "He has done me the honor to marry me. You must not be unkind, for he will keep me safe from Ewan."

"Och, aye, and is that the way of it?" He looked from one to the other, searchingly, then said abruptly, "Where are the bairns?"

"There," Mary said, gesturing toward Chuff and Pinkie, who were chattering happily in the midst of a group of other children.

When the dwarf had gone to speak to them, Duncan said quietly, "Tonight, madam, we will make certain that you are safe from MacCrichton."

She moistened her lips nervously, then said, "Very well, sir."

He could not seem to keep his eyes off her after that. The short trip back to Balcardane seemed longer than ever, and upon their arrival, when Serena said politely, "If you will come with me to the saloon now, Mary, I will show you that stitch you want to learn," Duncan wanted to throttle her.

He nearly stopped them, but tempted though he was to tell Mary the stitchery could wait, he recalled that dinner would be ready to serve as soon as the cook and her minions could attend to such finishing touches as they had left until their return from the kirk. Therefore, he contained his soul in patience, an act that required so great an effort as to make him feel rather virtuous.

The whole family gathered in the saloon before the meal, which was to be served in the hall again, where the more important members of the household would dine with them. No one dawdled, for the odors wafting from the great platters as they were carried in were too enticing to ignore. Duncan managed to suppress his other appetites in favor of the excellent food, although he found himself watching Mary throughout the meal, approving of her dainty manners and the easy way she conversed with others at the table.

Serena held herself aloof, as if it were beneath her to talk to MacDermid or to Martha Loudoun when she joined them, but Mary was at ease with everyone. It was a knack he had noted before, and one that pleased him. He also approved of the fact that she had removed her cap again, allowing candlelight from the chandeliers to set golden highlights dancing in her beautiful hair.

His fantasies came to an abrupt end when a clamor in the courtyard announced the arrival of riders. Balcardane and Duncan leapt to their feet at the sound, but before they reached the door, four men rushed in led by Bannatyne.

He cried, "They've attacked Dunraven, my lord! They set the outbuildings on fire." Turning to Duncan, he added, "These lads say they used fire arrows, sir. They think it was most likely the MacCrichton."

"Tell the men to saddle horses," Duncan ordered. "We'll ride at once."

Serena exclaimed in dismay, "You cannot leave us now, Duncan. It is dark outside, there is snow everywhere, and there is undoubtedly a new storm brewing!"

Bannatyne said quietly, "The sky is clear, sir, and they say the pass is still accessible. It will be slow going in places, but if we don't get to Dunraven—"

"You have your orders," Duncan growled.

"Aye, sir." Bannatyne left the hall at once.

Signing to the newcomers to help themselves to food, Duncan

said to his father, "I don't know how long I'll be away, sir, but we cannot allow such a criminal act to go unpunished." He looked at one of the men taking a place now at the table, and said, "Did you send elsewhere for help, as well?"

"Aye, sir. We sent riders to Inver House and to Castle Stalker. Like as not them from Stalker will get there long before Lord Caddell's people do, though."

"Good work." He turned to Mary. "I'm sorry about this, lass, but you ought to be safe enough from MacCrichton if he is making mischief in Campbell country."

"Aye, sir," she said quietly. "Keep safe yourself."

Her words warmed him. He kissed her forehead again, denying himself anything more; but as he rode into the night with his men, he found himself wishing he were not riding away from Balcardane.

The men had not exaggerated the state of the pass or that of the narrow trail winding down through Glen Creran, and it was nearly daybreak before they reached Dunraven. There Duncan found lingering chaos. Soldiers from the Campbell stronghold at Castle Stalker, strategically located on its islet near the confluence of Loch Creran, Loch Linnhe, and the Lynn of Lorne, had reached Dunraven the previous evening. But although they had apparently prevented further damage to the castle and its occupants, they had not succeeded in laying the raiders by the heels.

Having eluded their pursuers only to find themselves blinded by snow and in danger of becoming lost as they attempted to make their way by a lengthy and devious route toward Balcardane, Ewan and Allan Breck and their followers took shelter at last with a cottager who had hidden Breck many times before.

Reassured though he was that their host would not betray them, Ewan was angry. "How the devil are we going to make Balcardane if this snow keeps up?"

"If we can't get there, neither can Duncan," Allan said calmly, taking a swig of whisky from a flask he carried with him, then offering it to Ewan. "Want some?"

Ewan accepted, growling, "Do you think the lass really married that devil?"

"I won't be surprised," Allan said with a grin. "My chap who told me said he heard she was doing it to protect herself from your suit. I won't be surprised either, though, if Mary had refused to bed Duncan. She's a stubborn lass, is our Mary, so if you can get to her before he loses patience and claims his rights, your suit may yet prosper, my lad. That's why I agreed to assist with your Christmas temper tantrum at Dunraven. We'll no doubt pay for such sacrilege in the next world, but it was bound to draw Duncan away from Balcardane no matter what enticed him to stay."

"A fat lot of good that will do us if we cannot get there," Ewan grumbled.

"I do not intend to let you fail," Allan said grimly. "I've had the devil's own time of it, trying to collect money owed to the exiled lairds, so I'll find a sour welcome awaiting me in France if we cannot recover what you've lost."

"What I've lost," Ewan pointed out, "belongs to me, not to you or the lairds."

"Aye, and you are welcome to what you need from it, but your anxiety told me long since that the treasure you misplaced must be a substantial one, and I expect a hefty share of it for helping you retrieve it, my lad."

Depressed and feeling as if he had made a pact with the devil, Ewan said, "Even if we arrive ahead of Duncan, what makes you think we can get to the lass?"

"I know we can," Allan retorted smugly. "My chap brought a message from her, agreeing to meet me. I need only tell her where and when."

Fifteen

Upon his arrival, Duncan ordered breakfast for himself in his book room, and a like meal for his men to be served in the hall. Learning that Stalker's captain had led the soldiers himself, he told Bannatyne to rouse the man from his bed. When his henchman hesitated, diffidently reminding him that Patrick Campbell had been up most of the night, Duncan said, "He can sleep when I do. Fetch him."

His food arrived before Patrick did, but he had eaten less than half of it when the other man entered without ceremony. He had clearly come from his bed, for his light brown hair was tousled and his hazel eyes red-rimmed and bleary. He had not had himself shaved, and he rubbed his bristly jaw as he glowered at Duncan.

"Have some ale," Duncan said, "and felicitate me on my marriage."

"I'd rather have coffee if you've got any. As to felicitations . . . you?"

"Aye." Duncan gestured to Bannatyne to fetch coffee. "Sit down, Patrick, and take that foolish smirk off your face. I'll tell you all about it if you insist, but first, tell me what you know about the damned raid. Your lads tell me they cannot be certain the raiders were MacCrichton's men."

"We don't know anything for certain," Patrick said, pulling a stool up to the table and breaking a chunk of bread from the loaf as he sat down. "I heard of your visit to Shian a few weeks ago. I hope you haven't stirred up a hornets' nest. We've enjoyed peace in these parts for more than a year. I'd hate to see it end."

Duncan shrugged. "It seems to have ended already. What makes you think it could have been anyone but MacCrichton?"

"I don't say it's likely to have been anyone else, but we've seen no sign of trouble at Shian. It's one place we keep an eye on, after all, and we will until he's paid the fine demanded as part of his pardon. We know Allan Breck is in the area, however, and it's odd that he's still here, because he usually returns to France before the snow comes. Perhaps he's been brewing mischief, but he'd have to be mad to tweak your tail."

"He would," Duncan agreed, not bothering to hide his antipathy. "Breck couldn't organize a raid like this alone, though, and I don't know many who would help him. He made more enemies than friends when he murdered my brother."

"MacCrichton may have linked up with him, though I can't think why he would," Patrick said, nodding thanks to Bannatyne when the man put a cup of coffee in front of him. "He's got reason to stay clear of a felon like Breck if he wants to keep his peace with the government."

"They may both think they have a common enemy, however," Duncan said. While they ate, he told Patrick about Mary, and then the two men retired to sleep for a few hours. When they awoke, the snow was still falling heavily. During the next few days, Duncan's men made makeshift repairs with the help of the soldiers from Stalker, and tended the injured. By Monday the weather had cleared enough to travel, and Patrick announced that he and his men would return to Stalker.

"Perhaps," Duncan said mildly, "you won't mind if I ride with you."

"Not at all," Patrick said. "I think it wise of you to go the long way, up the Loch Linnhe shore road, rather than trying to make it over the hill pass."

"Oh, we'll make it over the pass," Duncan replied with a slight smile.

Patrick met his gaze and sighed. "I suppose you want me

and my men to ride round the end of Loch Creran with you to
pay a visit to Shian Towers."

Duncan grinned.

He was no longer grinning, however, when they reached
Shian Towers and found that its master was not in residence.
The guards at the gates could not say where he was. Suddenly
Duncan felt an urgent need to get back to Balcardane. "What
if the raid on Dunraven was but a ruse to draw me away?" he
demanded.

Patrick frowned. "Do you think he would dare attack Balcardane?"

"Why not?" Then, thinking more sensibly, he said, "even
with my men gone, he won't think he can take the castle, and
he must know he could never hold it. It's Mary he wants, Patrick.
I must ride, and swiftly. Thank you."

"Do you want us to go with you?"

"I'll welcome your help if I have to search for her."

"Then so be it."

Duncan gave spur to his horse, leaving the others to follow.
Snow almost obliterated the path up the glen, but he forced his
way as much by instinct as by any other means, plunging on at
a reckless pace. Pushing hard, giving quarter neither to himself
nor to his mount, he pressed on. Thus it was that when he approached Balcardane at last, riding down the wind-swept hill
toward the main gates, and saw a man who looked suspiciously
like Allan Breck disappear into the woods west of the castle,
and a woman in a gray cloak with a fur-trimmed hood waving
to him from the ramparts, fury exploded within him.

Recognizing Duncan, the castle guards threw the gates wide,
and he barely waited to turn his horse over to a lad before
striding angrily across an unusually busy courtyard to the entrance. Pushing open the door, he entered the hall.

The first person he saw was Mary, looking composed and
serene in the dark blue wool gown that she had worn to the kirk
the day he had left Balcardane. She stepped forward, and before

her expression changed to wariness, he would have sworn that she looked glad to see him.

He did not pause to wonder at that, however, or to note that she was not alone in the hall. Closing the distance between them in a few long strides, he grabbed her by the shoulders, intending to shake her until her bones rattled.

She continued to look at him, still wary but unafraid and with that damnable serenity radiating from her silver eyes. He paused then, his fingers clutching spasmodically at her shoulders. "I cannot believe you are not even breathing hard, madam," he said curtly. "You must have run downstairs from the ramparts, but I don't doubt that fear of my anger lent wings to your feet."

"I have been in the hall since my cousin arrived, sir," she said calmly. "What makes you think I had any cause to run downstairs?"

"Your cousin?" Fighting rage, he snapped, "How dare you speak so casually of that villain to me! Aye," he added when her eyes widened, "I saw him haring toward the woods, and it is a measure of my fury at *your* betrayal that I came to find you rather than chase him. Two of my men were close enough behind me to see him, however, and no doubt will have trapped him by now."

"But my cousin is right here, sir. You have met Neil before, of course, but perhaps you did not notice him just now when you came in."

Caught up sharply, Duncan looked at the other men standing nearby, and realized for the first time that several were strangers. One was not, however. He had indeed met Sir Neil Maclean before, but he remembered him as a boy about Ian's age, and the dark-haired young man standing before him was no stripling. Maclean was lean and lanky, and as Duncan recalled when he looked into his stormy dark eyes, possessed of a temper almost as quick as his own.

Duncan stood his ground but watched Maclean as he said to Mary, "I would have a word with you in private, madam. At once, if you please."

"I have no secrets from Neil, sir. He rode all the way from

Perthshire to be certain of my safety—and my sanity, I believe," she added with a wry smile for her cousin. "It would be most discourteous to leave him to his own devices so soon, particularly since he is our first visitor of the new year. Is it not fortunate that his having dark hair means this house will enjoy good luck all year?"

"You will not want anyone else to hear what I have to say to you."

"I can think of nothing that I have done, sir, to warrant your anger. Whom did you mean, if not Neil, when you referred to my cousin?"

Frowning, he wondered for the first time if his eyes could have deceived him, but he said bluntly, "Did you not receive Allan Breck here in my absence?"

She looked astonished. "I would not do such a thing even if the men would allow him inside these walls, sir. Whatever made you think I had?"

"You cannot deny that he has twice sought a meeting with you."

"You know he has, but you know I did not meet him. Nor have I invited him to visit me. I have not heard from him since you suggested setting a trap, sir."

"Look here, Duncan," Neil said, his tone as curt as Duncan's had been, "you must know that Mary does not tell lies. If she says she has not laid eyes on that scoundrel, then she has not."

"But I saw her, and him. That is," he amended, "I saw a man who looked like him running toward the woods on the hill between here and Ballachulish village."

"You saw someone who looked like me?" Mary's gaze, meeting his, was still as calm as it had ever been. "Where?"

He felt his temper ebbing quickly. Realizing that his hands still gripped her shoulders, he relaxed them, letting one fall away but moving the other just a little, unwilling to step away from her calming influence just yet. He drew a deep, steadying breath, grateful that no one else spoke. Everyone was watching him.

His father had entered the hall from somewhere in the nether regions, and stood just inside the door beneath the stairs. Two other men, apparently servants or companions, stood near Maclean, their demeanor wary but unthreatening.

Footsteps and a rustle of skirts drew Duncan's attention upward. Serena stood poised on the stair landing, looking down.

Turning back to Mary, Duncan grimaced ruefully and said, "Aye, lass, she looked like you. She stood at the wall, on the battlement, waving at the fellow. She wore your gray cloak, the one with fur round the hood."

"The only cloak I have, in fact," she said, "but I was not wearing it, sir. If you saw it within the past half hour—"

"Here now," Neil said, interrupting with a frown. "I saw that wench hurrying toward the postern gate when we rode up, and I saw some chap walking away from her toward the hill. I wondered what the devil they were doing, for it seemed like a dashed odd place for them to have parted company, I thought."

Ominous silence greeted his words, and Duncan looked at Mary again.

She was gazing thoughtfully at his belt or stomach, but she looked up just then, right into his eyes, and any lingering doubt he might have had vanished in a blink. He drew her nearer, giving her a slight hug.

"One of the servant lasses, meeting her lad, I suppose," he said with a sigh.

"In Mary's cloak?" Neil said skeptically. He was not looking at Duncan, however. He was gazing thoughtfully at the stair landing.

Sweeping up her skirt with one hand, Serena descended the remaining steps, saying, "Why did no one tell me that we had company?"

Balcardane stepped forward then, saying brusquely, "They seem to have kept it a secret from us all, lass. How did you find things at Dunraven, lad?"

"In need of a great many repairs, sir," Duncan said bluntly. "We can discuss all that later."

"Indeed, we will. I must say, I don't know why you've kept

these men standing here in the hall. I don't think I know them all, do I?"

Mary said quickly, "I beg your pardon, sir. I believe I need not introduce my cousin Sir Neil Maclean to you."

"Of course not," the earl said, "though I hope you have not left his mama standing about somewhere outside in the cold whilst you chatted."

His light tone did not fool his son (or anyone else, he suspected). The Lady Anne Stewart Maclean was no favorite with Balcardane. Her tongue was too sharp to suit the earl's notion of proper feminine submission to masculine authority.

"No, sir," Mary said, smiling. "My aunt is still with my cousin Diana in Perthshire. Surely, someone has told you that Diana expects to be confined soon."

"Good gracious," Serena said. "Is everyone having babies? My sister-in-law also expects to be confined soon, too, Sir Neil. It's prodigiously tiresome, however, because Juliet has already had five daughters, but it is the same every time, and since everyone at Inver House remains in a constant state of alt, I left."

Balcardane moved to pull the bell cord near the fireplace. "Well, take them into the saloon, and I'll order some refreshment. I daresay her ladyship will be as pleased as I am to offer Sir Neil and his men the hospitality of Balcardane."

"There will be a few more," Duncan said, watching his father warily. "Patrick Campbell and a company of his men are not far behind me, sir." Balcardane gave him a sour look but said only that he supposed Patrick would not stay long.

Neil dismissed his followers, and Duncan went outside with them long enough to learn that the man heading into the woods had escaped, and to order arrangements for removing Sir Neil's baggage to a guest chamber and housing his men. While he was thus engaged, Patrick Campbell and his men arrived.

Patrick laughed when Duncan told them to put up their horses and stay the night. "We'll stay the night and thank you," he said, "but I won't impose upon your father's legendary generosity any longer than that. We'll leave at first light."

* * *

When Breck ran to join Ewan in the woods, the much larger man grabbed him by the shoulders and would have shaken him, had Breck not snapped, "Someone saw me! I think it was Duncan. Run, man. Thank the lord I thought to tell everyone to muck about all over up here while I was gone, to hide our tracks."

"Where is she? Damn you, I knew it was a mistake to let you meet her. I should have gone myself!" But Ewan released him.

"Nay, then, you dared not. I know a sight more about covering my tracks than you do," Breck pointed out, pushing him ahead. "Go up toward the ridge. They'll expect us to head for the road. Where are the others?"

"I told them to scatter and meet us at the cottage. That's nearer than Shian, and I wanted an escort for when we took the lass. Why did you not bring her?"

"Wrong lass," Breck told him, chuckling. "If you want to abduct Caddell's daughter, instead, you'll do it without me."

"Caddell's daughter. The Lady Serena?"

"The same, and a vixen if ever there was one. But she's hot for intrigue, my lad, so we may find a use for her in the end. She does not like our Mary. Said she wanted to meet me to tell me that, and so she fixed it with the maid. Promised to keep a still tongue in her head, too, but we won't trust her for that. Hurry, man!"

"We'll never get near that castle again," Ewan protested, puffing.

"Don't despair. We'll take shelter at the cottage for a few days more, and set men to keep watch from the hillsides around here. We may yet get our chance."

"And if we don't?"

"Grief seems to stir that gift of hers a bit. We'll just make her a widow."

* * *

Taking Patrick inside with him to join the others in the yellow saloon, Duncan found his father absent and his mother making a valiant effort to play hostess despite a red nose, watery eyes, and every sign of an incipient fever.

"Faith, ma'am," he said, "are you ailing now, too?"

"I'm afraid so," she said hoarsely. "Serena's maid seems to have passed her illness on to a number of people. It happens every winter, of course. How splendid to have more visitors, though," she added, smiling at Patrick. "I was just telling Sir Neil that I should not have recognized him, for I believe I have not seen him since last May—the Beltane festival, you know—and he has changed a good deal, I believe. Why, you were quite young then, Sir Neil, and not nearly so . . . so—"

"So old," Duncan interjected as Neil, visibly struggling with acute embarrassment, tried to think of a polite reply.

Mary chuckled, but Serena said, "Don't be rude, Duncan. That is not what your mama meant, and well do you know it. I might add, sir, that no one has yet presented Sir Neil or this other man to me. Must I beg them to present themselves?"

Annoyed by the knowledge that he ought to have presented Neil to her at once, in the hall, Duncan introduced both gentlemen rather curtly.

Patrick bowed politely, but Neil made a profound leg, saying in dulcet tones, "Lady Serena, I have heard of you, I believe."

"My father is the Earl of Caddell," Serena informed him complacently.

"Ah, yes," Neil murmured, adding shrewdly, "Do you, perhaps, know of any *other* female here who would have the temerity to wear my cousin's cloak?"

Serena gasped, and Mary exclaimed, "Neil!"

"I was watching her in the hall, lass," he said. "She stood there with a little smile on her face, enjoying the fact that Black Duncan was angry with you."

"How dare you!" Serena's hands clenched, her cheeks grew fiery, and her dark blue eyes flashed sparks of anger.

Neil returned the look, his own eyes smoldering. "I think you tried to make it look like Mary had a clandestine meeting with Breck. I saw that meeting myself, and while I cannot swear it was he, I cannot swear it wasn't, either. In any event, no servant would have taken Mary's cloak, and I have heard no mention of any other gentlewoman in the castle. If you did take it, it was an unspeakable thing to do. You must have run up to the ramparts to wave, just hoping someone would report it to Duncan. It can only have been by the greatest mischance that he saw you himself."

Mary said, "Serena would not do such a thing, Neil. You must be wrong."

Stifling a cough, Lady Balcardane agreed. "I am persuaded that Serena would never borrow someone else's cloak, you know. She has any number of quite lovely ones of her own, so she has no need to do such a thing."

Duncan was watching Serena, and when he saw her relax, his own suspicions stirred to life. She glanced at him and stiffened again, raising her chin defiantly.

Neil said, "If I am wrong, ma'am, I will apologize; but, Mary, before you hand me my head on a platter, tell me who else could have taken your cloak."

Lady Balcardane tried unsuccessfully to smother another coughing fit.

Serena snapped, "If anyone took Mary's cloak, it must have been a servant."

"Oh, no, my dear, not our servants," Lady Balcardane said, emerging from her handkerchief. "They are all quite honest and loyal, I promise you. Balcardane would not keep one who wasn't."

"No, he would not," Duncan said, still watching Serena. He was certain now that Neil was right, and Serena had tried to make trouble. He said grimly, "Who was the man with you, Serena? One of our own? Does he know he might have been shot, or did you even bother to tell him why he was meeting you?"

Serena glowered. "I'm sure I don't know what you are talking about."

"It might really have been Allan," Neil said. "I've heard rumors ever since I entered Argyll again that he's somewhere in the area. Does she know him?"

"I do not," Serena said indignantly. "Nor do I care who he is or where he is. If my father knew how you have been treating me, Duncan, he would be furious."

"What's Duncan done now?" Balcardane demanded from the doorway.

Serena pouted. "Not only does he not want me himself, my lord, but now he is determined to poison these gentlemen's minds against me. He has led poor Sir Neil into making the most absurd accusation against me, and out of no more than wicked speculation. It is too bad, too," she added with a long-suffering sigh, "because Sir Neil is quite the handsomest young man I have met in many a long month."

Lady Balcardane gasped, "Serena! You mustn't say such things."

"What did he accuse you of?" Balcardane demanded.

"Oh, pray, sir, don't ask," she begged, turning swiftly to Lady Balcardane to add, "I know I should not have said that, ma'am. Sometimes, my tongue just goes like a fiddlestick. Young ladies are supposed to be as meek as nun's hens, and never say what they think, but I have always spoken my mind, I'm afraid."

"That's true enough," Balcardane said, chuckling indulgently.

"Come and sit by me, Serena, and behave yourself," Lady Balcardane said, glancing uncertainly at Duncan. "I am sure you have done nothing to harm anyone. Oh, good," she added with relief when a lackey entered with a decanter and glasses.

Balcardane said, "You will take a glass of claret, Neil—you, too, Patrick—although, come to think of it, since we dine in an hour, perhaps you'd rather repair to your bedchambers for a change of clothing. We will certainly excuse you."

"You will excuse me, as well, I trust," Duncan said. "The legs of these breeches are still damp and beginning to steam, as you can see. Come along, you two," he added to Neil and Patrick. "I'll show you where they've put you, and you can have your wine later. You come, too, Mary. I still want a word with you."

She got up at once and excused herself to Lady Balcardane.

"Oh, yes, my dear, you run along. I daresay you and Duncan have much to say to each other after being apart for so many days. We'll dine in the parlor tonight, but everyone else will just wait here until you are ready to join us." Hastily clasping her handkerchief to her face, she sneezed again, then coughed.

When she raised her head again, her brow wrinkled with obvious pain, Mary said anxiously, "You should go to bed, ma'am. I can fix you a tisane, if you like."

"No, no, my dear. Thank you all the same, but not with visitors here."

Mary hesitated while Duncan held the door for her patiently. Glancing at him, she gave it up. When he and Neil followed her from the room, they found Chuff waiting just outside in the hall. "What is it, my dear?" Mary asked him.

Looking important, Chuff said, "Hardwick said I was tae tell Himself that Captain Campbell should stay in his usual room, and Sir Neil in the chamber just doon frae yours, Miss Mary. Not Master Ian's room, he said, but on the other side."

Duncan opened his mouth to tell the lad that he should not call her Miss Mary, but he shut it again. He would have something to say to her about the fact that she clearly had not moved yet, but she would tell the boy how he should address her. There was no reason to correct him in front of Neil and Patrick.

Instead he said, "Thank you, Chuff. I wager you have chores to do."

"Aye, master, I'm off."

The boy took to his heels, and Patrick said, "I must see to my men before I change my clothes, if you will excuse me."

As he left, Neil said with a chuckle to Mary, "Who is your latest conquest?"

"That was Chuff," she said. "He helped me escape from Ewan." She glanced up at Duncan. "Neil and I have agreed that he will not tease me to death about my stupidity in falling under Ewan's spell, sir, and I will not scold him for risking his neck, riding here in such treacherous weather."

"How was your journey?" Duncan asked him, wondering if Mary hoped her husband would not do any scolding, either.

Neil grinned. "Exhilarating. We had the devil's own time in some places, I can tell you, and the snow caught us more than once, but I'd do it again in a trice. There is just something about fighting nature that makes a man feel alive."

"Take care that you haven't overestimated your capabilities," Duncan said. "Nature wins such battles more times than she loses them."

"Aye, but it was not so bad, and Mary's letters had put my mother in such a dither that it was either come and find out whether the lass had taken leave of her senses or stay and listen to Mam and Diana worrying about what she had done."

"By marrying me, you mean," Duncan said evenly.

Neil chuckled again. "You needn't look so black. Lord, I can see how you got your name, despite Ian's always saying it was only because of the color of your hair and eyes. It was not just you," he added hastily. "At least, not entirely."

"It was my fault," Mary said before Duncan could demand a clearer explanation. "I'd written two letters to them, you see. The first was to tell them I had decided to marry Ewan straightaway and not wait until spring as we had planned. He urged me to do it almost the minute they had gone."

"Then you had a letter saying she was going to marry Mac-Crichton followed by one a few days later saying she was going to marry me," Duncan said. With a touch of mockery, he added, "I wonder which one caused the most consternation."

"I've brought you a letter from your cousin, Rory," Neil said, grinning again. "Before you spill that sarcasm all over me, you might just read what he has to say to you. He does not believe that marrying you was any notion of Mary's, I'm afraid."

"Where is this letter?"

"In my bags somewhere. I'll give it to you straightaway."

Duncan grunted. He was not eager to read what his cousin had written. Rory Campbell, as a baron of the Scottish Court of the Exchequer, had never been one to hide his opinions or couch them in tactful phrases. Moreover, he liked Mary.

They reached the room allotted to Neil, and waited for him

to fetch the letter. Then, leaving him, Duncan and Mary turned toward her room.

"I want to fetch my shawl, sir," she said, reaching for the latch. "I will join you downstairs in the saloon."

He let her open the door, but when she stepped inside, he followed her. She moved back quickly, looking momentarily surprised and then resigned.

He shut the door, aware by her changing expression that she had been tempted to tell him he should not be there. But although he waited, she remained silent. The wary look returned to her eyes.

"You have not moved to a room nearer to mine," he said.

"No, I saw no real need, and I like this room. Please, Duncan, I hope you—"

"I know you did not meet Breck," he said bluntly.

"Well, I hope, as well, that you don't really think it was Serena dressed in my cloak," she said. "I cannot believe she would do such a thing. In any case, whom would she meet? She cannot know anyone hereabouts."

"I don't know the answer to that," he said. "I don't even much care, because I do believe her primary interest was to cause trouble for you. No doubt she cajoled one of the herds or some other poor chap into helping her. We know she is not happy with our marriage, and that she thinks only of herself. Now that we know what she is capable of doing, she can do no harm. We will do better to ignore her."

"Is that what you wanted to tell me, sir?"

"No," he said, reaching for her and drawing her into his arms. "I wanted to tell you that I missed you, lass. When I realized that MacCrichton was not at Shian Towers, I had the most horrid fear that he had raided Dunraven merely to draw me away from Balcardane."

"You think it was Ewan who led that raid?"

"Aye, although we cannot be certain," he said, describing briefly what little they did know, and assuring her that the damage would all be repaired. "The garrison at Castle Stalker is not far away, and Patrick Campbell is a distant cousin of mine, as you may know," he said, "so when he received word of the attack, he lost no time in getting to Dunraven. He agrees with me not only that that MacCrichton is the most likely one to have led it but that he and Allan Breck might have sufficient cause to have joined forces against me."

Mary frowned. "That is so, I suppose. Bardie told me that Allan stayed for a short time at Maclean House, and Ewan said once that Allan had told him about my gift. I don't see how that helps us though. Allan has eluded capture for years."

"Aye, and that brings me to the other matter I wanted to discuss with you," he said. His arms encircled her loosely, and he resisted the urge to tighten them. He wanted to kiss her, to taste her lips and test her response to him, but although she felt relaxed in his embrace, he did not want to frighten her.

She looked puzzled.

"When you look like that, I want to kiss you," he said without thinking.

She smiled. "It is your right, sir. You may."

He did, and she responded hesitantly at first, but he was gentle, his lips coaxing hers. He felt his body stir.

Easing his hold on her, he said, "We had better stop, lassie, if we are going to join the others for dinner. We'll continue this later."

"Very well," she said with a smile, "but what was it you wanted to discuss?"

"It's not really for discussion," he said with a sigh. "Mac-Crichton is up to something, and Allan Breck's being in the area and in a string with him does not make me happy either. You just remember to stay inside the castle walls. You are not to go outside them for any reason. Do you understand me, Mary?"

"Aye, sir," she said, making a face at him.

He kissed her again then, and hurried off to change for dinner. Afterward, however, when Mary bore Lady Balcardane away to put her to bed, Duncan remained with his father to entertain Neil and Patrick. The four men talked and drank whisky until one of them suggested a few hands of cards. By the time they decided at last to retire, half the night had disappeared.

Going straight to Mary's bedchamber when he parted from the other men, he was astonished to find the room empty. He looked for her in his own room, and then, on a hunch, in his mother's. There he found Lady Balcardane sleeping fitfully with Sarah hovering in attendance and Mary curled up in a chair, sound asleep.

Sarah moved silently to meet him, murmuring, "The poor lamb just fell asleep, sir. The mistress has been ailing for three days now, but this is the worst."

"Can you manage without Mary?"

"Aye, sure, sir, and she's given me things to help when the mistress wakens."

Duncan picked Mary up in his arms, and as she rested her head against his shoulder, murmuring in her sleep like a child, he felt a sense of protectiveness—or some other, more unfamiliar feeling—the strength of which he had never known before. When her eyelids fluttered, he said, "Sleep, lass. I'm putting you to bed."

He did not ring for Ailis, nor did he attempt to undress Mary, knowing he would waken her and certain she needed to sleep. He put her to bed in her clothes, smiling when she scarcely stirred except to snuggle into her pillow. He did take time, however, to light a candle at the fire, find paper and ink, and to leave her a message, telling her that he would leave for Fort William at first light, riding as far as the Ballachulish ferry with Patrick and the men from Stalker.

Duncan explained that he had learned the man he had sent to Fort William to present their marriage lines to the court had not yet returned. Though his tardiness was undoubtedly due to the bad weather, and Duncan fully expected to meet him along the way, he had decided to ride all the way to Fort William himself, if necessary, to make certain all was in order with the magistrate. He would return as soon as he could. Adding a postscript, reminding her yet again that she was not to leave the castle, he glanced wistfully at the sleeping figure, then snuffed the candle and went straight to his own room, and to his solitary bed.

Sixteen

Ailis, bringing Mary's chocolate later than usual the next morning, found Duncan's note and handed it to her mistress when she awakened her.

Reading swiftly, Mary looked up and said, "Have they gone, Ailis?"

"Aye, mistress, at dawn. Master Duncan said no tae wake ye till now."

Settling back against her pillows, trying to ignore a surge of disappointment, Mary read the note again, smiling a little at the reminder to stay inside the wall. She did understand his concern for her safety, and she truly meant to obey his order. Indeed, she had obeyed it since the day he first had issued it.

Downstairs, she found Balcardane, Serena, and Neil already enjoying their breakfast. For once Serena, clearly determined to beguile a resistant Neil, seemed perfectly amiable, exerting herself to be pleasant to everyone. She was bright, cheerful, and sweet-tempered while the gentlemen were at hand; and, when they had excused themselves, she seemed more interested in plying Mary with questions about Neil than plaguing her with the barbed comments she had favored before.

When Mary had finished, she left Serena to her own devices and went to look in on Lady Balcardane, finding her awake and sitting up, looking better than she had the night before. Nonetheless, Mary knew her appearance was deceiving.

Sarah agreed. Looking as fresh herself as if she had enjoyed a full night's rest, the woman took Mary aside and said, "I do not know how to keep her in bed, ma'am. Seems as if she always feels better when she gets up, but she is so tired, she does not think straight, and this morning the fever is still with her and she complains of a sore throat. She never sleeps in daylight, ma'am, and I warrant she won't sleep again the night. She's ever so much weaker. You can see that much for yourself."

"Aye, I do," Mary agreed. "She needs to sleep." Though she greeted Lady Balcardane cheerfully, the woman's flushed cheeks and feverish gaze distressed her.

The cold that had plagued many of the castle inhabitants had hit her ladyship hard. The poor woman had been fighting it for days now, sitting bundled by the fire in the saloon or in her own little sitting room to keep warm, with her tambour frame and needle to occupy her hands. She loathed isolation, however, and strongly felt her duty to oversee her dinner table despite a fever that eased during the morning hours only to spike again each afternoon. Although Mary had brewed more than one ti-sane of angelica with lemon and honey to comfort her, the cold had clearly grown much worse. Her ladyship's cough was now hacking and deep.

At the first sign of that cough, Mary had given her coltsfoot and treacle lozenges brought from Maclean House, but the stubborn cough persisted. She knew more drastic remedies were necessary.

She had brought the coltsfoot and angelica with her, and the latter, in particular, was always good for a feverish cold. A gorse toddy would have been more effective, but it required fresh flowers, and gorse did not bloom in winter. There were other powerful remedies, however, and remembering the celandine, nettles, and dandelions she had seen during her walk by the loch with Duncan, she decided at once what she would do.

Had Duncan been at hand, she told herself, she would have explained her plan and enlisted his support. He was not there, however; and when she looked for Neil, she learned that he, the earl, and a number of the other men had taken advantage of a break in the weather to go hunting, hoping to augment the castle's depleted stores with some grouse or moor hens.

Since Duncan had taken his usual escort with him, the castle guard was thus greatly reduced, and Mary decided that gave her sufficient reason not to ask any of the men to go with her. She did not consider asking Serena, nor did she want to send a servant to collect what she required, for she knew it would be nearly impossible to describe the location of the plants and she trusted no one else to gather exactly what she needed in any case.

When she realized that in fact she wanted to go by herself, that she missed the solitude she frequently had enjoyed at Maclean House, she wrestled a little with her conscience, but in the end, she decided to go alone, reassuring herself that it was a matter of judgment rather than disobedience. She would be away just a short time, to walk to where the burn entered the loch, and she would remain within sight of the guards at the main gate and atop the battlements. She had no intention of discussing her plan with Jock or anyone else, however. To do so would only lead to argument.

She knew that even the early-blooming celandine would not bloom for another two months, but it was an excellent time to gather rootstock and stems, and the roots, ground up and added to a nourishing nettle or cress soup, would provide a soporific effect that would help her ladyship rest more comfortably. Watercress grew year round, of course, and she knew she would find some near the burn.

With her hood up and her basket in hand, it proved easy enough to slip out through the postern gate. She had feared Duncan might have posted a guard there after the previous day's events, but if he had, the man had stepped away. No one tried to stop her, and she was not surprised after that when no one called her back. Her cloak, after all, had been outside only the day before. Gathering it around her, she hurried toward the loch, taking a side path that she knew would lead her to the burn where she had seen the plants with Duncan.

Woods and dense shrubbery lined the course of the brook as it tumbled down the hillside. Knowing that the cress generally grew at the water's edge, she pushed through this shady barrier and soon found a good patch. Picking enough watercress to make a good soup, she turned toward the spot where she had seen the nettles and celandine. A sudden cracking sound from behind startled her, and she whirled to find herself confronting Ewan MacCrichton.

He said, "When my lads told me Black Duncan left this morning, I hoped I might get lucky. I'd just begun to think you'd never come out of there, lass."

Since he stood uphill from her and towered over her, he looked even larger than usual, but he did seem to be alone.

Realizing belatedly that the shrubbery hid them from anyone at the castle, she felt a tremor of panic but ruthlessly suppressed it to affect a confidence she was far from feeling. She stepped away from him, hefted her basket as if she considered it a weapon, and said sharply, "Leave me alone, Ewan."

"Nay then, lass, that is no way to talk. My lads and I have been keeping a close watch on this place for over a week, and I'm tired. I thought we had you yesterday, but turned out it was the wrong lass. That's of no consequence now, though, for you'll come back with me to Shian and we'll settle it all between us."

"I am married, Ewan."

"Aye, I heard, but unless Duncan's taken to flying, I doubt he's anywhere near at hand now. I saw him myself, being poled across the narrows on that damned tipsy ferry this morning, and the earl has gone up toward the head of the loch with the bulk of his men. It's a fine day for hunting, too. They'll be of no help to you."

"I won't go with you." Still fighting her fear, she tried to sound firm.

He said flatly, "You have no choice." He reached for her then, but she eluded him, and as he lunged toward her, a snowball crashed against the side of his head.

"Run, Mary! Run!"

It was Pinkie's voice; and, at the same moment, a whistle sounded loud and long, the same notes Mary had once heard Duncan use to signal his men.

"Damnation," Ewan exclaimed when another snowball struck him on the forehead. "Come on, lass, *now!*"

But by the time he brushed the snow from his eyes Mary had dropped her basket, snatched up her skirts, and run. Ignoring bushes and branches that grabbed at her clothing, she dashed headlong from the woods toward the castle. She heard him following her, but suddenly, just as she emerged onto open ground, all sound of his pursuit stopped. When she looked up to see Jock Burnett and his men running toward her from the castle, she knew she had no more to fear from Ewan.

Looking back, she saw him leaping through shrubbery near the burn. Even as she spotted him, though, he disappeared. Drawing a breath of relief, she turned back to get her basket of cress, just as Pinkie and Chuff stepped out of the trees.

The boy held his rawhide belt wrapped around one hand, the oddly shaped brass buckle swinging freely, like a weapon at the ready.

"We frightened the laird away," Pinkie said, laughing.

"Where did you two spring from?" Mary asked.

"Chuff saw you go out the gate and thought we'd do weel tae keep watch," Pinkie said proudly. "He said the laird might be on the watch for ye."

"Chuff is wiser than I was," Mary said, smiling at the boy, who was fastening his belt round his waist again. "I never thought the laird would dare."

A half dozen men from the castle reached them then, and the burly Jock charged on with three of them in pursuit of Ewan. Mary set the other two to gathering nettles and dandelions while she harvested her celandine roots.

The children helped, laughing and boasting of their prowess with snowballs until one of the men threw one at Chuff. The boy heaved one back at him, and the battle was on. When the others returned to report that Ewan had had a horse waiting in the woods, a snowball struck Jock head on, drawing them all into the fight.

Mary joined in with enthusiasm, and the warriors pelted one

another until everyone was wet and their hands were either stinging or numb from the snow.

Laughing, she said at last, "Much as I hate to stop, I think we had better go back and get warm."

The others agreed, and they trudged happily up the hill together. Just as they reached the gate, one of the men glanced back. Pausing, he shielded his eyes from the sun setting low on the western horizon, then muttered under his breath.

Mary looked then, too, and felt a shiver that had nothing to do with the cold.

Despite a sheepskin cap and bulky greatcoat, she easily recognized Duncan as one of the leaders of a large party of men riding toward them. Recognizing the earl and Neil on either side of him, she realized that the hunting party must have met up with him near the ferry. She paid no heed to his companions, however.

"I don't suppose you could help me slip in without his seeing me," she said.

No one asked which rider she hoped to elude. No one spoke at all. The six men and two children just looked solemnly back at her.

She sighed. "You are right, of course. Very well then, I just hope he doesn't murder me."

"More like tae murder the lot of us," Jock said dourly.

Seeing Duncan spur his horse ahead of the others, Mary knew that he had seen her. Turning to Jock, she said, "Shall we go inside? There can be no good reason to stand here waiting for him."

"Aye, mistress," he said, shooting another wary glance at the approaching rider. "It ha' been a long while since the young master said ye were no tae leave the castle, and in all the excitement, I plain forgot about it. He's bound tae be wroth wi' all of us, ye ken. We left verra few behind tae guard the castle."

Mary said, "Chuff, you and Pinkie take that basket into the kitchen for me, will you? Perhaps one of the men would like to go with you."

Several of the men, casting worried glances at the approaching rider, were quick to volunteer, but Jock named one and ordered the others to remain.

As the children hurried through the open gate, Mary said, "Tell Martha I said the nettles and watercress are for a soup. She can begin to make it without me, but warn her to set the celandine aside until I can deal with it myself."

"Aye, sure," Chuff said. "I'll tell her. Come on then, Pinkie."

Following them into the courtyard, Mary and the remaining men had only a short time to wait until Duncan rode through the gate they had left open for him. He swung down from his saddle before his horse had come to a complete halt and tossed the reins to the nearest man.

Mary waited, her heart pounding, her hands folded tightly at her waist so that he would not see them tremble.

"What the devil were you doing out there?" he demanded. He did not grab her shoulders as he had done the day Neil had arrived, but he looked as if he might do worse than that if she provoked him.

"Your mother is worse," she said steadily. "I went a short distance to collect some things that will help her get better, that's all."

"How ill is she?"

Relaxing a little, she said, "Her condition is not grave, sir, but her cough is much worse, and I fear her lungs may be inflamed. She cannot sleep, which makes it worse, so I went to collect some of the celandine we saw that day you walked with me down to the loch, and some other things as well."

"Then where is the stuff you collected?"

"Chuff and Pinkie took it to the kitchen to give to Martha Loudoun."

"Oh." To Jock, he said. "I'm glad you and your men went with her."

Hesitating, Jock glanced at Mary, clearly reluctant to betray her.

She said quickly, "They did not escort me, sir."

"What?"

"Since I did not expect to go beyond sight of the castle, I

decided that such an escort was unnecessary, especially with so few men here at the time."

"I thought I had made my orders perfectly plain, madam."

"You did, of course," she agreed, "but I am not a child, sir. I am quite capable of judging such matters for myself." Unfortunately, the memory of Ewan's sudden appearance and her near escape reared its unwelcome head just then, making it impossible for her to meet Duncan's angry gaze.

After a heavy silence, during which she could feel him watching her, he said grimly, "If these men did not escort you, why did I see them returning with you?"

Mary bit her lower lip.

"Well, Jock?"

She heard Jock clear his throat, and knowing he did so to give her time to speak first, she decided that if the bad news was going to come from anyone, it ought to come from her. With a sigh, she said, "Please, sir, don't blame Jock."

"Why not?"

"I slipped out through the postern gate. I did not tell Jock or any of the other men, because I did not want to waste time arguing with them."

"So you defied me," he said flatly.

His voice seemed loud, and she was sure that every ear in the courtyard was cocked to listen, but she could hardly deny that she had brought it all on herself. The gates remained open, and obliquely, she saw the rest of the riders approaching, but she did not turn. She gazed straight ahead at nothing in particular, but her attention remained riveted to her husband.

Forcing herself at last to look at him directly, she said, "I wish I could say that I simply forgot your order, sir, and was thinking only of your mother's health."

"But you cannot say that, can you?"

"No, sir, but if you want to talk more about this, may we go inside? I am beginning to feel a bit chilled."

"Your cloak is wet, and you have snow in your hair, so I'm not surprised that you are cold. We are not going inside, however, until I get an answer to my question. Why did Jock and his men leave their posts if not to escort you?"

The silence this time was so thick she thought she ought to be able to touch it, but she knew that if she did not answer him, he would force Jock to do so. That would only make matters worse.

Balcardane, Neil, and the others had ridden into the yard and were beginning to dismount, but Duncan ignored them. Clearly, he intended to have her answer before he acknowledged anyone else.

"I . . . I met with some difficulty," she said, avoiding his gaze again.

"Come, Mary," he said impatiently, "don't equivocate. This is not like you. Tell me the truth, and tell me at once, if you please."

Again she hesitated, certain his fury would erupt when she told him.

He sighed. "Was it Allan Breck or Ewan MacCrichton?"

Grimacing, she said, "Ewan, sir. He was waiting. He told me that he has been watching the castle, hoping I would leave its protection."

"The devil he has!"

Hoping yet to forestall the explosion, she said, "He saw you ride out this morning. So, when Neil, your father, and the others left as well, and then I stepped out, he thought no one remained to protect me."

She heard the earl mutter, but Duncan's words overrode his.

"He was right, wasn't he, thanks to your decision to defy my order? You will not do that again. I think I warned you what would happen if you did."

"I got away from him," Mary pointed out. "He did me no harm, sir."

"You look as if he rolled you around on the ground!"

"Well, he didn't. We . . . we had a snowball fight."

"You and MacCrichton?"

"No, of course not." Feeling her temper stir, she wondered

if he was being purposefully thick-witted. "The children threw snowballs at him, and I got away."

"You are saying that a snowball fight erupted between the children and MacCrichton? Do you expect me to believe that?"

Hearing surprised murmurs from a number of others, she said, "Please, sir, let me explain. You see, I had forgotten that the trees by the burn would hide me from the castle guards, but Chuff whistled for them, and they . . . they gave chase."

Duncan turned his attention again to the unhappy Jock. "Where is he, then?"

"He had a horse waiting in the shrubs, sir. We were afoot, o' course, so he got clean away, I'm sorry tae say."

"Get some men out straightaway to look for him. They can look for Allan Breck, too, while they're about it. I want them to scour the countryside this time until they find that precious pair."

"Aye, master. I'll see to it."

Mary had taken advantage of the respite to collect herself, but when Duncan remained silent after this last reply, she looked at him in surprise. He was still looking at Jock, his expression grimly thoughtful.

At last he said, "You and your men are all rather damp, are you not?"

"Aye."

"The children, are they wet, as well?"

"Aye."

Silence fell again as Duncan turned slowly back to Mary. "I think you had better give me a complete explanation," he said, his words measured in such a way that she knew he held his temper now by only the slenderest of threads.

Striving for calm, she said, "There is little more to tell, sir, but if you want to discuss it at length, I would suggest again that we go inside." She glanced around pointedly at the interested audience, hoping he would realize that such a discussion between a husband and wife should more properly be private.

If he did, the realization did nothing to soothe his temper.

"By heaven," he said again, reaching for her at last, his grip tightening on both shoulders, "I ought to shake you till your teeth rattle or put you right across my knee. Are you daring to admit that so little did you all heed the danger you had been in that you and these idiot men engaged in a childish snowball fight?"

"I would not have put it quite that way," she said.

"I'll wager you wouldn't! Surely you see now why you must stay inside these walls. Damn it, Mary, he might easily have made off with you!"

"He did not, however," she said, feeling her temper leap and struggling to suppress it. "Really, sir, the danger was not so great as all that. Even if Chuff and Pinkie had not thrown snowballs to distract Ewan so that I could run away, Jock and his men would have got there in time to prevent his doing me any harm."

"You cannot know that," he snapped, his grip tightening. "What if he had had a host of men with him? What if he had dragged you off and thrown you onto that horse he had, and simply ridden off with you?"

"He does not have a host of men," she reminded him. "I never saw more than seven or so, and Chuff has never mentioned more than that. As to dragging me—"

"You don't know! That's just my point," Duncan said, giving her a shake. "Think, lass! If he had had even two men, or one— What if they'd had weapons? Who would have dared to interfere with them then?"

"You would," she said.

The explosion came then, and it was all that she had feared it would be, except that he released her. He took his hands off her shoulders in such a way, though, that she knew he was afraid that if he did not he might hurt her. His fear of that, she knew, was much greater than her own. She would not have put it past him to put her across his knee to teach her a lesson, but she knew he would never strike her in fury. She did not know how she knew it. She just did.

She did not try to stop the flood of words, but she was constantly aware of their audience. Therefore, when he stopped bellowing at her and began talking more grimly, telling her that she would do as he bade her because she was only a woman and needed others to protect her, her own temper snapped at last.

"Only a woman, sir? You dare fling that in my teeth after I have lived all these years with no one but my aunt to protect me! How dare you say such a thing when you and others of your ilk killed the men who once protected me? It was Camp-bells, I remind you, who fought against my family and my un-cle's family, Campbells who conspired with the Crown to steal our homes, and Campbells who brought that butcher Cumber-land here to kill our families and burn our lands!"

"We did not bring Cumberland," Duncan snarled. "We got rid of him!"

She ignored him, too angry now to care if she was wrong. "All you think of is your stupid orders," she cried. "You go in and out without a thought for danger, yet you believe I am such a fool that you cannot trust me to make simple decisions. Do you have so little faith in the men guarding Balcardane that you think Ewan could bring a party of horsemen close to the castle without their knowing?"

"That is beside the point." His tone was curt and his hands were on his hips, but he regarded her warily, as if she had turned into someone he did not know.

"That is *not* beside the point. It *is* the point. If I erred, it was in not keeping my eyes open, in becoming so engrossed in my task that I failed to hear or see him coming. You are right to take me to task for paying no heed, but one scream from me would have brought Jock and his men running. I was no more than a hundred yards away from them, Duncan. Moreover, Chuff and Pinkie—"

"Having also managed to sneak up on you . . ."

"I already agreed that I should have paid closer heed. If you want to scold me more for that, you have every right to do so, but this is not the place."

His eyes narrowed. "I will decide that."

"You want to decide everything for everybody," she snapped, "but you are not God, Duncan. The sun will not rise or set for you." Hearing gasps from her audience, she grimaced with remorse. "I should not have said that."

"No, you should not," he agreed grimly. "You should not have said a good deal of what you have said."

"Perhaps not, but I said it, and though I spoke in anger, sir, I meant every word. I will not let you order me about as if I were two years old. I have a brain in my head, and have long been accustomed to using it. I am not, however, used to having a man around who thinks he will order every step of my coming and going. You try to tell me what to wear and what not to wear, what to think and what not to think, what to say and what not to say. I cannot live as if I were no more than your echo or a pattern card you have devised from skin to skirt!"

"Damn it, Mary, be silent. I am your husband, and since you vowed before God to obey me, I mean to see that you do, not because I am a tyrant but because you are a woman and therefore weaker than any man. I am sorry that your father and the others died, so that you lacked men to protect you, but—"

"She had me," Neil interjected indignantly.

"Stay out of this," Duncan snapped.

"If that isn't just like you," Mary told him. "You begin this out here in the yard with the whole world watching and listening, and then when one of your audience dares to speak, you shout at him to keep silent."

"I did not shout!"

"Yes, you did. Moreover, you called me weak. I am not weak, Duncan Campbell. In fact, I am as strong in my own fashion as any man here is in his."

"Don't be daft."

"You doubt me?" She turned to Jock. "Forgive me for dragging you back into this, but if you fell ill and needed help, whom would you call?"

Jock glanced uneasily at Duncan.

"Answer her."

"They say the young mistress has healing in her hands," Jock said quietly.

A murmur of agreement buzzed through the courtyard.

"I'll grant you have knowledge of remedies," Duncan said, "but if you want to go outside the castle walls, you will ask my permission first. You are too small to look after yourself, lass, brains or not, and you simply cannot deny that women are weaker than men and need their protection."

"Oh, no?" Stunned by an outrageous idea that seemed to fly up from deep within her, she hesitated, wondering if she dared adopt it. Deciding that he deserved punishment, if for no reason other than having berated her in so public a manner, she said quietly, "I am no weakling, sir, and to prove it I will wager that I can carry a load in a wheelbarrow across this courtyard that you cannot wheel back."

"Nonsense, you couldn't do it. You'd only hurt yourself."

She looked at Jock. "Have we got a wheelbarrow?"

"Aye, mistress."

"Have someone fetch it. Unless," she added when Duncan began to sputter, "you fear that you cannot carry the same load that I do, sir."

"Exactly the same load?"

"Aye, the exact same one. No substitutions."

"And if you win?" Showing a touch of amusement now, he looked around the yard, inviting the men to join in his disbelief. "What then?"

"If I win, you will exert yourself to treat my judgment with more respect. I do not expect miraculous changes," she added. "After all, you have spent your whole life making decisions for everyone around you and offering them advice, even when none is required. Therefore, as a second penalty, you will try—at least upon occasion—to seek advice from others."

Again he glanced around the courtyard, but this time his demeanor was more challenging, as if he dared anyone to show so much as a hint of amusement. A few men looked hard pressed, but no one laughed or smiled.

He turned back to Mary. "Very well, lass, you've asked for it. Do I get to tell you what I will demand when I win this wager?"

"Aye, sir." She swallowed, knowing he would not win, but having a few uncomfortable second thoughts nonetheless.

"Good," he said. "I shall expect a willing and submissive wife, one who never questions my orders and obeys them absolutely. I shall further expect you to accept due punishment when you fail to obey me, and to accept that also without question or complaint. Do you agree to my conditions?"

"Aye."

"Excellent." He rubbed his hands together. "Bring out the wheelbarrow."

One of the lads came running with one, apparently having decided that its need had been inevitable from the moment of Mary's suggesting it. Its big iron wheel rattled loudly on the cobblestones.

Mary pretended to eye the barrow with misgiving. Its wheel was wide, and cloth bindings wrapped its handles, so they would not be slippery. She had wheeled many a load in a similar one at Maclean House when more work existed than hands to do it. She doubted that any of those loads had been as heavy as the one she contemplated now, but she believed she would manage easily enough.

"How far must we wheel this load?" Duncan demanded abruptly.

"Second thoughts, sir? You may set the distance if you like."

With a slight smile, he said, "So I shall, then. And just to show that I won't take unfair advantage, you need not wheel it the full length of the yard. Bannatyne, stand yonder by the well. Is that too far, madam?"

"No, sir."

"Good. Now, tell the lads what to load into the barrow."

"That will not be necessary," she said.

"Not necessary! Do you think you can conjure a load out of the air?"

"No, sir."

"Then where will you get it?"

In a firm, carrying voice, Mary said, "Climb into the wheelbarrow, Duncan."

Seventeen

After a moment of stunned silence, the men in the yard burst into laughter, many of them bending double or holding their sides.

The earl, laughing as loud as any other, finally contained his mirth enough to say, "By heaven, she's got you, Duncan. If she wheels you in that barrow, you cannot possibly carry the same load back."

Duncan was not laughing. That she had confounded him was clear. That he did not enjoy the men's laughter was equally clear. His eyes narrowed ominously.

The laughter ceased almost as abruptly as it had begun. An icicle falling from the stable eaves sounded unnaturally loud in the ensuing silence.

Mary gazed steadily back at her husband. "Well, sir?"

"You think you have been mighty clever, I expect."

"I offered a challenge that you accepted, sir. If you are a man of your word, you will not back out now."

Someone coughed.

"You men, get about your business now," Duncan said.

"Willna ye let her push ye in the barrow, then?" Chuff said as the others began to stir obediently. Hearing his voice, Mary looked at him in surprise. She had not seen him return from the kitchen.

"I will not," Duncan said. "You go and help the lads in the stables."

In the split second before he grabbed her, Mary realized from his voice that he had stepped nearer, but she had no time to elude him before he scooped her up and put her over his shoulder.

"Put me down," she cried, holding her hood off her face so she could see. "Whether you make me push you or not, I have won the wager, sir. Put me down!"

"I'm not convinced that you can wheel me in that barrow. You certainly can't if I don't cooperate, and I don't mean for the pair of us to provide a spectacle for everyone, so there's an end to it. And since you have wheeled nothing—"

"Unfair," she cried, releasing her hood to pound his back with her fists. "Put me down, I say!" His hard shoulder cut painfully into her midsection, and the indignity of her position inflamed her temper again. Reaching back to grab a handful of his hair, she yanked hard.

He muttered, "If you don't want to feel the flat of my hand on your backside, let go of my hair and behave yourself."

Knowing that after what she had done to him in front of his men he would not hesitate to punish her before them, she let go of his hair at once, clenching her fists in helpless frustration, glad that her hood hid her face again.

She heard Neil say, "You know, Mary is right. You agreed to the wager. You even taunted her. I say she won fairly, and you should honor your pledge."

"When I want your opinion, I will ask for it," Duncan snapped. "Your cousin needs a lesson, and I mean to see that she gets one."

Turning his back on them, he strode across the courtyard toward the main door, and Mary had all she could do to keep herself from bouncing painfully on his shoulder. His arm felt like a vise across her legs, but it was the knowledge that her backside, riding high in the air, would be the first thing seen by anyone he approached that made her want to murder him.

She could not remember ever being so furious with anyone, but at the same time, she feared what he might do. He had said he would teach her a lesson, and as her husband, he had every right to beat her. She had no doubt that Ewan would have done so under similar circumstances. Suddenly, the fact that she had married Black Duncan not just as a judicious recourse but for life struck her with stunning force.

As he carried her across the hall, she heard Serena exclaim in surprise, "Lud, Duncan, why are you carrying Mary? I heard all the ruckus in the courtyard, and I was just coming down to see what had happened. Has she been hurt?"

Mary shut her eyes tight, not wanting to see the derisive look on Serena's face, or to see her at all for that matter. Not that there was much fear of either from her present position, she thought, not with the hood covering most of her face.

"It's nothing," Duncan replied curtly. "She is not hurt."

Mary could almost hear him add, *yet*. The thought sent shivers through her body, and she made the mistake of opening her eyes when he started up the stairs. The first thing she saw was Serena standing below, in the center of the hall, grinning from ear to ear. "Witch," Mary thought, squeezing her eyes shut again.

They met no one else, and in far too short a time, he stopped in an unfamiliar corridor. She felt him reach, then heard a latch click when he opened the door. A moment later, he kicked it shut behind them.

He stood still for a moment, and despite the lingering embers of her fury, she felt no desire to speak. She was uncommonly aware of his arm across her legs, of his shoulder beneath her belly, and she was uncomfortable, but she ignored these discomforts, too apprehensive of what would happen when he set her on her feet.

She was looking down at a red Turkey carpet, richly patterned in blue, green, and gold. Though she had not seen it before, she knew she was in his bedchamber. The knowledge did not quell her apprehension, but she experienced new awareness, a physical sensitivity to her surroundings and to the man who had carried her there.

"You are very quiet all of a sudden," he murmured.

She did not speak.

He shifted her so deftly off his shoulder to stand on the floor that she found herself wondering if he often carried women so. Before she could voice the thought, however, she detected concern in his eyes. It vanished even as she defined it.

"I thought perhaps you had fallen unconscious," he said.

"No."

"Take off your cloak."

Silently, she let it slip to the floor.

Removing his sheepskin cap and shrugging off his greatcoat, he tossed them, along with his gloves and riding whip, onto the stool in front of his dressing table. "At least your temper has cooled a bit," he said.

"It is not *my* temper that concerns me."

"That is as it should be. I should have put you straight across my knee, lass. My father and the others will be laughing at me for weeks."

She bit her lip at the memory his words conjured up of what she had dared.

His eyes narrowed ominously. "I hope you are not also laughing," he said.

"N-no, sir." She was struggling, though, and could not imagine how she had allowed her sense of the ridiculous to stir at such an inauspicious time. She looked away, no longer able to meet his stern, unyielding gaze.

"Mary, Mary," he said with a sigh, "I had no notion of how impertinent you can be. I see that I must quickly cure you of that fault." He sounded sorrowful, as if he genuinely regretted what he was about to do.

The tone caused her to look at him again, half expecting to see him pick up his riding whip. To her astonishment, she saw deep amusement in his eyes.

That did it. First she gurgled, still trying to repress pent-up laughter; then she gave way to it completely. Memory of the look on his face when she had told him to climb into the wheelbarrow painted an image in her mind that made her laugh until she had to catch hold of a bedpost to keep from collapsing.

Duncan watched her, shaking his head. Then he reached for

her again, gently but inexorably drawing her upright and into his arms.

She leaned against him, weak with laughter, feeling his breath on her hair.

"Such impertinence," he murmured. "What am I going to do with you?"

"Nothing horrid, I hope. I confess, I'm glad you no longer seem so angry."

"I was, though, amazingly. Even Ian could not have infuriated me so." In a more solemn tone, he added, "No man likes to be shown for a fool, lass."

"I was angry, too," she said to his chest.

"To think I used to believe you had no temper," he said with a sigh. "I seem to bring out the worst in you, lassie, but you bring out the best in me. I wanted to throttle you, certainly to give you the skelping you'd asked for. Then I looked into your eyes, and I was lost. You looked so calm, so serene. Serena may bear the name, but she does *not* bear the characteristic. You give the word its true meaning."

"Oh, Duncan, I was anything but serene at the time. For a moment I feared you *would* put me across your knee in front of your men."

"Aye, well, I was sorely tempted," he admitted.

"I don't know why you didn't."

"I don't either. Something happens, though, when I look at you or touch you. I don't understand it, but I can be in a fury one moment, and then I look into your eyes or I touch you, and the fury vanishes. I've long thought your eyes bewitched men. I was right. You are a witch, sweetheart."

"I'm not, either, and I'll thank you not to say I am. Even our enemies never called me so."

"I'm surprised no one has suggested that your gift might be a product of witchcraft," he said more seriously than he had spoken yet.

"Highlanders understand the Sight for what it is. Sassenachs may sometimes fear it, but they soon learn from others that they need not fear me."

"I should think that many a man would fear the woman who could see his death in her dreams," he said thoughtfully.

"They are not dreams, Duncan. When it happens . . ." She shuddered.

He hugged her. "That is not what we are going to talk about now, in any case," he said. "There is still one matter that we must get clear between us."

"I am sorry if you think I made a fool of you," she said, looking at him, "but no more than you liked that did I like being scolded in front of your men."

"Is that what made you angry?"

"Aye, that and what you said about me being only a weak female. Think about what my life has been, sir. My father and brothers died when I was fourteen, my mother long before that, and the person who came to my rescue was my aunt, for my uncle had also died by then."

"Your aunt is a formidable woman, true enough."

"Aye, she is, and not weak, sir. I drew my strength from her. Neil is the only male with whom I have had close contact, apart from the herds and farmers who looked after things at Maclean House, but I never thought of him as protective."

"He's grown some and filled out since last I saw him," Duncan said, "but from what I know of that lad before now, he was not much use to you at all."

"He was younger then, sir, and resented his position. He is chieftain of the Craignure Macleans, after all, but the title is empty. He is a man without land of his own or the power bestowed by a host of loyal followers. Most of the Craignure men died with his father, fighting for the prince."

"That is all the more reason to let me protect you, lass. It's the reason you are here at Balcardane and the reason we married. If you insist on defying my commands, I cannot guarantee your safety."

"We have already plucked that crow, sir. You agreed, however, that if I bested you, you would treat my judgment with more respect, and even occasionally seek out my advice, or that of others, before making a decision."

"I don't remember anything about my decisions entering into it," he said.

"Would you quibble, sir, or will you keep your word?"

He looked steadily at her for a long moment, then shook his head and said with a sigh, "I cannot believe that I have to affirm it, but I will keep my word."

She smiled. "I never doubted that you would try to keep it."

"You won't win against me the same way twice, lass."

"I know that," she said, "but it served you right to lose. You have never accused me of being stupid, but you've never believed in my intelligence either. Perhaps you will think twice now before assuming I don't know what I'm doing."

"Perhaps I will," he agreed, "but don't read too much into that. You are still not to leave the castle alone. I don't care if you are going only ten feet from the gate. You will tell me or Jock or Bannatyne, and—"

"Tell? Not ask?"

"Tell," he said, smiling again. "I'll grant that I've been a bit dictatorial in that respect; however, you still must promise that you won't go beyond the walls alone."

"You are being generous, sir, so I will confess that I knew the moment Ewan appeared that I had acted stupidly. My hood was up, so none of the men saw my face before I got outside. Then, of course, they saw only my cloak, and although they clearly kept an eye on it, since they responded to Chuff's whistle so quickly, they did not try to stop me. I did not think they would." She paused, then took the plunge. "You see, I came to realize that you took no one to task yesterday when someone in my cloak left the castle. You cannot blame them for allowing it today."

"For that alone you should be skelped."

"Aye, perhaps."

Suddenly, she could not seem to take her eyes from him, and the way he looked back felt like he had touched her. She felt vulnerable, alone yet not alone. She had told him that he was not the center of the universe, and he was not, but presently he seemed to fill her immediate world, at least.

He stood for a long moment in silence, watching her. Then, without a word, he went to the door and opened it slightly. She heard a click; then he shut it again.

Turning back, he said, "No one will disturb us."

She swallowed. "N-no one?"

"No one."

"Do you have the only key?"

"Even a key would not help anyone trying to enter from the corridor. This room, my mother's and father's bedchambers, her drawing room, and the library are all fitted with such locks. They ensure privacy when privacy is wanted."

"I . . . I see." A tremor of anticipation shot up her spine. "I am wholly at your mercy then. Is that what you are telling me?"

"It is. Are you cold?"

"N-not anymore."

He reached for her again, but to her surprise it was only to lay his palm against her cheek. His hand felt very warm.

"Your skin is chilled," he said. "I'll build up the fire."

Nothing remained of it but embers, so the task took him a few moments, but she liked watching him. His movements were deft and efficient. Clearly, he did not depend upon servants to tend all his needs. He showed patience, too, waiting until the smaller bits caught before he added larger sticks and logs.

When at last the flames began licking at the logs, he straightened and said, "Come here, lass, and warm yourself."

She hesitated only a moment, then went to stand beside him, holding her hands out to the fire.

A moment later, he said, "Look at me."

Slowly, she turned toward him. "Yes, sir?"

"It is time, Mary."

"Time, sir?" She understood him though, and heat that had nothing to do with the crackling fire raced through her body. "We need not, sir, truly. Ewan knows that we are married. He told me so. And since you are here, you must have learned that all is well in Fort William."

"Aye, I met my lad returning."

"That should be enough then."

"Did MacCrichton say he's willing to forget about you?"

"N-no, he said . . ." She looked away, unwilling to repeat Ewan's words.

"Just so," Duncan said. Putting a hand beneath her chin, he made her look at him, adding in a husky voice, "We are not doing this just to protect you from him."

"No?"

"No. We are doing it because I want you, lass. Would you deny me?"

Wordlessly, she shook her head. A fleeting thought of Ian sped through her mind, a hint that she was being disloyal to his memory. He had been thoughtful, gentle, kind, and considerate, a charming boy who—had his life not been cut short so unfairly—would have grown into a charming man. But she knew that as much as she had loved Ian, she had never felt physical passion for him, and she knew, too, that knowing his family would never allow a marriage between them had kept her from questioning or testing her feelings for him.

A suspicion stirred, that Duncan had been right all along in saying that Ian had attached himself to her simply to defy Duncan's orders. Not that it mattered, for in any event, Ian would not blame her now. He had always assumed that she was capable of taking care of herself.

The man before her was rarely gentle, thoughtful, kind, or considerate. He made no attempt to charm, and he was more likely than not to insist that she was wholly incapable of looking after herself. But just the thought of his touching her, and of being able to touch him back, awakened a delicious fascination within her.

These few thoughts flashed through her mind in the seconds that his hand cupped her chin, but when it moved to stroke her cheek again, she could think only of his touch. His palm still felt warm, although not so warm as it had before he built up the fire. Then she had been conscious only of warmth. Now she felt its roughness. It was not a gentle hand, but it moved gently. One finger traced her left cheekbone, moved to the wispy curl in front of her ear, then to the ear itself, tracing a line up and along its curve, down to the lobe.

"You should have ear bobs, lass. I'll buy you some."

She licked her lips, aware of sensations in her body that she had never felt before, a stirring in its center, a warm melting feeling that spread all through her.

His finger moved to her neck, and she felt two more fingers now, touching just below her hairline.

She moaned low in her throat, leaning back almost involuntarily, arching her neck and pressing against his fingers until she felt his whole hand cradle the back of her neck.

He pulled her to him then, his other hand slipping around her waist, his lips hungrily claiming hers.

She could not doubt his desire for her, but she sensed, too, that he was holding himself back, as if again he feared he might hurt her. His hands moved over her body possessively, touching her as no man had touched her before. All the while, his lips explored hers, tasting, nibbling, licking them. He kissed her cheeks, the tip of her nose, and her forehead. Then he kissed her hard on the mouth again.

His hands kept moving, and beneath them her body surged to life. One cupped her right breast, a thumb moving over the nipple in a teasing caress that stopped the breath in her throat. A finger tickled bare skin at the edge of her bodice.

When she gasped, he scooped her into his arms and carried her to the high bed. Heavy blue velvet curtains hung from a full tester overhead. The matching coverlet felt soft to her touch.

"I'm going to unbutton your dress," he said.

"What about your clothes?"

"We'll worry about them later." His hands were at her bodice, his fingers nimbly undoing the buttons that marched in a line from the straight, square-cut edge of her stiff bodice to the point at her waist. She watched his eyes, but her emotions riveted themselves to the sensations his fingers awakened within her.

The room was growing darker. Firelight played on the walls. The windows, like the ones in her room, were tall, set deep in

the thick wall, and very narrow. Little light came through them
now.

"Won't it be time to dress for dinner soon?" she asked.

"Shhhh." He placed a finger against her lips.

Resisting an urge to kiss it, she kept silent.

Opening her bodice, he paused for a moment, looking down
at her.

She could feel heat in her cheeks, but she did not mind his
looking, for it seemed to give him pleasure, and it stirred more
delightful sensations inside her. When his gaze flashed up to
meet hers, she smiled.

He smiled back. "Don't move," he said.

She had no wish to move. She felt languorous, as if she had
been sipping wine. She watched him carry the candlestick from
the bed table to the hearth, where he knelt to light it, taking
time to put another log on the fire. With that candle he lit others,
two in a wall sconce, a branch of three on a writing table, yet
another on the dressing table. The walls seemed to dance in a
golden glow.

"That's better," he said. "I want to look at you. Are you still
warm enough?"

"Aye."

For once he took her at her word. Reaching for her, he helped
her sit up, then pushed her dress off her shoulders.

"It's easier if I stand up," she murmured, "even easier if I
do it myself."

"I want to do it." Nevertheless he helped her to her feet,
watching while she pushed the dress down over her hips.

She turned around. "My petticoat ties in the back," she said.

He untied it, and the knot of her stay laces as well, but when
she began to turn back, he stopped her with his hands at her
waist and she felt his lips touch the nape of her neck.

Slowly, his hands moved around and up, cupping both breasts
above her stays, teasing their nipples with his thumbs through
the thin material of her chemise.

She leaned against him, savoring the warmth of his body.

A rattle at the door startled them both, but when Mary jumped and would have snatched up her clothing, Duncan stopped her. "Relax," he murmured near her ear, "it's Hardwick. He didn't know we were here, and he's just come to set out my clothes for dinner. He'll go away, and he won't come back until I ring for him."

"Does he know what we're doing?" The thought dismayed her.

"He won't concern himself with that. Hardwick knows better than to waste his time trying to imagine my activities from one moment to the next." He loosened her stay laces as he talked. "How can you stand to be so tightly laced?"

She chuckled. "They are not so tight, sir. I'd rather breathe than boast of a fashionable half-yard waist."

"I can almost span yours with my two hands," he said. "It cannot be much more than that."

Grateful for the release, she drew a deep breath, then pushed stays and petticoat down to join the dress that lay crumpled on the floor.

He said curiously, "Are you just going to leave them there?"

"I am not going to play maidservant just so that you can watch me walk around in my chemise, if that is what you mean," Mary retorted.

He chuckled. "Such a disobedient wife. You do need a lesson, sweetheart. I think you will go without your dinner tonight."

Since she had already deduced that she was going to forfeit her dinner, the news did not come as much of a surprise. She held out one foot. "Are you going to unfasten my shoes?"

He chuckled again, and instead of reaching for her shoe, as she expected, he reached up under her chemise for her garter. His hand felt cold against her thigh, making her squeal and jump away. Duncan caught her and pulled her back, kissing her, then picking her up and laying her on the bed again.

Catching her lower lip between her teeth, she lay still while he untied her garters and removed shoes and stockings, leaving her clad only in the thin chemise.

"We'll have that off now, too, I think," he said.

"I'll freeze!"

"No, you won't. You can get into bed while I take off my clothes."

Since she had feared he might command her to perform the same service for him that he had performed for her, she breathed a sigh of relief.

Duncan chuckled again. "If I weren't in a hurry, lass, I'd make you do it."

She gasped. "How did you know what I was thinking?"

"It's a gift," he said, teasing her. He shrugged off his coat and waistcoat, shaking out the lawn ruffles on his shirtsleeves.

Hastily pulling the covers over herself, up to her chin, she stuck out her tongue at him.

"Don't do that unless you mean it as an invitation," he said, leaning against the bed to pull off his shoes.

"What do you mean?"

"Grant me one minute more, and I'll show you." He pulled off his neckcloth and unbuttoned his shirt, then unbuttoned his breeches and tugged them off.

When Mary realized that he had taken his drawers off with the breeches, she averted her eyes, albeit not so quickly that she failed to notice that he was aroused.

She heard him chuckle again. He said, "There is nothing wrong with looking, lass. I don't mind."

She did not move.

A whisper of cloth told her he had removed his shirt. He was naked now, she knew. She still wore her chemise. Carefully keeping the covers over herself, she wriggled to the far side of the bed.

She felt it shift with his weight, and then his bare leg touched hers beneath the coverlet. She jumped again.

"Don't be afraid of me, lassie," he said, his mouth near her ear. "You have less need to be frightened at this moment than you ever have in the past."

"I'm not," she said, knowing the words were true. Indeed, if she were to speak the whole truth, she would admit that she was trembling with anticipation of what he was going to do, of what they were going to do. She turned her head a little, looking

at him, thinking it odd to find his face so near to hers, as if for
once they were the same height.

Duncan kissed the tip of her nose, and his hands found her
beneath the covers. "You've still got your chemise on," he said.

"Aye." Her breathing had increased. Her hands seemed to be
in his way, and she did not know what to do with them.

One of his hands touched her bare knee and moved up under
her chemise. Her breathing stopped altogether for a long moment. The hand paused.

Duncan kissed her. Then, leaning on an elbow and looking
down at her, he said, "Stick your tongue out at me again."

Still breathless, she shook her head.

He kissed her, lightly, on the lips. Then he kissed her cheeks
and her eyelids, then a cheek again, and an earlobe. The hand
on her thigh twitched, then moved, but to her surprise it left her
bare skin and moved atop her chemise, higher up, gliding over
the fork of her legs to her stomach, caressing her lightly and
moving upward to cup her left breast. She started breathing
more normally again.

Everywhere he touched her he awakened nerves to life, and
every awakened nerve sent waves of pleasure through her body.

A finger touched the tip of one breast, and at the same time,
he kissed her again, and his tongue touched her lips, as if he
tasted them.

Her hands remained still.

"Touch me," he murmured.

"Where?"

"Wherever you like. I want to feel your hands on me."

Obeying, she moved her free hand to touch his bare shoulder,
stroking his skin. Reflection from the firelight turned it golden.
Her hand moved toward his neck. He had left his hair tied, and
she found the ribbon. With a new sense of power, she untied it,
freeing his hair to fall loosely around his shoulders and face. It
was thick and wavy, and it tickled her fingers, then her cheeks.

She could feel his breath against her lips, then his tongue
again, stroking her lips, caressing them. His fingers teased her

breast. She moaned deep in her throat, and melting warmth surged through her body.

Her lips responded hungrily to his, and his tongue dove into her mouth. At the same time, his right hand moved to her stomach, pressing more firmly, inching downward. Her whole body leapt in response.

He shifted his weight, and she felt both of his hands at the hem of her chemise. Tugging it upward, he raised her and stopped kissing her long enough to pull it off and toss it to the foot of the bed.

The covers had slipped, and she reached to pull them up, but he stayed her hand. "I want to look at you," he said, "to taste you with my eyes."

He had straightened up to raise her, and although he had put her down again, he stayed where he was, looking at her. A log shifted in the fire, and the resulting burst of flames heightened the golden glow coloring the room.

"Does it bother you, my looking?"

"No, Duncan." She liked feeling as if his eyes were touching her. "Do you think me wanton, sir, to like such things?"

"Never." He bent and kissed the tip of one breast, taking the nipple gently in his lips.

Mary gasped, arching her back and burying her hands in his hair. At least one aspect of marriage to Duncan Campbell was, she decided, exceedingly pleasant.

A sudden knocking at the door jolted them both. With a sound perilously near a growl, Duncan raised his head and shouted, "Go to blazes!"

"We know where to find MacCrichton, Master Duncan." It was Bannatyne's voice. "They say Allan Breck is with him, sir."

"I'm coming," Duncan shouted. "Tell them to saddle horses."

"Already done," Bannatyne called back. His footsteps sounded loud as he hurried away. Marry wondered why they had failed to hear his approach.

Duncan left the bed and began hastily to put on his clothes, saying with a grimace, "Sleep here tonight, lassie. I want to find you in this bed when I return. We'll finish then what we've begun."

"Is it so important to catch Allan just now, sir?"

"Aye, it is. I want the pair of them now, but I'll be back soon."

Pulling the covers back over herself, Mary said, "I may just stay here then. I don't really want to go down to dinner alone."

"Suit yourself," he said, adding with a grin, "but if you don't go down, they'll most likely think I've beaten you and sent you to bed without your dinner."

That thought, and the thought that Hardwick would come to tidy the room if he learned that Duncan had gone, spurred Mary to grit her teeth and decide to face the family. Only then did she remember Lady Balcardane and the celandine still in the kitchen. Guilt-ridden, she jumped out of bed the moment Duncan left, dressed herself hastily, then hurried to her room to ring for Ailis.

Eighteen

Duncan drew his greatcoat more tightly around him, cursing MacCrichton and Breck under his breath and hoping the horse beneath him would not lose its footing on the slushy track. Bannatyne's torch up ahead, and others borne behind them, did little to light the many hazards they met. More important to Duncan, however, was the plain fact that as much as he wanted to lay hands on the scurvy villains, he had not wanted to leave Mary. That reluctance, he told himself (more than once), had been a matter of wanting to assuage awakened lust and nothing more. Still, he had been loath to leave her.

For some time his men, judging his mood accurately, stayed behind him, but Neil had chosen to accompany them, and after a while he rode up alongside. He said, just loudly enough to carry above hoofbeats and harness jingling, "Do you think they'll still be there?"

"They'll have left a trail if they are not."

Silence hovered between them for some moments before Neil said, "Dare I say that I hope you didn't murder the lass."

"Did you think I would?" His memory of the way he had left Mary made him smile a little.

Neil, eyeing him, said, "I wasn't certain. In truth, I haven't trusted my thoughts since she wrote to say she had agreed to marry you. I won't conceal that we all feared then that the lass had completely lost her mind."

"Perhaps she did."

"I don't know that. She seems content enough, and you seem quite different somehow. Rory said she would be good for you if—" He broke off, and even by torchlight Duncan could see the deep color wash over his face.

Faintly amused, he said, "Don't stop now. Your comments were just becoming interesting."

"You won't like it," Neil muttered.

"I daresay I won't. Tell me anyway," he said, adding with a mocking look, "unless you are afraid."

Glaring, Neil said bluntly, "He said marrying her might be the making of you if she could teach you to think of someone other than yourself for a change."

Feeling his temper waken, Duncan suppressed it, saying, "I can't think where Rory got the notion that I think only of myself. Mary knows better, I promise you."

"So you didn't murder her. I hope you didn't . . ." Shooting another look at Duncan, he appeared to think better of finishing the sentence.

Thought of Mary having relaxed him again, as such thoughts increasingly were wont to do, Duncan's sense of humor asserted itself. "I did not beat her either, Neil. Not that it's any business of yours if I did," he added.

"No, of course not, though perhaps it should be. She is my cousin, after all."

"She is my wife, however."

"Just so," Neil admitted. Yielding the point, he said, "How far is this place we're heading for? I don't know all of these side glens well."

"It's near Glen Ure, where your late Crown factor lived," Duncan said. "I'm told that rather than return to Shian to re-plenish their stores MacCrichton and Breck have begun raiding their clan members' farms, and others, as well. One of their victims, a Campbell man, rode to Balcardane to demand aid. Evidently the villains have got a half dozen men with them, and they take all they can lay their hands on."

"Well, I just hope we can catch them without losing a horse or two, or even a man," Neil said. "Though we've got moonlight, those clouds keep hiding it, and our torches don't help all that much."

"Fall back and ride with the torchbearers if you are going to fret about it," Duncan recommended.

"No, if your nag and Bannatyne's can manage, so can mine. I just hope we find those worthless rogues. Serena told me MacCrichton struck Mary. Is that true?"

"Aye," Duncan said, making no effort to resist a new surge of temper, "and from what she told me, when he cornered her at Maclean House, he wanted to beat her witless. I mean to discuss that with him at length before he's much older."

"I'm surprised that you didn't do so at once."

"I had Mary to look after. That was more important."

Neil glanced at him, but evidently thought better of speaking. They rode in silence for a while before Duncan asked him a question about his visit to Perthshire that initiated a conversation having nothing to do with MacCrichton or Mary.

Although Duncan and most of his men believed they would find their quarry that night one way or another, they soon discovered that Breck and MacCrichton had outwitted them again. Duncan's men were able to follow the trail easily from one cottage to another, but just as they thought they were closing in, they found tracks leading off in eight directions, like spokes from the hub of a wheel.

"They've separated," Neil said. "Which one do we follow?"

Duncan sighed. "We could follow any one of them and perhaps find them all when they regroup, but that may not happen for days." Raising his voice, he said, "That's it for tonight, lads. We'll turn back. Bannatyne, see that the folks in this cottage have food and fuel to see them through the next storm."

"Aye, Master Duncan," Bannatyne shouted back.

"We could ride to Shian," Neil said, clearly unwilling to give up so tamely.

"We could, but I'll warrant we won't find them. MacCrichton is too smart to go back to his lair when he knows I'm on his heels." Cheered at knowing that they would be at Balcardane in less than two hours, Duncan signaled his men to ride.

* * *

Although Mary hurried, and Ailis did all she could to help her tidy herself quickly, by the time she had visited the kitchen to add celandine root to Martha's soup and seen it on its way to her ladyship, much time had passed. Balcardane and Serena were already at dinner when she joined them, and it soon became clear that Mary would have to exert herself to get through the meal with her dignity intact.

From the first, Serena made no effort to conceal a near-gleeful air of satisfaction, and she could think of no way to diminish it without declaring outright that Duncan had not remained angry, let alone done anything to punish her.

As she sat down, the earl said, "What kept you, lass? Duncan left long ago."

"Taking Neil with him," Serena said crossly. "He need not have done that, and it will doubtless all go for naught, but I daresay," she added in a more earnest tone, "that he was still frightfully angry, so it's just as well, is it not?"

"I daresay Neil wanted to go," Mary said, ignoring the rider. Then, to the earl, she said, "I went to the kitchen to see about some soup for her ladyship."

"That was kind," he said. "I'd have gone with them, but Duncan said I need not, and in this unpredictable weather, I don't mind leaving such chores to him. He'll deal with those villains. I just hope he don't beggar me in the process."

"Poor Duncan," Serena said, casting a look at Mary. "He seems to have had much to deal with today."

Fidgeting, the earl said, "We'll say no more about aught else, if you please. Duncan told me those villains have raided some farms. Like as not, he will draw from our supplies to restore what they've lost, so I'll have to keep an eye on him."

Ignoring his attempt to change the subject, Serena said sweetly, "You waited till he left before you came to dinner, Mary. Did he say you could do so, I wonder?"

Balcardane said in surprise, "Bless my soul, lass, why would

he stop her? Are you referring to that fool wager? Because if
you are—"

"What wager?" Serena looked from one to the other, her air
of bewilderment reminding Mary that she had not witnessed
the events in the courtyard.

Balcardane grimaced ruefully, then said, "I expect you'll hear
it all before long anyway." He explained, and then, while Serena
gaped in amazement at Mary, he added, "I admit, Duncan was
put out, and that temper of his can be dangerous."

"Do you think so, sir?" Mary asked, taking care to avoid
Serena's gaze.

Balcardane considered the question, then said with surprise,
"Now that you ask, lass, it occurs to me that since you came
to live with us, he has not been so easily thistle-pricked. He's
always been short-tempered, of course, even as a lad, and more
than ever since Ian's death. He blamed himself, you see, though
no one else did."

"Ian would not have blamed him," Mary said. Hearing herself, she felt guilty, remembering how often in the past she had
blamed Duncan for Ian's death.

Balcardane said heavily, "Duncan said he was not stern
enough, that he should have made certain Ian feared him too
much to defy him. I know he blamed me, as well, thinking I
ought to have controlled the lad."

"No one controlled Ian, sir," Mary said gently. "He did as
he pleased. I own that for a time I blamed Duncan, although
for a different reason than he blames himself. Ian enjoyed going
among the people of Appin. He did not see them as his enemies,
or as enemies of his clan, sir, only as friends and comrades. I
thought that if Duncan had not been so bent upon protecting
him, and not drawn the bonds so tight, perhaps Ian would not
have felt so strongly the need to break free."

Serena looked from Mary to the earl in evident confusion.
"But how can any man control another," she demanded, "unless, of course, he imprisons him?"

"You are right, of course," Mary said. "In any event, Ian died
simply because he chanced to be in the wrong place at the wrong

time. I don't know if anyone ever told you, my lord, but Allan Breck told us afterward that Ian's death was an accident. He never meant to kill him."

"Aye, Rory told us as much, for your cousin Diana told him," Balcardane said, "but it makes no difference, lass. Allan Breck is guilty of murder. I know how passionate you can become in defense of those you care for, but I hope you won't try to defend him just because he's kin to you."

"I won't, sir. He was already wanted by the law, and he fought Ian because he feared Ian would hand him over to the authorities. That alone makes Allan guilty, and I don't hold with murder. I think he killed Colin Glenure, too. I think—"

"I know you still think we hanged an innocent man when we hanged James Stewart," Balcardane said irascibly, reading her thoughts with apparent ease. "You're dead wrong about that lass, and I don't want to hear any more about it."

"Very well, sir," Mary said, turning her attention to her dinner.

"Carve me some more of that ham," Balcardane said to a hovering lackey.

Serena said a moment later, "Now I understand why Duncan carried you in over his shoulder, Mary. I thought it was a very odd thing indeed at the time."

Feeling an urge to strangle her, Mary said, "He was funning, that's all."

"Lud, that seems prodigiously unlike him, I must say."

When Mary pressed her lips together, Balcardane said evenly, "Duncan's temper is a hot flame that burns quickly. We'll say no more about it now, lass."

"As you say, sir, of course, but I thought he looked mad as fire," Serena said. "I'll wager he did more than just carry her upstairs."

Mary looked directly at her. "You are mistaken," she said firmly.

"Oh, I—"

"I said that's enough, Serena," Balcardane said curtly. "Eat your dinner. We don't let food go to waste in this household."

Serena obeyed at last, but Mary was aware of her oblique glances throughout the meal and looked forward to its end, hoping she could go straight upstairs. The earl foiled that hope, however, by saying that in the absence of everyone else, he would accompany them to the saloon. They soon adjourned to that room, and Mary felt no surprise when Duncan's name came up again almost at once.

"I wonder when the men will be home," Serena said with an innocent air.

"Bless me, lass," Balcardane replied, "they'll be here when they're here."

"Well, I was just thinking, you know, that Mary might want to retire early," Serena said. "Just in case Duncan returns sooner than she expects, that is."

"I don't know why she'd want to leave us," Balcardane said. "Duncan will find her here as easily as anywhere else."

"In that case, sir, perhaps you would care to play a few hands of Piquet." The mischievous look she shot Mary said as clearly as words that Serena thought she was trapping her into staying. She certainly still believed that Mary had disobeyed Duncan's order to forfeit her dinner, but she reckoned without the earl.

Mary could scarcely conceal her delight when he said he was in no mood for cards but would play a game of draughts if one of them would accommodate him. "I know Serena will be delighted to play, sir," she said, getting up at once to fetch the board and pieces. She had no wish to spend the next hour or more as the target of Serena's barbs, and although she had not yet decided whether she would obey Duncan's command to await him in his bed, she had a perfect excuse to go upstairs.

"Oh, don't go, Mary," Serena said when she began to excuse herself. "I'm sure his lordship did not mean to chase you away."

Seeing indignant protest on the earl's face, Mary said with a smile, "No one is chasing me, but if you don't mind, sir, I'd like to look in on her ladyship."

"Aye, lass, you run along," Balcardane said. "Serena plays a good game of draughts, so we'll not miss you. When you come back, you and I can have a game."

Mary had no intention of returning. She just hoped Serena would not come looking for her when the earl grew bored with the game and retired to his library, as she knew he soon would. It occurred to her then that Duncan had not considered the difficulties she would face if she tried to slip unnoticed to his bedchamber, but the thought brought a smile to her face. She did not think he would consider such difficulties of much importance even if she pointed them out to him.

Her visit to Lady Balcardane was brief, for she found her sleeping peacefully. Sarah, sitting quietly by the fire, got up, holding a finger to her lips as she moved swiftly to meet Mary. "Like magic, it was, ma'am," she said. "She drank up her soup, and it wasn't but ten minutes later, she declared she would go to bed."

"I am glad of that," Mary said. "If she should waken, Sarah, don't hesitate to give her more. I will nip down to the kitchen now and warn Martha Loudoun."

Finding Jessie overseeing the kitchen clean-up, with Pinkie flitting here and there to help, Mary conveyed her instructions and then went up to her bedchamber.

When Ailis came in response to her ring, she ordered a bath set before the fire, hoping that if Serena did come to her room, and found her bathing, she would go away again. It occurred to her that Duncan might arrive and come looking for her, but she doubted that he was likely to return so quickly.

Nearly half an hour passed before the servants brought and filled the tub for her, but at last she was able to relax in warm water and let Ailis scrub her back. No one disturbed her, but the maidservant made no secret of her belief that Mary was crazy to bathe at night in wintertime.

Mary laughed at her. "I'll be careful not to take a chill, Ailis, I promise."

"Aye, well, it's your lookout, mistress. Just dinna be telling Master Duncan that this bathin' was any o' my notion, that's all."

Ready for bed at last, still sitting at her dressing table, Mary sent Ailis away. It was possible, she realized, that Duncan might not return that night, but she knew, too, that he would do so if he could. He had not wanted to leave her.

She stared at her reflection in the mirror, as if it could help her decide what to do. If he did return and she was not in his bed as he had commanded, he would come looking for her. Or he might not. She told herself that would be just fine, but then, with a sigh, she shook her head and looked her reflection straight in the eye.

"Mary Maclaine Campbell, you are a fraud," she said. "The plain and simple truth is that you don't want to take a chance that he won't come running if he doesn't find you where he expects to find you."

Getting up, drawing her dressing gown close, she peeped into the corridor. Finding it empty, she hurried to Duncan's bed-chamber.

As she had expected, Hardwick had been there and gone. The fire burned cheerfully on the hearth, and the bed had been tidied again and turned down.

Taking off her dressing gown, clad only in her long, lace-edged, lawn night shift, she climbed into the bed, drawing the bed curtains in the event that the manservant returned before Duncan did. Though she was certain that she would not sleep a wink, before she finished saying her prayers, her eyelids drooped, and within minutes after her head touched the pillow, she fell fast asleep.

It was late when the riders returned. Dismissing his men, Duncan went with Neil into the library, half expecting to find his father there, waiting for their report. Balcardane had retired, however, and the fireplace was cold.

"If you want claret or whisky to warm you, get some from one of the decanters on the table yonder," he told Neil as he cast his heavy greatcoat, gloves, and sheepskin hat onto a chair for a servant to put away. "I'm for bed, myself."

"I think I'll go up, too," Neil said. "My man will have a fire burning in my bedchamber, and he'll have whisky at hand, too. Good night, Duncan. I'm sorry we didn't catch them."

"We will," Duncan said.

They parted on the stair landing, and Duncan hesitated only a moment before heading toward his bedchamber. He had made himself a silent wager that Mary would not be in his bed. It wouldn't matter, of course, because he would simply go to hers, but he hoped he would find her in his.

He knew the minute he opened the door that she was there. He could smell the herbal scent she used, and his loins stirred at once. He heard her move, restlessly, and he wondered then if she was awake, waiting for him.

She did not speak, however, and the fire had died down, so he went to stir it to life. As flames leapt high, he heard a whimper that stilled him where he knelt.

She sobbed, then cried out; bringing him upright and swiftly to the bed, where he swept the curtains open. The fire cast barely enough light to see her, but he saw at once that she was writhing, tangled in the bedclothes. Dampness glistened on her cheeks, making him fear that she had caught his mother's fever.

She cried out again and seemed to fight the blankets.

"Mary, what is it? Mary, wake up!" He caught hold of her shoulders, hoping a firm touch would still her, but she tried to fight him, twisting more, and crying out again. Sitting on the bed, he pulled her upright, hugging her tightly against him. He could think of nothing to say but, "You're safe, love. I'm here now. Hush."

She clutched at him wildly, then opened her eyes, cried out, and tried to wrench herself away again.

He let her pull back but held her so that she had to look at him, then forced himself to speak calmly, saying, "It's me, Mary. It's Duncan. You're safe, sweetheart. You had a bad dream, that's all."

He saw awareness dawn briefly in her eyes before she flung herself, sobbing, into his arms.

He could not remember anyone, least of all a woman, ever doing such a thing before, and he was not certain what to do about it, but he seemed to have no choice. He held her, letting her sob, while he pushed the bedclothes aside and eased onto the bed beside her. Then, gathering her close, he drew the covers back over them both and let her cry until she could cry no more.

She was silent at last, but he held his tongue. Though he felt tempted to ask what had upset her, he thought he would do better to wait until she spoke.

Instead, she grew quite still and a little stiff in his arms.

He waited.

"I-I'm sorry," she murmured at last against his chest.

"You had a nightmare," he said quietly, stroking her hair. "That is nothing for which to apologize."

"I've got your bed all in a tangle," she muttered.

"I'm wearing my boots in the bed. Which is worse?"

He felt her relax.

"Tell me about your dream."

She shook her head.

"Don't be foolish, lass. Tell me. It will make it seem less frightening."

"You'll laugh at me."

He did not dignify that statement with a reply.

After a moment, she tilted her head to look up at him, her eyes searching his. "You look grim. Are you vexed with me again?"

"I don't like things that disturb your serenity, lass. Today I have seen you angry, and now well nigh hysterical. Tell me about your dream."

She relaxed again, laying her head against his chest, and for a moment he thought she meant to remain silent. Then she said, "I was in a deep, dark cavern."

He felt her shudder. Her whole body quaked with it, and he remembered the way she had looked the day he had suggested she slip down into the dark, narrow crevice to help Pinkie when the child had got stuck.

"You're afraid of dark holes." He made it a statement, not a question.

"Aye. It's foolish, I know, but I cannot seem to help it."

"Have you always been afraid of them?"

She shook her head. "Only since Butcher Cumberland came to Lochfuaran."

"What happened then?"

"I-I hid in the barn, under the hay in the loft, but I could see them."

"You saw everything they did?"

She nodded, and he heard her sob. "I was afraid. I couldn't help them!"

He stroked her gently. "You would have been foolish to try, lass, but that's past now. You accused me of being allied with Cumberland, but I hope you know it's not true. It was Argyll and the Campbells who got that malicious brute recalled to London. No one with a claim to human feelings could stomach what he did."

"Aye, I do know, but I still see them. The images just come!"

"Is that what you saw in your dream tonight?"

"No, it's different and quite horrid, Duncan. I've dreamed it before, you see, more than once, and each time something is added. Tonight I was at the bottom of the cavern, and it was as dark as could be and smaller than before. I could touch walls all around me but no ceiling. The sides are slimy and horrible to touch, but I'm terrified to move, because I don't know what I'll find. I can hear a child crying. I think it's Pinkie, but I am not certain. Once before, and again tonight, there was someone dead on the floor, someone I know, a . . . a man. I was terrified. At first, when I awoke and saw you, I did not know where I was and . . . and I thought—" She sobbed again, catching her breath with a rasping sound.

"You're safe now," he said, "but it just goes to show that even you know you need me to protect you." When she stiffened in his arms again, he waited.

She glared at him. "How dare you, Duncan Campbell! If you think for—"

He laughed. "That's better. Sit up, lassie. I'm going to get you a wet towel to mop your face. Then I'll straighten this bed and get into it properly."

"Duncan, I—" She broke off, and he sensed that she was reluctant to go on.

"We'll sleep, lass, just sleep. We've waited this long for the rest. We can wait a bit longer. I don't take advantage of exhausted or unwilling women."

When she did not reply, he knew he had guessed her feelings correctly. Resigned but feeling rather noble, he went to put more wood on the fire and then to dampen a towel at the washstand. When he returned, she had straightened the bedclothes and was lying propped against the pillows, waiting for him.

"Thank you," she said, taking the towel and holding it to her face.

He got quickly out of his clothes and, leaving the bed curtains open, climbed into bed, putting an arm around her to draw her close. She smelled good, and he wished she hadn't worn her night shift. At least, he thought, she had not worn one of her foolish caps. If her hair was tangled, he did not care a snap.

It felt good to hold her. Unfortunately, a certain portion of his body clearly agreed, for he felt it stir hopefully. The more he tried to ignore it, the more it stiffened, stirring the covers as it made its desires known.

She moved slightly, no doubt simply shifting to make herself comfortable, but her movement made matters worse. He stifled a groan, commanding himself to control his urges, to have just a little resolution.

Her fingers began tracing idle patterns on his chest. She probably was not aware of the movement and would not understand if he asked her to stop. Moreover, he did not want her to stop. He wanted her to do much more, but after her nightmare and her heart-rending distress, only a villain would demand such things of her.

Her hand slid lower, toward his stomach, making him instantly aware that he had erred badly in not wearing a nightshirt. Since he rarely did, it had not occurred to him. It ought to have occurred to him, though, he told himself savagely. He was a fool, an idiot. When her hand slipped lower, he caught it with his, drawing in a deep breath, trying to steady raw, agitated nerves.

Mary snuggled against him, giving the hand that held hers a friendly squeeze. Her warm cheek lay against his chest, her parted lips mere inches from a nipple. He could feel her breath on it—soft, warm breaths, one after another, after another.

Staring at the tester overhead, he tried to concentrate on the shadowy dark patterns etched in its underside. He could not really see them, but he had stared at them many times over the years. He knew them by heart. Concentrate . . .

"Duncan?"

"Aye." The single word rasped, as if his voice refused to work properly.

"There is something I haven't told you. Something you should know."

"What's that?" His body stirred at the sound of her voice, at each warm little breath against his chest, making it hard to pay heed to what she was saying.

"It's about Ewan, about why he wants me."

She had his attention now. "Why?"

"He's searching for the MacCrichton treasure. He and his father and brother hid it before they went out in the Forty-five, so the Campbells would not find it."

"But if they hid it themselves—"

"His brother notched the tree where they hid it, he said, then marked hundreds of other trees near it, as well. His father and brother died, of course, and now, he cannot find it. He thought I would be able to, on account of the Sight."

"He's a damned fool then. Ian explained to me once that you can see only death, and not even that beforehand, only when and as it happens."

"Aye, that's true. I sometimes have odd feelings about things, though, and folks believe I have healing in my hands. Many attribute those things to being a seventh daughter, but I've never tried to locate something, or had a vision that told me where to look. Ewan believes I can, nonetheless. That is why he wants me."

He was silent, thinking. Her words explained many things.

She shifted her position slightly, looking up at him. "I should have told you."

"Aye, you should. Why did you not?"

She was silent.

"Trusting goes both ways, lass. I'll try to remember you've got a brain in your head if you will try to remember that I am no villain."

"That is why I knew I had to tell you now," she said.

"When you told me that Ewan admitting knowing we had married, you knew that would not deter his resolve to recapture you, didn't you?"

"It would stop his trying to marry me, though, don't you think? He said he wanted marriage because otherwise a question might arise over ownership of any treasure I found."

"You did not answer my question, Mary."

"Please don't be vexed," she murmured. "I want you to kiss me again."

"I dare not," he said, trying to ignore the instant fire in his loins. "If I kiss you, sweetheart, I won't want to stop. It will lead to other things."

Quietly, she said, "I don't mind, Duncan. I want you to make me your wife."

He required no further urging. Though he had been ready to explain firmly that she had been wrong to distrust him, the point was irrelevant now. Without a word, he helped her take off her shift. Then he kissed her, savoring her soft lips, pressing his tongue against them until they parted, then plunging it into her mouth.

When she moaned, he caressed her with his hands, squeezing her soft flesh lightly, then harder, teasing her nipples and kissing them, tracing his kisses farther down her body, then using his fingers to open her, holding her when she squirmed. He kissed her everywhere, exploring every curve and soft mound of her body with his fingers, lips, and tongue, encouraging her to stroke him, to touch and kiss him, and to hold him. When he thought she was ready, he entered her carefully, stroking slowly at first, until her body adjusted to his.

She cried out only once, but he had been expecting it, and he kissed her softly, saying, "The ache will pass, sweetheart. After this there is only pleasure."

He finished quickly after that, then lay back, holding her tenderly.

"Is that all there is to it?" she asked a moment later.

Detecting a note of frustration in her voice, he smiled. "Not quite, lassie. Give me a minute to catch my breath, and I'll show you more."

It took longer than a minute, but when he began again, she left him in no doubt that his efforts gave her pleasure. After that, he helped her clean herself and they slept soundly until morning; however, since he had forgotten to set the clever little lock, Hardwick wakened them both when he came in as usual to light the fire and open the curtains.

Nineteen

When Mary awoke for the second time, to find herself en-closed in darkness, she experienced a flash of panic before she remembered that she was alone in Duncan's bed with the bed curtains drawn again to keep out the morning light.

Reaching out, she touched soft velvet, then paused to listen, wondering if anyone else was in the room. Sitting up, she re-alized she was still naked, and since she did not know where her night shift was, she hoped she was alone. The memory of waking to find Hardwick there stirred her embarrassment to life again. Opening the curtains enough to peep out, she saw an empty bedchamber, and barely glowing embers in the fire-place indicated that no one had been in for some time.

Memories of the previous night washed over her, and she decided she was glad that Duncan had risen and gone. Warmth flooded her cheeks again at the memory that when their exer-tions had caused her to bleed, he had dampened the towel again and gently helped her clean herself, as casual about that as he had been earlier when he had fetched her the same towel to mop her face.

Putting the disconcerting thought aside to open the curtains more, she saw her night shift folded neatly at the foot of the bed, and her wrapper draped over the dressing stool. Snatching up the former, she put it on; and, feeling much less vulnerable, she got out of bed to get her wrapper.

A note lay on the dressing table from Duncan, telling her

briefly that he had not wakened her because he knew she would want to sleep, and that when she pulled the bell, Ailis would come to her. Profoundly relieved that she would not have to make her way back to her bedchamber, she pulled it at once.

The maid brought clothing with her, and was reassuringly businesslike in her attentions. Mary wondered at the lack of question or comment until Ailis said matter-of-factly, "The young master said ye'll be moving in here today, mistress, so in future ye're tae give the bell two tugs when ye want me, and one for Hardwick."

Tempted though she was to tell Ailis she would do no such thing, Mary held her tongue. He was doing it again, making decisions about her life without so much as a word to her, and she was not at all ready to live in his bedchamber.

"This room is rather small," she said.

"Aye, but the adjoining one is tae be yer dressing room, he said. Hardwick slept there when Master Duncan was a lad, but we're tae put your clothes in there, he said, and there's still the wee bed there, too." She chuckled. "He said he could use it on nights that ye were too wroth with him tae let him share your bed."

Ailis clearly believed that no woman would dare deny Duncan his connubial rights, but the minute Ailis had gone, Mary examined the clever lock on the corridor door. Once she had ascertained its movements, she went to examine the second door Ailis had mentioned.

Just as the maid had said, the next room contained a narrow cot. A blue carpet covered the floor, a fireplace backed against the one in Duncan's room, and the other furnishings included a large wardrobe, a plain table, a chair, and a stool. With satisfaction, Mary found that the door between the two rooms locked in exactly the same way that the corridor door did. She smiled at the discovery.

She was not eager to go downstairs, because images from the night before filled her mind again, and her body seemed to come alive with them, making her certain that someone would notice the difference in her. Another, more welcome thought followed, however, that Duncan might already have given her a child. Hugging that thought to herself, she decided she could face anyone.

Going down to the dining parlor, she found Serena reading a letter to Lady Balcardane, who looked vastly improved after a good night's sleep. Speaking at once in a tangle of words, they told her the letter had come from Inver House.

"A messenger came this morning," Serena said with a sigh. "Juliet was delivered of a son four days ago, and it finally occurred to my father to inform us that my brother has an heir at last."

Lady Balcardane said happily, "Isn't that delightful?"

"Oh, yes, how very pleased they all must be," Mary said.

"Lud, there will be no bearing it," Serena said. "I only wish I need never go home, for Juliet will be forever in alt now over her prodigious accomplishment."

"But surely you are happy for her," Mary said. When Serena looked at her blankly, she added with what she hoped was not too much unseemly enthusiasm, "Must you go home at once, then?"

"My papa writes that I have stayed away long enough," Serena replied, pouting. "He says he misses me, but I daresay that is rubbish, since he also writes that Juliet cannot seem to decide whether to laugh all the time or cry all the time. Doubtless he simply wants me to look after her and keep her out of his way."

"Being delivered of a child takes some women that way, I'm told," Lady Balcardane said. "I would not know, for I am sure I was as pleased as anyone could be after each of my sons was born." Her face clouded momentarily, but she cheered up at once, adding, "I quite look forward to seeing Juliet's wee laddie."

A sense of foreboding touched Mary. Wondering at it, she glanced from one woman to the other as she said, "Do you intend to see the baby soon, ma'am?"

"Oh, yes, indeed!"

"My father writes that my brother wants to have wee Donald

christened within the month," Serena said. "He said there has been a furor because of certain unsuitable persons performing baptisms; so he wrote Balcardane, too, asking him to stand godfather to the bairn and to bring the Ballachulish parson to perform the ceremony. You are all invited to attend the christening party, of course."

"Even Balcardane agrees that it is the most sensible thing to do," Lady Balcardane said, "although, as you might expect, he has already begun complaining about the expense of taking a party to Inver House at this time of year."

"He would complain about that at any time of year," Duncan said with a chuckle from the threshold.

Mary jumped at the sound of his voice, and feeling instant heat in her cheeks, she could not wonder when Serena looked at her more intently than usual.

Duncan bent to kiss her cheek. "Good morning, sweetheart. I hoped you would sleep later than this."

"Goodness, sir, I cannot think why," she said, thinking she sounded like a goose. "I am always up before now."

He looked about to say more, and she hoped he would not blurt out why he thought she would sleep late, but Lady Balcardane said in surprise, "Have you not had your breakfast, Duncan? I am quite sure that Jessie told me you ate hours ago."

"I did, but I wanted to know how you are feeling, ma'am, and I found that I had grown hungry again." He grinned at Mary, making her feel hotter than ever. Then he added, "I left my father in the stable, complaining at length about how poor he is and how he hoped Caddell does not expect him to bear the parson's expenses. He don't want to feed the poor man for the best part of two days and a night."

"Perhaps my papa ought to have sent money with his letter," Serena said, "but it would not have occurred to him to do so, you know."

"Don't fret about it," Duncan recommended. "Even he knew he had gone too far when Chuff asked him if everyone in the castle will soon go hungry."

Mary choked back a laugh, but Lady Balcardane did not hide

her concern. "How dreadful! As if my lord, or you, my dear, would ever let our people starve."

"I do think the lad embarrassed him," Duncan said with a smile. "He went all brusque—you know his way, ma'am—and told everyone he would look after them if it meant spending his last groat, that they had nothing to fear."

"Will we all go to the christening party?" Mary asked.

"Aye," Duncan said. "It's to be a week from tomorrow, so we'll leave for Inver House Saturday morning unless the weather fails us."

When Lady Balcardane asked how long they would stay, Mary made a swift mental survey of her meager wardrobe, wondering what, barring her wedding gown, she could furbish up sufficiently to make a suitable christening-party dress.

"Lud, where is Sir Neil?" Serena asked. "He must come, too. Papa did not know of his presence here, or I am certain he would have invited him."

"He's out in the stable," Duncan said. "We'll ask him, but he may prefer to retire for a time to Maclean House, you know. He has spent no time there yet, and he may have matters of his own to attend to."

"I mean to ask him, in any case," Serena said. "I hope you won't be so prodigiously cruel as to refuse to let him accompany us."

"Don't be ridiculous," he said curtly, turning back to Mary. "Have you finished your breakfast?"

"Aye," she said, though he could see for himself that she had not.

"Then come for a walk with me. I want to talk to you."

Serena said archly, "I hope you are not still displeased with her, sir. I thought when she came so late to supper last night that she looked sadly distressed, and I know you were angry with her before then."

The ensuing silence seemed to vibrate. Mary said nothing.

Duncan drew a long breath, then said sharply, "You are a great deal too busy, Serena. What passes between my wife and me is none of your business, and if you know what is good for you,

you will cease your foolish efforts to stir trouble between us. No, don't bother to deny it. I would not believe you. Come, Mary."

She let him take her hand, excused herself to the countess, and left the dining parlor with him. He turned toward a nearby corner service-stairwell.

"Where are you taking me, sir?"

"Upstairs to our room."

She said gently, "That is a matter we should discuss first, I think."

"Nonsense, you cannot have liked having to ring for Ailis to bring your clothes. I already told her to put your things in the room next to mine. Hardwick used to sleep there, before I went away to school."

"Yes, I know. Ailis told me, but should you not ask what I want, Duncan? If you visit me in my room, I will not have to send for my clothes afterward."

"We'll talk about it upstairs," he said.

Talk was not the first thing on his mind, however, for he set the lock on the door before he shut it.

"What are you—"

He silenced her by catching her in his arms and kissing her. "I've been thinking of doing that since I woke up this morning," he said. "You looked so beautiful lying there that I had all I could do not to waken you and take you again. Today, madam, you may take my clothes off. I will help you," he added, casting his coat and waistcoat across the room and undoing his neck-cloth.

She chuckled. "Don't you have work to do?"

"It can wait. I am taking a party of men out later to see if we can get news of MacCrichton or Breck's whereabouts, but I don't want to go hungry, lass." He kissed her again. "I might not get home till late again. I'd have to wake you up."

Although she made no effort to stay his hands when he began to unfasten her dress, she said gently, "I think we had better talk first, sir. I must warn you that I have thought of a way I can punish you for your domineering ways."

"What domineering ways?" He pushed her gown from her shoulders and began loosening her stay laces.

"You ordered Ailis to move my things, sir. Since they are my things, I should decide if and when they will be moved."

"I want you here, lass, sleeping with me. Your room is too far away. I could have them set up the room next door for you, I suppose, but that would be silly. I want you in my bed. We can arrange for adjoining rooms later, or find you one nearer to this one if you insist, but for now, surely my plan will do. Just how did you intend to punish me?"

His hands slid around to her breasts as he asked the question, making it hard to think, so she turned to face him, and to still his hands, she began unbuttoning his shirt as she said, "I looked to see how the locks on the doors worked. I was going to—" She gasped when he caught her hard by the shoulders and gave her a shake.

He said grimly, "Mary, if you don't want to see what I'm like when I lose my temper, don't even think of locking me out. Not ever. Not out of this room or any other where you are. No lock would stop me, lass, not for an instant."

She believed him. Licking suddenly dry lips, she said, "I won't do it then, of course, but am I to have no say, sir? Am I simply to let you order my coming and going, to do my thinking for me, and never again to take a part in making decisions that affect my life? You promised me that would not be so. You know you did."

He did not reply. Taking a deep breath instead, he released her and stepped back shrugging off his shirt, then flinging it to join his coat and waistcoat. Mary remained where she was, with her dress and stays riding loosely on her hips. He stood silently, watching her for a long moment. Then he said, "Come here."

"Duncan, I—"

"Come here, lass. I won't bite, I promise. I'll even admit that you are right. Before I told Ailis to move your things, I should have discussed it with you."

Keeping her eyes fixed on him, she slowly pushed the clothing down. As dress and stays dropped in a heap to the floor and she stepped free of them, she said, "Will you promise me you won't ever do such a thing again?"

"No. Come here."

With a wry smile, she did as he commanded, saying as he enfolded her in his arms again, "I knew you would not."

"Then you should not have asked such a foolish question. I can but try, Mary. I don't make promises I know I won't keep. That doesn't mean I won't try to show how much I value your opinions. It just means that I know I have developed a habit of making decisions without requiring much discussion." Reaching for the hem of her chemise, he pulled the garment off over her head, adding, "Do you object to sleeping in the same bed with me?"

"N-no, sir."

He stroked the curve of one naked breast, touching the tip of it with his thumb. "Do you object to having your clothes nearer at hand?"

"No, but do you understand why I was annoyed?"

"I do, but you will have better luck teaching me to heed your wishes if you can point out my mistakes without infuriating me in the process. There are two buttons on my breeches. You may unfasten them."

After that, their activities continued with a sense of urgency, but she could not complain that he ignored her wishes, for he seemed more concerned than she was that she might still feel discomfort from the previous night. He was gentle, yet demanding, and she found that she liked the combination very much. He taught her new ways to please him, and showed her more ways that he could please her. When it was over, she lay beside him, sated, content, and relaxed.

The woods through which they rode seemed eerie and oddly still under a gray sunless sky. Even their horses' hooves made no sound on the snow-covered track. The trees looked black, not just the leafless varieties but even the evergreens, as if Satan's hand had touched them and turned them to charcoal. The shrubbery was dark and dense. No leaf stirred. No icicle dripped. No sound, anywhere.

The track forked ahead. One branch followed the river, the other wound into a shallow side glen. The river flowed silent and calm beneath a thin sheen of ice.

A crack shattered the silence. Then stillness swallowed the scene again. Foreboding overcame her and grew to terror, though there seemed to be nothing in such a place to frighten anyone. No forest creature stirred, no beast, no hobgoblin, not even a kelpie, the water-sprite that delighted in trying to drown wayfarers.

She had no control at all. She could not speak or make herself move a muscle. She felt nothing, not the horse beneath her—if, indeed, there was such a horse—or the chill in the air. She could only watch, and fight increasing fear.

Her gaze seemed riveted to Duncan, riding ahead with Neil and Bannatyne, all apparently unconcerned with danger. Though she could see no one but the three, she was aware of a party riding with them. As that awareness made itself known, a ray of sun broke through the gray, diamonds fell from the sky, and the woods erupted in sound and fury. Men charged from every direction, overcoming the men ahead as she watched, helpless. Swords flashed, and Duncan fell lifeless to the ground.

Mary opened her eyes to find herself sitting bolt upright in bed, staring into Duncan's concerned face. She was shaking. Her palms felt damp. Her lips were dry, and her throat was parched. She could hear the echo of a hideous cry.

"What is it, lass, another nightmare?"

"Aye, I think so. I-I don't know. Did you not say you mean to ride out with your men to look for Ewan and Allan? Don't go, Duncan. Please, don't go!"

"Do you think it was a vision? Mary, you were just dreaming. You haven't even been asleep long, only for a few minutes, but I'll swear you were asleep. Your visions don't take you like that, do they?"

"N-no. At least, they never have in the past, but it was so real, Duncan!"

"Tell me."

She described it in as much detail as she could remember, and she thought she remembered it well, though she had to admit that some of it seemed absurd.

He listened with apparent concentration, and when she had finished, he said, "Do you mean to say there was utter silence until the ambush?"

"Aye. I know that sounds impossible, like diamonds falling from the sky."

"Both are impossible. Are your visions ever silent?"

"No," she said, shuddering. "Never."

"Then it was just a dream, lass, a nightmare like the other. You had better take more care with what you eat before you sleep, that's all."

"Perhaps you are right," she said, but she still felt frightened.

He kissed her, smoothing her hair back from her face. "I am always right," he said. "I'd offer to comfort you more, but if I do, I'll end up staying in bed all day."

"I wish you would."

"Wanton woman, would you drain my strength?"

She smiled but said, "I'd feel better, that's all. I don't like knowing you will be riding out with your men after such a horrid dream."

"We'll be armed, lass, don't worry. I've told you, I prefer you wrapped in serenity. Now get up or you'll soon earn a reputation for being a slug-a-bed."

She obeyed him, glad to note that the fear was dissipating; but when she watched him ride out with his men an hour later, anxiety stirred again. Perhaps though, she told herself, it was no more than normal wifely concern for a husband's safety. She could hardly deny that she was coming to care much more for Black Duncan Campbell than she had ever thought she could.

Finding that Ailis had moved most of her clothing to the room next to Duncan's, Mary busied herself for the next half hour, searching through the gowns that Lady Balcardane had given her, trying to decide what to take to Inver House. She had become deeply involved in this task when a light rapping heralded the entrance of Lady Balcardane's woman.

Sarah said deferentially, "Begging your pardon, mistress, but her ladyship would like you to visit her in her dressing room. We have been looking at some gowns she thought might suit you for Inver House."

"Oh, how kind she is," Mary said. "I will come at once. I own, Sarah, I have been racking my brain, trying to think which of these will do for such an occasion."

"Those dresses are for simple wear," Sarah said with a sniff. "My lady still has some lovely ones from when she was young. They may not be the height of fashion, but we think we can furbish them up with a little needlework."

Mary went with her to Lady Balcardane's dressing room, where they found that her ladyship, still coughing a little but clearly much improved, had cast a number of lovely gowns out of her wardrobe and onto any piece of furniture that would hold them.

"I think the blue brocaded satin, and the gold alapeen polonaise," she said when they entered, just as if they had all been taking part in a conversation.

Mary spent the next twenty minutes trying on one gown after another before all three decided that her ladyship's choices were correct.

"A nip here and a tuck there, and with a bit of new lace, the blue will be perfect for the christening itself," she said. "Then, if there is to be a grand party afterward, the gold will do very well. We need only remove those faded silk posies, Mary, take some of the fullness out of the skirt to accommodate a smaller, flatter hoop, and find you a lacy petticoat to wear underneath. We shall begin at once."

Sarah offered to begin the alterations when they had removed the trimmings, so while she tidied the room, Lady Balcardane and Mary carried their work down to the saloon, where they could be more comfortable. As a hall boy built up the fire for them, Lady Balcardane took her favorite seat near the windows overlooking the loch, and began removing lace trim from the blue gown.

Mary, drawing up a chair, both to be near her and to take advantage of light from the windows, set to work taking the silk flowers off the golden gown. She thought Duncan would like it. The material was nearly the same color as her hair, and although Lady Balcardane had suggested that she ought to powder it for such a grand occasion, she knew Duncan would prefer that it remain unpowdered.

She was indulging herself in a fantasy, where he danced with her in a roomful of strangers, making every other woman turn green with envy, when Lady Balcardane said, "I wonder where Serena has got to, my dear. She could be making a list of the accessories you should wear with these rigs."

"I haven't seen her since we had breakfast," Mary said.

"She went out soon after you and Duncan left the dining parlor, saying she could tell when she wasn't wanted, which was an extremely foolish thing to say. I'm sure I never said anything to make her think such a thing."

"I'm sure you didn't, ma'am. She is upset about Juliet's baby. Furthermore, do you not think it possible that she still resents Duncan's having married me?"

"I don't know what Serena thinks, my dear," she said, smothering another cough. "From what I have seen of her these past few days, I should think she has set her cap for your cousin, Sir Neil. Perhaps she has gone in search of him."

"Perhaps," Mary agreed, "although I supposed he had gone with Duncan."

"Did he?"

Realizing that the only reason she had thought so was that she had seen them in her dream, Mary flushed and said, "I don't know who went with him."

They worked for another half hour, and since Lady Balcardane kept up her usual stream of chatter, Mary had little to do but listen, add a comment from time to time and attend to her work. If her thoughts strayed from time to time, her lack of attention did not disturb her companion in the least.

When the drawing room door opened and Serena swept in, her cheeks aflame and her eyes bright with strong emotion, both women regarded her with surprise.

"Goodness, have you been outside, my dear?" Lady Balcardane said.

"I have, and what I was doing is quite my own affair, and not *any* affair of people who seem to think I ought to beg their permission for everything I do."

Feeling instant sympathy with the complaint, Mary said, "Oh, dear, Serena, have you suffered a run-in with Duncan?"

Serena lifted her chin. "I have not. Duncan has nothing to say about what I do. He had his chance. But if a person wants to go for a walk outside the gates, I cannot see why that should disturb anyone."

"But if it wasn't Duncan, who was it?"

"Indeed, Serena," Lady Balcardane said, "you ought not to go beyond the gates alone. Whatever possessed you to do such a thing?"

"Mary did it, and no one said anything," Serena said sulkily, "and I . . ."

"You know that is not true," Mary said when she appeared unlikely to finish the sentence. "You know perfectly well that it's not. I went out when you were ill, ma'am," she explained when Lady Balcardane looked bewildered. "To gather things to help you sleep so you would feel more the thing."

"And so I do, my dear, to be sure, and I shall take another cup of soup tonight, but you must have known Duncan would not like it."

"I knew the men on the walls could see me," she said. The words stirred a memory of the adventure her cloak had taken the day before, and putting it together with Serena's unfinished sentence, she stiffened. To cover her reaction, she added quickly, "Duncan was merely being overprotective, ma'am, that's all."

Before Lady Balcardane could reply, they heard a masculine voice shout, "Serena!" It was Balcardane's voice, and the earl soon followed it in person. "What the devil were you doing out there, lass? Have you lost your mind?"

"I am quite safe, sir, I assure you. I did no more than walk a short way up the hill to stretch my legs."

"You can stretch them well enough in the hall, or in the courtyard!"

"It's not the same," she said, lifting her chin. "The courtyard cobblestones are slippery, and in the hall one does not benefit from the fresh air."

"Then, devil take it, ask me or Duncan to provide you with an escort. Who was that lout who accosted you up there?"

"He was no lout, I assure you, sir. It was but one of the villagers from Ballachulish who desired to assure himself of my safety. He said he was not accustomed to seeing young women of quality out walking alone."

"Nor should he be, damn his impudence! Who was he?"

"I'm afraid I do not recall his name, but I can point him out to you in kirk tomorrow if you like."

"By God, I hope you are telling me the truth, lass. I remember that Neil—"

Before he could finish, a childish shriek from the hall startled them all. "Miss Mary, Miss Mary, come quick! Oh, where are you? Where are you?"

Recognizing Pinkie's anguished voice, Mary leapt to her feet and dashed for the open door. Balcardane stood still, apparently too astonished to react, but she pushed past him into the hall, crying, "I'm here, darling! What is it? Is it Master Duncan? Oh, Pinkie, has something happened to Master Duncan?"

"He said tae fetch ye," the child cried, flinging herself at her and trying to drag her toward the door. "Our Chuff's gone and fell in tae the burn. Oh, miss, I couldna get him oot when he fell. He was trying tae catch fish tae give the laird, and his foot slipped and he went straight in. He near drowned, our Chuff did, but Himself dragged him oot. He tellt me tae run and fetch ye straightaway."

"Himself!" Balcardane had caught up with Mary. "What the devil is the child blethering about?"

"It's what the children call Duncan, sir. There was a slight misunderstanding at the outset, I'm afraid."

"Did she say the wee lad was trying to catch fish for me?"

Pinkie gazed solemnly up at him and said, "Aye, laird. Chuff did say we must earn our keep, so we'd no be a charge on your wee puny purse."

Balcardane groaned. "Come, Mary, we must hurry to see what can be done."

"If you don't mind, sir, you go, and take blankets from the stable. I will go to the kitchen, and take Pinkie with me. If Duncan has got Chuff, he does not need me there, but he will need my help if the boy has taken a bad chill or injured himself."

"Himself did say Chuff hurt his leg, Miss Mary," Pinkie said urgently. "When I hurt mine, ye made it better. I think ye should go tae him the noo."

Putting an arm around the little girl, Mary said quietly to the earl, "Tell Duncan to treat the leg just as he would if one of his men were injured, sir. Then, if it's all right with you, he can carry Chuff up to the old nursery."

"Aye, he can do that, right enough." The earl still sounded distraught.

"Thank you, sir. I can look after him more easily there, and Pinkie can stay with him there, as well. They will want to remain together, and although some may think it odd to consider children's feelings in such a way, I have a special interest in these two, you know."

"Never mind what others think, and don't spare any expense, lass. May the devil take me, but I never thought my frugality could result in the death of a child."

"He won't die, sir. Not if I can help it. Now, go."

"I'll go, but you see before you a changed man, damme if you don't."

Mary believed him. Never had she seen a man so shaken.

Twenty

Having ordered fires kindled in both the schoolroom and the nursery, and a kettle of hot water carried up so that she could brew a hot toddy to warm Chuff after such a dangerous chilling, Mary sent Pinkie running for her remedies. Then she set blankets to warm in front of the fireguard for the little cot in the night nursery.

Duncan himself carried Chuff into the schoolroom a quarter hour later as Mary was taking the kettle off the hob.

"Strip off his clothes," she said, "every stitch. I don't know what we can put on him, but he can't stay in those wet clothes. And mind his leg."

"I don't think it's broken," Duncan said, "but he gashed it when he fell in. He nearly drowned. It's a deuced good thing I was delayed leaving, lass, or we would never have heard Pinkie calling for help, though she screeched like a banshee."

"She's a good lass, Pinkie," Chuff muttered without opening her eyes.

"She is," Duncan agreed in a harsher tone, "and I shall want to know before you are much older, just what you were thinking to take her near that burn. For that matter, I told you after your last encounter with the MacCrichton that you were not to go out again without permission. Did you ask anyone's leave to go?"

Eyeing him warily, Chuff shook his head.

"You can talk about all that later," Mary said firmly. "We've got to get him warm, Duncan, or it won't matter that he didn't drown."

Duncan did not argue, carrying the boy into the nursery, stripping off his wet clothing, and toweling him dry. Chuff protested that he was hurting him, but when Duncan would have stopped, Mary urged him to be sure the boy was dry. "There is some linen there to wrap around his leg, sir, to stop the bleeding."

"Do you want to look more closely at it? His ankle is swollen, too, but I think he merely sprained it."

"Then I need not examine it yet. Just put him to bed so he can get warm. I have warm blankets. Have you got an old shirt that we can put on him?"

"Aye, I'll find something."

Pinkie returned with Mary's satchel as Duncan left to find a shirt, and Mary left the little girl to keep Chuff company while she went to brew him a toddy. He still seemed very cold when she carried it in to him, but he sipped obediently.

He was resting more comfortably when the earl surprised them by coming all the way upstairs to see for himself that the lad had taken no lasting injury. "You young fool," he growled, smoothing Chuff's hair back from his face, "I can look after my people here without your interference."

"I thought I could help with a fish or two," Chuff said, looking at him warily. "I didna mean tae fall in tae the burn, laird. My foot slipped on some ice."

Shooting a rueful look at Mary, Balcardane said, "You're a good lad, Chuff, but if I gave you to understand that I think it's too expensive to keep you and your sister here, I apologize. I'm an old fool, that's all, and I hope you will forgive me."

Flushing, Chuff said, "Nay, then, ye mustna say such things, laird. 'Tis right that Pinkie and I should earn our keep. Flaming Janet allus said so, and our daddy would ha' wanted it that way, as weel."

"Who was your father, Chuff?"

The boy shrugged. "Flaming Janet calls him George, but we say Daddy."

"And he's dead?"

"Aye, he died in the fighting, Flaming Janet said. That's why she said it were the laird's job tae look after us."

"He must have been a MacCrichton tenant," Mary said quietly. "Ewan mentioned a handfasting, but he said Chuff came well after the year and a day."

"Aye, well, you are not to worry now, lad," Balcardane said. "I'll look after you and your sister. You just rest and get better now, you hear?"

"Aye, laird," the boy answered sleepily.

Although Balcardane had sworn that he would change his ways, no member of his household really expected him to do so, least of all his undutiful son. Thus, the earl caused a sensation Monday at breakfast when he announced that he would go to Maryburgh, the little town that supplied the garrison at Fort William, to buy a christening gift for Juliet's baby.

Duncan expressed everyone's amazement. "Today, sir? But the herds are predicting heavy weather in the next few days. We'll be lucky if it clears before Saturday so we can get to Inver House." He saw Mary hide a smile, and hoped no one else realized that he was far more interested in restoring Serena to the bosom of her family than he was in celebrating the birth of Juliet's son.

"Faith, lad, I have lived with heavy weather all my life," the earl said heartily, turning to demand of his loving spouse, "Have I not, my dear?"

"To be sure, sir," she said promptly, "you have survived many a Highland winter in fine style, but do you think it necessary to travel so far? Surely, for a lad so young, a wee gift from the shop in Kentallen would do very well."

"Ah, but I cannot purchase a silver christening spoon there. Moreover, would you think fabric from Kentallen's wee shop would suit you as well as fabric from Cameron of Maryburgh, my lady?"

The countess stared at him as if she regarded an apparition

rather than a human male. "Fabric from Cameron of Mary-burgh, sir? For me?"

"Aye, madam. You won't have time to make up a new gown before we depart for Inver House, but I warrant you can find a use for some prime stuff nonetheless, and perhaps a few ribbons and furbelows, as well."

Speechless for once in her life, she gaped at him.

Plainly taking pity on her, Mary said, "To be sure she can, sir. How kind of you to think of that! She can use a new shawl, I know. A pretty blue one to go with the gown she has refurbished would cast all the other women in the shade."

"You both will put them in the shade, my dear, for I mean to rig you out in style, too, if your husband don't forbid it." He grinned at Duncan.

Duncan said mildly, "Do you want me to accompany you, sir?"

"What? Don't trust me to dress your lady? I ain't even asking you to pay for it." He patted him on the shoulder, adding, "You have matters to attend to here, lad. Moreover, with Sir Neil here, one of us must act as host. I don't want Caddell accusing me of allowing his daughter to be taken advantage of under my roof."

Neil blushed fiery red, making Duncan glad that Serena had not joined them yet in the breakfast room. Exchanging a glance with Mary, he said, "I'll stay then. There are certainly things I must attend to, since we will be gone for several days."

"Then you won't object if I choose for Mary, too?"

"No, sir, certainly not. Choose something pink."

Balcardane snorted, turning to Mary. "Have you any preferences, lass?"

Smiling, she said, "None at all, sir. I trust your judgment completely. How very kind you are."

"Tush, now," the earl said, coloring. "I am nothing of the sort. Where are young Chuff and that small shadow of his this morning?"

"They had their breakfast in the schoolroom," Mary said. "Chuff is still not up to dashing about, so Pinkie is bearing him company. The schoolroom is warm, and Duncan agreed that he would be more comfortable there than on his pallet."

"Duncan was right. I like the thought of children in that schoolroom again. There is something about young Chuff, too, that makes him seem to belong up there amongst books and such like, rather than in the servants' quarters."

"Well, don't put that idea in his head," Duncan said. "Frustration and trouble are all that lie ahead of him if he develops notions above his station in life."

"Aye, I know, but if he goes on the way he's begun, dashed if I won't do what I can to see that he amounts to something when he grows up. No reason he can't be educated, you know. Look at James of the—" He broke off, looking ruefully at Mary. "Sorry, lass, spoke without thinking."

"Don't apologize, sir," Mary said. "Despite his unfortunate end, James is an excellent pattern card for Chuff to follow, for he took every opportunity to better himself and was much respected in Appin. If Chuff could do as well, he could grow up to be very proud of himself."

"Well, I don't see why he shouldn't," Balcardane said.

Duncan said, "When do you want to leave, sir?"

"I've already told them to hitch up a team to the coach."

"You'll not ride, then."

"Nay, lad, I'm wiser than that. Let the coachman freeze his whiskers off. I'll stay cozy and warm with furs piled over me and hot bricks at my feet."

Lady Balcardane said, "Can you make Maryburgh today?"

He chuckled. "More like tomorrow, I'm thinking. It's all of fifteen miles or more, and in such weather as they are predicting . . ."

"You don't want to get caught in a blizzard," Duncan said.

"Nay, I'll take care. I'll pass the night with MacLachlan at Coruanan. He's always got horses he wants to sell me, so he'll be right glad to give me a bed."

"Are you leaving us, my lord?" Serena stood on the threshold in an elegant blue round gown. She had hesitated, Duncan noted, until all eyes turned her way.

He said dryly, "We had begun to think you were going to lie abed all day."

"I couldn't sleep. I want chocolate," she added when Jessie entered from the passageway just then. "Fetch me some hot, straightaway, Jessie."

"Aye, mistress." The maid hurried away.

Serena took her place at the table, smiling at Balcardane. "You did not answer, sir. Do you leave us?"

Before he could reply, Lady Balcardane said, "He has sprung a most delightful surprise, Serena, dear. He means to travel all the way to Maryburgh to buy your new wee nephew a silver christening spoon."

"And to buy her ladyship a new dress length," Balcardane put in cheerfully. "Do you want me to bring you anything, puss?"

Serena's eyes opened wide. "Good gracious, sir, I never thought you—"

"She is amazed by your kindness, my lord," Neil interjected swiftly, "but I warrant there is little that Lady Serena wants that she does not already possess."

Serena tilted her head and said saucily, "What very pretty manners you have, Sir Neil. Is it your general habit to interrupt ladies when they are speaking?"

"Only ladies whose tongues skirl like bagpipes," he said, smiling lazily at her. "That's a most becoming gown you've chosen this morning."

"Do you like it? I rather thought you would. It is Duncan's favorite."

"Then I am right to admire it," Neil said. "Duncan's taste is impeccable."

"You flatter me," Duncan said, adding untruthfully, "I don't recall seeing that dress before, Serena. Are you sure that I have?"

"Good gracious, sir, I have been here nigh onto two months now. I warrant you have seen every stitch I own."

"Oh, surely not every stitch," Lady Balcardane said, chuckling. "Even Duncan is not so forgetful of his manners as to pry into your unmentionables, my dear. As a matter of fact, though, Duncan, I do recall your having complimented Serena not long ago on that very gown. Of course, it may have been another of the same color, but I distinctly remember that you said something about those cerulean ribbons. So becoming with her lovely eyes, I think, but it might be that she wore those same ribbons with another gown. Do you think that might be the case, Serena? I never can remember, myself, which ribbons my Sarah puts with which dresses, for I am sure she would never turn me out looking a dowdy—except insofar as my gowns have hitherto been sadly out of fashion—and that is all that matters. But I must not complain, must I, for here is Balcardane, promising to provide me with a fine new gown to make up after the christening, and Mary kind enough to say that with no more than a new shawl I shall put everyone else in the shade."

"Well, if Mary said that—"

"She was very likely right," Neil said quickly, adding to Balcardane, "If you have already ordered your coach, sir, perhaps . . ." He paused pointedly.

"Right you are, lad. Mustn't keep the horses standing. 'Tis likely their hooves will freeze right to the ground, and then where should I be?"

"I'll walk out with you," Duncan said, pushing back his chair.

"Excellent," Balcardane said, standing. Smiling at Mary, he added, "You run up and tell those children I mean to bring them each a wee present from town. That will give them something to think about these next few days."

"Aye, sir, I'll tell them, and thank you."

Mary watched the two men go, then turned her attention back to her breakfast. Neil and Serena continued to engage each other with verbal swords, while Lady Balcardane maintained her usual gentle flow of commentary, to which she seemed to expect no particular response. Mary was able to keep half an ear on what she was saying, enough to murmur appropriate noises in the appropriate places, but the exercise was not strenuous enough to interrupt her thoughts or her breakfast.

She assumed that Neil and Serena enjoyed their prickly sparring, and for the most part she had no objection to it. At least, she thought, Neil's arrival had occupied Serena's thoughts sufficiently to keep her from making more trouble.

When she had finished eating, she waited until Lady Balcardane came to a pause in her discourse, then said, "Did you not say that you want to write some letters, ma'am? I will accompany you to your sitting room if you like."

"Yes, indeed, for I promised several people that I would tell them the instant Juliet's son arrived—although, of course, I had no assurance that he would be a boy—but somehow I have not yet seemed to get around to those letters. I am feeling much more the thing today, however, so I must write to Ellen Campbell, and to . . ."

Going right on with her list, she got up from the table and accepted Mary's arm as they left the room together, then broke off in the corridor to say, "You don't suppose we ought to have waited for Serena, do you, my dear? I keep forgetting, but perhaps her mama would not approve of her being left alone with Sir Neil."

"Serena can take care of herself, ma'am, and so can Neil. I don't see why you should put yourself out at this juncture for either one of them."

"Well, if you are quite sure."

Mary chuckled. "You could ask Jessie to remain in the dining parlor with them if you are reluctant to leave them alone."

"Oh, no," Lady Balcardane exclaimed. "How Serena would hate that!"

"Just so, ma'am. I think you may rest easy. And pray, ma'am, do try to rest a bit today. Shall I light your candles or fetch your writing desk?"

"No, no, I shall sit at the table to write, I believe."

"Then I'll leave you to your task while I look in on the children," Mary said.

She found Pinkie and Chuff playing spillikins by the school-room fire. They looked up with smiles when she entered.

"We've still got our own fire," Pinkie said happily, getting to her feet. "We've had one for three days now."

"So you have," Mary agreed. "How do you feel today, Chuff?"

"I'm gleg enough," the little boy said stoutly. "I tellt that chappie Hardwick that I didna need tae stay indoors the day, but he wadna tak' tellin'."

"I do think you would be wiser to keep to your couch today," Mary said with a speaking look.

Chuff regarded her sagely. "Is Himself still in a pelter wi' me, then? He ha' said naught else, so I hoped he had forgot."

"You took a foolish risk, Chuff. He understands that you meant well, but you disobeyed him. Master Duncan does not take kindly to disobedience."

Pinkie shook her head, watching Chuff with wide and worried eyes.

He reached out and patted her hand. "Dinna fash yersel', lass. Let the tow gang wi' the bucket."

Mary chuckled. "You must not teach her such phrases, Chuff. He means to say that you must let matters take their course, Pinkie, and however he says it, his advice is sound. He will have a few unpleasant minutes with Master Duncan before he can put this all behind him, but I have brought you both welcome news, too. His lordship has gone to Maryburgh in his coach, and he said to tell you both that he will bring you each a wee gift from town."

"Will he, then?" Chuff said. "That's fine, that is. I never had a gift afore."

"Coo," said Pinkie. "What will he bring us?"

"You'll see when he returns," Mary said. "In the meantime, Chuff, you must be a good boy. If you like, I will read you both a story, and later, when Jessie brings your dinner, you can eat here by the fire again."

"And Himself?" Chuff spoke casually, but he did not fool Mary.

Gently, she said, "I don't know, Chuff. He will either come to you here or send for you. In either case, he won't eat you, you know."

"Aye, so ye say." Chuff sighed heavily, and Mary, hiding a smile, turned away to find a story to read them.

When Jessie came up with their midday meal, Mary left them and went outside in search of Duncan, finding him in the stable, talking to one of his men.

He greeted her with a smile. "Your cheeks are rosy, lass, but I'll warrant your feet are cold in those thin boots."

"They are warm enough, sir. May I speak privately with you?"

"Aye, of course." He dismissed the man and put an arm around her. "Do you want to walk, or shall we go into the house?"

"I'd like to walk. It feels good to breathe out here."

"Enjoy it while you can. Those clouds yonder are brewing up a blizzard. I just hope my father doesn't drive straight into it."

"He will watch the sky, sir. He is not a fool."

"No, but I always worry when he takes the coach. The ferry men at Ballachulish are accustomed enough to taking heavy loads across, but I still fret whenever I'm not at hand to see that they handle the thing properly."

"You fret, sir, whenever you cannot order everything to your liking."

He chuckled. "Perhaps you're right, but I have been trying not to act the ogre, lass. Have you come out to tell me I've failed the test again somehow?"

"No, sir, I came to ask you if you won't please be gentle with Chuff. He truly did not mean to vex you, although he did disobey your order. He did it because he thought only of pleasing your father. He is just a child, and he misunderstood him."

"Nevertheless," Duncan said, "he must learn obedience. If he grows up thinking he can ignore orders and go his own way, he is bound to learn his error in a much harsher way than I will teach it to him."

Mary swallowed hard. "Please, sir, he won't do it again, you know. It is not a misdeed anyone is likely to repeat, and he has paid a frightening price already."

"Mary, look at me." His hand was gentle on her shoulder as he turned her to face him, and to her surprise, she saw that he was amused. "Do I look like the sort of man who would beat a child to teach him obedience?"

"You threatened often to thrash Ian," she said. "Did you never do so?"

The amusement disappeared, and she nearly regretted her question when she saw the pain she had caused him, but she forced herself to hold his gaze.

Stiffly, he said, "I cannot say I never struck Ian. We were brothers, and I thought I knew what was best for him. You know my temper. So did he. He rarely provoked me to violence, but he felt the rough edge of my tongue more than once."

"Rather frequently, I think."

"Yes. I was wrong, Mary, and I treated him badly at times, but I never did him any real harm. Moreover, he was eight years younger than I, not twenty like Chuff is. I will make it plain to the lad that he must not fish an icy stream again until he is much bigger and stronger, but that is all I mean to do this time."

"This time?"

"He is a mischievous lad, sweetheart, so I am not going to promise never to skelp him. The fact is that I, or one of the other men, probably will occasionally, but today you can be sure that I'll do no more than talk to him."

"Then do it quickly, sir. He'll be uneasy till he knows how angry you are."

"Well, I won't say he doesn't deserve to worry, but I'll speak to him this afternoon. Now, come and walk with me to the loch. I want to see if any ice has formed yet."

She enjoyed their walk, and whatever passed between him and Chuff later that afternoon, she did not know, for neither of them spoke of it afterward. Chuff seemed relieved, however, and he was up and about the next day as full of energy as ever, so she assumed that Duncan had not been too harsh with him.

The predicted storm set in that evening, dropping a foot or more of fresh snow, and making them all worry about whether Balcardane would reach Maryburgh the following day or not.

On the third day, when the sky cleared and the temperatures warmed considerably, Duncan delighted Chuff by giving him a telescope and installing him in Serena's bedchamber at the top of the tower, where he could see across to the Lochaber road and watch for the returning coach. Another day passed, however, before Pinkie, who had been keeping Chuff company during this special mission, came pelting down the stairs to tell Mary that he had seen the coach.

" 'Tis on the far shore, our Chuff says, and the ferry be a-coming tae this side, so it will be a time and all, our Chuff says, afore the laird crosses over."

Duncan was out riding with some of his men, and Neil and Serena had taken advantage of the improved weather to go for a walk. Mary had scarcely set foot outside the castle since the day she had walked to the loch shore with Duncan, and she decided at once that she had remained inside entirely too long.

"Quickly, Pinkie, fetch your boots and meet me in the hall. We'll walk to meet his lordship's carriage."

"Will Chuff come, too?"

"No, darling, not this time. You and I will get one of Jock's men to go with us, but Chuff should rest his leg at least one more day."

Jock received her request for an escort with wary hesitation. "I could send Wull with a pistol, I expect," he said, "but I doot that I should, mistress."

"Master Duncan said only that I should not go out alone, Jock," she reminded him, "and we are bound to meet his lordship quite soon. It's only a half hour's walk, after all. We should meet the coach before we reach Ballachulish."

Jock agreed then, but although Wull did not join them as quickly as Mary had hoped, they did not meet the coach. After they had passed through the village, she increased their pace. As they strode briskly along, their feet crunching with each step, she listened for an approaching vehicle, but all she heard were occasional bird songs and the cry of a lone gull soaring overhead. Once she could see the north shore, she realized the ferry had been delayed. Not until she and the others reached the forested area just east of the narrows did it begin to drift away from the shore.

Pinkie said, "Isna that the ferry coming the noo?"

"Aye, it is," Wull replied.

"If we walk quickly," Mary said to the child, "we can meet his lordship when it lands and see what he brought you." Hurrying now, she kept her eyes on the snowbound roadway, so as not to slip, and held tight to the little girl's hand.

Suddenly, Pinkie slowed. "Mistress," she said in an odd voice.

Wull gasped.

Mary looked at them. "What is it?"

Pinkie said, "I'm thinking that ferry looks a wee bit queerish."

"Mercy on us," Mary murmured, seeing at once what the child meant and feeling her heart leap to her throat. The ferry platform was listing, and it looked to her as if the coach atop it was rolling. The two ferrymen had dropped their poles, and were straining to hold the heavy vehicle, but it moved slowly, inexorably, toward the edge, its shifting weight causing the platform to list even more.

Striving to remain calm, Mary said, "Run back to the village, Wull, just as fast as you can, and tell the first person you see to bring help at once. They will need ropes, men, and horses. Don't wait for them, but go straight on to the castle and tell the men the ferry is sinking. Tell them to hurry!"

"But his lordship—"

"He will be quite all right," Mary said firmly. "Run now, and don't look back. You must run faster than you have ever run in your life. Go!"

Wull did not question her order but left at a dash. Turning back toward the landing, Mary caught up her skirts and ran, too, knowing the effort was futile, that there would be little, if anything, she could do. She knew that Pinkie was right behind her and wished she could have sent her with Wull. She had not wanted to burden him, however, and hoped now only that the child would see nothing horrid.

So intently was she watching the drama unfold on the water that she nearly missed seeing movement above her on the hillside, but some instinct made her glance up, and she saw horsemen emerging from the Lettermore Woods. Recognizing their leader at once, she screamed, "Duncan, hurry!"

He had already spurred his mount and, with the other riders, plunged down the steep track at a dangerous pace. Mary reached the landing at nearly the same time they did, to find one man alone on the landing stage, twisting his hands.

She said, "Is there nothing we can do?"

"Nay, mistress, the rope did freeze right up and snap, but they was fine till the laird's coach begun tae shift. Ay-de-mi, there she goes!"

"Give me that rope," Duncan snapped from his saddle, indicating a coil on the landing stage. "Pinkie, get back," he added harshly. "This is no place for you."

"Bless ye, Master Duncan," the man on the dock said, "that rope isna long enough tae do a lick o' good."

"Mary, quickly, hand it to me!"

Snatching up the coil, she handed it up to him and caught Pinkie's hand to draw her back off the landing. "What will you do, sir?"

He did not answer, and with her heart in her mouth, she watched him urge his horse right into the water until it was swimming with him. At that moment, coach, horses, and ferry slid under water. Clapping a hand over her mouth to keep from screaming, Mary turned to the four men who had been riding with Duncan. "Don't just stand there, you! Go with him. He will need your help."

For the next half hour, she watched with Pinkie, her spirits sinking more with each passing minute. People came from Ballachulish village, carrying blankets and ropes, and the men did what they could to help, but many could not swim, and there was nothing they could do but shout encouragement and help with the ropes.

They saved the horses, and one of the men whom Mary had ordered to join Duncan rescued one of the ferry men, but the other disappeared after frantically splashing about for some time and she did not see him again. Pinkie remained silent.

Duncan and his men managed to tie ropes to the coach, but when Mary saw him slide off his horse into the water, she had all she could do not to scream at him to get back on. She could see what he was trying to do, but she could not believe he would succeed. A village woman tried to draw her away, but she said fiercely, "I'm staying. That is my husband out there. Take the child, though, and thank you."

Other men arrived with more ropes, and before long, the entire top of the coach rose into view. Though she knew that a relatively short time had passed, it seemed like hours before Duncan emerged with Balcardane in his grasp. Men reached to help, and they passed the earl hand by hand to the shore. Mary rushed to him, snatching a blanket from an onlooker to wrap him in.

Balcardane's face was blue and mottled. At first she thought he was dead, but then she saw his chest heave. A moment later, Duncan knelt at her side, dripping icy water, and she could hear his teeth chattering. "Get more blankets," she snapped, "and one for yourself, as well. Do you want to perish of the cold?"

"Gently, lass," he said. "I won't freeze, but he was under a long while."

"He still breathes."

"Aye, there was air trapped for a time in the top of the coach, and he had the sense to breathe it, I think, but he wasn't breathing when I first hauled him out. Can you help him?"

"Oh, Duncan, I don't know! We *must* get him warm, and there is not so much as a hut nearby. Can your men build a fire?"

"Aye, they can, but if we can get him on a horse, we can hustle him home to his own bed, or at least to the village."

Leaving him to make any arrangement he could, Mary turned

back to Balcardane and saw that his eyes were open. "Mary, lass, I'm spent," he muttered, gasping for air and shivering violently.

"Please, sir, stay with us," she said, gulping as she piled blankets atop him and tried to rub warmth into his icy hands. "We'll do everything we can for you."

"Don't let them leave the coach long in the water. The fabrics will spoil."

"Don't fret about them, sir. Please, don't. You are far more important. Keep breathing. They are going to find a way to get you inside somewhere and warm. You'll soon be as right as rain again."

"You're . . . wrong, lass," he gasped. "I'm . . . f-for it. I c-can scarcely t-talk for this damned shaking, which I c-cannot control."

"You will not die," she said fiercely, flinging herself across him, trying to press warmth into him with her body. "Come, everyone," she cried. "If you are dry, come down here with us and use your bodies to help me get him warm!"

Though some hesitated, others moved quickly to help her, and willing warm bodies soon surrounded the earl.

"There, you see," Mary murmured close to his ear. "You will live to see your godson, and later a grandchild if we're lucky. Please, you must live, sir."

He murmured something, and she was sure she knew what it was. "Aye," she said, hoping she spoke truly. "You will have a grandchild come summer, sir. Duncan does not know, only you. It's only a strong feeling now, the sort I have learned to trust. I wanted to wait to be certain, but you should know."

In a surprisingly firm voice, he said, "The children's presents, Mary. They are in the coach, too, but there is something in my pocket for Duncan. He'll know what it is. Take care that he don't let it rust."

"You will tell him yourself. Did you hear what I told you before?"

"Aye." His voice was weaker. "You're a . . . good lass. I wish he had f-found you long ago." A harsh rattle sounded in his throat.

Recognizing the sound, she cried, "No, you mustn't!" Determined not to let him die, she shook him. "Breathe! Oh, please, sir, they are coming for you now. Breathe!" She was still shaking him when Duncan pulled her gently away.

Twenty-one

The party accompanying Balcardane's body met Neil and others from the castle along the way, and by the time they reached Balcardane, the crowd had grown larger. Other people they met had turned to walk with them, many, Duncan knew, fearing in the old way that if they did not, they, too, would die soon.

Although he had stripped off what he could of his wet clothing and borrowed what garments his men had been able to spare, he was still wet and cold; but, riding at the head of the procession, he ignored the discomfort. He had taken Mary up before him, and Bannatyne, just behind them, held the silent Pinkie. The others followed.

Duncan was pleased that Mary held her head high, although she was clearly fighting back tears. Otherwise, he felt numb, as if his mind could not take in what had happened. In his free hand, he clutched the watch she had told him he was to take from the earl's pocket. Balcardane had always said he meant to leave it to Ian.

As they passed through Ballachulish village, he put the watch in his pocket and took out money for one of his men to give the church sexton, to pay bell-ringers and defray other expenses of the funeral preparation. The passing bell was already tolling, and he knew it would toll for the funeral and again at this hour for days to come, to keep away evil spirits and ensure the earl's safe passage to the next world.

Despite centuries of Roman and Protestant teaching, many

Highlanders still believed that the devil and his minions waited to seize a man's spirit as it set out on its last journey. Therefore, Balcardane, like many of his ilk, had hedged his bets. Despite his parsimonious nature, he had set money aside to tend both his Celtic spirit and his Christian soul, and Duncan intended to honor his wishes.

He could hear people behind them singing a hymn of sorrow and felt grateful that they, many of whom were Stewarts and Macleans, would express sadness at the death of a prominent Campbell. It was a sign, perhaps, of slowly shifting tides.

The gates of the castle stood open. Servants who had not raced to the landing had gathered in the courtyard, anxious and eager for news. He could sense their distress, and the moment they realized that his father was dead.

"Take him into the hall," he said to Bannatyne, adding to another, "Tell someone to mix black paint for the door."

"Aye, my lord," the two replied in unison.

Duncan felt Mary stiffen, and he knew that he had reacted, too, for it was the first time anyone had addressed him by his new title. It reminded him sharply that he was now the fifth Earl of Balcardane. That moment to which he had once looked forward had slipped past him during the crisis and seemed now to present an awesome burden. Swinging to the ground, he caught Mary by the waist and lifted her down beside him, touching her shoulder gently to usher her inside.

Neil followed silently behind them.

In the hall, Duncan saw his mother hurrying down the stairs, holding her wide skirts high so they would not impede her. Her gaze was stark with shock. He strode halfway across the hall before her eyes focused on him.

"Duncan? They said— Oh, Duncan, what happened?"

"An accident, ma'am." Seeing her sway, he moved quickly to meet her at the foot of the stairs, steadying her and blocking her view for that moment. There was no way to protect her from what was coming and no easy way to say the next words, so he said them baldly. "He's dead."

"Dead? But that's impossible! He is too young to die." She

searched his face, clearly looking for some sign that he had made a dreadful joke. "Your hair is wet."

He said gently, "The carriage went off the ferry, and he was trapped inside. I was near enough to see it happen, and we did all that we could, but the water was cold, and by the time I reached him, he had been under a long time. His heart just stopped beating, ma'am, but Mary was holding him. He did not die alone."

"Oh, Mary, bless you, my poor lamb!" Lady Balcardane hurried to her, enfolding her in her arms. "What a dreadful thing for you, but how glad I am that someone who cared for him was at hand to feel his last breath."

"Aye, ma'am," Mary said quietly. "Many were with him."

"Did you know before?"

Duncan saw Mary look confused for a moment. Then, slowly, she shook her head. "No. I . . . I should have felt something, perhaps, but I did not." She looked at Duncan, her eyes widening, and he knew without a word what she was thinking.

"Your dream was just a nightmare, nothing more," he said firmly. "Not only was it I who fell in it, and not my father, but if you begin reading hidden meaning into every dream you have, lass, you'll soon go mad. Go now, and tell the servants to fetch mourning cloths to hang over looking glasses and pictures in every room. It is only a gesture, but perhaps it will comfort those who fear that his spirit might otherwise take off in the wrong direction."

"Surely, they must believe that his spirit fled his body somewhere between here and the ferry landing," she said.

"Those who cling tightest to the old beliefs won't. Such simple folk believe the spirit waits until he is safe at home before it abandons him."

"Send for Martha Loudoun and Jessie when you attend to that, my dear," his mother said, visibly gathering herself. "They can see to it that he is properly laid out." When Mary had gone, she said, "Duncan, did you speak to the parson when you passed through Ballachulish?"

"It seemed wrong to stop, ma'am," he said. "I sent bell-pennies to the sexton though, and I'll speak with Parson later. He will come to us as soon as he hears."

A clock began to chime, only to be hastily muffled. Duncan glanced over his shoulder and saw that one of his men had stopped its movement.

"Don't let them shut the front door," Lady Balcardane said anxiously.

"They won't, ma'am. It is far more likely that they will try to turn this place into an icehouse by opening all the windows. I mean to let them open one in the saloon and leave the doors to the hall open, but you are not to let them open any windows in your sitting room or any other rooms upstairs."

"Such orders may offend some of our people," she said fretfully.

"I'll deal with them," he said. "I don't want you falling ill again."

A string at the back of the hall alerted him to Mary's return. Martha and Jessie followed her, and soon took matters in hand. However, when Mary, at a nod from him, tried to draw Lady Balcardane away, the dowager stood firm.

"I'll not leave him yet," she said. "My place is here."

"Duncan," Serena said imperiously from the landing, where she stood poised with one hand on the banister, "I am glad you are here, for one of your people has been telling the most dreadful falsehood. She said his lordship— Lud, sir, is that him on the table?" Abandoning her pose, she snatched up her skirt and ran down the rest of the stairs. "What happened? Is he truly dead?" Staring at the body, she clapped a hand to her cheek in apparent shock. "He cannot be!"

"He is," Duncan said, making no attempt to soften the news. "It was good of you to come down, Serena. You can be of help here, I believe."

"Oh, I couldn't," she exclaimed, backing away, her gaze shifting hastily from the corpse. "I don't know how you can ask such a thing of me! What are we going to do about Juliet's baby? Does this mean I don't have to go home now?"

Stunned, he could only stare at her, leaving it to Mary to say calmly, "We can discuss that later, Serena. If you do not want to help us lay him out, perhaps you will feel more comfortable in her ladyship's sitting room or in your bedchamber."

"How dare you tell me what to do! Just who do you think—?" Breaking off, Serena stared at her in shock plainly greater than any she had felt over Balcardane's death. Then, recollecting her anger, she added, "What *am* I saying? Oh, this is too cruel! I suppose you expect me to address you as *my lady* now that you are a countess. Well, I won't do it! It's too unfair. Oh, how could this happen to *me?*"

"That will do, Serena," Duncan snapped. "You are never to speak to my wife like that again. Nor shall you inflict any more of your self-serving complaints and reproaches on this household if you do not want to suffer the direst consequences of my displeasure. Now, seek your room and stay there, for I have had all I can stand. You are quite the most self-centered, unwomanly, ill-mannered, and spiteful—"

"Enough, Duncan," Neil interjected quietly from behind him. "She is just upset. I'll attend to her now, so you can look after his lordship and your mother."

Duncan fell silent at once, shocked at his outburst, for despite a lifetime of experience with his unpredictable temper, the swiftness and strength of the fury Serena had provoked had surprised him. Even now, although Neil's intervention had recalled him to his senses, he still struggled to reclaim control of himself.

As if drawn by a lodestone, his eyes shifted toward Mary's face.

She stood by the table where the men had laid his father, but she was looking at him, and her steady silvery gaze calmed him as it always did.

He looked back at Serena, a little surprised to see that the color had drained from her face. Neil stood beside her, evidently awaiting his permission to withdraw.

"Take her upstairs," Duncan said. His gaze remained fixed on Serena as he added sternly, "I am grateful for your assistance, Neil, but make it clear to her that whatever I decide, she will do as I command."

"Aye, my lord," Neil said, adding gently, "Come away now, lassie."

Serena clung to his arm, avoiding Duncan's gaze.

When they had gone, Mary said, "You should get out of those wet things, sir, and then you have much to do, I know. I will stay with your mother."

He nodded absently, already making a mental list of necessary tasks. Turning away, he realized that one was paramount and turned back to say, "We must send a messenger straightaway to Inver House. They expect us to arrive on Saturday."

"I should think they will want to attend the funeral," Mary said.

"Aye, perhaps, but not only will snowbound roads make it hard for those at any distance to get here, but an influx of Campbells into Appin country would likely start another war. Moreover, I'd like to get him underground as quick as we can, before the ground freezes hard." A thought struck him that offered a possible compromise. "We could take him to Dunraven, I suppose."

Lady Balcardane said hastily, "He wanted to be buried here, Duncan. You know he did. Though he was not born at Balcardane, he was raised here. He always thought of this castle as his home."

"Aye, ma'am, I know."

"My lord," Chuff said carefully from the open doorway, drawing everyone's attention, "Jock said tae bring these rush lights, and he bade me remind ye tae put a pan o' salt at the laird's feet."

Martha Loudoun put her hands on her hips and said indignantly, "You just put those lights where the men can deal with them, laddie. Then tak' yersel' back out tae that Jock and tell him no tae be telling me my business."

Pinkie, peeping out from behind Chuff, said in a small voice, "Is the laird dead, then, for sure? I thought they helped him, but Chuff said he died anyway."

"Yes, Pinkie, he is dead," Duncan said.

Her eyes widened with fear. "Will the deevils come here after us, then?"

Feeling Mary's gaze, Duncan said gently, "No, lassie, I won't let them."

Though Pinkie looked slightly reassured, Mary said, "If you like, you and Chuff can sleep by the schoolroom fire tonight, and Jessie will stay with you."

"They did say ye be going away, Miss Mary, and Himself, too." Pinkie's lower lip began to tremble. "Ye willna leave us here alone, will ye?"

Mary opened her mouth, shut it, and looked beseechingly at Duncan.

He said, "We'll see, Pinkie. Right now I don't know what any of us is going to do, but no one will go anywhere tonight, I promise you."

The child regarded him solemnly for a long minute, then nodded.

Chuff said, "Must she go tae the kitchen the noo, or can she bide with me?"

"She can stay with you," Duncan said. "You look after her fine, Chuff."

"Aye, I do that," the boy said, handing his rush lights to one of the men.

With a gesture Duncan dismissed the children, then hurried up to his room at last to rid himself of his wet garments. Not until he began to remove them did he realize how chilled he was, but Hardwick, having anticipated his needs, handed him a hot toddy. The drink and a roaring fire soon warmed him.

Downstairs again, he issued orders to prepare the castle for mourning. Men had already brought black paint and paper for the door, and willing hands began hanging the mourning cloths, while Jessie and Martha attended to the earl.

Mary's gentle voice served a blunt contrast to Duncan's curt tones when she asked two men to set up screens, then asked others to bring water to wash the body.

Noting her appearance then for the first time since their return, Duncan said, "Go upstairs and change your clothes before you deal with all that, lass. I failed to notice before, in all the upset, but your skirt is still damp from holding him."

"It is only the outer layer, sir. I'll change when I can."

"The parson is here, my lord," Bannatyne said from the open doorway.

Suppressing his annoyance at Mary's refusal to take care of herself, Duncan greeted the clergyman's arrival with relief, inviting him into the library after he expressed his condolences to the dowager. He knew that although he had managed to avoid speaking sharply to Mary, the impulse to speak so, and his earlier burst of temper with Serena, proved he was less in control of himself than he wanted to be. It was a good time, he decided, to seek some advice, just as he had promised to do.

He was able to relieve some of his pent-up feelings by making it clear to a lackey who had begun to extinguish the fire in the library that he wanted it built up instead. "And don't let anyone put out the fire in her ladyship's sitting room," he growled. "Freezing ourselves to death will aid nothing."

"It be custom, my lord. The fires must be smothered tae protect his spirit."

"Not this fire, or any upstairs. Do you understand me?"

"Aye, my lord." Red-faced, the lackey bowed and took himself off.

"Dinna be harsh with your people, lad," the parson said. "They believe they are doing the right thing. Old customs ingrain themselves deep."

"Do you want whisky, sir?" Duncan asked, moving toward the decanter.

"Aye, and I thank you kindly, for 'tis brisk out the day. When do you want to hold the funeral?"

"I need some advice about that," Duncan said, finding the admission easier than he had expected. Pouring out two glasses of whisky, he went on, "As you know, Caddell expects us all to take part in his christening party on Sunday. Normally, I would send word of my father's death hither and yon, then await those who wish to pay their respects, but at this time of year . . ."

"Aye, well, my lord, you must send word to Lord Caddell

that your father's death will delay the christening, that's all. Seeing a man out of the world is more important to the folks in these parts than seeing one in."

"They'll fear for the bairn's soul, too, won't they?"

The parson chuckled. "Though they'll draw censure for it, they will just ask a midwife to do the honors. She will sprinkle three drops of water on the bairn's forehead—one for the Father, one for the Son, and one for the Holy Ghost—to protect him against evil spirits and fairies until we can get there. Depending on her beliefs, she'll use plain water on the wee laddie, or her own spit."

Duncan handed him a glass of whisky. "Then I expect we should discuss what I must do here before we can go to Inver House. Sit down, Parson."

Mary did not mind helping prepare the earl's body. Like most Highland women, she had assisted with such rituals before. She knew that he would lie in state in the great hall for a day or two at least, for the lakewake—the watch over the dead—so that any who wanted to pay last respects could do so in their own way.

She had not spared a thought for Juliet's child until Serena had spoken of it, nor did she give it another thought afterward. Clearly, Balcardane had to come first. Caddell would understand that, whether his daughter did or not. In any event, Mary knew she could trust Neil to look after Serena.

The thought startled her, but she realized that she had come to accept him as an adult, even more since his arrival at Balcardane than before.

She had watched him grow from a surly, bitter adolescent into an intense young man full of resentment at the situation in which he found himself through no fault of his own. She had not expected him to come to Balcardane, certainly not for her. That he had done so spoke much of his increased maturity.

She recalled his initial meeting with Serena with an amusement that she had not felt at the time. That he had proved to be right about Serena's activities with the gray cloak showed that she had not fooled him; but she also tantalized him, and it came as no great surprise to realize that she intrigued him now more than ever.

Mary could not imagine what the Earl of Caddell would think of Serena's attraction to a landless chieftain of the Macleans. He had, after all, intended her to marry Duncan, who now controlled the powerful earldom of Balcardane. Mary had a notion that Caddell would not approve of Neil, but since Serena seemed able to wrap her father around her thumb, perhaps it would not matter what he thought.

When it became apparent that despite the parson's presence at Balcardane neither Martha Loudoun nor Lady Balcardane had given a single thought to the evening meal, Mary took Jessie aside and asked what remained to be done in the kitchen before they could feed the household.

"Will we eat then, my lady? Martha didna say and I didna like tae ask."

"Certainly, we must eat, Jessie. We gain nothing by allowing ourselves to grow weak or ill. Do you send one of the other maidservants to help us here, so that you can look after things in the kitchen. I will tell Martha."

"Aye, well, I'll see to it then. Will we be setting the table in the dining parlor then, or down here in the saloon, what wi' the parson and all?"

"Set things up in the dining parlor," Mary said. "It will be warmer there than in the saloon." Shivering as she spoke, she realized that her dress was damp through now, not just from holding Balcardane earlier but from helping to wash his body.

As she turned away, meaning to go upstairs and change, Lady Balcardane said, "Mary, love, go and tell Duncan we need coppers to put over my lord's eyelids. Without them, folks will fear he might open his eyes and demand a companion for his journey to the next world."

"Aye, well, and he might, too," Martha Loudoun murmured. "And, too, he'll no mind the expense o' two wee coppers the noo."

Sniffling, and blotting her eyes with her handkerchief, Lady

Balcardane said, "Every time I recall how often I yearned for him to loosen the purse strings I begin to cry again. Who *ever* would have believed that generosity would get him killed?"

"He was kind and considerate to me from the day I arrived here, ma'am," Mary said. "I came to love him like a father. Indeed, you both have been kinder than I ever imagined you could be."

"You became a member of our family, and I think he liked your spirit, my dear," the dowager said. "Do go now and ask Duncan for the coppers, will you? One of the men has already gone to fetch salt to put at his feet. We never did that in my family, but I know folks here believe it keeps evil from overtaking them if they touch him in farewell, and we do not want to upset anyone."

"No, ma'am. I'll fetch the coppers for you."

Crossing the hall, she opened the library door, savoring the wave of warmth that welcomed her. "Duncan," she said, "forgive me for intruding, sir, but your mother would like a pair of coppers if you have them."

"Aye, I do," he said, getting to his feet. Then his gaze came to rest upon her, and his eyes narrowed. Flicking a glance at the parson, he added, "I'll just take them to her myself and see if she requires anything more."

"Really, sir, I think—"

"Parson, you won't mind if I leave you to enjoy a second glass of whisky here by the fire, will you? I won't be gone above a quarter hour or so."

"Run along, lad, run along. I'll just find myself a book to read."

"Help yourself," Duncan said. "Come along, Mary."

"Your mother and Martha have everything in train, sir, I promise you," she murmured as they left the room. "You should not leave Parson alone like this."

"I am quite sure that my mother and Martha know what they are doing, but my wife clearly does not," he said, putting an arm around her shoulders and urging her past the screens toward the stairway.

"The coppers, Duncan. Don't forget them!"

"I won't. Here, ma'am," he said, giving them to the dowager. "I am taking Mary upstairs to see that she changes her clothes. She is soaking wet and does not seem to have enough sense to do anything about it without urging."

"You see to her then," Lady Balcardane said. "Martha and I have little left to do here, and then I will just sit quietly with him, I think, until they serve dinner."

Mary opened her mouth to say that she would return to bear her company, but Duncan gave her a little push, and she shut it again until they reached the first landing. Then she said, "Really, sir, I can take care of myself. I am not nearly as wet as you seem to think. I had my cloak on over my dress before, and—"

"Go," he said, giving her another little push. "We've had enough sickness in this place. I don't want my wife catching her death from the cold."

She did not attempt to argue more until they had reached her dressing room. Then she turned, and with hands on her hips and arms akimbo, she said bluntly, "Do you intend to undress and dress me yourself, too?"

With rueful smile, he said, "I dare not, lass. I've too many things to do to let you distract me more than you already have."

"Then give me credit, sir," she said evenly. "I admit that my gown was still damp before, and has grown a trifle more so. I'll also admit that I've grown chilly, but I did not like to leave your mother alone with only Martha to support her."

"You told me to change *my* clothes," he pointed out. "You've got to look to yourself, too, lass."

"You had been in the water," she reminded him. "You borrowed a jacket, a hat, and perhaps even a shirt; but your breeches, undergarments, and hair were still soaked. I know I must take care, Duncan. I am not a simpleton. But remember, sir, you promised to treat me like your partner, and not simply issue orders for my guidance and protection. Before you can keep that promise, you must be willing to let me accept the consequences of my decisions if they prove faulty or foolish."

"Turn around, Mary," he said.

A little shiver shot up her spine. "Why?"

"So that I can unbutton your gown for you. You will be that much quicker out of it. Although," he added gently, "you would be well served if I were to suggest that you already have consequences to face as a result of decisions you have made."

"What decisions?"

He turned her so that her back was to him as he said, "Specifically the one that took you away from the castle today with only Pinkie to bear you company."

She could not tell from his tone if he was angry, but she knew that a simple explanation would serve better than revealing her exasperation. Accordingly, she said, "In fact, Wull was with us until we saw in what danger the coach lay. He had a pistol, too. Jock was hesitant to let me go, sir, but since we expected to meet his lordship before we had gone far, he agreed. Perhaps I ought to have gone back with Wull when he ran for help. Would you prefer that I had not stayed?"

"You know I am grateful that you were there," he murmured. His warm breath caressed her neck, and she knew he meant to kiss her.

Impulsively, she turned, hugging him tightly when she felt his strong arms close around her. To her surprise, she felt him tremble.

"There was a time when I thought I disliked him," he said. "I never felt really close to him, and never expected to feel such bereavement at his death. I was wild with grief when Ian was killed. This is different, but still . . ."

"I know," she said, holding him tight and wishing she could comfort him the way she was able to comfort Chuff or Pinkie. "A brother is a brother, and very dear, but one's father is the source of one's own existence, sir. His mortality reminds you of your own far more forcibly than Ian's did. Thus his death strikes deep."

"You're a kind lass, Mary, and a good wife," he said, kissing her on the forehead. "I know you can never love me like you loved Ian, but I want you to know that I have no complaint and think myself most fortunate to have married you."

"Duncan, I—"

"No, let me finish, because much as I want to, I cannot linger, and I must say this lest you think any rules have changed. Your good opinion becomes increasingly important to me, lass, and I promise I'll do what I can to treat you as you desire, but your new status may lead you to dismiss some of those rules. You say you'll accept any consequence, but MacCrichton and Breck still pose too much of a threat to your safety for me to risk letting you put yourself in harm's way. Therefore, you will stay inside our wall, lass, or face the consequence of answering to me."

Kissing her lightly, he left before she could think of an appropriate retort. Since she had hoped he would discuss his feelings at greater length, he had caught her off guard again. Not only had he apparently dismissed her attempt to soothe him but he had instantly contradicted his promise to respect her abilities by ordering her yet again to obey his command without question.

Taking her warmest gown from the wardrobe, she pondered her lack of outrage. By rights, she ought to be indignant, even angry, but she was not. Having seen the closed look on his face as he turned away, she believed she understood him better than he understood himself, for she had seen that look once before, after Ian's death. It was as if Duncan had closed and bolted the shutters to his soul. Before, she had assumed that he was just a hard man devoid of human feeling, but she knew now that she had been wrong. Duncan felt things as deeply as anyone she knew. He simply did not allow others to share his feelings, or exploit them.

As she stepped out of the damp dress, she considered this new viewpoint of her husband, and she considered, too, one of the things he had said before issuing his command. Had she loved Ian too much ever to love another man?

Ian had been a delightful, lovable laddie, to be sure—a gentle, caring soul, whose thoughts dwelt more frequently on birds and other wild creatures than on his family or friends. He had loved her, certainly, and she had loved him and had been devastated by his death, but had she really expected to marry him? Remembering that she had considered the point once before, she remembered, too, the circumstances, and wondered if sexual passion might have overridden the truth.

The more she thought, the more certain she became that her instinct that night had been correct. Ian's dreams of marriage had always seemed a bit fantastic, and although she had listened to them complacently, just as she had listened to his complaints about the unfeeling ways of his father and brother, she could not recall sharing his anger or his resentment at seeing his dream thwarted. In truth, she had discounted his complaints in much the same manner that she had discounted Neil's.

It was a shock to realize that she had ever viewed Ian in the same light as Neil, but she saw now that each of them had railed against his particular situation in life without doing anything about it. Both had been youngsters then, of course, and just as it had startled her to realize that Neil had grown up, so did it shock her now to realize that she had never thought of Ian as a man, only as a dearly loved laddie.

In contrast, she was finding it easier to imagine Duncan as a boy. Before, she had not thought of him as ever having been youthful or (until recently) lovable. He had been only Balcardane's black, rather dangerous shadow; yet, when she tried to imagine being married to Ian instead of to Duncan, her imagination boggled. Not only would Ian have failed to recognize that Ewan could prove dangerous, but he would have greeted proof of that danger just as he had greeted any opposition. He would have railed against it, but he would have done nothing to counteract it.

As these thoughts paraded through her mind, Mary slipped into the fresh gown. Its thick blue wool felt soft against her skin, but the snug bodice boasted a line of tiny cloth-covered buttons all the way up the back. She had managed the upper ones, and several near the waist, but the ones between defeated her and she was just about to ring for Ailis when a door opened in the adjoining bedchamber. Peeking from the dressing-room doorway, she was surprised to see Pinkie.

The child's lower lip trembled, and her big blue eyes welled with tears.

Mary hurried toward her. "What is it, darling? What's amiss?"

"Chuff said ye *will* go away," Pinkie wailed. "He said he's tae go wi' ye, tae help look after the horses, but I'm tae stay here. Och, mistress, I be afeared tae stay here without Chuff, and without ye or Himself tae look after me! What if the auld laird's spirit comes tae fetch me? What'll I do then?"

"Martha and Jessie will—"

"Nay then, they'll only tell me tae stop mumpin', and what can they do against the laird's spirit anyway? It fair shoogles up me internals tae think on it. It'll tak' me away, it will!" With that, she cast herself, sobbing, into Mary's arms.

Holding her almost as tightly as she had held Duncan, Mary murmured, "There now, no one will take you away, Pinkie. If Chuff is to go with us, then you simply must come, too."

"But Chuff said Himself said I canna go, that Chuff can go only because he can mak' himself useful."

"You shall make yourself useful, too," Mary said firmly. "Indeed, I will tell Himself that I have urgent need of you."

Her sobs hushing at once, Pinkie pulled back to look up into Mary's face. "But what can I do?"

"You can help me," Mary said firmly. "You can be my maid."

"But Ailis—"

"Ailis was never meant to go," Mary said truthfully. "We will take few if any servants because his lordship—Himself, that is—will want to take men at arms, and this time of year even an earl's household will not willingly house a host of guest servants. If Lady Balcardane were going, we would share a maid, but I think she will stay here now, so we are more likely to carry extra food than extra servants."

"I dinna eat much," Pinkie said, "but I dinna ken a maid's tasks, neither."

"You can learn all you need to know," Mary assured her. "You can begin now by buttoning the buttons I could not reach by myself, and do it quickly, dear, for I must get back down to her ladyship. Oh, and do not say anything about this plan,

Pinkie—not even to Chuff—until I have had a chance to tell Himself."

Attending efficiently to the buttons, Pinkie said doubtfully, "D' ye think he'll allow it, mistress? Chuff said—"

"Never mind what Chuff said," Mary told her. "I'll deal with Himself. First we must attend properly to his papa's funeral, but then we will put sadness behind us for a time to welcome a new soul into this world. We'll have a fine time at Inver House, Pinkie. You'll see."

Twenty-two

The next evening, in the candlelit great hall at Shian Towers, Ewan leaned back in his armchair at the head of the huge table and glowered at his unwelcome guest. "I don't know why you've come back," he growled. "I don't want you."

"I bring news, my lad," Allan Breck said, casting his coat and scarf onto a bench and beginning to remove his gloves. He looked around the hall, adding, "I don't know why you don't set some of your folks to furbishing up this place. No wonder Mary didn't want to stay."

"One does not do much furbishing without gelt," Ewan said, lifting his mug. "Help yourself to whisky if you want it. What's this news of yours?"

"Balcardane is dead."

Frowning, Ewan said, "Is he now? Do you expect me to attend his funeral?"

"I did think we might take advantage of the upset, but I've learned something that will do us more good than that. Our little dove might well come right to us."

"What the devil are you talking about?"

Breck was pouring himself some whisky, and he did not reply at once. When he had filled a mug for himself, he moved toward the fire, saying critically, "You don't need much gelt to see this floor polished up, or the soot cleaned from the stones round the fireplace. What sort of weaponry have you got here?"

"What do you think? Soldiers from Stalker searched the

whole place before I got back from France. It's a wonder they didn't take those lances off the wall."

"Where are their tips?"

Ewan shrugged. "My father carried them with him when we left. He said lances could be fashioned anywhere, but steel tips would be hard to come by."

"Well, you can buy new ones when we find the treasure."

"Generous of you. Just how much of it do you intend to leave me?"

Breck smiled, moving to put one foot up on the bench beside the table.

"I wish you would stop looking at me as an enemy, Ewan. I want only to help you find it. Duty demands that you contribute your fair share of it to the cause, of course, and I mean to see that you do, but first we must find the damned thing."

Ewan sneered at him. "After that, friend, I'll decide for myself what to do with my own treasure. You won't even get the chest open without me."

Breck raised his eyebrows. "What makes you so sure?"

"The chest itself. Have you ever seen an Armada chest?"

Frowning, Breck said, "I don't know. Have I? What's one like?"

"It's iron-bound," Ewan said, "and the locking mechanism in the lid looks like clockwork. Without the right key, no man can open it."

"And where is this key?"

"You don't really expect me to tell you that," Ewan said, smirking. Having not found the chest, he had not yet had occasion to look for the key, but he knew right where his father had always hidden it. To divert Breck from plaguing him over its whereabouts, he said curtly, "You said the lass will come to us. How so?"

"I told you before, I've got eyes and ears everywhere, my lad, and there is no better informant than one with a score to pay. There is to be a christening party at Inver House, which means, unless the weather turns much worse, they will be coming through Glen Creran."

"But when? Do you mean to camp in the glen until they do?"

Breck smiled. "Unnecessary. We shall receive a signal, my lad."

They talked of other things until they retired to their bedchambers, but Ewan's thoughts kept returning to the key. When he was certain that Breck would not stir from his chamber again that night, he went to fetch it. The key was gone.

Two days later, watching men lower the coffin into the ground, Duncan decided that, come spring, he would order a proper tombstone put up, perhaps even a small chapel. His father had mentioned more than once that this hillside provided a perfect setting for a family chapel. An old Stewart graveyard in the woods near the burn held a number of the previous owner's kinsmen, but Balcardane had long since made it clear that he did not want to join them.

"I'll want the sun to shine on my resting place, lad," he had said, "and I'll want a devilish good view of the loch."

Well, Duncan thought, here he would have both when the dark clouds overhead had moved on. The slight warming spell that had begun the day of the accident had surprisingly continued, so rain was possible rather than snow, but he hoped it would not rain. There was too much snow higher up that could melt and turn nearby rivers into torrents threatening anyone who traveled through the glens.

Hearing the soft sound of feminine weeping, he looked for the source and saw one of the maidservants sobbing into her sleeve. Involuntarily, he frowned.

"Let her cry," Mary said gently beside him. "It has been long since anyone hereabouts has howled the dead into their graves."

He nodded, unsurprised that she had read his mind. It had become something of a habit with her. His cousin Rory, who had traveled miles with Argyll, had once told him Englishwomen did not attend burials, but Duncan was glad Mary was with him. His mother was there, too, at his other side, watching them lower the coffin.

"Did they have difficulty digging the hole, Duncan?" she asked.

"Less than I'd feared," he said. "Coulter said the ground was hard for only the first few inches. Are you sure you are warm enough, ma'am?"

"Oh, yes. Listen, someone is playing a fiddle. How mournful it sounds. That must be Simon Stewart playing again, I think."

Duncan knew who it was, because the same dour Stewart clansman had played more cheerful music from time to time during the lakewake. Although the church frowned on the Highlanders' ancient practice of dancing exuberantly around a coffin—as, indeed, it frowned on many of their oldest customs—the cheerful music had persisted. Even now the onlookers, of whom there were about fifty, began quietly to sing. As Duncan stepped forward to throw the first shovelful of dirt onto the coffin, the rain began to fall.

It was a light rain, barely enough to make itself felt at first, and not until the music stopped could he hear the raindrops hushing on nearby shrubbery. Other men took their turns at the shovel, and soon the sad deed was done. Everyone turned back toward the castle.

Inside, the windows were shut again and the hall fire roared. Serena said, "Thank heaven we can have done at last with freezing ourselves. That fire feels absolutely wonderful! I shall hate to leave it in the morning."

Neil glanced at Duncan. "Do we still leave tomorrow? This rain could—"

"We'll start early," Duncan said. "Unless this drizzle grows much heavier, it should pose no great threat to us, but I want to be well into the glen and along before the day has time to turn warmer."

Watching Duncan, and listening, Mary knew that he was more concerned than he was admitting, and she did not have to ask why. She, too, had seen what a warm rain could do after snow had blanketed the Highlands. A quick melt overfilled the rivers and burns, sending them quickly into dangerous spate, raising the levels of the lochs and lifting any ice that had formed on them. Conditions would soon grow too treacherous for travel, and she knew that Duncan wanted to avoid offending Caddell any more than he already had by rejecting his daughter.

Thoughts of Serena overtook her again when their guests had departed, which they soon did, for they, too, had concerns about the weather. Serena had left the hall by then, and Mary hoped she was packing.

Leaving the servants to clear away the remains of the funeral feast, she went upstairs to the tower bedchamber, determined to make certain that Serena would not delay the morrow's departure. Opening the door without ceremony, she surprised her in the act of setting a lamp in the deep stone window embrasure.

"Lud, Mary, you nearly made me drop this! What do you want?"

Having noted that Serena's maid was also in the room, sorting clothing, Mary did not comment on her tone but said calmly, "Don't place that lamp too near the glass, Serena. Rain or no, it's cold outside. The lamp's heat may crack the window."

"Much I would care," Serena said, turning with a swirl of her skirts to sit on the dressing stool. She did not invite Mary to sit. "Why did you come up here?"

"To be certain you know that Duncan wants to leave early in the morning."

"I know he does, though we'll all be soaked to the skin by this rain."

"I don't think so. The shepherds say it's turning colder, and I agree. The rain outside will turn to snow by morning, but the day may warm it to rain again if the sky doesn't clear, and Duncan is worried about the river we must cross."

Serena shrugged. "If he is worried, we should wait. There is no great hurry."

Aware that Duncan had even more interest in returning Serena to the bosom of her family than in greeting Caddell's new grandson, Mary rejected a wicked urge to tell her so, saying instead, "Your parents will be delighted to see you, Serena, and you must know that much heavier snows are bound to come soon. When they do, they will make travel impossible. You will not like to be stuck at Balcardane then."

Serena hunched a shoulder, avoiding her gaze.

Turning to the maid, Mary said firmly, "Please see that you finish packing Lady Serena's things tonight, other than what she intends to wear tomorrow. Then have them taken downstairs to the hall before you retire for the night."

"Aye, my lady, I'll see to it."

"Good night, Serena." She did not wait for a response, which was just as well since none was forthcoming. Shutting the door behind her, she went to the schoolroom to be sure the children were in bed.

Finding them well tucked in, with Jessie in a chair by the fire, telling them a story, she bade them sleep well.

Pinkie said anxiously, "Will we all go even if the weather turns worse?"

"If it gets too bad, no one will go," Mary said, "but if we go to Inver House, you may be certain that you and Chuff will both go with us."

Remembering that she had not yet imparted that information to Duncan, she said good-night and went immediately to the chamber she now shared with him.

Finding that he had not yet come upstairs, she rang for Ailis to finish packing her clothes for the journey. Then, before the maid grew too busy in the dressing room, Mary donned her night shift and took the pins from her hair.

"You need not brush my hair tonight, Ailis," she said. "I'll take my brush into the bedchamber and do it myself by the fire."

"Aye, mistress. I'll no tak' long here, I'm thinking." Ailis smiled. "That wee lass, Pinkie, has flitted up and down the stairs the day, keeking into your baggage, insisting she wants tae ken where all is kept so she'll ken where tae find things when ye reach Inver House. D' ye really mean tae take her with ye?"

"Aye, but do not fear for your position, Ailis. His lordship does not want to impose on Lord Caddell's hospitality, so we'll take mostly men at arms, and Chuff is to help with the horses. Doubtless they think he'll eat less than a larger lad."

"They dinna ken that laddie's appetite then," Ailis said with a chuckle.

"At all events, I want to keep the children together," Mary explained. "They have only each other in this world, you know."

"Aye, mistress. Does the master ken aught o' this yet?"

Seeing a twinkle in the maid's eyes, Mary realized that it had been nearly three days since she had promised Pinkie she could go, and yet she had not heard a single word whispered about that promise within the household.

"Ailis, have you formed a conspiracy to keep it silent?"

Still twinkling, the maid shrugged. "We didna ken, ye see, but we didna think it would be Master Duncan's notion tae tak' the wee lassie along."

If she had needed proof of her acceptance by the inhabitants of Balcardane Castle, Mary thought, she had received it. She wondered what other secrets Ailis might be keeping for her. There was at least one other that she might have deduced.

With a little shake of her head, Mary said, "You put me to shame, Ailis. I should not be the cause of your keeping secrets from his lordship. I will tell him tonight. It . . . it just went out of my head, I'm afraid."

She believed she spoke the truth, but since she had slept in his bed and enjoyed his sexual attentions every night, and thus had had plenty of occasions to tell him, she felt like a coward nonetheless. Remembering that she had known even at the moment of telling Pinkie she could go that the decision would test Duncan's promise, Mary wondered if her failure to tell him about it was truly inadvertent.

Keeping her other secret was not a matter of cowardice. Until she was sure of it herself, she had no intention of telling him. She would not do so before they returned from Inver House, in any event, because he had already decided the journey would be too much for his mother. At the merest hint that his wife might be bearing his child he would order her to stay behind as well, and Mary did not want him to have to face Caddell alone.

Taking her brush and donning a warm dressing gown over her night shift, she went into the bedchamber and drew a stool close to the fire. As she removed her cap and took the pins from her hair, she wondered if she feared his reaction.

"I am not afraid of him," she murmured at last to the leaping flames. "I just did not want to add to his worries."

Bending forward to let her hair swing down in a curtain before her, she brushed rhythmically the way her mother and sisters had taught her in childhood, counting quietly, letting her mind free itself of all thought but the number of strokes. As always, she felt her body begin to relax. It did not matter who did the brushing, Ailis or herself, so long as she did the counting in her mind.

So lost was she in that world between counting and full consciousness that she did not hear him enter and did not realize he was near until she heard him speak.

"Is that my wife or someone else?"

Starting, she straightened and flipped her hair back to look up at him, noting new lines at the outer corners of his mouth and eyes. "Come sit by the fire," she said. "Ailis or someone brought wine earlier. I'll pour you a glass if you like."

"Pour another for yourself, lass." Drawing the armchair near the fire, he sat wearily and began to pull off his boots. "Has Hardwick finished packing my gear?"

"I have not seen him, but I am sure he has, sir. Ring for him if you like."

She saw his lips twitch. "I have your permission, do I?"

"Aye," she said, pouring two glasses of claret from the decanter on the side table. "He must have brought the wine. I do not think Ailis would have thought of it without someone's having asked her."

He was silent; and Mary, conscious of his gaze, wondered why she hesitated to tell him about Pinkie. She told herself she was waiting for the best time to break the news to him, perhaps when he had relaxed a little.

A window rattled. "The wind is picking up," he said.

"From which direction?"

"Southwest." He grimaced. "I hope it shifts before morning and that the rain does not grow worse."

"I am sure Caddell would understand," she said gently.

"Blast Caddell. I want to give him back his daughter."

Surprised into a gurgle of laughter, Mary hastily stifled it, but Duncan grimaced. "I see nothing funny about that."

"I know you don't. I was laughing because I was thinking only a short time ago that Serena was the primary reason for your concern about the weather. I am growing to know you rather well, I think."

"You read my mind," he said. "I've noticed it more than once. Are you going to make me get up for my wine, or do you intend to serve me?" There was a new look in his eyes, and he no longer seemed quite so tired.

Demurely, she said, "I will serve you gladly, my lord." Moving toward him, holding both glasses carefully, she let her wrap fall open.

He reached for her. "I can teach you still other ways to serve me, lass."

Putting his glass in his outstretched hand and stepping back before he could grab her with the other, she said, "First there is something I must tell you."

He sighed. "I knew it. You are angry with me."

"Angry!"

"Aye, don't trouble to deny it. I've known it for days, but what with keeping watch over my father and attending to my mother, as well as making preparations for tomorrow's journey, and all the rest, I just didn't want to deal with that, too. You seemed easy enough to divert," he added with a smile, "but we need to talk it out, lass. I warned you that I'd not change overnight."

"Duncan, what are you talking about?"

His eyes widened. "Don't you know? I was sure you were incensed because I'd no sooner told you I would trust your judgment than I scolded you unfairly for leaving the castle and then commanded you not to do it again."

"Well, I am not angry," she said. "Still, I'm glad that you

feel a bit guilty, because what I want to tell you is that I told Pinkie she can go with us."

"Then you can just tell her you were mistaken," he said instantly. "Such a journey is no place for that child. My mother is not even going."

"Duncan," she murmured, moving close again. When she caught his eye, she shook her head gently. "I already told Pinkie that she can go. I am not taking Ailis, and Pinkie needs to stay with Chuff. She is afraid to remain here alone."

"Then the boy can stay with her."

"Don't be horrid. You would never take back your promise to him, and I do not believe you mean to take back your promise to me, either."

He sighed, reaching out to take her hand. "Keeping it is proving more difficult than I thought. Somehow I guess I thought the choices you'd make would be ones I would make anyway. I keep forgetting you have notions of your own."

"You will learn."

"Will I?" He set his wineglass on the floor and drew her closer.

"Aye, sir, you will." Taking care not to spill her wine, she sat on his lap and leaned against his shoulder, pulling her hand free to stroke his cheek. Demurely, she said, "Would you like to put my glass down by yours?"

"You can give me a sip instead," he said, adjusting his arm to make her more comfortable. His hand moved up under her hair, and his fingers tickled her neck.

A stirring of warmth spread through her. "Then Pinkie can go?"

"Aye, if you want her. I don't want to hear any complaints from you about a lack of proper service, however," he added sternly.

She chuckled. "I'll have more service than without her," she pointed out. "Are you taking Hardwick?"

"No. He looks after my gear well enough, but Coulter and Bannatyne are far better with sword or pistol."

"Does no one ever remind you that arms are forbidden to Highlanders, sir?"

"Only one sharp-tongued lass dares say such things to me. A Campbell going unarmed in Stewart country would have to be a fool, sweetheart. I am no fool."

"Well, I confess that I shall feel better knowing you are armed," she said. "I still don't like your traveling. That dream was so horribly real."

"It can have nothing to do with this journey, however. As I recall your description, the sun was shining while diamonds fell from the sky. If we see any sun tomorrow, I shall own myself greatly surprised. As to diamonds . . ." He chuckled.

She sighed. "I'll say no more about it then. I daresay you are right."

Taking the wineglass from her unresisting hand, he swallowed the rest of its contents and set it down by his. After that she soon forgot her nightmare. Half an hour later, when she snuggled against him in bed and closed her eyes to sleep, she felt replete and utterly relaxed. Thus it seemed most unfair that she endured the awful dream again just before she awoke early the next morning.

"It wasn't diamonds," she exclaimed, shaking Duncan urgently. "It must be rain, Duncan, because there is a rainbow!"

He muttered grimly, "You had better hope the hour is later than I think it is."

"The clock says half past five," she said, turning the one on the bed table so it caught the glow from the embers. "You said you wanted to start early, sir, and it will begin to grow light in an hour. Did you hear me. It wasn't—"

"Aye, I heard you," he growled, "and I don't want to hear it again. It was a dream, Mary, that's all. Have you found yourself in any caves lately?"

"I know that one was a nightmare brought on by my fear of small places," she said, "but it wasn't like this. This is the second time I've had this dream."

"You've had the other more than once, too, have you not?"

"Aye, several times, but this is—"

"Different. I know you think it is, but you are wrong. You fretted about me when I rode out looking for MacCrichton, and I came to no harm. This time you are doubtless disturbed because you know I have concerns about the weather. That's all, Mary. You've said yourself that your visions don't come like this."

"That's true, they don't," she admitted, "but still—"

"That's enough," he said curtly. "I don't want to hear another word. I have enough on my plate today, as it is, and that's Hardwick's step at the door now."

Duncan was glad he had heard the footsteps, because Ailis was with Hardwick when he entered the room. Hardwick carried the tray with their breakfast, and the wench pulled the side table out so he could set it down.

Glancing at Mary, Duncan saw that she had composed herself, but she did not look at him, and he knew that she was both annoyed and disappointed. Though he felt a stab of remorse, he consoled himself with the thought that she would get over it, and that he did, indeed, have too many other things to worry about.

She ate little and did not speak, so when she and Ailis retired to her dressing room, he finished his meal quickly and dressed himself, then went to hurry the others along. He need not have worried about his men, however, for Bannatyne assured him that they were all well along with their tasks.

"It was that Chuff," his henchman said with a grin. "He woke everyone an hour ago, my lord, and he's been dashing around like a collie with a feckless herd of sheep. I thought Coulter was going to give him a clout when he told him to stir his stumps. But when he threatened to, the lad just snapped back at him that he could do so if he pleased but that Himself would no be happy if the men were not saddled and ready to ride when he wanted to leave. That silenced Coulter, I can tell you."

Duncan grinned, his spirits lifting at once, and when he discovered that Chuff had also seen to it that his sister was ready to leave, he clapped the boy on the shoulder. "It seems I should make you my second in command," he said.

Chuff flashed a smile. "I'd like that fine in a year or two."

"Would you like to ride with me?"

The rapturous look on the lad's face was answer enough. When the others were ready, Duncan swung him up behind, seeing without surprise that Mary carried Pinkie before her.

She still did not look at him, nor had she spoken to him since their exchange earlier, but he could not afford to let his thoughts dwell on it. He nearly told her to give the child to one of his men, but knowing she would resist, he held his tongue. He did not want the men to suspect that all was not well between them.

"Bannatyne," he said abruptly. "Tell her ladyship that she and Lady Serena are to stay in the midst of the men. I know she would prefer to ride up here with me, but it will be safer if others ride ahead of her to clear her path."

"Aye, my lord."

Duncan did not wait to see if Mary would obey. He knew she would. Looking up at the still-dark sky, he saw not a single star. As the herds had predicted, colder night temperatures had turned the rain to a light snowfall. He sent a pair of men with torches on ahead to lead them, and fell in behind them. The rest followed in twos, some leading pack animals with their supplies. He was taking as much as he could afford to take. He did not want to be beholden to Caddell.

Wind soon extinguished the torches, but it grew significantly lighter by the time they reached the pass. Just the other side, however, snowdrifts slowed them down, and although men soon cleared the way, the delay chilled them all.

"This is madness, Duncan," Serena said pettishly. "I'm freezing, and we are not likely to grow warmer. What if this snowfall turns into a blizzard?"

"Then we will take shelter," he said, striving to keep his temper. He knew he was not really angry with Serena. She was acting as he had expected her to act.

He was prickly because Mary still had not spoken to him. He wanted to go to her and shake her, tell her she was behaving badly and to stop it. But even as the thought formed in his mind, he knew it was untrue. He wanted to go her and hold her, to feel her holding him, to know she was not angry with him. Her good opinion of him had somehow, over the past weeks, become not just important but vital.

The little party continued down through the glen, their progress steady but slow, hampered as they were by the new, light snow atop ice that had formed after the previous day's rain. Footing, even for Highland ponies accustomed to the worst, was treacherous, and twice his horse slipped, nearly casting him to the ground.

"Hold tight," he warned Chuff.

"Aye, my lord, I will. D' ye think Pinkie will be warm enough?"

"The mistress will see that she is."

"Aye, sure, she will. She is kind, the mistress."

Duncan felt a knot tighten in his throat.

Lost in his thoughts, he scarcely noted the warming temperature. They had been riding for several hours when the snow turned to sleet. Little wind touched them in the glen, and though he could see that it still blew above them in the treetops, the roar of the river Creran drowned out any sound it made. Indeed, the river's roar was so loud now that he could scarcely hear anything else.

Not until they had passed the trail leading into Glen Duror, near where he had first met Mary and the children, did Duncan notice that the sky had lightened. Suddenly, the sleet ahead of him began to sparkle as an errant ray of sunlight pierced the clouds to create a path of diamonds against a rainbow.

In a flash, he remembered Mary's dream, and turned his head in time to see a surge of movement from the woods. As he swept Chuff from the saddle behind him, Duncan felt a stab of sharp pain and fell into darkness.

Hearing the gunshot and seeing Duncan and Chuff fall, Mary screamed, but it was too late. Men leapt from nearby trees and shrubbery to surround the party and drag the men from their saddles. Not one managed to draw his weapon, and they soon found themselves trussed together like so many bales of hay.

To Mary's astonishment, Serena slipped at once from her saddle, caught up her skirts, and ran to Duncan, who had tumbled downhill toward the river. When Mary moved to follow, a hand caught her horse's bridle, and Ewan MacCrichton said harshly, "Stay where you are, lass. You're coming with me."

"But I must get to Duncan," Mary cried. "He hasn't moved! He must be badly injured."

"He's dead, Mary," Serena cried. "Duncan's dead!"

"No! Oh, Serena, you must be mistaken." Looking into the girl's anguished face, Mary felt overwhelming grief. Tears poured down her cheeks, burning when they froze. She wanted to shriek and wail. More than that, she wanted to run to Duncan and gather him into her arms. Not until now had she realized how much she loved him. But when she tried again to free herself, Ewan held her.

Pinkie whimpered, and just then Chuff ran at Ewan with a knife held at the ready. But another man, bundled in a hood and warm jacket, caught him up by his jacket from behind and wrenched the knife from his hand.

"Bring him," Ewan said curtly. "I've a wee score to settle with that laddie."

As the second fellow tucked the squirming, struggling boy under his arm, he glanced up at Ewan, and Mary recognized Allan Breck.

Twenty-three

After that single break in the clouds, they snapped back together again, blacker than ever. The temperature plunged, and the storm increased with a vengeance. Wind howled, the day darkened to evening, and thick snow swirled around the riders long before the walls of Shian Towers loomed into sight, but not long after that the gates swung wide to receive them.

The children had not spoken, and after one attempt to talk her captors into letting her say a proper farewell to Duncan, Mary, too, had fallen silent. Neither Allan nor Ewan tried to engage her in conversation.

Although with Allan leading her horse, she had little to do but stay on her saddle and hold onto Pinkie, she had found it difficult to think. Tears trickled down her cheeks, freezing before they had run their course. Her face stung from the cold, and the hairs in her nose crackled when she rubbed it. Snowflakes clung to her lashes, and dusted the little girl's hair.

When Pinkie coughed, she murmured, "I hope you are not coming down with a cold now, darling."

"Nay, ma'am, the breath just caught in my throat. I've got my scarf up now."

Chuff remained stoically silent.

The men talked in low tones, saying nothing that she wanted to hear, but she forced herself to listen, hoping to keep at bay the image of Duncan as he had fallen. The attempt was useless. No matter what she did, no matter what she tried to think about, all she could see in her mind's eye was his figure, sternly upright in the saddle one moment, falling dead the next.

She felt numb, as if it had all happened to someone else, as if she were a spectator, except when that image filled her mind's eye. Then she wanted to burst into tears and wail like a banshee. The ancient custom of howling for the dead had always seemed overdramatic to her. Now it seemed like a natural reaction.

She could not cry. She had to think of the children. Even more, she had to think of the child she believed she was carrying, Duncan's child, the child she had not even told him about, for fear that he would forbid her to attend the christening.

By keeping the news from him, she had kept him forever from knowing that he was to be a father, and she might have jeopardized the Balcardane succession, as well. Indeed, she might be solely responsible for the line's end. The thought that she might easily bear a daughter occurred to her only to be rejected. Fate could not be so cruel as to let her survive and then give her a daughter who could not inherit the Balcardane title. God could not think her small act of omission so horrendous as to punish her by cutting off the Balcardane branch of the clan Campbell tree.

As the riders passed through Shian's gates, she looked dully at the tall tower house and knew that she might not even live long enough for Fate to decide if she should bear boy or girl. Allan and Ewan were bent on finding the treasure, and since they both believed that she could somehow divine its whereabouts, she was under no illusions about what they would do when she could not.

Ewan had not hesitated before to use his strength against her. He would not hesitate now, and she doubted that Allan would try to stop him. They might even kill her, for Ewan could not risk her testimony against him in a courtroom. Neither he nor Allan would want to leave witnesses, and while Duncan's men and Serena could not know their attackers' identities for certain, Chuff and Pinkie did.

That thought chilled her to the bone.

They drew to a halt. Looking over her shoulder, she saw that the huge iron gates had swung shut again, and armed men stood guard beside them. Others moved about in the courtyard, their heavy boots crunching in the icy snow.

She made no effort to dismount, waiting until Ewan jumped from his horse, put his hands at her waist, and swung her abruptly to the ground. Chuff and Pinkie soon stood beside her. When Pinkie's small hand crept into hers, Mary gave it an encouraging squeeze.

Roughly, Ewan grabbed Mary's shoulder and pushed her toward the stairs leading up to the main entrance. The wooden steps were icy, and she held tight to the rail with one hand and to Pinkie's hand with the other.

Behind her, Chuff muttered, "Ye needna shove a fellow. I'm going!"

"Mind your manners, brat," Allan growled, "or you'll feel my whip across your shoulders."

Mary pressed her lips tightly together. To let Allan bait her into defending the children now could do no good. Besides, Chuff could take care of himself. He had shown that more than once over the past weeks. She could hear his feet clomping on the steps behind her.

Pinkie, clutching her cloak shut with her free hand, did not look back.

Moments later, they entered the castle, and Ewan urged Mary up the circular stone steps into the hall. She noted that the place looked just the same. Freshly lit candles, and a roaring fire on the hearth showed that the floor and paneling still needed polish. The big table in the center held congealed remnants of a meal served some time before, and the pointless lances in their racks made shadow patterns on the walls where light from the fire danced around them.

Ewan, coming to a stop beside her, said brusquely, "As you can see, lass, there is much for you to do here."

"To what purpose?" she asked quietly.

"I've made you a widow, Mary Maclaine, but you'll not be one for long. God intended you to be my wife, and so you shall be, just as soon as I can make proper arrangements. It will then be your task to see to the furbishing of your home."

"This never will be my home," she said between gritted teeth.

Before Ewan could reply, Allan said, "Let's get on with it. I want to be away before Black Duncan's men besiege us or this weather makes travel impossible."

"They'll not besiege us," Ewan said. "None saw our faces but the lass here and the bairns, and even if they should suspect who planned the attack, no one remains with sufficient power to besiege this castle."

"Argyll could," Allan said sourly. "That's why we didn't kill them all."

"Because all Campbell country would have risen if we had," Ewan replied, "but the duke had no great liking for Black Duncan, and if you are thinking Rory Campbell will fly to avenge his death, think again. He's a member of a high court, not a soldier. Moreover, by the time he and Argyll can put their heads together, the incident will be forgotten and the depths of winter full upon us. There will be nothing they can do then before spring, and if you think they'll harbor strong feelings that long over Black Duncan's fate, I say you are wrong."

"Perhaps," Allan said, "but I don't want to be stuck here till spring, so make her tell you where the damned treasure lies, and make her tell you now."

Ewan shook his head. "Language, language."

"Don't play your games with me, MacCrichton," Allan snarled. "You don't want me for your enemy, believe me. How will you make her work for us?"

Ewan glanced at Chuff and Pinkie, who were whispering together in the window alcove. "She cares more for those misbegotten brats than anyone should," he said slowly. "I thought perhaps we might spit one and turn it slowly over the hall fire until—" He fell silent, smiling at Mary, letting her fill in the rest for herself.

She stiffened angrily. "If you think that by harming those children you can force me to do anything, Ewan MacCrichton, you had better think again. What you are suggesting is barbaric, and if you kill them, I promise I will let you kill me, too, before I will lift a finger to help you."

"Ah, but we don't mean to kill them, lass, only to roast them a wee bit. How long do you think you can bear to hear the wee one scream before you agree to do anything I command of you?"

Her blood chilled, but she faced him squarely. "If you still think I can call up my gift at will, you are a fool. And if you think the information you seek will come to me while I am distraught over the torturing of an innocent child, you are mad."

"We'll see. They are mighty dear to you, I think."

"The gift visits me, Ewan," she said, striving to sound calm. "It does not work by my command. I have not had a single vision in a year, and I might not have another for many years to come. If I could control it, or if it simply came whenever someone dear to me lay in danger, it would have warned me of Duncan's death." With a catch in her voice and a hope that God would forgive her the lie, she added firmly, "It did not so much as nudge me to expect any trouble."

Ewan grimaced. Glancing at Allan, he said, "I hadn't thought about that. Why did she not know about the ambush if she can call such things into her head?"

Allan shrugged. "Who is to say why it works or fails? I say she never loved Black Duncan enough to stir the Sight. How could she? The man was a menace. Don't tell me that life with him was a pleasure for our Mary, for I won't believe it. In fact, we know it was not. He cared more for another, and Mary frequently defied him, so why should her visions warn her about harm coming to him?"

"I did care for him," Mary said, her throat aching. "I cared very much."

"So you say now, when your future lies in jeopardy if you can't make us believe the Sight ought to have saved him," Allan said, jeering. "I see how it is, you know. You don't want to stay here with Ewan. Well, that's just too bad for you."

"She'll stay, right enough," Ewan said, nodding.

"You should be glad he wants you," Allan told her. "He'll make you a good enough husband, and no one will even object that he should have waited a decent time after he takes you to his bed. Neither Rory nor Argyll will give a damn about you once you've lain with Ewan, nor will any court. It is not rape if others claim you went to him willingly, and they will. A host of them will, for we've seen to that."

She believed him, and again chills shot up her spine. Even if her cousins, her aunt, Rory Campbell, and the Duke of Argyll all believed every word she told them, there would be nothing they or anyone could do after she had been with Ewan for months, lying with him as his wife. There were even those who would be willing to believe he had stolen her heart long before Duncan's death, or that she had given it.

Allan was watching her, no doubt shrewdly judging her reaction to his words. The harsh look on his face relaxed. He said, "You know I'm right, Mary, lass, for I know you well." He looked at Ewan. "She would give her life for those children if she believed her death would save them, you know. However," he added looking slyly back at Mary, "while she may be unable to draw on her gift if you make her fret herself to flinders over *them,* what if we can arrange it so the only one she frets about is herself?"

Ewan frowned, and Mary felt herself tensing. She did not like to think she was a coward, but if Allan was thinking of roasting her over the fire in place of the children, she was certain they all would soon discover just how weak she was. Not that such brutality would help them in their quest, for she could scarcely have visions or report them if she was screaming her head off in agony.

Clearly Ewan thought the same, for he shook his head. "I've no objection to taking a few minutes to remind the lass that she must do as I tell her, but if you are suggesting I use the same techniques against her that Butcher Cumberland used to get information from his enemies, you'd best think again, Breck."

Allan chuckled, no doubt reading Mary's mind again. Just the mention of Cumberland had shaken her. Instantly, the images of her father, brother, and sister rose unbidden to her mind. That men could do such things to other men was horrid enough.

That her sister had fallen victim still appalled her. That men could even think of doing such things to women and children in peacetime was much worse.

"I would never stoop to Cumberland's methods unless I chanced to get the Butcher himself into my clutches," Allan said. "Then I would forget the rules, and gladly. I was thinking that there are other, far more useful tools at our command."

"And what tools might those be?"

"Use the lassie's own greatest fear to stir her gift to action."

"I do not follow your reasoning, man," Ewan said impatiently. "Be plain. What would you have me do to her?"

Instead of answering directly, Allan said, "Before Culloden, Baron MacCrichton held the power of the pit and the gallows, did he not?"

"Aye, for centuries. The pit lies under yon rug by the stairway door."

"It is entered from this level of the castle, then?"

"Aye, it is. There is no entry below, just walls six foot thick that help support the house. The trap door lies under the wee rug yonder. The pit beneath it is nigh onto twenty feet deep."

"Dark is it?"

"Aye." Looking bewildered, Ewan said, "Full dark with the trap shut."

Mary's skin began to crawl. She backed away from Ewan.

From the window, Chuff demanded, "What will ye do tae our Mary?"

Both men ignored him. They were watching Mary.

Ewan said, "Why did you want to know about the pit?"

"Because I happen to know," Allan said, his mocking gaze fixed on Mary, "that dark, enclosed places terrify her. I'd wager my last meal that her gift will stir to life right quick if we drop her down that pit and leave her alone there overnight."

Ewan was still watching Mary, and try as she did, she could not conceal her fear. It threatened to overwhelm her, making her palms feel so clammy that she wiped them on her cloak. Her lips felt dry and cracked, and despite her earlier attempt to force Duncan's image from her mind, now she tried with all her might to recapture it. She failed, for she could think only about the dark threat of unending confinement in the pit.

Smiling, Allan went to the small rug, bent, and whisked it away from the trap door. Gripping an iron ring, he raised the trap. "I cannot even see the bottom," he said. "Twenty feet, you say?"

"Aye, maybe thirty," Ewan said. "Well, lass?"

She could not drag her gaze from the open trap door.

Allan called for a torch, and one of the men lit one for him at the fire. Plunging the flame into the pit, he said, "Are those bones I see below?"

Ewan laughed, a harsh dry sound. "Nay, we cleaned them out years ago. Don't go frighting the lass more than we need. She's as pale as dust, as it is."

"What will ye do tae our Mary?" Chuff demanded again, fear making his voice shrill.

"You shut your mouth if you don't want to feel the back of my hand," Ewan snapped. "Take your sister and go upstairs or down to the kitchen. You don't belong here in the hall with your betters. I'll deal with you later, I will."

"We're as good as ye, laird. Flaming Janet said so! Our daddy and mam were handfasted, they were, and that's as good as married, she said."

"Not when they broke the handfast before you were born, it isn't," Ewan snarled, "and not when the parson never spoke words to make it right. Now go!"

"Mistress Mary and Himself were kind tae us," Chuff said stoutly. "They didna mak' us stay in the kitchen."

"More fools they, then. I don't want to hear your voice again, or see your face." Ewan glanced at Mary, who had been wondering what had possessed the boy to challenge him, and why Chuff's words had angered him so. "Pay him no heed, lass. He doesn't know what he's talking about. Moreover, it's time for you to go down in that pit unless you've changed your mind about helping us."

Allan had been watching her thoughtfully, and he said now, "It may well be, you know, that she's already had a vision and failed to tell anyone about it. What about that, Mary? Mind, you tell us the truth now."

Wordlessly, she shook her head. She would not tell them of her dreams.

Ewan said sharply, "Do you think she's lying?"

Allan chuckled, but there was no humor in the sound. "I don't know that she's ever told a lie in her life," he said, "but you can easily see that she can't think about anything now but the deep, dark hole beside me. You're for it, Mary, lass, unless you agree to help."

"I won't. I-I can't." For a moment, she wished that she could, but then the thought of what Allan meant to do with the treasure steadied her. She could not let him take it with him back to France. Even if a vision should come to her, she could reveal the treasure's whereabouts only if she was willing to see England and Scotland at war again. Drawing a long breath, she said, "Do what you will."

Allan dropped the trap door to the floor, leaving the black pit gaping, and moved toward her. At the same time, Ewan grasped her arm and urged her forward.

"Wait," she said, her courage failing at the sight of the yawning blackness. "If you drop me twenty feet, I might be killed. Is that what you want?"

The two men looked at each other. Ewan grimaced. Then, over his shoulder, he shouted, "One of you men, fetch us a good stout rope!"

Mary could see down into the pit's blackness now, and shivering, she tried to pull back, but Allan held her. Chuckling, he shoved her sharply forward, making her lose her balance so that the only thing that kept her from falling into the pit was his grip, and Ewan's, on her arms. Involuntarily, she screamed.

"Dinna hurt our Mary!" Chuff shrieked, flinging himself at them, his hands clutching at the men's fingers on her arms, trying to pry them loose. "Let her go!"

"Begone, lad," Ewan snapped, knocking the boy away.

Chuff fell backward, but he jumped up again and hurled himself at Ewan.

"Ye'll no hurt our Mary. I'll murder ye, ye great ugsome brute!"

This time it was Allan who struck the boy away, hitting him hard.

"Don't hurt him," Mary cried, struggling wildly to free herself when she saw Chuff go head over heels then lie still. "He only wanted to help me!"

Already the boy was stirring, trying to sit up. He looked dazed.

Allan's fingers bruised her arm. Ewan's grip was lighter. He was watching one of his men approach with a coil of rope.

Chuff leapt to his feet again and charged them, pushing past the man with the rope to hurl himself again at Ewan.

Allan moved to intercept him, but Ewan shouldered him aside, striking Chuff again with his free hand and snatching Mary back just as the blunted end of a lance sliced toward Allan, striking his throat a glancing blow. Jerking back in startled amazement, he lurched against Ewan, who was still trying to fend off Chuff.

Mary, trying desperately to wrench free of Ewan's grasp, realized—just as a sudden terrified scream filled the hall, followed by a hollow thud and silence—that Pinkie held the lance. A moment passed before her shock allowed her to sort through the confusion and tell her that Allan, twisting to avoid the lance and propelled by Ewan's shoulder, had stumbled screaming into the pit.

Solemn and silent, Pinkie still held the lance, pointed now at Ewan.

All motion in the room had stopped. The man with the rope stood as one turned to stone. Chuff sat on the floor, staring wide-eyed at Pinkie. The little girl stood quietly, still holding the lance she had evidently snatched from the wall to protect her brother. Ewan stared into the pit, from which came only silence.

He was the first to recover. He looked at Mary, his expression difficult to interpret. She had felt him push Allan with his shoulder. Now she wondered just how hard Ewan had pushed him, and if he had intended to kill him.

"Bring me that rope," Ewan said harshly to his man.

"Be quick," Mary said. "We must see what we can do for him."

"There is nothing we can do," Ewan said flatly as he took the lance from Pinkie's unresisting hand and tossed it aside to clatter on the floor. "No one could survive such a fall. He's dead, and I, for one, won't mourn his loss."

"You must want to make certain," she said dully.

"Why?"

"Then what do you want with the—? No! No, you can't! Ewan, no!"

Her struggles were fruitless. Knotting the rope around her waist, Ewan and his man lowered her into the pit. Mary grabbed at the rope end to hold herself upright and fought against rising panic.

When her foot touched Allan's body, she snatched it up only to put it down again at once when she realized that she would end up sitting on him if she did not do something to prevent it. Reaching out frantically with both feet, she managed to find the stone floor, and although she stumbled and nearly lost her balance, by steadying herself with a hand against the wall, she avoided falling on him.

Standing rigid, pressed against the damp stone wall, she shut her eyes, trying desperately to imagine open fields and wide blue skies, to forget the stones pressing in around her, to forget the corpse at her feet. Suddenly, she realized that Allan might not be dead. The instant the thought flashed into her mind, she bent, only to have the rope bring her up short. "Give me more rope, Ewan. I cannot reach him!"

"Untie yourself, lass," Ewan ordered, his voice bouncing off the stones in eerie reverberations.

"I will not." Her voice sounded hollow when it echoed back to her.

To her shock, the rope fell, tangling itself around her, and panic seized her at the thought that Ewan might not have another, that she would remain in the pit through all eternity. Then she remembered Allan and, fiercely suppressing her fear, she knelt beside him, searching for any sign of life.

There was none. Sickening warm stickiness oozed from his head, and once her eyes accustomed themselves to what little light there was at the bottom of the pit, she saw that he lay in a crumpled heap, in a contorted position that no living man could or would maintain willingly.

"Please, God, no," she murmured, seeking comfort in the sound of her voice. There was none to find, however, for she knew he was dead and he would not come back to life merely to provide her with company. Fighting another fear now, the oldest of all, she swallowed hard and moved carefully away from the dead body.

Then the light disappeared, plunging her into total, terrifying blackness.

She screamed long and loud, turning to claw in panic at the wall behind her, seeking hand- and footholds, finding only dampness and slime.

Appalled by the hideous sound of her voice ripping back at her from the wall of the pit, she forced herself at last to stop screaming and stood rigid, pressing her head, back, shoulders, and palms hard against the wall. Her breath continued to come in harsh sobs. Terrified to stay where she was, more terrified to move, she could not seem to think.

Mental images that had haunted her for six long years hurled themselves into her mind's eye. As clearly as if it were happening again, she saw soldiers drag her father and brother from the house, saw them beaten, kicked, and tied to posts for flogging. She heard their screams, and again she saw her sister run shrieking from the house, saw soldiers grab her, fling her to the ground, and take turns raping her.

Still sobbing, Mary clapped a hand over her mouth to stop herself from screaming again. The horrid smell of slime from the pit wall shocked her and sent her senses and thoughts reeling. She jerked her hand down, squeezed her eyes tight shut—as if by doing so she could make the images go away—and tried to think of Duncan as he had been before his death.

To her astonishment, his image came easily and swiftly, as if it had waited only for her call. He was there with her, and suddenly, she could hear him saying, as he had before, "It's the past, lass. Let it lie in the past. Let go, Mary."

Drawing a deep breath, ignoring the horrid smell, ignoring the presence of Allan's body at her feet, she tried to keep her mind on Duncan, to keep him with her. For as long as he stood at her side, she had nothing to fear. His love for her and hers for him would sustain her.

The last thought nearly led to her undoing, however, for it occurred to her that she had never told him she loved him, and he would never stand at her side again. He had as good as said the words to her, but she had let him die thinking she had loved Ian too much ever to love another man. Tears came then, and more sobs, and she crumpled to the ground, hugging herself, no longer able to care that she was in a pit with a dead body.

Overwhelming grief pushed every other thought or image away, and she gave herself up to it, letting the tears flow. Pressed against the slimy wall and clutching her knees to her chest, she sobbed, rocking a little, back and forth, her fears submerged in anguish. Then exhaustion took its toll at last, and she slept.

The terrors returned full force when she awoke. At first, she could not think where she was, and it was as if she had awakened to find herself blinded. She cried out without thinking, reaching out with both hands, expecting to touch a coverlet or bed curtain. Instead the back of her left hand hit slimy rock wall. When she gasped, the flood of terror washed over her again.

How, she wondered, fighting it, had she slept? Focusing her frantic mind on the fact that her legs had cramped, she nearly moved to stretch them before she remembered Allan. Stifling a shriek, certain that even a little one would explode into the same panicked screaming that had overcome her before, she fought to regain control of her sensibilities.

Suddenly, with a clatter and thud, welcome light filled the

pit, and she heard Chuff's excited whisper. "Mistress, there's boats a-coming! I saw them myself!"

Hope surged through her, but then she heard Ewan's voice. "What the devil do you think you're doing, brat?"

Twenty-four

Mary saw Chuff stand to face Ewan, and heard the boy say clearly, "There's boats a-coming, laird. Someone is coming tae rescue us, and ye'll be sorry, ye will! I wager that Himself isna dead at all, and he'll pitch ye straight into hell tae do the devil's work, he will. Here now, let go o' me!"

Mary gasped, seeing Ewan swing the boy out over the pit. "Don't drop him," she cried.

"Can you tell me yet where the treasure lies, lass?"

"No, I cannot. I can scarcely think in this horrid place."

"Then I'll drop you a wee companion. Mind you catch him now."

Almost before she realized what Ewan meant to do, he lay down on the floor and, dangling Chuff by one arm, lowered the boy as far as he could.

"Mercy, sir, are you mad? You can't just drop him down here!"

"He is nothing to me, lass. If you value his worthless hide, catch him. Here he comes. Now!"

She had no time to think, only to react. Reaching up to catch the boy, she tilted her head back, bumping it yet again against the stone wall.

Chuff crashed into her, his foot thudding against her ribs and scraping down along her left hip and leg as she struggled to break his fall. Staggering with his weight, she managed to hold him as she slid down against the wall to the floor. When she touched Allan's body, she recoiled, hugging the boy to her. Gasping, for his kick had knocked the wind from her, she felt him wriggle to be free.

"Are you all right, Chuff?"

"Aye, I think so. Cracked my head against your shoulder, I think, but I'm all of a piece at least. Hark though, that's Pinkie shrieking. If that brute hurts her—"

Mary's breath stopped in her throat. Pinkie was crying out, her voice coming from a distance, echoing off the walls of the pit, and the combination of details was suddenly, overwhelmingly, familiar. Except for the few moments before she had slept, when she had forced her mind to focus on Duncan's voice and her love for him, the image of him falling and her terror of the pit had filled her mind to the exclusion of rational thought.

Memory of her cavern nightmare flooded in now. She was reliving it, but it had not been a cavern at all. The slimy stone walls closing around her in the dream had been the walls of this very pit.

Her terror had vanished the moment Ewan held Chuff over the pit. Thought of the boy's fears and the danger to his life had banished her fears like mist in the wind. Now, recalling her dream, knowing it had not been a simple nightmare after all, she knew exactly what it must have been. The Sight had never touched her so before, but it could be nothing else.

"Chuff, help me move Allan Breck's body up against the wall yonder."

"Is he dead then?"

"Aye, he is, and he is very much in the way."

"I dinna want tae touch a dead man."

"Then I shall move him myself," she replied calmly. "I want to do it while I can still see what I am doing, and Lord Mac-Crichton is bound to slam that trap door shut the moment he remembers it is open."

Grabbing the arms of the corpse, she tried to drag it, but she found it hard to gain purchase. The space was not large enough to allow much maneuvering. After a moment, during which she wondered if she would have to give up the effort, Chuff got up and began to push from the other side.

"That's it," she said. "Just a little more now. I want to pull some of these stones out, Chuff, and we will need some space to set them down. With three of us down here, there is not much room, I'm afraid."

"Will we try tae climb out then?"

The question startled her. "Climb out?"

"Aye, will we pull out them rocks tae make footholds?"

"We're pulling them out because . . . because I think we should."

"Aye, sure, then. Which ones?"

"I-I don't know." Then she realized that she had moved Allan instinctively, as if somehow she had known where he would be out of the way. Trusting that instinct, she said, "We'll try the ones in the wall in front of us first."

Almost at once, she knew it was the right wall, for the dirt was loose enough to scrape out with her fingers. After a few minutes and two broken nails, however, it occurred to her to see if Allan had anything on his person that might help with the task. With the dirk from his boot top, the work went more quickly. The first stone proved reluctant, but once they freed it, the others came out easily.

"I ken how it is," Chuff said a few moments later. "We're diggin' a tunnel through the wall. We'll be oot o' here in a twink, mistress."

"I hope so, Chuff," she said quietly.

"Them boats . . . That *would* be Himself coming for us, aye?"

"Perhaps," Mary said quietly, not wanting to betray her belief that the hope was a futile one. Indeed, perhaps Neil had survived the attack and was coming for them with those of Duncan's men who had also survived. She was as certain as she could be that Allan had been wrong in thinking the men would not know who had attacked them, whether they had seen faces or not.

Interrupting these thoughts, Chuff said, "Then why are we diggin'?"

"Because I believe we must," she said.

A chuckle drifted to them from above. Looking up, she saw

Ewan standing at the pit's edge, hands on his hips, grinning. "What are you doing there, lass?"

Glad the dirk was out of sight in the hole, she kept still and said nothing.

"What did ye do tae our Pinkie tae mak' her cry?" Chuff shouted.

"Nothing yet," Ewan said. "The little bitch ran away and hid. I'll teach her better manners when I've more time to attend properly to the matter."

"Did ye see them boats then?"

"I did. Would you like to hear about them, Mary, lass?"

A note in his voice warned her that he brought bad news, so she said nothing, and for once Chuff kept silent, too.

"I'll wager you hoped they were coming to rescue you."

Grimly, she said, "I collect from your tone that they are not, however."

"They are not. And why not? Because what he saw is a funeral procession, that's why. There are five sailboats, all decked out with banners and black ribbons."

Her heart sinking to her feet, Mary said dully, "The snow has stopped then."

"It has. There's even sunlight peeping through the clouds to shine on the lead boat. That one flies the Dunraven banner and bears Black Duncan's body in state on its deck. It's his funeral procession, that's what it is, taking him across the loch."

Chuff gasped, and Mary felt tears spilling down her cheeks. She did her best to stifle her sobs, but hearing Ewan chuckle, she knew that he had heard them.

"They'll sail from Glen Creran straight to Dunraven," he went on smugly. "Presently, they've formed a wee line at the head of the loch, which is no doubt why the lad did not immediately perceive their dark purpose. Oh, aye, and speaking of the dark . . ." The trap crashed shut again, plunging them back into blackness.

* * *

As the little flotilla of boats sailed down the loch, Duncan lay as still as he could. His shoulder ached where the bullet had struck it, and his pride ached at the memory of his ignominious fall from his saddle. He had lost some blood, and had had to sustain himself through certain uncalled for remarks by Bardie Gillonie, who, having heard the gunshots, had come upon them soon after the ambush. He rode in the second boat now.

Bardie still had no respect for his betters, Duncan thought grimly. Still, it had been Bardie's herbs that had stilled the throbbing pain in his shoulder, and Bardie's brews that had put him on his feet again so quickly—Bardie's brews and his own thoughts of what MacCrichton might well be doing to his precious Mary.

"How are you doing?" Neil asked, moving up beside him and kneeling. He crossed himself. "For the love of heaven, don't open your eyes. Someone may see."

Obediently, Duncan shut his eyes. "Going to pray over me, are you?"

"Seemed the least I could do to improve the scene. After all, MacCrichton might have a telescope or two up there on the ramparts. Are you still in much pain?"

"It's eased, but lying here is a damned penance," Duncan muttered, keeping his lips as still as he could, in case someone was watching through a telescope.

Neil stifled a chuckle. "Mary would say you deserve to do penance, my lord. I think she will be glad to see us both, however."

"So help me, Neil, if that bastard has touched her—"

"Aye, I'll want a piece of him myself. But still your fury for the present, Duncan, or you will spoil our pretty scene. I'll warrant the murderous bastard is watching us, gloating over your apparent death."

"Let him gloat. He'll stop soon enough when he faces my sword."

"If he's law-abiding, he will be unarmed, you know."

"All the better," Duncan growled.

"Would you spit him even as he yields to you?"

Duncan snorted in derision but stifled it quickly to say, "I am perfectly willing to promise you that if he does yield I won't lay a finger on him."

"I find that hard to believe," Neil said sardonically.

"It will never come to the test. MacCrichton's bastards were all armed to the teeth, remember, and he'll not give up now without the devil of a fight."

"By heaven, I think you are looking forward to it."

"I am. Did you tell the lads to dip their banners to the villain?"

"Of course I did, since you commanded it. It goes against the grain with every one of them, but they'll do it. We are beginning to tack inland now. Lie still, my lord, and for the love of heaven, keep your eyes shut."

"I'm getting damned cold," Duncan muttered. "Though the sun shines on us from time to time, I'll be as stiff as my sword if we don't get there soon."

"I thought of that," Neil said. "Here, Bannatyne, bring that plaid and lay it gently over his lordship. "A fine bit of wool, my lord, in pretty Campbell colors. It should warm you, and MacCrichton will think only that it is a mark of clan respect, so as long as no one in authority learns of our activities this fine day . . ."

"If they hear, they'll do nothing about it. Ah, that's better," he added when Bannatyne draped the plaid over him. Opening his eyes just enough to see through his lashes, he added, "Is there still ice near the shore?"

"Not enough to matter," Neil said, looking toward Shian. "The boats will break through it easily. I'm more concerned about Patrick Campbell and his lads approaching the castle from the forest. Do you truly think no one will see them?"

"I think MacCrichton has made such a great thing of his delight in my supposed demise that his men will take their lead from him. If he is celebrating, they will be celebrating, and that means they will all want to see the parade, especially since you say you heard him proclaim himself the new lord of Loch Creran."

"He did, the rogue, shouted it to all of us as he was riding away. If we hadn't guessed at once who our attackers were, we'd have known then for sure."

"Still, he should bask in our little show of respect," Duncan said grimly.

"I hope you're right," Neil said, standing to make way for Bannatyne to take his place beside the supposed corpse. He moved back, ducking to avoid the boom.

Duncan wished he could see exactly where they were, but he knew that Neil was right about the possibility of a telescope or two. They would not be powerful enough for a watcher to have seen his lips move, and if one had seen Neil speak, he would assume only that he was praying. But Duncan was not a patient man.

The thought nearly made him smile. How Mary would agree with it. He hoped she had managed to stay out of MacCrichton's filthy clutches. If she had not, if the scoundrel had raped her . . . That thought was too awful to contemplate. If he let his mind dwell on such possibilities, he would be unable to remain still, and their entire plan depended upon that. Beneath the plaid, one hand gripped his short sword. Ewan MacCrichton would rue the day he had set eyes on Mary Maclaine.

Beside him, the kneeling Bannatyne murmured, "We near the shore, sir."

"Excellent."

The next few minutes passed slowly, but at last, he heard the sound of his banner coming down the mast. It stopped halfway, where someone tied it.

That would give MacCrichton pause, he thought. Properly, they should raise it to the top again. Would MacCrichton think they stopped it as a sign of their grief? He knew the other boats would do what their leader did. Gripping his sword tightly, he hoped his limbs had not stiffened too much. The dull, persistent ache from the flesh wound in his left shoulder would not affect his swordplay.

* * *

"Hoots," Chuff said. "I canna see my hand in front o' my face the noo."

Mary said, "You can still feel the rock wall, can you not?"

"Aye."

"Then keep helping me, Chuff. We must make this hole much bigger."

The boy remained silent for a long moment while Mary scraped dirt from the next stone and began to ease it from its bed. Then he muttered, "I dinna like it doon here. I'm afeared tae be in the dark wi' a dead corpus."

"He cannot harm you now, Chuff," Mary said.

"Pinkie killed him."

"No, he died in an unfortunate accident."

"She poked him wi' that lance, she did. Got him right in the neck."

"I don't think the lance actually touched him, Chuff. The laird pushed him out of the way, and then Allan Breck stumbled. He just tripped over his own feet, and if the two of them had not opened the pit to drop me into it, the accident would never have happened. You must never tell Pinkie that you think she—"

"Och, then, I wadna! But she may think she did, even so."

"Then we shall simply tell her that she did not," Mary said firmly.

"Aye, sure." Chuff's tone remained doubtful, but a moment later, Mary felt his hands alongside hers, prying, scraping, and pulling.

"Take care that you don't get your hands too near the dirk," she warned.

"Aye."

As she set down the dirk to brush some dirt to the floor, she heard metal scraping against rock. "What's that noise, Chuff."

"I took off my belt," he said. "The wee charm my daddy left us fits between the rocks, and it's stronger than my fingers for the diggin'."

"Perhaps it will bring us luck then," she said, using the dirk again.

"Aye, maybe." Shortly thereafter when another rock came

free, he said, "Will the laird no see all them rocks when next he looks doon here?"

"I don't think so. The stones are much the same color as the dirt on the floor, and recollect that Allan Breck had to hold that torch well down into the pit before he could see the bottom—if he could even see it then. He said it was littered with bones, remember?"

"Aye, and it isna, which I'm right glad tae ken, I tell ye."

"I'm glad, too, Chuff."

Another stone joined the others, and another, and yet another. Ewan came twice more, gloating, to report on the progress of the funeral procession. Each time, when the trap door opened, Mary and Chuff stopped working to look up. Ewan did not seem to notice anything amiss.

The next time he came, he said, "You'll be pleased to know, lass, that the captains of yon sailboats know their duty."

"Do they, indeed?"

"Aye, they've drawn close to shore to dip their banners in respect to one they all recognize now as lord of Loch Creran. They raised them only halfway afterward, too, proving Duncan is dead. No one remains now to challenge my authority."

"When will you let us out of here, then?"

"Now that's not up to me, that isn't. You'll stay down there, lassie, until you've done as you were bid. Have you had no visions yet?"

Wondering if the Lord would ever forgive her for the lies she had told, she said firmly, "I have not."

"Then—"

A shout interrupted him, and he straightened, leaving the trap open.

"Master, they're landing! The boats are landing!"

"Damn them," Ewan snapped. "Call out the men!"

Another shout, unintelligible to those in the pit, sounded from a distance.

"Soldiers! They've tricked us," Ewan screamed.

* * *

Duncan's nerves were singing, and he remembered the feeling from previous battles. War was dreadful, but fighting did something to a man. Energy surged through him, and he welcomed the lurching shudder when the boat crunched against ice and then solid ground. He did not think he could have kept still much longer.

With a roar, he sprang to his feet, feeling no pain at all. Leaping ashore with his sword aloft, he shouted the ancient Campbell war cry, *"A Cruachan!"*

Echoing the cry, his men charged toward the gate, and before they reached it, it opened. Patrick's lads had successfully scaled the rear walls.

Fighting in the courtyard was already fierce when the men from the boats charged in to join the fray. Duncan saw two MacCrichton soldiers dashing toward the wooden stairway that led to the castle entrance.

"At them, lads! Don't let them burn the stairs!"

As Duncan reached the foot of the stairway, a large key clattered to the ground beside him. Astonished, he bent to pick it up.

When he straightened, he saw that his men had those who would have burned the stairs in custody. Looking up, he saw a child's hand waving from an arrow slit. He smiled.

Sudden silence filled the courtyard. Turning, he saw that his men and Patrick's had gained control. He waved to Neil. "Come see what I've found."

Neil hurried to his side, staring in amazement at the key. "What the devil—?"

"Don't blaspheme, my lad," Duncan said. " 'Tis a gift from above. Shall we see if it fits the door?"

As they hurried up the stairs, Neil said, "I thought MacCrichton would be out here with the others, but they say he is inside."

"So he's a coward as well as a scoundrel. Let's have at him." Realizing that MacCrichton would not be alone, he shouted to the men below, "Who's with us?"

The prisoners had been herded into one corner, and a number

of his men were already moving toward the stairs. Patrick Campbell waved. *"A Cruachan!"*

"MacCrichton is mine," Duncan muttered to Neil.

The younger man made no comment.

As Duncan fitted the big black key into the lock, he caught sight of Bardie Gillonie lumbering toward the stairs in the wake of the other men. Knowing the dwarf was unarmed, Duncan hoped he would keep out of the way.

The big door swung wide enough to hit the yett, but the heavy iron gate yielded to the same key. In moments, with swords and pistols at the ready and with no attempt at stealth, the men clattered up the spiral stone stairs to the great hall.

Pausing in the doorway, Duncan saw MacCrichton and two other men. Ewan held a sword in one hand and a pistol in the other. His companions likewise bore arms. There was no sign of Allan Breck, however.

"So the lass lied to me and you're not dead, after all," Mac-Crichton said gently. "I'll have to remedy that wee mistake."

In a quiet aside, Duncan said to Neil, "Tell the men to watch out for Breck."

"Aye," Neil murmured, turning to speak to Bannatyne and Patrick, just behind him.

"If you are going to shoot me again," Duncan said, "you'd better do so at once, MacCrichton, but it is only fair to warn you that our men are all armed and will not hesitate to shoot you down like the villain you are. Where is my wife?"

"We can discuss that if she is not a widow when our little scene is played out here. That way I know you won't simply shoot me."

"Your men are prisoners, MacCrichton," Patrick Campbell said from the doorway. "The only ones still with you are the two standing yonder."

"So you think, but I have a bargain to put to Black Duncan."

"You are scarcely in any position to bargain," Duncan told him.

"Do you think I cannot shoot you and Maclean where you stand before any other man reaches me? Do you think we cannot account for a few more before they take us? Look up, Duncan. One of my lads is in the minstrel's gallery yonder with a brace of pistols. He's aiming one at you now."

"He won't save you, MacCrichton. He cannot shoot more than one of us before you die."

"Fight me, Duncan. If you win, I'll tell you where Mary is."

"She is Lady Balcardane, if you please. What if you win?"

"Then you guarantee my release."

Duncan laughed. "I'd fight you for nothing, MacCrichton."

"Aye, sir, you would that," Bardie Gillonie said from the minstrel's gallery.

MacCrichton whirled, raising his pistol toward the dwarf, and Duncan lunged forward, striking it from his hand with the flat of his sword. MacCrichton leapt back, smoothly shifting his sword to his right hand. With a growl of fury, he lunged toward Duncan.

"Stand back, men," Duncan cried. "He's mine!"

Aware that Neil, Patrick, and Bannatyne had moved swiftly to disarm MacCrichton's two companions, Duncan fixed his attention on his foe, and for the next few minutes the clash of steel against steel rang through the hall.

MacCrichton was well taught, but Duncan was the better swordsman. Had his injury not weakened him, the fight would have been swiftly over. As it was, MacCrichton nearly nicked him once. Even so, it was only moments before Duncan saw an opening; and, expecting to pink MacCrichton's sword arm, he took it. As he lunged forward, MacCrichton moved to parry, and before Duncan could draw back, the sword pierced MacCrichton's chest. He fell, gasping.

"Where is she?" Duncan demanded, kicking the man's sword away and standing over him.

"Find her . . . yourself. I'm . . . sped."

"Damn you, MacCrichton, don't die yet! Where's Mary? Where's my wife?"

"Please, sir," Pinkie said from the gallery, "she and Chuff are in the floor." With his last gasp, Ewan muttered, "Damned handfast brat."

Twenty-five

Eerie, dully thumping echoes reverberated around the stone hall as two men pulled rocks and dirt from the pit wall below, widening the hole Mary had found. Patrick Campbell and his men had gone, taking their prisoners with them.

Someone had pounded rods into the pit wall halfway down, to hang lanterns, and the orange and golden glow turned the workers from dark shadows into recognizable figures as they moved into the spill of light and out again.

"They'll be done soon," Duncan said, putting a hand on Mary's shoulder.

Glancing up at him, she saw that the late afternoon sun coming through one of the high windows had drawn a halo around his head. The thought of Duncan having heavenly connections of any sort surprised a chuckle from her.

"It is good to hear you laugh, sweetheart, but it is not wise to laugh at your lord and master."

She grinned. "You've grown a halo, sir."

"A what?" He looked astonished, as well he might, she thought. Then his dark eyes lit with laughter. "Your ordeal in that pit has unhinged you, I fear."

"Master, we've got it!"

"We'll lower ropes," Duncan called down to them.

Mary said, "Do you think that's how Daft Geordie got the chest down there in the first place?"

"Aye, it's the only way. That pit's all of twenty feet deep or more. He must have lowered the chest first, then himself. It's no mean feat for any man."

"He wasn't as daft as Ewan thought him then, and he certainly must have been very strong."

"Aye." Duncan's reply sounded absent-minded. He was busy with ropes. "Stand opposite me," he said to Bannatyne. "Once they get it tied, we'll hoist it up."

After that, it was but a matter of minutes before they swung the heavy ironbound chest onto the hall floor. Taking it by handles at either end, Duncan and Bannatyne left others to help the men from the pit, and carried the chest to the table in the center of the hall.

Neil moved toward them from the great fire, where he had been chatting with Bardie and the two children. "It's not nearly as big as I'd expected," he said with a frown. "It cannot be but a foot and a half high, nor yet three feet wide."

"It's heavy enough," Duncan said. "How big did you think it would be?"

With a rueful look, Neil said, "Judging by Ewan's passion to find the thing, I'd expected something at least the size of a coffin."

"Aye, sure," Bardie said. "That's all well and good, but what's in the devilish thing? Open it, will ye? I'm fair awash wi' curiosity."

"Me, too," Chuff said, moving closer.

"Me, too," said his small, ubiquitous shadow.

Mary smiled at the children, then at Duncan. "Well, sir?"

He smiled back. "Well, my lady?"

"Do we not need the key to open it?"

In answer, he gestured to one of his men, who stepped forward to hand him an iron bar. Taking it, Duncan said, "This, my dear, is a universal key, for it will open almost any lock." He tried to insert an end into the narrow crack between the chest's lid and body, but his efforts proved useless. "I cannot get purchase," he said.

"Let me try," Neil said, taking the bar.

When he failed, they studied the lock. After some moments

of this exercise, Duncan said with exasperation. "You'd think Daft Geordie would have had sense enough to bury the key with the chest!"

"Please, sir," Chuff said, "Flaming Janet allus said folks should no call him daft. She said our mam didna like it. She allus called him George, and—"

"Aye," Pinkie murmured. "He was no daft, she said."

Mary and Duncan exchanged astonished glances.

Duncan said, "Do you mean to say that Daft Geordie was your father?"

"George," Chuff said firmly.

Touching Duncan's arm, Mary said gently, "Was his full name George MacCrichton, Chuff."

"I dunno that," Chuff said, frowning. "I thought it must be MacLachlan, the same as Red Mag and Flaming Janet."

"But his name *was* Daft Geordie." Seeing the protest leap again to Chuff's lips, she added quickly, "Other people called him that, did they not?"

Grudgingly, Chuff muttered, "Aye."

Duncan said thoughtfully, "Did Flaming Janet have red hair, Chuff?"

"Aye."

"Did your mam?"

The boy shrugged. "I dinna remember her."

Mary said, "Her name was Red Mag, Duncan, and both children are blond, like Ewan. I never knew his brother, but even if the children are his, Ewan called them handfast brats. He said Chuff was born after the handfast was broken."

"He may have lied about that," Duncan said. "He called Pinkie a handfast brat with his last breath, did he not, and Daft—" He glanced apologetically at Chuff, then went on, "George must have died before she was born. That would seem to indicate a continued relationship. Not that it matters. We know a handfast existed, and if a child came of it, even after the year and a day, that child is its father's legitimate issue." He looked thoughtfully at Chuff.

Mary, too, had been looking at Chuff, and an idea struck her now with some force. "Where is your charm, Chuff? You did not leave it in the pit, did you?"

"Nay, then, just stuffed it in my breeches when they hauled me up." He reached in and pulled out the twisted length of rawhide he used as a belt. Dangling at the end was the grubby, oddly shaped metal piece that served as its buckle.

Mary caught the swinging bit of metal and held it up. "Duncan?"

"Aye," he said, "it might be the key, though it doesn't look like one. Let's have it, lass."

A moment later, the chest was open.

"Ooh," Chuff said, his eyes wide.

Mary was certain hers must have looked the same, for the little chest was full of jewelry and gold coins. "It is easy to see why that iron bar failed to open it," she said, gazing at a locking mechanism that filled the entire inside surface of the lid. Hook-like bits all round the lip fitted into opposing slots in the body's rim. Without the key, the chest would defy any attempt to open it.

Pinkie reached in and touched some of the coins, stirring them curiously.

"So the treasure is real," Mary said, still staring at it.

"It would seem that it is," Duncan said.

An odd note in his voice dragged her rapt attention away from the treasure clinking through Pinkie's fingers. To her surprise she saw that he was amused.

"What?"

"My father," he said, meeting her gaze. "I was thinking what a pity it is that he did not live to see this."

With a sudden sinking sensation she said, "I-I daresay the authorities will confiscate it, or . . . or . . ." She could not put into words the thought that the Campbells would most likely demand custody of it.

"Still don't trust me, sweetheart?"

His tone was light, and when she met his gaze again, the deep understanding in his eyes banished the last vestige of worry from her mind.

"What will happen to it?" she asked.

"Here's a letter," Pinkie said in surprise. "It was buried in the coins."

Taking it from her and opening it, Duncan showed it to Mary. Written in crudely formed letters, it contained the following message: *If ye find this without me, Ewan, I am dead and ye got the key from the lad. He is my son, and there is another bairn coming soon. I charge ye to raise them both as proper MacCrichtons, to look after Mag, my wife by handfast.* It was signed, *George MacCrichton.*

Duncan looked at the children. "As I understand this, Geordie MacCrichton never broke the handfast, so now that Ewan and Geordie are dead, Geordie's son is the rightful heir to the title, to Shian, and to all that may be found inside its walls."

"Chuff?" Mary said.

"Me?"

"Coo," Pinkie said when Duncan nodded.

"In the end, Geordie did a wise thing," Duncan said, kneeling to sort through the items in the chest. "There does not seem to be much here to identify these things as MacCrichton property, and he says nothing in the note to identify it as such. Had it been found in the forest, anyone might have tried to claim it, but the fact that we found the chest inside the castle walls puts its ownership beyond question now."

Mary said, "Won't there be a fuss?"

"Not if I take Chuff and Pinkie under my protection. I think I can persuade Argyll that it's the most logical solution. He certainly won't want to turn the castle or the treasure over to Jacobite sympathizers; and, with Chuff here being underage and the last of the MacCrichtons, a veritable horde of them are bound to claim kinship and offer to look after him and Pinkie. Argyll is most likely to agree that I should do so instead; and, with an estate just across the loch, I'm in an excellent position to run this one until Chuff is old enough to take over."

She was silent.

"I won't let him down, Mary, or you either."

"I know you won't, but are you certain Argyll will permit it?"

"He will, because he knows he can trust me to see that young Chuff here grows up without having his head stuffed full of rebel notions. He's a good lad, Chuff is, so if you are thinking he might be a burden—"

"Never!"

Duncan smiled. "Well, be that as it may, sweetheart, I mean to send him to a good school. He is going to need a proper education."

"Pinkie, too," Mary said firmly.

"Aye, if you like, but you'll not want to send her away. We can hire a governess for the wee lass."

He turned away to give orders about taking the chest under guard, and watching him, Mary felt a glow of something much stronger than pride.

She saw Neil watching her, and smiling at him, she said, "Did it occur to anyone to send Caddell an explanation of our absence from the christening?"

"Aye, it did," he said grimly. "We sent Serena and her wench with two of Duncan's men to tell them. She did not want to leave us, and we could ill spare the men, I can tell you, but when I explained what would happen to her if she stayed, she did not question which was the better choice."

"Goodness, what did you tell her?"

"Only that if she did not take herself out of my sight at once, I could not answer for the consequences. She believed me."

"I can see why she would," Mary said, repressing a shiver. "You looked like Duncan at his most forbidding just now when you said that."

"Mary, I wanted to strangle her. At the very least, I would have beaten her till she screamed for mercy. The only reason I did not do so at once is that she had saved Duncan's life."

"She did?"

"Aye. When she told Ewan that he was dead, Ewan believed her."

"That's right, he did. I wonder why."

"Because she was the one who told them where and when to find us in the first place, that's why. She said something that made me curious, and when I taxed her with it, she admitted that her maid had told them about the christening party, and Serena herself signaled them the night before we left."

"The lamp in the window! But why? I know she was upset when Duncan married me, but I thought it was becoming a case between the pair of you."

"It was not. Serena would flirt with any man. If I seemed to respond, it was only to keep her out of your hair and Duncan's. She knew I was not interested."

"Well, if she saved Duncan, I can forgive her nearly everything else," Mary said. "I expect she told Ewan he was dead because she still cares for him."

"I don't think so," Neil said with a sigh. "It's true that she had a notion once to become a countess, but she told me that Duncan frightens her. I think, in the end, she just balked at murdering him. She was jealous of you, because the old earl's death made you a countess, but I think she meant only to punish you. She did not foresee any other consequence to her actions. She just didn't think, that's all."

"I think she does care for you, though, Neil."

"Perhaps she does," he agreed, "but I don't want a wife who could even think of doing the things she has done. I told her that much when I sent her home, and I told her, too, that she had better confess to her father what she had done, for I mean to tell him if she does not."

Mary nodded, agreeing that Caddell had every right to know. She looked for Duncan and saw that he was talking to two of his men near the door.

Neil said quietly, "You love him, don't you?"

She said simply, "More than I ever thought it I could love anyone."

"More than Gentle Ian?"

She smiled reminiscently. "Ian was very dear to me, Neil. He made me feel beautiful and loved, and he taught me to care deeply for the creatures of the land and for people in need. Before, although I tried to be kind, it was because it was my duty, but I don't think I cared from my heart. I had held myself apart for too long from everyone who was left to love me. Ian took me out of myself."

"You did love him, Mary."

"Oh, aye, I loved him very much."

Behind her, Duncan said lightly, "I hope you're speaking of me, sweetheart."

A little guiltily, she said, "We were talking about Ian."

"He can rest in peace now that Breck has gone to hell."

"Still, I'm glad that Allan's blood is not on your hands, sir," Mary said.

He put an arm around her shoulders. "I'm glad of that, too, lass. I'd have spitted the devil without a blink, mind you, but it was better done as it was."

"Do you mean to report his death to the authorities?"

"I'll drop a word in Argyll's ear, and Rory's, but I think that's all I'll do. We do not want a full inquiry, after all."

Mary glanced at the children, back near the fire again with Bardie, warming their hands. "No, we don't," she said. "I'm not certain what did happen, it was so quick, but Pinkie and Chuff certainly had a hand in it. I think it likely that Ewan pushed him, but I don't want the children questioned."

"No," Duncan said, "because from the way you've described it, it might as easily have been you who fell into that pit, sweetheart, and I don't want them realizing that, either. In any event, we can't know exactly what happened."

"With Allan dead, we'll never learn the truth about James of the Glen now, either," she said sadly.

"No," he agreed. "Where is your cloak?"

"I don't know," she said. "Are we leaving now?"

"Aye, I want to get you home before dark."

"We will never make Balcardane so quickly."

"We are going to Dunraven," he said. "It is time you saw the one place that has always been mine. I've got boats waiting for us at the dock."

"Where did the funeral boats come from, Duncan?"

"From all around the loch," he said, grinning. "While Bardie fixed me up, Neil got Serena and her wench on their way and

then he, the lads, and I devised our plan. Bannatyne rode to
Stalker to get Patrick and his lads, and explained their part to
them. The rest of the men went in search of boats and the where-
withal to turn them into a funeral parade. We weren't sure it
would work, because the weather has been so unpredictable,
but I must say that I'm glad it did."

"Why didn't you just leave it to Patrick, since you knew who
attacked you?"

He smiled. "Because I didn't want to leave it to Patrick. I knew
MacCrichton would try to keep you alive, hoping you could find
his treasure for him, but I could not be certain he would not use
you as a shield or threaten to murder you if he saw soldiers
preparing to attack Shian. Our little diversion allowed us to take
him by surprise, which kept him from thinking much at all. Now,
come along, lass. We can talk all you want later."

Leaving Neil and Bannatyne behind to supervise the clearing
up at Shian (with Bardie's sharp-tongued assistance), Duncan
took Mary and the children to the dock, where they found that
one of the boats had been stripped of its funereal decorations
and made ready to carry them across the loch.

The sun was shining on new fallen snow that blanketed the
land, and it sparkled, too, on the bright blue waters of the loch.
A stiff breeze blew them across to the southern shore in no time.

"What do you think of it?" Duncan asked when they stood
at the entrance of the tall, lime-washed castle, looking up at the
Campbell arms carved into the lintel.

She smiled at the pride in his voice. "You want to live here,
don't you?"

"Only part of the year, and only if my wife does."

"Then, let's go in and find out how well she likes it." As she
linked her arm with Duncan's, Mary knew she would live with
him wherever he chose.

Chuff's eyes were big with amazement. He stood looking at
the castle with his hands on his narrow hips. "It is bigger than
Shian," he said.

"Aye, but it isna so beautiful," Pinkie said loyally.

"Perhaps not," Duncan said, smiling at them, "but its mistress is the bonniest lady in all Scotland, and I love her with all my heart." Looking into Mary's eyes, he said softly, "I do, you know."

"I know," she said. "That knowledge sustained me when they put me in that horrid pit, that . . . that and my love for you, my lord, and one more thing, too."

Duncan caught her tight in his arms. "Are you sure you love me, lass?"

"Aye, sir, and there is something else you should know."

"That's all I want to know, sweetheart. It is everything to me."

Chuff said suspiciously, "Are ye going tae kiss our Mary?"

"I am," Duncan said, suiting action to words.

Mary held his head when he would have straightened. "There truly is something else you should know, sir, something I should have told you before now." Then, whispering into his ear, so he would hear the news privately first, she told him the secret she had been hugging to herself.

He held her away, looking into her eyes, his own alight with excitement. "Are you sure, lass?"

"I shouldn't be sure yet, but I am. Perhaps it's the Sight, or—Duncan!"

He swept her up and swung her around, laughing his delight, but then he put her down again, and stood looking at her as if he could not get enough of looking.

"Are ye going tae kiss our Mary again?" Chuff asked with disgust.

Without bothering to reply, Duncan caught Mary around the waist again and kissed her thoroughly, an exercise to which she responded with enthusiasm.

Chuff groaned, but Pinkie abandoned her long habit of always agreeing with him, and giggled, saying, "It's a fine thing, it is, for Himself tae kiss our Mary!"

Dear Reader,

I hope you enjoyed *Highland Treasure.* Since many of you
continue to express interest in the history behind the romance,
you may be as interested as I was to learn that there really was
a Black Duncan Campbell. Moreover, he actually built Barcaldine Castle in Argyll, the castle that provided inspiration for much
of *Highland Secrets* and *Highland Treasure,* and provided archi-
tectural detail for Shian and Dunraven, both of which are otherwise purely fictional. Balcardane Castle is patterned after Huntly,
however. The pit at Shian is from Castle Stalker.

Originally, I was intrigued by the name Barcaldine, but I did
not want to use the real castle or the name, because I could
discover very little about it. So the Balcardane earldom was
born in *Highland Secrets.* Then, this fall, my husband and I
went to Scotland and discovered that Barcaldine had recently
been opened to the public. The present heir and his family want
to keep it in the family, and have refurbished it and opened it
in hopes of making enough money to keep it going. It's a wonderful place, but imagine my amazement when I came across
a portrait of Black Duncan Campbell on one of the walls there
and discovered that he had built the original castle. Here I had
already written one book with my Black Duncan as a character,
and was well into another with him as my hero.

The real Black Duncan was Sir Duncan Campbell of Glenor-
chy. His lands in the late 16th century stretched from Barcaldine
(on the site of Dunraven Castle in *Highland Treasure*) to Tay-
mouth Castle on Loch Tay in the east. He also built a string of
seven other castles, including Kilchurn on Loch Awe (also open
to the public). The Barcaldine Castle guidebook describes him
as "a very vigorous and forceful character but also an accomplished man, having travelled abroad, patronised art and litera-
ture, and instigated tree planting schemes on his lands."

The Armada trunk described in *Highland Treasure* was a

forerunner of the modern safe. Many of them still exist, and at Fyvie Castle, when the key was misplaced, it took modern, skilled locksmiths weeks to figure out how to open it.

As for James of the Glen, the controversy rages on. His cadaver fell to the ground in January 1755, and the authorities ordered that the bones be reconnected by wire clips and the remains restored to the gibbet. It remained so for many more years while the skeleton slowly disintegrated. We visited the site of his memorial, the site of the murder of Crown factor Colin Glenure, and Glenure's home.

Allan Breck Stewart is known to have escaped to France after the Appin murders, and many suspect that he returned to Scotland at least once afterward. But then he disappeared. One legend has it that he fought against Wolfe's troops in Canada in 1758, but there is no proof of this. Other evidence exists that suggests he lived in France to a ripe old age under a pseudonym. It is just as likely, however, that he disappeared forever after that next visit to Scotland, a victim of his own felonious nature.

If you enjoyed *Highland Treasure* and would like to read more books of a similar nature, please look for *Highland Secrets* (Zebra, October '97) and *Highland Fling* (Pinnacle, February '95) at your local bookstore, or ask them to order the books for you. Also, in February 1999, please watch for *The Mayfair Madam* (Zebra), which details what happens when Lady Letitia Deverill—whom some readers will remember as a child in *Dangerous Angels* (Pinnacle, January '97)—inherits a house in Mayfair that turns out to be a brothel.

Letty is all grown up now, but she still has her pet monkey, Jeremiah, and her savoir faire. She needs all she possesses of the latter to deal with monkeyshines, mayhem, and with Justin, Viscount Raventhorpe, who is not only the wealthiest man in London but a gentleman who believes that every woman needs a strong man to guide her. His great-aunts, two eccentric but surprisingly discreet elderly ladies, are Letty's inherited tenants in the best little house in Mayfair.

Determined to show that she can manage her own affairs, Letty soon finds herself faced with the need to protect the old ladies (and herself) from social ruin, and—by the way—to prevent the assassination of Britain's new monarch, the young Queen Victoria. It's proving to be a fun story to write, to say the least. I think you will like it.

Sincerely yours,

Amanda Scott

Other Books by Amanda Scott

HIGHLAND SECRETS
HIGHLAND FLING
DANGEROUS ANGELS
DANGEROUS GAMES
THE BAWDY BRIDE
DANGEROUS ILLUSIONS

<u>BOOK YOUR PLACE ON OUR WEBSITE</u> <u>AND MAKE THE</u> <u>READING CONNECTION!</u>

We've created a customized website just for our very special readers, where you can get the inside scoop on everything that's going on with Zebra, Pinnacle and Kensington books.

When you come online, you'll have the exciting opportunity to:

- View covers of upcoming books

- Read sample chapters

- Learn about our future publishing schedule (listed by publication month *and author*)

- Find out when your favorite authors will be visiting a city near you

- Search for and order backlist books from our online catalog

- Check out author bios and background information

- Send e-mail to your favorite authors

- Meet the Kensington staff online

- Join us in weekly chats with authors, readers and other guests

- Get writing guidelines

- AND MUCH MORE!

Visit our website at
http://www.zebrabooks.com